AN ETHICAL GUIDE TO MURDER

AN ETHICAL GUIDE TO MURDER

Jenny Morris

SIMON & SCHUSTER

London · New York · Sydney · Toronto · New Delhi

First published in Great Britain by Simon & Schuster UK Ltd, 2025

Copyright © Jenny Morris, 2025

1 3 5 7 9 10 8 6 4 2

Simon & Schuster UK Ltd
1st Floor
222 Gray's Inn Road
London WC1X 8HB

Simon & Schuster Australia, Sydney
Simon & Schuster India, New Delhi

www.simonandschuster.co.uk
www.simonandschuster.com.au
www.simonandschuster.co.in

A CIP catalogue record for this book
is available from the British Library

Hardback ISBN: 978-1-3985-3440-7
Trade Paperback ISBN: 978-1-3985-3441-4
eBook ISBN: 978-1-3985-3442-1
Audio ISBN: 978-1-3985-3444-5

Typeset in Sabon by M Rules

Printed and Bound in the UK using 100% Renewable
Electricity at CPI Group (UK) Ltd

MIX
Paper | Supporting
responsible forestry
FSC
www.fsc.org
FSC® C171272

For Caroline, who deserved to live forever.

AN ETHICAL
GUIDE TO
MURDER

Chapter One

*I've never wanted to kill anyone, but I can't just
let good people die when I have the power to
save them. All I can do is make my decisions as
fairly, and as ethically, as I can.*

I have an awful feeling that Ruth is going to die today.

We are sitting at our kitchen table, drinking freshly squeezed orange juice and eating cereal. Ruth is engrossed in the *British Medical Journal*. I am scrolling through TikTok.

'Pass the Cheerios, please,' I ask.

She looks up from her reading, a little dazed. It takes her a moment to realize the Cheerios are sitting right under her nose. 'Sorry, here you go.'

I take the box, accidentally brushing her hand as I do, and that's when it happens. It's like a static shock, but on steroids. A high voltage punch to the heart. And I'm left with the irrational but nevertheless undeniable certainty that my best friend of seventeen years is going to die. Tonight. At 11.44 p.m. When she touched me, the date and time appeared in digital clock format, just once, in a flash of light seared inside my eyelids.

I drop the box, and the circular puffs spill out across the soft cream tiles.

'Thea, are you okay?'

I blink hard, several times, trying to test for Ruth's estimated time of death. Nope, just darkness. Then I check how many fingers I have. Five on each hand. Chipped green nail polish semi-intact.

There's a faint smell of burning toast, but other than that everything's fine. People don't predict death over their morning Cheerios. This is just what happens when you combine an overactive imagination and sleep deprivation. It's even less convincing than the time I woke up certain that I was not a failed lawyer but Amal Clooney, and that George was downstairs making me a lovely Nespresso. No such luck.

I crouch down and start scooping the Cheerios back into the box. 'Yeah, I had the weirdest feeling ... but ignore me. I'm tired. Nothing a good night's sleep won't fix.'

'Oh, I see, this is a ploy to get out of tonight, isn't it?' She grins. 'Well, I'm not having it. I prescribe paracetamol, water and a quick nap before we head out.'

Tonight, after work, we are celebrating the end of Ruth's FY2, which means she's a properly qualified doctor now. It's the culmination of five years of medical school and I'm determined she'll enjoy every second of it. I shake my head, trying to throw away the last of my temporary delusion with it.

'Not a chance, it's going to be a great night. Everything is a hundred per cent completely and utterly fine.'

My office is in central London, two Tube rides and a short walk away from my flat. I'm reliably late as a person, and today I'm true to form. It's not my fault. I've got a background throbbing in my brain that paracetamol can't touch. I stand at a turnstile trying to use my coffee loyalty card as an Oyster for a good few minutes before a kindly older gentleman straight out of a Dickens novel helps me out. And I've forgotten my access card and have to ask reception to buzz me into the building. They insist on checking my ID – which they are clearly only doing to make a point because this is the fifth time this month that I've forgotten my card.

I work in human resources. At a bank. Absolutely no one has ever asked me a follow-up question as to what that involves. The office is set over one large, open-plan floor. There are long rows of desks in the middle section, and glass-walled rooms along each side for meetings and senior staff offices. Our team occupies one of the desks, and a little patch of wall that my boss, Zara, has covered with a huge whiteboard. She's split it up into columns, each headed by a name, and there is a list of tasks underneath. Under my name, this week's tasks are half-ticked off and the four frowny faces that Zara drew glare at me. I'm currently on thin ice because I approved a job posting for a *terrorist advisor* instead of *anti-terrorist advisor* (got to make sure we're not accidently funding Isis. It happens). I admit, it's not a great look for the company. And the traction it got on social media was less than ideal. But it was also basically a typo and didn't warrant her calling me a waste of time and energy.

'You're late . . . again,' Zara says. She gets up and adds a fifth frowny face in red marker that seems even angrier than the last.

'Sorry, I can stay late if you want.'

'And I'm sure you'll love telling Ruth that I made you late for our night out. Just make up the time at lunch.'

In an unfortunate turn of events, Zara is Ruth's other best friend. I'm not sure why. They dated for all of two months, three years ago, before Zara had the audacity to turn Ruth down. And I can't see they have much in common besides generational wealth. Yet here she is, a constant in both of our lives, more stubborn than a fungal toenail.

In her defence, she's also the reason I have a job at all. A favour to Ruth rather than any underlying tolerance towards me, but still, I'm not entirely ungrateful about it. So I bite my lip, put my head down and concentrate on reviewing the employee mental health evaluations. Without looking, I know word for word what the evaluations will say: We're all bloody stressed, so stop adding mindfulness workshops to our already overpacked schedules and tell IT to stop 'improving' the finance system. I make good progress compiling the responses and by lunchtime I've completely forgotten about this morning's events.

Then I'm asked to sign for a delivery. The woman presses a pen into my hand and the same jolt shoots up my spine. *Ten years*. She's going to die at 3.04 p.m. on 2 August. I snatch back my hand. It's exactly the same. Electricity. Date and time. Burning toast.

Hmm, maybe I'm having a stroke?

My favourite and only work friend, Eli, helps me google symptoms and we rule out the stroke. But something is definitely not right. At this point I reckon my body is pulling an elaborate psychosomatic plot to get out of an evening with Zara. I'm not going to let this clearly irrational but nevertheless horrible feeling, like something is burning a hole in my stomach, ruin Ruth's night. So I wrap up my essential tasks, go home and get straight into bed. Can't have intrusive paranoid thoughts if you're unconscious. Take that, brain.

My win is short-lived, because I forget to set an alarm and sleep straight through until 9 p.m., at which point Ruth wakes me up by knocking on my door. 'Thea, are you ready?'

'Nearly,' I lie, trying not to curse as I unstick my mascara-clumped lashes. They crusted together while I slept.

'The taxi will be here in five.'

We're late going out because I can't decide what to wear. Zara is always decked out head to toe in designer clothing. Knowing she's coming with us makes me look at the contents of my wardrobe and wonder why I choose to dress like a seven-year-old. I'm like a magpie distracted by every sequin and pattern I see, and as such I take for ever to find an inoffensive blue dress, tights – because it's January – and some heeled boots. The boots are half a size too big (on sale, couldn't say no), so I need socks too. Unfortunately, the only pair I can find have a picture of hammerhead sharks in party hats alongside the phrase, 'Let's get hammered.' I'm trying, sharks, I'm trying.

We meet Zara and two more of Ruth's friends at a bar on Clapham High Street called Supernova. Zara has clearly already had a few because the only thing she says to me is, 'You look all right.' And I'm glad that I pushed the animal socks down under my boots.

Supernova is a glorious celebration of disco and cheese. It's basically compulsory to buy the overpriced glow sticks from the bar. Before they died, my parents brought me up on a healthy diet of nineties pop (from my mother's side) and seventies rock (from my father's side). Usually, I love nothing more than to show off my extensive lyrical and choreographical knowledge of S Club 7 and Queen, but tonight my old favourites have lost their shine.

Every time I bump against someone on the dance floor, the time and date of their death flashes through my mind brighter than the neon lights at the bar. The woman in the red dress who won't stop doing slut drops: *twenty-five years*. The man shyly watching the slut-drop woman from across the room: *fifteen years*. The couple who are using each other as human spittoons: *five and fifty years*.

It's 11.27 p.m. I'm sweating but the hairs on my arms are standing up. This isn't some entertaining quirk anymore, and while I'm aware that believing any of this would make me certifiable, I can't shake the doubtful voice in my voice that says, *What if? What if you're wrong and this is real, and Ruth drops dead at 11.44 p.m.?*

I keep my eyes firmly locked on Ruth, as if nothing bad can happen to her while she's in my line of sight. And I remind myself there's no reason to think anything is really going to happen. She's the picture of health: glowing skin and honey-brown curls shining under neon light. I keep bobbing along to the music as best I can, but I'm struggling because my socks keep bunching – I pushed them down too far in my attempt to hide them from Zara. I take advantage of a lull in the song to bend down and pull them up. Before I manage, the Wicked Witch herself takes a wrong turn and charges into me, dropping her cranberry vodka on the dance floor.

'What the hell, Thea? What are you doing?' Zara holds her hands up incredulously, as if *I'm* the one in the wrong, when it's her drink soaking into my tights.

The other partygoers are glaring at us. We bob and weave through the maze of bodies and find a quieter spot to take a breath. Neither of us speaks for several long moments.

I break the silence first. 'It was an accident.'

'It always is with you, Thea.'

'You're not supposed to have drinks on the dance floor. That wasn't my fault.'

Zara sighs. 'If you weren't so careless, maybe you wouldn't make so many mistakes.'

Of course, I should have known Zara wouldn't be able to let the *terrorist advisor* incident go, even for one night. 'It was a bloody typo. And I've already apologized.'

'It was seen by thousands of people. Do you have any idea how embarrassing that was for the company, and for me?'

I'm not sure what else I can say. Thankfully, Ruth interjects. 'Hey, gals, all good?'

Zara shakes her head. 'I can't deal with her. I'm going to get another drink.'

'Don't drop it this time,' I say, enjoying the freedom of poking the bear, knowing she won't turn round and bite me in front of Ruth.

'What happened?' Ruth asks.

'Nothing, I could do with some air though.'

Around fifteen people at various points along the drunk and disorderly spectrum crowd the fenced-in smoking area. Even so, it's peaceful. Relative to the sweat-infused musk of the club, the smoke feels fresh, and the hum of chatter is kept low by people pausing to inhale their cigarettes.

A guy around my age stumbles over to us. His eyes are completely glassy, and it's like he's trying very hard to focus them on us. 'Hav'ya got a cigarette?'

'No, sorry,' Ruth says.

We only came out here for a break. Ruth doesn't smoke because she values her health. I just can't afford it.

He continues, 'Come on, I bet ya do.'

'We haven't got any,' I say, my tone sharp.

'All right, was only asking, you don't have to be a bitch about it.'

I let it go because he promptly tries someone else. 'Tosser,' I say under my breath to Ruth.

'He's okay really, just a bad drunk. Zara knows him,' Ruth says.

'Hmm, a friend of Zara, great.'

She gives me a knowing look. 'I seem to remember you promising to play nice, no?'

'She started it,' I say, not caring how childish I sound. 'Never mind, I won't be working for her soon, so there'll be nothing to fight about.' Unsurprisingly, working in human resources for someone I intensely dislike has never been my dream. But seeing as I failed the bar, I had to make do. HR seemed legal-adjacent enough, so I thought it would make an okay stepping stone.

'Really, that's great. Have you got an interview?'

'Well, no, but I'm signed up to this webinar about alternative routes into law that looks really good.'

'A webinar?'

'You're pulling a face.'

'I know you, Thea. Can't fail if you don't really try. I also know that if you really did try, you could do it. Zara's got some great contacts in the legal world. I'm sure she'd help.'

'You're right, she would love to be rid of me.'

She gives a small smile then goes quiet before saying, 'I appreciate you coming out. I know you're not a big fan of Zara, but it's been a great night and it means a lot to have all my friends together.'

I mean to say something nice when I notice Ruth's watch. 11.44 p.m.

'Is that the time?'

'Yeah, it's running a few minutes ahead though. Trying to get myself in the habit of arriving everywhere early before my shifts at the hospital start next week.'

She's cut off by a scream. The bouncer perks up, but he can't seem to locate the source of the problem. I get an elbow in my back and notice the tosser from earlier – the one who asked for a cigarette – squaring off against a bloke much bigger than him. He looks like a puffed-up chihuahua who has picked a fight with a Rottweiler. Little dogs like that never know when to stop. He throws a punch that looks like it takes all the strength he has, but it only has the effect of irritating the bigger guy. The Rottweiler exchanges a quick glance with the girl beside him and sends the chihuahua flying with a single shove.

Straight into Ruth. She's down on the ground. I can't see her through the maze of bodies.

'Move!' I yell at them and fling myself to her side. Broken glass on the ground cuts through my tights and into my knee. The sting makes me wince, but I ignore it. 'Ruth?'

She doesn't react. There's blood on the single concrete step into the club, blood on the tarmac under her head and blood darkening her honey brown curls. I touch her wrist to check for a pulse, and it's there, but I feel the truth of it deep in my bones: she's dying. Less than two minutes left.

The bouncer has disappeared, no doubt running off to find the police officers who wait outside Supernova on Friday nights ready to disperse those who don't know when to go home. I don't know when I started screaming, but the crowd has backed away, pressed up against the constraints of the metal smoking area fence. No one is actually smoking anymore but no one dares to put out their cigarette. It's as if everyone has decided that if they stay very still and very quiet, then time will slow down and everything will be okay.

I look from person to person, waiting for a solution to magically appear. Then I catch a glimpse of my socks. Stupid hammerhead shark socks. And I realize this is all my fault. I knew she was going to die, and I said nothing, then we were late going out because I fell asleep and couldn't find normal-looking clothes or a decent pair of socks, then I tripped Zara trying to adjust said stupid socks, which led to us being out in the smoking area at this very moment.

The person I love most in the world is going to die because I couldn't find a matching pair of fucking *socks*.

Someone breaks the line and crouches down beside me – a man, the tosser from the fight. His voice trembles as he speaks. 'Is she all right?' He looks so much younger than he did moments ago. The cocky grin evaporates, and the puffed-up chest deflates. 'I didn't mean to push her, you know that, right? It was an accident, not my fault.'

Ruth isn't even cold, and he's already trying to shift the blame. I could reach across and rip his throat out with my bare hands. Anything to stop him from talking. Suddenly I realize this is not my fault. It's his. He started that stupid fight. He took it too far. His careless lump of a body is the one that knocked hers to the ground.

Ruth, who I have known since primary school, who has always played fair and has always seen the best in others, dead. It's simply too much to bear. My heart is already twisting itself into knots, crushing me with the knowledge of what is to come: the grief, the pain, the loss. I can't survive it. Not again.

One minute.

Ruth's soon-to-be killer reaches out and grabs my arm. 'Say something, please!'

I know he wants me to tell him it's all okay, that he hasn't just killed my best friend, as if I give a shit what happens to him. But I look down at his hand on my arm, and that same sense of dread washes over me: he has five months to live. That's five months longer than Ruth.

What happens next is difficult to explain because I have no

idea what I'm doing. His hand is still on my arm, and I can feel his life force the same way I can feel breath filling up my lungs. I pull at the thread of it, and it comes loose. His life is mine to take. He jerks back his hand, eyeing me with distrust.

Ruth twitches on the ground. I imagine her funeral, and the dark abyss her death will leave behind. I can't let her go.

I have dissociated from my body. Some deep, primal instinct or dormant muscle memory is guiding me – or at least that's what I'm telling myself, because I need to believe someone else is doing this. I take his hand in mine, close my eyes and wrap my mind around his life. This time, I pull hard. Energy courses through me. Electric. Every cell of my body is alive, like I've stepped into the ocean in winter. Then, a moment later, the water settles, lapping over my skin in warm waves. I drop his hand and place mine on Ruth's shoulder. The same energy flows from me to her. Her skin warms under my touch.

I look back to the man, who's looking more like a boy with every passing moment. And somehow, even though it makes no logical sense, I know exactly what I've taken from him. 'It's okay, it'll all be over soon,' I say. Then I add in a hushed croak, 'And I'm sorry. I didn't have a choice.'

He's visibly paler but drops his head into his hands and breathes a sigh of relief.

All of this takes place in the time it takes for the bouncer to call the police over. The metal fence scrapes as the bouncer pulls it back. Police herd the crowd away. A paramedic drops to Ruth's side and asks me to give them some room. Ruth's eyes flicker open. She takes a shallow breath and tries to pull herself up.

'Stay down,' the paramedic says. 'It's important you don't move until we've examined you.'

There's a patch of blood on the concrete, but they can't find the head wound.

The boy, Ruth's would-be killer, turns around, clearly looking for his friends. He takes a step towards them, then his legs buckle. It looks like someone has taken a bat to his knees, except there's no one standing remotely near him. He falls down and lies still. One of the paramedics rushes to his side, then the second, leaving Ruth to her own devices. They try CPR for several minutes, continuing their rhythmic attempts to save his life until a crack echoes through the air. A rib. I tell them it's no use. He's dead. He was gone the moment I touched him.

Chapter Two

There's no single reason that makes someone deserving of death. But the more items on my list ticked off, the better. Well, not better for them, obviously ...

Our flat is silent. When I first wake up, all I can think about is my head pounding as I try to navigate the ten feet from my bedroom to the kitchen. I flick the kettle on, lean against the kitchen counter, watch the water boil and try not to vomit on our nice clean tiles.

It's like any other Saturday morning. Then I remember last night. Ruth. Dead.

My heart, already under strain trying to process the alcohol from last night, works overtime and I can feel it drumming against my chest. I clamber up the stairs to Ruth's room, using my hands as front legs to keep me steady. I raise my arm to knock on her door, then stop. I can't hear anything. Maybe she is dead after all, and everything else has been my brain constructing a new reality I can actually cope with. If I don't knock on the door, she might not be dead. But she also might not be alive. It's like that stupid cat in a box thing Ruth once tried to explain to me.

I knock and call out softly, afraid of the response. 'Ruth?'

'I'm awake, come in.'

I open the door and there she is, propped up against the headboard with a sleepy smile on her face but very much alive and well. I take what feels like my first real breath since I woke up. It's then I notice the state of her room. It usually looks like the inside of an IKEA advert, but today her clothes lie scattered across the floor, and there is a tipped-over glass on her bedside table.

'How are you feeling?' I ask.

'Exhausted. You?'

I give a small smile. 'Hanging.'

'I can't stop thinking about Greg,' she says. When I don't respond she adds, 'The guy from last night.'

Greg. Knowing his name makes it so much worse.

Ruth continues: 'It's all people are talking about on the group chat. I didn't realize what a nice guy he was. He used to volunteer every summer at . . .'

Odd how people suddenly remember the good stuff – grief-tinted glasses will make them forgive anything – but all I can picture is the idiot who got drunk and started a fight in a crowded, enclosed area. I don't want to hear anything else about him. I *need* to not hear anything else. A boy died of a heart attack – tragic, but nothing to do with me.

'So sad. Such a horrible accident,' I say.

Ruth sweeps back her hair and does a double take as she picks a fleck of dried blood out of her curls. 'You know, I'm still hazy about last night. What actually happened?'

I shrug. 'I couldn't tell you. Alcohol, right?'

'Right.'

I'm not lying about the hangover – it's a miracle I remember anything at all. The headache and nausea are bad enough, but it's the cold that's really getting me. It's strange. Usually, I wake up in a fluster, my body sweating out toxins, but today I'm frozen to the bone. Like someone has sucked all the life out of me.

I edge towards the door and say, 'I'm making coffee, want one?' Ruth mutters a reply, but I'm out the door before she can pull me back into a conversation about last night. Ruth is alive, that's all that matters.

I spend the rest of the weekend attempting to repress Friday night. Every time Ruth brings it up, I say I can't remember and change the subject. And it works. I'm starting to believe that what I thought had happened was nothing more than a product of alcohol and an overactive imagination. That's the logical explanation here – the only explanation. By Sunday evening, we're both focused on the week ahead. Ruth is starting work in the intensive care unit, and I've got a busy week too. Soon, Friday night will be nothing more than a hazy memory.

Back in the real world, I'm coming up to the end of my probation period and, lacking any alternative, I would like to keep my job. Someone has to fund my coffee bill. On Monday morning I pick out the most boring cream blouse I own and blue trousers with only a little bit of pattern on them. I force my blonde mess of a bob into a bun, even though it's too short to go up properly and it takes half a pack of hair slides to hide all the stubborn escapee wisps. I hate wearing it like this, but Zara constantly comments on the importance of appearance. She's usually staring at me when she says this.

After our spat on Friday night, I'm expecting the worst from Zara. But she starts the day by wiping away my collection of red frowny faces on the board.

'Let's start fresh this week, shall we?' she says, attempting a small smile. It humanizes her a little. Between her taut ponytail and fitted black suit, her soft side usually remains hidden.

The others arrive a few minutes later. There's Eli, my office partner in crime; David, who retired last year then came back part time (I think he just likes having a reason to leave the house); and Kate, a mum of two a few years older than me.

Zara assigns tasks for the week. I'm in charge of payroll. The singular worst task because it's both important and mind-numbingly boring. However, I would like to pass my probation, so I tell Zara, 'Thanks, I'm excited to get started on such an important project.'

I'm sure she must be able to hear my lack of sincerity, but she seems pleased by my response. Maybe this is all work is: pretending not to hate every second of it with every fibre of my being. I remain engaged in our morning briefing, asking questions and answering her prompts. By the end of it, I have a green smiley face on the board, and Eli is eyeing me with suspicion. Briefing over, the others return to their computers.

Zara has another meeting to attend, but before she leaves, she calls me over.

'Thea, I meant to thank you for wrapping everything up well on Friday before you left, even though you weren't feeling well. I'm sorry I snapped at you at the club. Sometimes it's difficult to balance professional and personal boundaries but I'm going to try harder. Life's too short to hold grudges.'

I'm baffled. Who is this lovely alien that has taken over Zara's body, and how do I keep her? She's even holding herself differently. Her nose less upturned, her posture less aggressive.

'That's okay, I'm sorry I messed up that job posting. You seem a bit . . . different today. Everything all right?'

She sighs. 'I'm a bit out of sorts after losing Greg. It was such a shock.'

I flinch at his name as if she's hit me. Of course – they were friends. Greg, the boy I may or may not have killed. Suddenly, Friday night is not a hazy memory. It is tearing its way back into my head in high definition. I remember the way his legs buckled, the crack of his rib as he died.

'I'm sorry,' I say, truly meaning it. And without thinking I reach out, give her arm a reassuring squeeze, and my fragile illusion of normality is torn apart by her death date flashing across my vision. *Sixty-five years left.* 'Fuck,' I say, out loud, at full volume.

'Are *you* okay?'

'Yeah, it's just so sad, isn't it? He was so young.'

'Yeah, it really is.' She's nodding vigorously as if I've said something insightful. Then she squeezes me back. 'Thanks, Thea. I'll see you later.'

Denial is not an effective strategy in this situation. I can't stop people from touching me and every time they do, I'm reminded that Ruth nearly died ... and that I may have killed Greg to save her. But still, what's more likely? That I have a supernatural ability or that I've gone insane? If I had actually passed the bar and become a proper lawyer, I would treat this like a case and gather evidence to get to the truth. So, that's what I'm going to do. Currently, I have correctly predicted death on one occasion. To prove that this is real, I need to do it again. And preferably a third time to be thorough.

I begin my hunt on the Tube ride home. There's an old lady sitting by the carriage doors, hunched over a plastic tartan shopping trolley. Her skin is like dried leather and she's missing several teeth. Perfect. I follow her all the way to the last stop, when she finally gets to her feet, hauling herself up on the shopping trolley. She's taking too long. The doors start beeping. But it's okay, I'm right behind her.

'Here, let me help you,' I say, hoisting her shopping trolley up and giving her my arm.

Twenty-two years. Christ, she's already a walking skeleton. How the fuck is she going to live another twenty-two years?

'Thank you for your help,' she says sweetly, making me feel a little guilty for my internal remarks. 'I don't suppose you could help me up the stairs?'

This is why I don't help people. You do one good deed and then you get roped in. 'Sure, happy to,' I say, even though she's entirely useless to me.

Turns out it's harder than you think to find someone who's about to drop dead. I spend my lunch breaks and evenings following old people about like one of those cats who can sense death. That's what gives me the idea to visit the retirement home at the weekend. I call several of the most conveniently located ones, asking if I can come to visit my grandma, Mary (I googled it, most common name for women born between 1920 and 1940). It's not long before a friendly voice encourages me to 'pop along any time. She'll be thrilled to have a visitor.'

And Mary really is thrilled. I find her sitting in a red velvet armchair in the front room of the home. She waves at me and exclaims, 'Hello, my beautiful girl!'

I enjoy this, very much so. Until she says the same thing to one of the carers, and the tabby cat that walks in.

Unfortunately, Mary has two years to live. When the carers are busy preparing lunch, I explore. It's not a bad place to wait out the end of your life. There's a fairly strong smell of cabbage, but the place is well ventilated so it's bearable. The front room has a television and a fake fireplace, and a big bay window that looks out onto a well-kept garden. They must take good care of their residents because everyone has an annoyingly long time to live. I noticed a sign outside that read 'Single room available now,' so presumably I've just missed an opportunity. After introducing myself to several of the residents, I realize the next vacancy won't be for six months.

I can't wait that long – not if this is real and I'm right about what happened the night of the accident. Ruth was supposed to die. Greg was not. Ruth is now alive. Greg is not. So, my current working theory is that I stole his five months and gave them to her – his death date is now hers. By the time the next oldie pops their clogs, Ruth will already by dead. Again.

Back to square one. I collect my coat and scarf from the cloakroom. As I close the door, the woman with the friendly voice I spoke to on the phone is waiting. 'Did you have a good visit?' she chirps.

I sigh. 'Sure, it was nice.'

'Don't be too disheartened. I know it's hard when someone you love can't remember you, but I'm sure they recognize us on some deeper level. It still means a lot that you came.'

Not exactly the problem here, but sweet of her to say so. She's one of those people that radiates warmth. Probably in her late fifties, still with rosy cheeks and a twinkle in her eye. She has dyed bright red hair and blue butterfly earrings.

'I'm heading out now too,' she says, reaching across me to grab her bright yellow coat. I jump as if she's hit me. *Thirty minutes*. Holy fuck. This wasn't supposed to happen. I wanted to observe a natural death, to test the accuracy of my abilities. I can't watch this delight of a woman die like this. But what am I supposed to do? I don't know how any of this works. I don't even know if it's real.

We walk to the end of the road together, then she waves

goodbye and goes in the opposite direction. I wait a few minutes, then follow her, staying fifteen feet behind at all times.
Which is incredibly difficult because she's a painfully slow
walker. I stop myself going on a mini mental tirade about it
because if she's really about to die, she can walk at whatever
pace she likes. We take a left onto a busy high street. People
are pouring out of the shops, cafes and restaurants after the
lunch rush and I'm thankful her bright red hair and big yellow
trench coat makes her so easy to keep track of. *Twenty minutes*. Nothing out of the ordinary has happened yet. There is
no concrete reason to think she's about to die other than the
lava in my stomach. Then, fifteen minutes before her predicted
death, she steps off the walkway and into an inlet by a coffee
shop. She's facing the wall, clutching at her chest. Shit. I'm
right. This is it. A heart attack.

What would a normal person do in this situation? There's
still time. Ambulance. I pull out my phone and call 999. She's
clutching the other side of her chest now. Kind of weird, no
heart there. But it's hard to tell exactly what she's doing with
that oversized open trench coat blocking my view. I don't give
my name, only the location and that I think someone is having
a heart attack. She drops to her knees. Her bag is on the floor
in front of her and she's leaning forward. Several moments
pass. Then, as I hang up the call, she takes out her phone from
her bag, puts in a pair of Bluetooth headphones and carries on
walking. Crap, she was looking for her phone, not clutching her
heart. I've called an ambulance because some woman wants to
listen to music while she walks. I'm an idiot.

An earthy aroma from the coffee shop tempts me, so I
decide to stop following her. Ironically, caffeine usually calms
me down, so I take my chance to cross the stream of human
traffic and grasp the door. Sirens blast through the street as an

ambulance tears up the road. I turn to look at it, full of embarrassment that I've caused all the cars on a gridlocked street to pull off into the bus lane. Then there's a flash of red, a flash of blue and a sickening crash.

I let the door swing shut and push my way through the crowd. The carer lies in a crumpled heap underneath the ambulance. My attempt to save her has cost her life. I check my phone: dead on time.

It also means that all of this is real. That I took a life to save my friend. And worst of all, Ruth only has five months left to live.

Chapter Three

It's definitely okay to kill Hitler or a cannibal.

Ruth and I have been friends since we were eight years old. My parents had just died, and I'd been shipped off to live with Grandad. And let's just say I didn't take the transition particularly well. Grandad looked after me well enough, but his parenting approach prioritized structure and discipline over warmth and affection. And it's not so easy to make friends halfway through the school year when the other kids have been told to be nice to you because of something they can't possibly fathom at that age. When you come into contact with death as a child, it others you. Most of my classmates avoided me completely. One girl told me she understood because her cat had died recently. Another boy wanted to know how it had happened, and whether I'd seen it.

Then I met Ruth. I'd just been removed from class for being too disruptive (learning the eight times tables was really hard for me) and made to wait out my punishment in the library. Nothing turns my stomach sour like the smell of musty books. I sat in the corner of the room with my arms crossed, refusing to do so much as look at a book. Ruth was sitting in the opposite corner of the room, hair plaited into pigtails, hunched over a textbook with a twenty-eight-pack of coloured gel pens and a purple notepad. The first time this happened, we didn't speak. She kept to her corner of the library and I kept to mine. And the second and the third time, nothing. On the fourth time, I finally caved. 'Why are you always in here?'

She looked up, gel pen cap between her teeth. 'I'm working.'

'Why aren't you in class?'

'Sometimes I don't feel well. It's easier for me to concentrate in here, away from all the noise of the classroom.'

'What's wrong with you?'

'It's rude to ask that.'

'Why?'

'Why are you always in here? You never do any work.'

'Hmm, I'm the noise in the classroom,' I said. 'It's not my fault. My parents died.'

'Oh, I'm sorry,' she said. 'I have leukaemia.'

My mum had been a nurse, and I'd heard her use that word before. Even at eight years old, I knew it was bad. And I knew it meant Ruth's bubble of childhood innocence had been burst, just like mine.

'Why do you care about doing your work if you're sick?'

'Because I want to be a doctor.'

It was then I noticed her textbook. There was a diagram of a skeleton. Next to it was a cartoon man in a white lab coat, providing an explanation about the skeleton via a speech bubble. He had a huge nose, wild grey hair and wonky glasses.

'Well, you'll be better than him. He doesn't look like a doctor.'

'Well, he is. Most doctors are boys. It makes me worried sometimes. I've spent so much time in the hospital that I'm already behind in class.'

'You know who also spends a lot of time at hospitals?'

'Who?'

'Doctors,' I said.

She smiled.

The next time I saw her, I swiped her textbook while she went to the toilet. I pulled out the pack of stickers I'd bought at the corner shop, and I went through her textbook at lightning speed, sticking a face of a girl with pigtails and freckles over the doctor's face, on every page, without fail.

Her eyes went wide when she returned and realized what I'd done. 'You can't do this!'

'I already did.'

She tried to peel off the sticker, but I'd sprung for the premium stickers, and it started to take the paper with it. She smoothed it back down and stared in disbelief. For a moment, I thought I'd made a mistake. That she was mad at me and now there were two rooms in the school where I wouldn't be welcome, but suddenly she snorted with laughter. A full-blown pig snort, nothing delicate about it. It wasn't not long before we'd both descended into laughter, enough to earn us a *sssshhh* from the librarian.

'C'mon, let me help you with your times tables,' she said.

From that moment on, we were friends. The next year, we were put into the same class. Ruth was bolder around me; I was calmer around her. All the teachers liked Ruth. She was a hard worker, quiet and obedient but, above all that, kind. When I was around her, I was good by association.

And if there's one thing I'm sure about, it's that she deserves to live.

But who deserves to die?

I remember someone asking a variation on this question

at a house party back at university. It was 2 a.m. Most of the guests had moved on to houses that hadn't run out of booze while I'd got cornered by a philosophy undergrad – white guy with dreadlocks, obviously – and had to suffer through his detailed opinions on the matter. Now I wish I'd listened, because this is not a hypothetical anymore and I have no idea how to approach it.

Somebody has to die. If I don't pick someone, then it will be Ruth in exactly five months and five days. This *thing* seems to be activated by skin-to-skin contact. I keep finding excuses to touch her, to make sure, and every time it's the same. I don't know where, I don't know how – I only know when. Ruth is hurtling towards her death. It's seemingly inevitable, except that she's already supposed to be dead. I've changed her fate once. I can do it again.

However, this is a completely different thing from what I did to Greg. That was an accident, but this is premeditated, intentional . . . murder? I don't like that word. I've never wanted to hurt someone, let alone kill them. And I don't think it describes what I'm considering doing here. If I'm really going to do this, which I'm still not sure I really am, then I've got to get it right.

I fetch a brand-new Moleskine notepad from my bookcase that I was saving for when I had something important to write. This is a project that justifies its own notepad. I write down the following:

Project Saving Ruth

1. *Can anyone truly deserve to die?*
2. *Who?*
3. *Can I really take another person's life?*
4. *How?*

Embarrassingly, the first action I take to answer question one is to . . . google it. I'm sitting in bed, eating matzah that Ruth left out because I haven't gone food shopping this week, asking the internet who deserves to die. To be fair to the internet, it provides me with an answer: Hitler. People seem to pretty consistently agree that it would be ethical to kill Hitler. Obviously, he's already dead, so this isn't much help to me. However, at least this provides me with a starting point: I can probably feel okay about taking someone's life if they've committed genocide.

In general, I'm surprised how many people are up for ending someone's life. I would say most people fall into one of the following camps: killing can never be justified, no matter what; we should kill those who are a continued threat to others, to prevent further harm; we should kill to punish those who have committed acts of evil.

Clearly, I'm not the only person who's thought about this and asked the internet. There are countless Reddit threads dedicated to the topic. This is a good thing because, hopefully, entertaining the idea of ending someone's life doesn't mean I'm psychopathic. I have a motive. I'm trying to save a worthy life, so all I really need to do is find someone worth less than Ruth. Should be easy.

The comments get weirder the further I go. For example, BigDickHal69 says: *women who lie and cheat on their partners deserve to die. My friend's girlfriend constantly cheats on him. She does this even though she knows how much he loves her and wants her to change. I think red-headed women are more likely to do this.*

Shitposter8 says: *Death to red-heads!*

I sigh and eat another cracker. Dammit, internet, I was just coming round to your way of thinking. Now I'm keenly aware

I'm taking life and death advice from a bunch of trolls living in Mummy's basement. I wipe the crumbs off my laptop keyboard and close it.

As I said, I haven't done any food shopping in a week. Thankfully, Ruth suggests we order in Thai. We sit on the sofa with our red curry (veggie for me), sticky rice and spring rolls.

'*True Crime USA?*' Ruth asks, but she's already navigating to it with the remote.

It's our default show. It has to be the American version because their crimes are so much more interesting than ours – must be all the British repression stunting criminals' imaginations. But I don't feel like it today.

'How about a comedy instead?'

'Like what?'

Our food is getting cold, and I cannot be fussed with channel flicking through endless options. 'Ahh, you're right, true crime is easier.'

She makes a fist and punches the air. 'Yes, there's an episode about cannibals.'

We start watching, but I'm focused on Ruth. It's bizarre to see someone so kind-hearted completely absorbed by morbid tales. Ruth is full of surprises. On her first day of medical school, they showed everyone a dead body to weed out the squealers. Ruth was at the front of the queue, utterly fascinated. She was born to be a doctor.

I think about that as we watch a behavioural analyst trying to explain why a man lured teenagers to his house and ate their organs. I want to save Ruth because I love her, but she also has true value. Spending their childhood in and out of hospital would break most people, or at least mess them up a bit (maybe if the cannibal had had bone cancer as a child, I would have more sympathy). Not Ruth. She barely even complained. Then she decided to dedicate her life to saving others because she wanted to give back in the best way she knew how. There are objective reasons why she should live – even if it costs someone else their life.

The cannibal gets the death penalty. The victims' families are ... not happy, exactly, but relieved. All except one. She's a woman in her sixties, defending the man that murdered her daughter.

'I'm so tired of all this death,' she says. 'I don't want his on my conscience, and if he dies, then he'll never get the chance to learn remorse for what he's done. He deserves to feel that pain.'

'That's ridiculous,' I say. 'Why don't they kill him already?'

'Bit quick to dole out judgement, don't you think? We don't even know why he did it yet,' Ruth says.

I realize we have been watching this show for very different reasons. I like seeing the bad guy get caught. Ruth wants to understand them.

'Who cares why? He ate people.'

'So, we make killers of ourselves in the process of punishing him?'

'It's not the same. Don't you think he deserves it?'

She shrugged. 'Who are we to decide? It's a line that shouldn't ever be crossed.'

'What if killing one person could save another?'

'Like the trolley problem?'

I nod. 'Sure, and obviously I know what that is, but for the benefit of others present . . .' I gesture to the out-of-place smiling porcelain cat that sits on our coffee table. I bought it at a flea market. Ruth thinks it's creepy and possibly haunted, but I think it has character.

She grins. 'It's a moral philosophy problem. The train is

heading for five people who are tied to the track. You can either let them die, or you can pull a lever and divert the train, but it will run over one person tied to the other track. What do you do?'

'I pull the lever.'

'That's what most people say,' Ruth says. She's in her element in situations like this. 'But the lever allows you to distance yourself from the killing. What if you had to do the dirty work yourself? If the only way to stop the train was to push a rock onto the track with one person, crushing them to death, would you?'

'Kinda like the difference between buying chicken from the supermarket or killing it with your own hands? I guess I'd still do it. Five people are worth more than one. It would be selfish not to.'

She laughs. 'See, I've sown some doubt already. It's tough when it comes to actually killing a person, which is what we're asking someone to do when we give out the death penalty. I've got an old textbook from a philosophy and ethics class if you want to read more about it.'

'Yeah, that would be great. Would you pull the lever?'

'I want to say yes. Most people think that's the moral course of action, but I'm not sure if I could.'

Ruth gives me her textbook before bed. It's over five hundred pages long and weighs a ton, but if I'm going to take someone's life, then I owe that decision the respect of reading a single book about it. Besides, I've got five months to get through it. I turn my bedside light onto the highest setting and sit up straight in bed, determined to read a hundred pages tonight. I get to page five before I fall asleep.

*

I wake up with Ruth's great lump of a book on my chest and my reading glasses still on. So far, all I've got is that it's probably fine to kill either Hitler or a cannibal. Although Ruth disagrees over the latter.

I'm ten minutes late to work, which is pretty good for me, but Zara still looks like she wants to wring my neck. 'You realize that your nine to five working hours are not a suggestion?'

Guess that's the end of soft, vulnerable, grieving-for-her-friend Zara. I thought as much towards the end of last week when she snapped at me for not washing up her favourite mug (I was going to do it . . . just later) but now I'm sure.

'Sorry,' I say, only just managing not to roll my eyes. Honestly, with my probation coming up I've been trying to play nice, but I'm dealing with matters of mortal consequence and Zara cares that I'm ten bloody minutes late. She needs to get her priorities straight.

Zara sighs and massages her temples. If she loosened that bun occasionally, she wouldn't get so many headaches. 'With annual reviews coming up, I've got no idea how we are going to manage. It couldn't be a worse time to be a team member down, and after all that time I put into recruiting her . . .'

She's talking about our latest hire, whose mother died on her fifth day working here. Our company allows unlimited unpaid compassionate leave – it's actually one of the policies that Zara advocated for – but I don't think she expected anyone to use it for this length of time. Our new hire has been gone for the past month now.

'It's not like she did it on purpose, Zara. You do know her mum's dead, right?'

She flinches at that word: *dead*. Why does everyone need to say lost, passed or gone? As if the words we use make the truth any less awful. It's odd to me how much effort people will put into avoiding something they will inevitably encounter, either as the victim or the griever. Maybe that's why death is always such a shock to people. Maybe I'm just cynical.

'I know that,' she snaps. 'Does this mean you'll have no complaints when I ask you to stay late tonight?'

I cross my arms to hide my clenched fists. 'Course not.'

'Oh, and I've been meaning to say, you sent out the wrong training evaluation form, so the last batch is invalid. You need to take care of it.'

I remember now. Zara updated the formatting and some of the question wordings. 'Why does it matter? Surely the answers will still be the same.'

'But they've been answering the wrong questions. It needs sorting. Can you handle that?'

She always speaks to me like I'm a child. 'I can handle some forms.'

'I only ask because if you could be trusted to do things correctly, this wouldn't have happened in the first place, would it? The details are important, Thea – you have to stop rushing into things without taking the time to ensure the job is done correctly.'

I'm boiling. Zara is the worst kind of person imaginable. Someone who takes pride in administrative procedures being as complicated as possible, because if she's the only one who knows how to navigate them, other people must cower before her. This is the only way she can achieve power in her small insignificant life. I took this job for the legal experience of dealing with employee contracts, but Zara won't let me near anything important. She specifically assigns me to the petty admin she knows I loathe. Perhaps it's a punishment because she regrets hiring me. I can't understand what Ruth ever saw in her. She actually cried when Zara dumped her – by text, claiming incompatible work schedules. That should have been the end of it, but they kept running into each other. Literally. Zara lives nearby and they share all the same running routes, so they became workout buddies. Then actual buddies. Now I'll never be rid of her.

'And please wear your ID tag around the office,' she says, passing me my lanyard.

I avoid wearing it because the photographer caught me with my eyes half closed, which makes me look permanently drunk.

Her bergamot- and sandalwood-perfumed hands skim mine and remind me of the sixty-five years she's holding. What did Zara do to deserve such a long life? There's something about that scent that sets off something inside me. And this part isn't her fault, because she wasn't to know that bergamot and sandalwood triggers memories I've tried hard to forget, but that knowledge doesn't stop the poison that comes bubbling up. I think about how cruel some people can be, the malice they contribute to the world and how undeserving of life they are. And it's an accident, I swear, but her life starts flowing into me. I snatch back my hand, dropping the lanyard to the floor.

Shit. I didn't mean to do it. I don't think I took the whole sixty-five years, but how the hell am I supposed to know what I did? This thing didn't come with an instruction manual.

Zara picks up the lanyard. 'What was that?'

'Static shock,' I say, and take a moment to compose myself. She passes it again, and I try to remember what I did with Ruth, let the energy flow, like it's water in a stream.

I think I managed to put it back. The energy feels ... gone. But I don't dare touch Zara again to check because she's doing that scrunched up thing with her nose like I'm a bad smell, and my venom towards her is rising again.

I hadn't realized how careful I need to be with this ability. My temper has always been more of a personality quirk than a problem – an ex-boyfriend once described me as an angry but-terfly. Now that it could kill someone, it doesn't seem so cute.

As a silent apology, I stay late every evening this week. My guilt makes me an exemplar employee, and by the end of the week I have more smiley green faces on the whiteboard than the rest of our team combined. I can hardly look Zara in the eye because every time I do, I'm reminded that I nearly killed her over an evaluation form, and despite my frustration towards her, I'm well aware she doesn't deserve to die. But someone has to. God, I wish someone would tell me what the right thing to do is here. I've made no progress on Project Saving Ruth. The ethics textbook she lent me remains on the empty side of my bed, with the corner of page five folded over.

At the weekend, Ruth decides to visit our hometown to see her family. They've got a … complicated relationship. She's the very youngest sibling of five, all of whom are wildly successful. Their family gatherings are more like performance reviews than a chance to spend quality time together. Still, she visits our hometown more often than I do.

'I can drop you off at yours if you want to come too. It's been a while, hasn't it?' she asks on Friday night.

I wince. Eight months. Last time I went home, Grandad and I fought. I'd been out in the next town having a few drinks with friends. I lost my phone. And my purse. Then it took forever to convince someone to lend me some cash for a taxi. By the time I finally got back it was two in the morning. I tried to sneak in with the grace of a drunk baby rhino. Grandad came running down the stairs in his pyjamas brandishing a sword as tall as himself – he's a history buff and the sword's ceremonial – but it was still an alarming sight to someone who had been drinking two-for-one cocktails all night and resulted in me smashing an antique vase. Cue yet another argument about my lack of trustworthiness and responsibility.

'We haven't spoken much since the fight.'

'You always fight, and you always make up.'

'I know. I just don't know why he always assumes such malicious intent when it comes to me. It's never, "Oh you did a selfish thing" but "You're a selfish person." Instead of accepting my apology, he wants me to change my whole personality. What am I supposed to do with that?'

'Just because he doesn't say it, doesn't mean he doesn't miss you.'

At Ruth's insistence, and on the understanding that I can pick the playlist for the car, I agree to go along.

But those aren't the only reasons I agree. Someone needs to die to save Ruth, and I don't think a book is going to help me. I might not have appreciated my corporal punishment-style childhood at the time (a mild exaggeration, I admit), but if there's one person who knows right from wrong, it's Grandad. Head of the neighbourhood watch, organizer of the local Help for Heroes group and the unofficial guardian of the community. He's never encountered a moral quandary he can't solve. I just need to figure out how to ask for the answers I'm looking for.

Chapter Four

You wouldn't go shopping when you're hungry,
so don't murder when you're angry.

It usually takes three trains and a taxi to get home, but in Ruth's Mini Cooper it takes just under an hour. Driving through the village reminds me of how we spent our childhoods. There's not much to see. A church, a pub, a grocery shop, two charity shops and randomly a nail bar, which I'm fairly sure is a front. But there's also the tuck shop where we used to get sweets and the playpark where we used to go after-hours back when we thought that was a cool thing to do. Ruth's ten years younger than her next youngest sibling and, as such, I pretty much had her all to myself most days.

We pass a copper statue of our village's founder and I tell Ruth to slow down. 'Do you remember what you did to that poor man, Ruth?'

'Don't remind me.'

'Traffic cone on his head, bright pink bikini and a spray-painted penis. Humiliating. He's probably still turning in his grave.'

'Don't try to blame the penis on me. You're the perverted one,' she says, feigning disapproval, but I can see the twitch of a smile.

Ruth may play the good girl, but there's a rebellious streak in there. That's why she puts up with me. She knows that without me she would have spent her whole childhood in the library.

'Whatever, you loved it,' I say.

'I can categorically say that I did not. Dick's hardly my thing.'

We both giggle, but as we draw closer to Grandad's house, I grow quiet and start shredding the last remnants of my green nail polish.

'He'll be glad to see you, Thea.'

'Easy for you to say – he thinks the sun shines out of your arse.'

Thing is that the fight has never been the problem. We've always butted heads. Grandad comes from a different generation: he believes central heating is a scam, the flu can be thrown off by strength of will alone and that the country has fallen apart without a war to fight. In his mind, children respect their elders – my being an adult has never had any bearing on that.

But there's something else, something I haven't told Ruth. It was when we stopped fighting and he said, 'Sometimes you're so like your father.'

I remember the soft defeat in his voice. The way he seemed to shrink, the orange and green floral wallpaper looming over him. We do not talk about my parents. Every time I've tried, it's like Grandad's throat seizes up. So, to hear him compare us and express such . . . disappointment . . . I couldn't understand it. I still don't.

That's why I left that part out. I don't know how to explain why it bothers me so much. It just does.

She rounds the corner, and the house comes into view. Two-bedroom, pebbledash exterior with white plastic windows. Every time I come to visit, it seems smaller, even though nothing has changed. And I mean nothing – there's a pinboard by the door that still has notices on from twenty years ago.

Grandad is crouched in the front garden, planting primroses. He looks well, bright blue eyes and a face flushed with a healthy glow.

'You better drive off before he spots you if you want to make it home before dinner,' I say.

Ruth lives in a sprawling country manor house, but it's over on the other side of the village – the nice side.

She nods and checks her watch. 'Good idea. I want to get there before the others.'

I open the door and throw my bag over my shoulder. 'It's not a competition, remember. And if it starts feeling like one, remember that Max is actually fucking boring, Ava definitely has a coke problem, Robin's wife told me he can't get an erection unless she slaps him, and Abigail ... actually she's kind of great. Anyway, your siblings are not better than you. Enjoy your weekend.'

I shut the door and Grandad looks up. I'm grateful he doesn't move to greet me because I couldn't handle knowing how long he's got left to live. One problem at a time. It seems easy enough to avoid finding out people's death dates by not touching them. I don't anticipate this will be an issue for me and Grandad because I think the last physical contact between us was when he checked a seventeen-year-old me's forehead for a temperature. I actually had a hangover, but he didn't need to know that.

'You're earlier than I expected,' he says.

'We made good time.'

He stands up, one hand holding his back as he carefully straightens. 'I hope Ruth was being careful. People come out of the city and forget you can't treat country lanes the same. And the potholes are just treacherous, utterly treacherous.'

I wince. We both know the fallout of dangerous driving, the irreparable damage done by someone who did not consider the consequences of taking a corner too fast or having one extra drink at the pub.

'It's Ruth – she's always careful.' There's a moment of silence, then I say, 'Well, I'll go and get settled.' I turn towards the back door.

'Thea,' he calls.

He puts down his trowel and stretches his neck. He looks at me for a moment. I wonder if he's going to say something about our fight. Or maybe I should? It's already present, at the front of my mind and on the tip of my tongue, so what's the harm in addressing it?

'Yes?' I prompt.

'Dinner is at six thirty.'

We have a roast. I always insist he doesn't need to make such a fuss, but he never listens. He also doesn't fully understand the concept of vegetarianism, so my roast consists of piled-up potatoes, carrots, broccoli and cauliflower cheese, smothered in gravy. I don't object. They're the best bits anyway.

We keep things light. He asks about work, and I say it's fine. I ask about the history museum he volunteers at twice a week, and he tells me long stories about people I've never met. They're also in the running to receive a donation of historical artefacts – a collection of medals and a soldier's diary. He's very excited about it. The house is already full of war memorabilia. An oversized painting of a Spitfire hangs in the dining room, yet there's not a single photo of my parents. The only visible memory is Grandad's black-and-white wedding picture, which sits above the fireplace in a small gold frame. How can someone who spends their time preserving the past try so hard to bury their own?

But I'm not here to talk about my parents. That ship has long sailed. I need Grandad's advice, but first I need to figure out how to ask for it.

If there's one thing that gets Grandad talking, it's planes. He was in the RAF. Mostly in ceremonial roles and desk jobs but I know he saw active service at one point – that's the part he's cagier about.

He finishes his second glass of red wine (he thinks it's his first, but I've been topping it up behind his back) and is telling me about one of the many 'fascinating' design features of the Vulcan bomber. I use this to steer to his time as a pilot, feigning interest in what kinds of planes he flew. And when he's settled into a rhythm, I ask what I really want to know: 'Did you ever kill anyone?'

He shakes his head. 'I don't know.'

'How is that possible?'

He stares into his empty glass. 'Probably.'

'What was it like?'

'I don't know.'

'What do you mean, you don't know? You must feel something about killing a person?'

'It does no good to think about how I feel. I did what my country asked of me but that doesn't make it right.' He goes quiet and I can tell his throat is seizing up. He coughs to cover it. 'Why are you asking me these things?'

'I don't understand. You love talking about war, so why won't you talk about your own experience?'

'I don't love talking about war, Thea. I think it's important to honour what happened, so that we remember the cost of it – even if it seemed like we were doing it for the right reasons at the time.'

'So, what are you saying – there's never a good reason to go to war? What about the Second World War? Surely that one was fair game?'

'Right and wrong are not mutually exclusive concepts. Having a good reason to do a terrible thing doesn't make it any less terrible. Especially if you're the one deciding what's moral and what's not. He shakes his head. 'Let's get these dishes in to soak.'

We clean up in companionable silence, and I'm in bed by 9.30. My room has the same orange and green wallpaper as the hallway, which I've tried to cover up with contrasting covers of my parent's old vinyl collection. Rolling Stones, ABBA, Blue Öyster Cult, Madonna, Queen and Carole King. With them looming over me, it's impossible not to think about what Grandad said: *you're so like your father.* Why should I not be?

I can't stop thinking about it. About them. Then, inevitably, how they died. That last evening I spent with them, when we drove up to the forest to have a McDonald's picnic – Dad's idea, he was fun like that, which is one of the clearest things I remember about him. We walked through the trees, Mum holding my left hand, Dad holding my right, swinging me over puddles as I giggled, until we found a quiet bench to watch the sunset. It was a perfect evening. Until the drive home, when my childhood was destroyed by flashing lights, screeching tyres and burnt rubber.

It's a memory I've worked hard to repress, but being back here makes that difficult. Getting blackout drunk has proved an efficient remedy for suppressing traumatic memories, and I find the headache preferable to the nightmares, but Grandad and I finished the wine at dinner. There's nothing else in the house but ouzo – even I won't stoop that low.

I wonder why I couldn't save them. This power came to me to save Ruth, but why not them?

No answer comes. Instead, I try to count sheep, to take deep breaths and to focus on the swirls of the Artex ceiling. Once again, the night is filled by the sound of my mum's scream and the image of her head hitting the dashboard.

I remember the headlights of the other car, illuminating the contents of the wreckage in painful detail. And an outline of someone walking towards us. The glass crunches under their feet, then they stop. The headlights blind me, and I can't make out their face. In my dreams I try to focus, as if I can find some fragment of memory that's been lost, rather than never formed. I've pictured them with so many faces that I've formed a near-human composite in my mind that is undoubtedly wrong and more terrifying than the real thing.

In my dreams I strain at my seat belt, trying to get a better look because maybe if I could have described them all those years ago, maybe they would have caught them, and maybe my parents' deaths wouldn't have gone unpunished. Sometimes they are male, sometimes female. Once I saw green eyes, at other times they are blue. Their nose has been straight, bumpy and crooked. Every time I think I've finally caught a proper glimpse, they duck their head and turn. The engine bursts into life and the car pulls away.

After the second nightmare that night I lie awake and think to myself, if I truly wanted to kill someone – not because I had to, but because I *wanted* to – it would be them.

*

The next morning, we go to church. I haven't been in years, but it's exactly the same. Red carpets, rows of carved oak benches and that signature religious musk that is really just lack of air circulation. Even the fabric banners hung above the pews are the same.

I used to go to Sunday school every week and sing hymns in choir, and I still wear a small cross around my neck. Grandad is to blame for the first two, although I do actually quite like the songs. 'All Things Bright and Beautiful' is a tune. The cross was a gift from my dad. It's silver and has a black tourmaline stone in the centre that is supposed to ward off dark spirits – seems like Dad was really trying to cover all the bases.

Grandad makes me attend Sunday service every time I visit, which goes some way in explaining why I don't come back that often. We're in the third row listening to the vicar's sermon. I'm not paying attention – they're all about love and forgiveness anyway. Instead, I'm wondering whether I can catch an earlier train back to London. This trip has been a bust. I don't know what I expected anyway.

I may not be listening to the sermon, but there's something about the booming vicar's voice and the church's oversized stone ceilings that makes me feel guilty. Like someone knows what I did to Greg, and what I almost did to Zara. I start to think that perhaps Ruth and Grandad are right and taking a life can never be justified. The Bible certainly seems to think so because the vicar's currently going on about turning the other cheek. Besides, if someone were going to be given the power to make this decision, why would it be me?

Then I remember that the Bible is full of violence. Seriously. Here's a list of things the Bible says people should be killed for:

1. Not listening to a priest.
2. Being a fortune-teller (stoning for this one).
3. Adultery.
4. Being gay.
5. Hitting Mum or Dad.
6. Cursing Mum or Dad (wow, this is clearly a parenting tactic).
7. Being a non-believer.
8. Having sex before marriage (stoning – but for women only).
9. Taking the Lord's name in vain (another stoning).
10. Working on a Sunday (actually, fair).

Oh, and if there's one person in a village who worships another god, kill the entire town to be on the safe side. To be fair, most of it is Old Testament; Book of Leviticus, to be precise, which most Christians are happy enough to ignore unless they get a bee in their bonnet about gay marriage . . . yet those same people seem happy enough to go on eating bacon and shrimp (which God considered an abomination in the Bible part one but apparently later backtracked on. I guess everyone gets to have character development.) Anyway, my point is that most religion is an inconsistent crock of shit and the world is lucky I'm not turning to it for advice.

There's a coffee machine in the room at the back of the church, and people like to mill about for at least an hour after the service, trading gossip and showing off about their kids. Not very Jesusy, if you ask me, but Grandad loves any opportunity to natter with the locals, so he makes us stay. Mrs Palmer corners me by a huge arrangement of carnations. I can't move without knocking either her or them over.

'Thea, darling, we've missed you at church. Please tell me you're taking care of yourself in the city?'

She says the word *city* with disdain. Mrs Palmer is the mother of a boy I went to school with who used to cut chunks out of my hair in arts and crafts. They had to ban him from using the scissors.

'It's not that bad, Mrs Palmer. I've only been mugged a couple of times. The trick is to stare them down, like bears.'

She clearly detects none of the sarcasm in my voice and takes a sharp intake of breath. 'How awful. You know, my Sebastian found a job right here in the village. Perhaps he could give you some advice. Let me find him for you.'

The moment she turns I escape, keen to avoid losing any more chunks of hair. I'm headed for the side door that leads into the cemetery because that's far preferable to being lectured on the benefits of country living by Mrs Palmer's twat of a son. I reach for the handle, but the door swings towards me and I'm hit with a great waft of bergamot and sandalwood perfume. A woman with sagging, mole-spotted skin, wearing a long floral skirt and plastic sandals, steps through. My chest freezes, my heart too shocked to beat. I'm staring into the face of evil. My old schoolteacher: Frances Wells.

Chapter Five

Anyone who hurts a child is more than deserving.

Frances Wells is a pillar of the community. Our village takes Bonfire Night pretty seriously, and every year Frances is at the helm. She organizes the procession floats, deals with the contractors and chooses the Carnival Queen to lead the parade. Every time I come home, I pick up a local newspaper and scan the obituaries in case she's dead.

She never is. I think she might be immortal, like a cockroach that survives a nuclear blast. She has a dog with her now. Dogs aren't allowed in church, but it's a golden retriever that wouldn't harm a fly if you smothered bacon on it, so nobody says anything. It's a fundamental law that people who love dogs are good people, but I think Frances knows this and uses the dog as a disguise.

She's still got one hand on the door. 'Well, don't stand there gawping, help me through.'

The door has a huge step up to it, and she's holding out her hand for me to take. I'm not sure how old she is – she's always looked like an old woman to me, even when I was little – but she's got the fragility of an eighty-year-old. Of course, that could be a ploy too. Anything to seem innocent and vulnerable. I want to refuse to help. She deserves nothing except a kick in the shins from me, but the words are stuck in my throat. As I touch her arm, I get that familiar sensation: *twenty-one years.* How is that fair? Ruth is going to die in five months while this hateful cockroach lives on.

After I haul her over the step, she places herself in the centre of the room. Soon enough she has a small crowd around her, and someone is fetching her a tea. She's the closest thing our village has to a celebrity.

I cannot stand being in the same room as her, so I duck outside like I originally intended to, and find my parents' headstones. They are side by side. Adam and Lucy Greaves. I don't like the idea of their bones in the ground – Grandad insisted on a proper church burial – so I prefer to talk to the tree that overshadows them. It's a beautiful oak that drops acorns around them. Sometimes I see squirrels here. Definitely the least depressing spot in the cemetery.

I sit down in the grass. There's a spot that's moulded to my bum over the years. I tell my parents about the last few days. About Ruth, about death, about Frances. I don't say these things out loud because that's completely mental, and they don't reply because that would be psychotic. But it helps to feel like I'm with people who understand. Nobody knows more about death than dead people.

If they were still alive, I like to think they'd be supportive about this whole death problem. I also like to imagine that if they knew who Frances Wells truly was, they would have killed her themselves.

*

Back at school, Frances liked brash boys and obedient girls. But I was neither of these things. More sullen and wilful. I used to do things like purposefully sew the wrong sleeves onto a dress. I didn't enjoy sewing very much.

But to be fair, my parents had died extremely recently. Most people cut me some slack. Not Frances.

She used to hold up my work as an example of what to avoid. She would take points away from whatever team I was on, so I always got picked last. And she would devise impossibly difficult questions, get me to stand up in front of my classmates and smile as I failed to answer.

Then, one day after class, someone left a pin on her chair. She sat on it and let out an almighty yelp. The classroom descended into giggles. Until she held up the pin – gold with a blue, flat plastic head – and demanded to know who had done it. It wasn't me, but she didn't bother to interrogate the others.

She didn't say a word, simply carried on with the class. Which was utterly terrifying. I remember my thighs sticking to those plastic seats and wondering if I could fake an illness convincingly enough to get me sent straight home, but Grandad would never have bought it. The bell rang. We put our chairs on our desks at the end of the day and I thought I was going to get out of there unscathed. Until she said, 'Stay behind, Thea. I need to speak to you.'

My little heart sank. I stared at the floor as I shuffled towards her. 'It wasn't me, honest.'

'I cannot stand liars. Children like you only understand one thing.'

I looked up. My voice had disappeared into the floor along with my confidence, so I couldn't ask what she meant.

'Hold out your hand,' she said.

I did. She pulled it into her lap and jabbed the pin into the fleshy part of my palm.

When you're eight, you haven't experienced much, so pain like that makes you think you are going to die. I screamed from the shock. She yanked me closer and said, 'Don't make such a fuss. You did something bad and now you've been punished. We won't speak another word about it, will we?'

Until that moment, no adult had ever harmed me. But this was another item in the list of things I was learning were not true: that my parents would always be there, and that adults would always protect me. I wasn't sure who else I could trust, so I stayed quiet.

But I still remember the fear every time I entered her class-room, the way my palms would sweat too much for me to hold a pencil, and the way her voice would make me jump harder than if she'd pinched me. I used to hold my breath in those classes, as if the simple act of my existence might be enough to earn her wrath.

I wonder if she would have done it if she'd known I'd one day have the power of life and death. Probably not. All bullies are cowards, especially the ones who pick on children.

I'm still in the graveyard when I smell her bergamot and sandalwood floral perfume wafting towards me on the breeze. She's shuffling – I can tell from the gravel beneath her feet. I wonder what she'll die of. The next twenty-one years might not even be happy or healthy ones, and yet she's got hold of them rather than Ruth. How is that fair?

I stand up, blocking her path. The sun is high in the sky behind me, and she shields her eyes with her hand to get a better look.

'Can I help you, dear?'

Dear, as if.

She lowers her hand. It's paper-thin with yellowish hue. She's less than the length of a ruler from me now; that's all it would take for me to reach out and take what Ruth needs.

But I can't. Grandad's words echo in my head: '*Doing a wrong thing for a right reason is still a wrong thing. Especially if you're the one deciding what the right thing is.*'

Murder is wrong – on that both the Bible and Google agree. But maybe I don't have to kill her? I didn't kill Zara. When I concentrated, I was able to put the life back into her, so maybe I have more control over this power than I first thought. The punishment should fit the crime and I reckon bullying children certainly warrants ... six months, a year even, off someone's life.

I reach out and encircle her wrist with my hand. It's thin as a twig and the skin is sallow. I imagine myself as a vengeful angel looming over her, and that she'll somehow know what I'm doing is divine retribution for what she did to me. She tries to shake me off, but I'm older and stronger now, and her life is mine to take.

And then ... nothing.

I close my eyes and scrunch up my face, trying to remember what it felt like with Greg and Zara, to feel their energy sapping into me like liquid. It was easier than breathing, so I can't understand why this isn't working now.

I push. I pull. I squeeze. It's like I'm desperate for a wee but it won't come out. Shit, is this my conscience?

'I don't owe you anything,' I say, more to myself than to her. 'I don't need to justify my actions to someone walking around with twenty-one years they don't deserve.'

'Stop, you're hurting me,' she says, her voice weak. 'Who are you?'

I loosen my grip a little. 'You don't remember me?'

She squints. Dark, soulless eyes. Squinting so small that they might disappear entirely, like they want to escape the flesh they're attached to. 'I'm sorry, dear, I've had many students over the years.'

'You should remember me – unless you abused all your students?'

'Abuse? In my day we called it discipline.' She looks away, eyes landing on my parents' headstones. 'I do remember you. You always did have an overactive imagination.'

I remember those words on my school report. Every detail of what happened is thoroughly seared into my mind, and yet she's looking at me with hazy focus, like I'm an outline that reminds her of someone she once knew.

'What's my name?'

'Dear, it's not easy for me to recall such details.'

'My name. What is it?'

'Oh, I suppose it was something like Tabitha or Teagan, wasn't it?'

I'm not concentrating. Sometimes I do wonder if I've over-blown what happened in my own mind, whether I really do have an overactive imagination. But I remember those names – she used to make a point of getting my name wrong in class, to which I always answered to avoid punishment. She's letting me know – right now – that she remembers exactly what she did to me and she doesn't feel a lick of guilt about any of it.

My hand is still on her wrist. Without warning, her energy surges into me. It takes a few seconds longer than last time, enough time for me to try to stop, but I don't. I haven't even considered how to stop, practically speaking. After one second, five seconds, twenty seconds? I can't tell how much I've taken. It's like a tap attached to a barrel of water I can't see, and I'm not even sure if there is a tap because maybe I've just punched a hole in the barrel instead. By the time these thoughts have raced through my mind, it's over. The barrel is empty. Her life is mine.

I could put it back, like I did with Zara.

'Tell me you're sorry,' I say to her.

'What have you done to me?' Red capillaries burst in her face, and she coughs up blood on her sleeve. I thought she would have simply dropped dead, like Greg, but I guess that's not how this works.

'Tell me you're sorry, and I'll make it stop.'

She splutters up more blood, wipes it with her sleeve and glares at me. 'You refused to learn any other way. I won't apologize for taking your education seriously.'

She's wheezing now, reaching out for me, but I step back and she falls onto the path. Her dog whimpers, but he's too simple and gentle to do anything of use. The birds are quiet in the trees, like they know something dark is happening.

Believe it or not, I don't actually want to kill her, but I cannot bring myself to return the life I've stolen.

Frances tries to speak but I can't make out the words. Perhaps she's finally uttering that sorry I asked for, but it's too late. I turn before she finds the strength for any last words, avoiding eye contact with my parents' headstones. In fact, I keep my head firmly down as I walk the path back to the church and enter through the side door, pausing only for a moment, long enough to see Frances flat on her stomach.

Grandad is ready to go anyway so we drive straight home. I struggle to hide the euphoria of decades of life pulsing inside me. It's raw power. I go for a run that evening and keep going until I'm drenched with sweat and my limbs ache. I had no idea it felt like this. Twenty-one years of life.

What are the chances that Frances Wells appeared to me in a *church* at the very moment I needed answers? Perhaps there is something more to this – why should guilty people live on while good people die young?

Maybe Ruth isn't the only one I'm meant to save.

Chapter Six

*The target must have taken no action to repent
and show no or little remorse for their actions.*

I can't stop touching people – not in a creepy way.

At the coffee shop this morning, when the barista passed over my usual avocado latte, I let my fingers touch his as he held out my leopard print reusable coffee cup. *Thirty-nine years.* On the train to work, I reached for the same yellow pole as a silver fox halfway through reading *Anna Karenina*. *Fifty-six years.* And I meet a little old lady on a park bench, and while usually I don't find the elderly appealing, this one compliments my 'snazzy' blue-checked trousers and I like her for that. *Seven years.*

Actually, maybe touching people to find out when they're going to die is a little creepy – but not in a sexual predator kind of way, and that should count for something. It's strangely addictive, like I'm walking around with the cheat codes to the game of life.

Which people deserve to have their life extended? And which deserve to have their years cut short? I'm no further along in answering this question, but my mind is brimming with possibilities.

I've been testing the parameters of right and wrong with my work colleagues. 'If you could take a year of life from a serial killer and give it to a child, would you?'

Eli leans back in his roller-wheel chair and pretends to consider my request. 'Sure, would you?'

'Yes. What about a non-serial killer and a random person?'

'Non-serial. Just your standard murderer, then? I guess so, if you're sure he's guilty.'

'How sure would you need to be that he's guilty?'

'Pretty sure.'

'What would you do to make sure?'

'I don't know, Thea, I'm trying to sort out this onboarding before our new recruits arrive.'

'Wait, just one more. What about someone who's just committed a couple of violent crimes? Would you take some life off them to save someone else?'

'What, no, I wouldn't do that,' Eli says. Without getting up, he swivels his chair and shimmies over to the neighbouring desk, over-ear headphones on.

Zara peers over her screen. 'You're perky this morning. Actually, there's been something different about you all week – what's up with you?'

She's not wrong. This week, I've been in bed before midnight every day without fail, I've arrived at work on time nearly as often, and I've spent my evenings updating my CV. My mind is clear. My skin unblemished. And the semi-permanent knots in my shoulders have finally released.

Holding twenty-one years of excess life will do that to you. Ruth decided to spend an extra day with her family, seeing as she had some spare time before starting in the ICU, so I had to take the train straight to work on Monday morning. I'm not worried. She's safe for another five months. I'll make the transfer as soon as she gets back. And I can't say I'm not enjoying keeping hold of her twenty-one years in the meantime. To be brimming with this much energy is intoxicating. It's not just the energy, though. Frances Wells is dead. I thought I'd feel guilty, but I simply don't. I feel lighter, freer than I have in years.

'Oh, you know, I've just been eating more vegetables.'

'Well, please send me your recipes. With the end of the quarter coming up, I've been working twenty-four seven, especially as we're still a team member down. I know that we need someone else, but I can't bring myself to just replace her. I know what it's like to lose a parent.'

'You do?'

'Yeah, my mum died a year ago. Didn't you know that?'

'No, I'm sorry.' I say those pointless words like a reflex, like so many people have said to me over the years.

'Thanks. Losing my mum, then Greg, in such a short space of time, I can't help but feel death is following me.'

Nope, just me. And she doesn't even know I nearly killed her over an evaluation form.

'I'm sorry I snapped at you the other day. The evaluation forms were my fault – I should have just apologized at the time. And I'm sorry for the recruitment post. I guess I've been a bit slack.'

'That's okay, I've not been myself either lately. And I know you've been asking to get involved in projects that offer legal experience. We're getting a lawyer involved in a potential unfair dismissal case we're dealing with. Do you want to help with that?'

'Of course. That would be great.' Wow, maybe I really have misjudged her.

By lunchtime, I've almost managed to trick myself into thinking I like my job. I finish processing payroll and start thinking about how to make the process more efficient for our freelancers. Usually, I'm so far behind a deadline I wouldn't have a spare thought in my head for how to be better at my job.

Towards the end of the week, Zara says to me: 'You know, I have an old friend who works at Tate & Grey. Maybe she could take a look at your CV and give you some advice on getting back into law. She's always happy to help.'

I'm not even mad that Zara has worked with me for eleven months and has only decided to tell me this now, because everything's finally coming together.

I'm putting good vibes into the world and they're coming back twice over.

My week of productivity continues. I declutter my wardrobe, alphabetize my bookcase and finally tackle 'the drawer', which is full of stuff I have no specific place for. If I haven't used something in six months, it goes in the bin. No exceptions.

Between me being on double speed and Ruth starting shifts at the ICU, we end up not seeing each other until Sunday afternoon. As I take another bin liner full of uncategorizable crap out through the living room, I find her dressed in purple and black Sweaty Betty running gear, stretching her hamstrings against the sofa. Back at school, I genuinely loved running through the woodlands with Ruth. Then life and work got in the way, and I was always too tired or too busy to run. Not Ruth. She does half-marathons for fun.

I know I should make the transfer now, but it's not like one more hour is going to hurt anyone. It's been years since we've run together, so I tell her I'll join her.

She looks at my inappropriate sneakers. 'Are you sure you're going to be okay running in those?'

I got them on discount from the supermarket clothes section, but today it's like someone has put springs in them. It's an effort to stay still. 'Trust me, they're just well worn.'

She makes a face. 'Okay, let's take it easy.'

She insists I stretch first. After each one I say, 'Can we go yet?'

'You'll get cramp if you don't stretch properly.'

I keep nagging until she gets bored and then we're off. We amble down the street, dodging two dogs, a group of teenagers who refuse to move aside and a woman with a pushchair. Even when the pavement opens up, Ruth refuses to go faster. Finally, we get to Clapham Common and into the park. Wide open space with nobody in my way.

'Race you to the bandstand,' I yell.

And I start running, really running. The ground falls away beneath my feet and air rushes against me. I run past the pond, past the hotel. I cannot be contained. Every muscle is strong, fibres working together to propel me forward. Mud splatters up my legs, my hair comes loose and walkers are eyeing me with a certain apprehension as I fly past. I do not care about any of it. I haven't felt this good since I was a kid, before I knew about back pain and hangovers and the dreadful shame of hearing 'credit card declined'.

The bandstand's blue railings and maroon posts are in view. It's small, but it makes a perfect winner's podium. I run straight up the steps, turn around and jump in victory. Ruth's not far behind. She holds onto the delicate fencing and catches her breath. 'Someone had their Weetabix.'

'I had a really good week. I even made up with Zara, you'll be glad to hear.'

'Wow, who are you?'

'She offered to put me in touch with a legal contact of hers and is giving me a better project. It really feels like everything is finally clicking into place. I can stop wasting time and get on with my life.'

'I haven't seen you this excited in ages. It makes me happy,' she says, sounding a bit wistful with a ghost of a smile. It's then I notice her normally clear skin is marred with dark circles; her unusually straight posture is slouched.

'And how are you doing? I've barely seen you.'

'I'm fine, just a bit tired.'

'Hey, we don't lie to each other. Remember?' I say, noting the irony.

If there's one thing Ruth can't stand, it's lying. When she was twelve, she caught her dad with another woman. Immediately, she told her mum, who was apparently more annoyed about Ruth telling her than about the affair itself. Her siblings had all moved out of the house by that time anyway, and they told her not to upset things. Then at every family event her dad would make a toast about their incredible marriage, and how grateful he was to have children he not only loved but liked (even though he could write what he knew about their personalities on a postcard). I think that's why Ruth's so principled. We either become our parents or go hard in the other direction. She made me promise then never to lie to her. I don't think I ever have, until now. Although it's more of a secret than an outright lie.

'It's just that working in intensive care is tougher than I expected. I saw my first patient die this week. Even though I was prepared for this, it's so different when it's real and happening in front of you.' She pauses, glassy-eyed and staring at a blade of grass like it's the only thing in the world. Then she catches me watching. 'I'm okay, honest, I just need a bit of time to adjust. And after what happened with Greg, I think I'm overly sensitive.'

'Zara said the same.'

'The funeral is next weekend. Maybe that'll provide everyone with closure.'

Why is everyone talking about Greg all of a sudden? It's not like he was part of our friend group before he went and died. And I can't spend the rest of my life feeling bad for what happened to him. I don't need to hear another thing about him, because he's not what's wrong with Ruth. I've selfishly been skipping around, high on life, while Ruth's been wallowing. Maybe that's what happens when your time's ticking?

I grin and hold out my hand in a mock gesture. 'Good race.'

She takes it and I make the transfer. The energy glides from me to her without instruction or effort.

'Once around the park and back home?' she asks. 'I'll try to keep up.'

Beating Ruth at anything is such a rarity that I take enormous pleasure in it. 'Sure, although I'm happy to slow down for you. You just have to ask.' My cockiness lasts exactly three seconds because I take a step forward and my legs crumble like they are made of gelatin. I grab onto Ruth. Pain shoots up the back of my calf and I grab it, pinching my nails into the skin to distract myself. 'Cramp!'

'Stretch it out like this.' Ruth sticks her leg out in front of her. I copy.

It feels like my muscles are elastic bands stretched over something too big. Cramp, stubbing your toe and paper cuts are all things that really seem like they shouldn't be that painful – no one has much sympathy for them – but they bloody hurt. I can't focus on anything else for what seems like several minutes. Ruth tries to massage it, but it feels more like she's repeatedly jabbing her fingers into my leg. The pain finally starts to dissipate, and I take a deep breath.

Ruth raises her eyebrows. 'I'm not going to say I told you so, but ...'

She's grinning and the colour has returned to her face. I wonder if it feels the same for her as it did for me, but she seems to be able to keep both feet on the ground. Perhaps it's because she needs those years to stay alive, but for me it was surplus. Not that I know how long I've got to live – my power doesn't seem to work on me – although maybe that's a good thing. She helps me hobble off the bandstand and back onto the path. We walk the entire way home. I'm already missing being so brilliantly high on pure energy, but at least it's done. Ruth is safe. Everything is completely fine.

I take a shower, then curl up on the sofa in my dressing gown and promptly fall asleep. As I slip in and out of bad dreams, I'm aware of snippets from *The Price Is Right*, an old cowboy movie and the shopping channel. The TV seems to have settled on the last when I wake up.

My bones are frozen. My limbs are lead. My head is a stone. And the remote is at least two stretches too far to contemplate reaching for, so I shuffle into a marginally more comfortable position and accept the shopping channel as my fate.

A woman in an aubergine dress and blow-dried blonde hair is proudly holding up a pink bottle of stain remover that looks suspiciously like Vanish but is instead called Disappear.

The woman chirps away with far too much enthusiasm for stain remover, 'Any stain gone in three minutes or less, or your money back – guaranteed!'

Then I swear she looks right at me. Bright blue eyes piercing into mine.

'Oh sorry, I didn't see you there, Thea. I'm afraid we've had to make an exception for you.'

Did that woman just say my name? The flat is completely dark, save the light from the television. Someone has covered me up with a blanket. Ruth, no doubt. It must be really late, and I'm imagining things. I try to tap my Fitbit to check the time, but I don't have the energy.

'Yes, I mean you!' the blonde woman says, grinning manically. 'Thea Greaves, recent murderess.'

'Excuse me?' I whisper, more out of reflexive politeness than anything else.

'If you take a look at the terms and conditions, you'll see that our three-minute guarantee doesn't apply to you.' The camera zooms in on the pink bottle, and sure enough my name is printed in bold comic sans. 'Some stains are more than skin deep. I'm afraid a little hydrogen peroxide won't be enough to wash yours away.'

This isn't real.

She responds to the voice in my head. Chirpier this time. 'Oh, but it is. Unforgivable crimes are just too hard to shift. There's absolutely nothing you can do but accept the slow and inevitable rot of your soul.'

I throw my weight forward to lunge at the remote. Nothing. The couch is holding me fast, eyes peeled open as the scene continues.

'And I have a co-host today. Please welcome Greg Ferguson.' The woman bursts into applause as Greg shuffles in front of the camera. His skin is grey, his eyes lifeless. He's like a reanimated corpse dragged out against his will. 'You'll have to excuse Greg; he doesn't talk much on account of his recent murder.'

He doesn't have to speak because the accusation in his eyes is clear enough.

'Stop it,' I strain through my clenched jaw.

'Do you still feel okay about this, Thea? Do you really think you did the right thing?' I realize what's familiar about those eyes. They belong to Ruth, and suddenly the woman shifts into her, her aubergine dress replaced with dark scrubs. 'Was it worth it?'

I don't know how long this goes on for, the faces of Greg and Ruth swirling around in my mind. Before long I see Grandad, Mum and Dad. I can't distinguish between them at all, or the anger and pain and disdain coming from each of them.

I'm still not sure if I'm asleep or awake, but finally my finger twitches and I manage to grab the remote. The room plunges into darkness and I can breathe again. I grab myself a glass of water and trail back into my room. It's then I notice my organizational overhaul hasn't been quite as organized as I'd thought. The contents of my wardrobe are scattered across the floor, and I've painted six different swatches onto the wall, with no idea of which one I picked.

It's possible that everything is not fine.

First thing in the morning, there's a man waiting on the steps to my flat. He's young, in his thirties perhaps, short but stockily built with a nondescript face.

'Can I help you?' I ask when he doesn't move aside.

'Miss Greaves, yes, I'm sorry to bother you. I was in the neighbourhood and thought it might be easier to drop by.'

'Er, who are you?'

'Officer Stewart, we met the night of Greg Ferguson's death. I had a couple of follow-up questions for you.'

I remember now – he took my statement outside the club.

Honestly one of the most forgettable faces I've ever seen. I take him through to the front room. He hovers for a while. I think he might be waiting for me to . . . offer him a tea? I do not.

'I'm not sure what else I can help you with. Didn't Greg die of a heart attack? Ruth isn't here, by the way.'

'Quite all right, it's you I wanted to speak with.'

He runs through the same list of questions as last time, and I can feel myself growing more irritable by the second. *How did you know the deceased? What happened before the incident? Did he say anything before he collapsed? Did you say anything before he collapsed?* To which I respond: *I didn't; a fight broke out; he asked if Ruth was okay;* and *no, I didn't say anything.*

He keeps breaking eye contact like he's nervous. Maybe he's younger than I thought; maybe he lost our statements and is too embarrassed to tell the truth.

'And you're certain about this. You didn't say anything to him?'

'Yes, I'm sure,' I snap.

He takes his phone and places it against an empty mug on the coffee table. 'Please could you watch this video.'

It starts with three girls I don't recognize doing shots. They're outside, giggling and jeering. Then the phone drops to the floor with a crash and a woman screams uncontrollably. All I can see is the dark sky and the outline of someone's barely covered bum.

Then I hear Greg's trembling voice. 'I didn't mean to push her, you know that, right? It was an accident, not my fault.'

I realize that scream was mine, although I can scarcely believe that banshee wail came from me. I go pale because I know what I'm about to hear next.

'It's okay, it'll all be over soon,' I say on the recording. 'And I'm sorry. I didn't have a choice.'

The recording continues to play. There's more jostling and noise, then more screams as Greg collapses. My voice again, telling the paramedics that it's no use. Greg's already dead. I watch it all, desperate to avoid the officer's gaze. He's watching me with a passive curiosity, like he can't figure me out. And I don't want to help him do that.

'Why did you say you were sorry?'

'I don't know.'

'Why did you lie about what you said?'

'I didn't remember. That night is a bit of a blur.'

'Can't you think of any reason you would be sorry? It seems like an odd thing to say?'

If I was still holding those twenty-one years, I'm sure I could come up with a perfectly reasonable explanation, but I was up all night and, without the excess energy, my brain is in buffer mode. 'Look, I don't know. I was drinking and, in case you didn't notice, my friend was dying on the floor, so I'm sorry if I don't know exactly what I said or why I said it.'

'Your friend was dying? It was a bump on the head. She didn't need so much as a single stitch.'

Oh shit. 'I meant she was hurt, and it felt like she was dying.'

'That's also a strange thing to say.'

'You can't just show up and start attacking me over word choices. I'm not a fucking dictionary. I didn't mean anything by it and, anyway, saying the wrong thing is not a crime.'

He looks taken aback. 'I wasn't attacking you. I just thought the video was strange and that you could explain it to me. If I was suspicious, I would have questioned you at the station.'

It's then I realize this isn't a genuine police enquiry, but I may have just turned it into one. 'Isn't the case closed?' I ask. 'He died of natural causes.'

'A lot of things can look like heart attacks,' he says.

'You know what, Stewart,' I say, purposefully using his last name without his title. 'Get out of my flat.'

He collects his phone and gets to his feet. 'Thank you for your time, Miss Greaves.'

Chapter Seven

If I stand by and knowingly let someone die, is this the same as killing them?

I wake up in the middle of the night every night that week with the horrible feeling I'm being watched. The moonlight peeks in under the curtains like the beam from a searchlight. Tonight, it has settled directly on a tea stain marking the wall (I never got round to actually painting my room) and I swear it's like an old man's face glaring at me. At first I think it's Stewart, then I think it's Grandad. There's no shortage of people ready to be disappointed in me.

My own words echo in my head. *And I'm sorry. I didn't have a choice.*

Why did I have to say that? People only say sorry when they've done something wrong. I could see it in Stewart's face; he might not know what I've done, but he knows something's off.

Stop it. It was an isolated incident. They are not going to open up a closed case because I've set off some junior officer's spider-sense. And even if they did, there's no way they could prove I had anything to do with the natural death of a boy I didn't know.

Then there's Frances of course. If they looked at my school records, they'd find a motive. But I read the obituary: liver failure. They simply couldn't pin that on me. No one would believe it.

Regardless, I'm feeling less confident in my plan to start dishing out life and death. If Stewart connects me to a third death, it will be more than a suspicious notion.

Nothing said while drunk or high should be taken very seriously. I'm claiming the same defence for my grandiose plans formed under the influence of twenty-one years of life itself.

And it's good timing too because something wonderful has happened.

I've been invited for an interview. Zara's contact came through. At first, we had a quick chat on the phone and talked about my options. Then she mentioned an opening, which is essentially for a glorified internship, but it doesn't matter. I'd asked her for a time and place before she'd even finished the job description.

My hands are shaking before the interview. Stewart's appearance in my living room has strongly reawakened my need to be on the right side of justice. I've lost count of how many legal interviews I've been through, but I remind myself I only need one person to give me a chance, and this could be it.

My interviewer, Svetlana Tate, is easily one of the most beautiful women I've seen in real life. She's wearing a cream pencil dress, sitting with crossed ankles rather than legs and a self-assured demeanour I can only dream of. She makes elegant notes with a fountain pen in a leather-bound notebook. After forty-five minutes of grilling my technical knowledge, she closes her notebook.

'Well done, you seem to have a good grasp of the law,' she says.

'Thanks. I've been trying to keep up with my studies where I can. I know I've had a bit of a career gap but several of my projects in my current job have a legal component—'

'Thea, you did a good job. You can stop trying to impress me. I don't want to hear about what's on your CV, I want to know more about you. Why do you want to be a lawyer?'

I let out the breath I've been holding for the past thirty minutes. Now that the technical part of the interview is over, I can relax.

'I know it's a cliché, but I just want to help people. It's been my dream since I was a kid. I can't stand to see justice going unserved, so I decided a long time ago I would dedicate myself to the law, to defending those who can't help themselves.'

God, I want to work for her so badly. When Zara said she had a contact, she neglected to mention that Svetlana Tate is one of the most successful domestic violence prosecutors in the country. I'm already imagining her becoming my mentor: how we'll bond over being strong working women in the boy's club that is the legal system, how she'll coax me into finding my own answers rather than giving them to me, and how she'll delight as I begin to find legal loopholes that even she'd missed.

'Thea?' she asks.

'Sorry, could you repeat the question?'

'I asked what justice means to you.'

Shit, I thought this was the easy portion of the interview. I'm not prepared for this – what should I say; what does she want me to say?

There's a glass water jug on the table. To give myself a moment, I lean forward, fill up my glass and take a sip. Shit,

I'm choking. It's gone down the wrong hole. I put my hand to my mouth, which is the only thing that stops me spraying water across the table.

Svetlana raises a threaded eyebrow at me. 'Are you okay?'

'Yep, sorry, had a throat tickle.' Jesus, I can't even drink water right. What did she ask me again? Oh right. 'Justice means doing the right thing, even when it's hard.'

She puts down her pen. 'I'm going to be honest with you – working for a not-for-profit firm like ours isn't for everyone. It's emotionally draining work, you will never be paid what you deserve, and a lot of the time, despite pouring your heart and soul into a case, despite everything you know is right, the guilty will walk free. Every day is an injustice, so you will need something deeper than some abstract sense of wanting to create justice to keep you going.'

My mouth goes dry, which doesn't matter because the words won't come anyway. She thinks I'm some baby graduate who's been swaddled in cotton wool, someone who would throw up at the first sign of blood.

'My parents died,' I blurt out. I wasn't prepared to talk about this, and it feels horribly vulnerable to say in front of Svetlana.

'I'm sorry.'

'I was young. It was a car accident. The person who did it drove off and left us there, and the police never found them.' My voice is cracking now, for real. 'Justice isn't just some abstract concept to me. I can't get it for myself, so I want to balance the scales where I can.'

Despite the wobble, I think the interview went quite well. Svetlana said she'd be in touch, but the waiting is physically excruciating. Every time my phone pings, my heart does a little somersault. It's like I'm a needy girlfriend waiting for my crush to text back, only worse. I haven't checked in seven minutes. No ping but I check my phone again anyway. Still no text.

When the phone finally rings it's not Svetlana, but Grandad. I tell him about the interview.

'I'm very pleased to hear it. Being a lawyer would be good for you.'

'Why?'

'You'll be helping people.'

'Yeah, but you said good *for* me.'

'Well, it's good work. You'll have a sense of purpose and structure. That's good for anyone.' I still suspect he specifically means me, but I let it go. 'What's wrong?' he asks. 'You don't sound terribly happy.'

I hesitate but decide to tell him anyway. 'Mum and Dad came up in the interview.'

I've played the dead parent card before, but that doesn't mean I enjoy digging into old wounds for someone else's benefit. Since the interview I've had this heavy feeling – I wonder what they'd think of me using their deaths to get a job. Even as I tell myself it was for a good cause, I keep imagining them floating behind me in that interview room, spectres of disappointment.

'I see. Perhaps not the right situation for that.'

When is? 'You're probably right.'

'Don't worry, there'll be other interviews. Always good to have a practice run.'

Nice vote of confidence from Grandad. Classic.

On Saturday, Ruth wants to go to an art gallery. Usually I'd refuse such culture, but today I'd welcome any distraction – plus I know I can convince her to stop for gelato on the way home. Besides, between her hospital shifts and my renewed interest in the law, we've hardly spent any time together since she nearly died. I know the transfer isn't a permanent fix because I'm hardly going to let Ruth die at forty-seven either, but it buys me plenty of time. So, for now, all I need to do is enjoy her company.

The gallery is almost silent, because nobody else is spending a rare sunny winter's day inside, staring at pictures on a wall. The plastic soles of my boots clip the floor every time I take a step, earning me a scowl from a middle-aged woman wearing a kimono who had previously been staring a hole through a round red sculpture that reminds me of Babybel cheese.

'What about this one?' Ruth asks, stopping in front of a painting of a man in a suit and bowler hat, his face hidden behind a floating apple.

The label reads: *The Son of Man* by Magritte. I wish they'd put a cheat sheet next to each painting explaining what I'm supposed to say. 'Sure, very nice.'

'Oh, come on, give me something,' Ruth says.

'What do you want me to say? It's a painting of a man with an apple.'

'Art is about interpretation. What does it mean to you?'

I shrug. 'That someone has made my life deliberately harder by putting an apple in the middle of a perfectly good painting.'

'See, that's an emotional reaction to the painting. You're irritated by not being able to see what's right in front of you, which is not far off Magritte's own explanation of the painting, that the truth is often hidden even when it's right in front of us.'

'Or maybe that's bollocks and Magritte was just hungry,' I say, wondering if Ruth will rise to the bait.

Ruth smiles sweetly, but I'd recognize that clenched jaw

anywhere. 'Well, there are no wrong answers in art. And there have been lots of interpretations of Magritte's work. Some people think it's about Jesus, or Adam and Eve.'

'Then what's the real answer?'

'That's what I'm trying to tell you, it's all about interpretation. There's no right answer.'

I grimace. 'This is why people hate art.'

Ruth laughs. 'One day, I'm going to find a painting that you actually appreciate, and I'm going to say I told you so.'

Thankfully, I do convince Ruth to stop for gelato on the way home. I get mint chocolate and raspberry; she gets honeycomb with white chocolate sauce. We walk to the park and sprawl out on the grass. It's only about ten degrees, but in the sun it feels much hotter and I take off my coat. Ruth asks me about work, so I indulge in a bitter rant – redacting Zara's name from my complaints. I go on for several minutes before I realize she's fallen asleep. I stop talking and leave her for a while, happy to sit in the cheery background hum of a London park on a sunny day. Then I notice a spider crawling up her arm, so I reach over to brush it off.

'I was listening, promise.' Ruth scrambles upright. 'Something about work being crap.'

'I'm always complaining about work, it's not hard to guess.'

'Sorry, I've hardly been sleeping lately.'

'Thought *I* was the insomniac. What's up with you?' I'm trying to keep my tone light, but I'm worried. Ruth is one of those insufferable people who never gets sick, actually likes vegetables and sleeps eight hours a night without fail.

'I really don't want to go into it. The new job has been a lot more stressful than I'd imagined. This is the most fun I've had all week.'

'Well, that's just sad,' I say. 'An art gallery and gelato cannot be the highlight of your week. Why don't we do something tonight, invite some people over to celebrate.'

'Celebrate what?'

'Surviving,' I say, although it comes out less good-humoured than I meant it to sound.

'Yeah, all right, I could use the distraction.'

I try not to worry about the resignation in her voice. What if I've done something awful to her? I've still got no idea about how this power of mine works. Frances Wells was an evil person, so what if that darkness is somehow spreading to Ruth? Maybe I should have spent more time testing the limits of my ability before unleashing them on the most important person in my life. I tell myself to stop it. Ruth's having a bad week and I've immediately spiralled into wondering if I've corrupted her immortal soul, even though I don't believe in any of that crap. Ruth thrives on other people. All I need to do is recharge her batteries with a good old-fashioned party.

Ruth's wasted as a doctor. I know she saves lives and all, but when she's in hostess mode, she truly shines. If I'd organized this get-together, there would be a bowl of Doritos on the table and I would have told people to bring their own booze. Maybe it's because she grew up rich, but Ruth has certain expectations.

There are three varieties of crisp laid out in neat bowls on the table, along with olives and hummus. The fridge is stocked with every colour of wine and anything else someone could possibly ask for. And a pre-curated Spotify playlist is already going on her retro speaker.

'Do you think people will want dessert wine later on?' she asks. 'I forgot but I could run out and get some.'

'You didn't get dessert wine? The party is ruined. Ruined!'

'Oh, do shut up, I want people to enjoy themselves. Can you put these in the oven, please? Twelve minutes at one eighty.'

She passes me a tray of vegetable samosas, spring rolls and mozzarella sticks. I put them onto the top rack and go to set the timer on my phone. There's a new email. It's from Svetlana's office. I've been so busy helping Ruth prepare the flat for guests I actually managed to forget about the interview for a couple of hours. I almost can't bear to open it, but I do, scanning the opening niceties as quickly as I can, until I find what I'm looking for.

> We regret to inform you that we will not be pursuing your application further.
>
> Thank you for your time and best of luck in your future endeavours,
>
> Bianca Istead

No explanation. No excuses. Just a blanket form letter rejection from her assistant. I shared the most traumatic moment of my life with that woman, and I'm not even worth rejecting to my face. And she said I did well at the legal portion of the interview, so it's personal. There's just something wrong with me.

An evening putting on a show is now the last thing I need, but the doorbell rings at eight on the dot. I've invited my favourite office pal, Eli. Ruth has asked two of her medical school friends and, of course, Zara. We stand in the kitchen while we wait for Ruth's snacks to cook. She cracks open some champagne. I drink two glasses before the others have finished their first.

I barely hear a word anyone has said until one of Ruth's

medical student friends, Alessandra, says my name. 'Ruth said you're a lawyer?'

Alessandra is a Grecian goddess sent to earth to make normal women feel inadequate. She has golden curls that fall past her waist, so perfectly coiled they almost don't look real. I find it extremely unfair that she has a face carved by angels, makes medical school look easy and is the heiress to an international biscuit empire. It's like she won the genetic lottery three times over.

Also, I've met her twice already. Although I'm not sure if she's ever asked me a question before. My response is a cross between nodding yes and shaking no. 'Kind of. I studied law at uni, but getting a position in a law firm is really tough so I'm in human resources for now.'

She replies: 'Really? My brother got a job before he graduated. Where's your degree from?'

'Southampton,' I say.

'Well, that's a halfway decent uni, so why can't you get a job?'

Not the bloody time, Alessandra. I throw my hands up a little. 'It's a mystery.'

Ruth opens the oven door, releasing a hot wave of spice, ginger and cheese. She arranges everything neatly on a grey slate plate and announces, 'Time for a game. Follow me.'

She shepherds us into the living room. Zara sits next to Ruth on the sofa. Closer than she has any right to be. And then Ruth puts us on the same team, which is just cruel. The games are suitably nerdy – Ruth has created a quiz and made sure there's something for everyone.

'What do people with Cotard's syndrome believe they are?' *Dead*, Alessandra answers.

'What's the address of Harry Potter's childhood home?' *4 Privet Drive* – Eli, a known Potterhead, gets this one.

'Which queen wore a white wedding dress, setting the trend for dressing brides in white?' *Queen Victoria*, from Zara, self-proclaimed fashionista.

For a little while, I have fun. The food is good, the music is good, Eli mocks Zara's outfit behind her back – she's wearing a black dress and a black feathered cape-like thing which apparently should be cool but makes her look like a crow – and I'm grateful to be surrounded by friends.

But then the night turns sour.

We're at match point. Whoever wins next takes the game.

Ruth reads the question. 'If caught, which fish – by *law* – must be offered to the reigning monarch?'

At the word *law*, everyone turns to look at me. I shake my head. 'A fish?'

Ruth nods gleefully. 'Come on, this one is for you.'

'I'm not sure – a salmon, maybe?'

Zara shakes her head. 'Pretty sure it's a sturgeon.'

I'm not sure what makes me so stubborn. I don't like how comfortable Zara is in our flat, how she knows where the glasses are kept and helps Ruth clear the plates. Or maybe after today I just need a win. 'No, trust me, my gut instinct is telling me a hundred per cent it's salmon.'

'I'm sure I've heard this at a pub quiz before and it's sturgeon,' Zara says.

'No, this is my question. And I always trust my gut. Salmon. Final answer.'

Ruth pulls a sympathetic face. 'Sorry . . . it's sturgeon.'

The other team cheers. A timer pings. Ruth diplomatically takes the opportunity to leave the room. Zara rolls her eyes.

'Oh, come on,' I say, and I mean the next bit to come off jokingly, but it's sharper than I intend it to be. 'It's not like any of us really know salmon from sturgeon.'

'I did, Thea, but you never listen, do you?'

'Hey, we all had our questions. The legal one was mine. It could have just as easily been salmon.'

Alessandra smirks into her champagne. 'Yeah, but you did go to Slowlent. All makes sense now.'

'What did you just say to me?'

'Just a little joke.'

'Explain it to me, then, because I didn't find it funny.'

'Oh, come on, you said you went to Southampton and conveniently forgot to specify Southampton Solent. They're hardly of the same calibre. The Solent used to be one of the old polytechs, so it's not even a proper university.' She snorts with laughter, but in an incredibly annoying way that is somehow delicate and appealing. 'My brother used to call it Southampton Slowlent.'

My wrath is not for her but for Zara, because she's suddenly fixated on her black sock boots and I'm not sure who else Alessandra could have heard that piece of information from, because Ruth wouldn't have said it. When did they find time to discuss my academic credentials? What else did they talk about? The rejection email burns brightly in my mind. Then I remember Svetlana is Zara's friend, which means Zara probably already knows exactly how my interview turned out. My skin feels hot. The champagne is forming big angry bubbles, bursting in my brain. I imagine them gossiping and giggling behind my back. *Thea couldn't get a job in law if it wrapped itself up and gifted itself to her. What do you expect? She did go to Slowlent after all.*

'Yeah, well, not all of us have Daddy's handouts to rely on. We have to make compromises.' I say this in reply to Alessandra, but I'm looking at Zara when I say it. I'm fairly sure her father is an oil tycoon. I think she's going to bite back but she makes an odd choking noise instead.

Ruth returns with churros and works hard to rescue the evening. She directs the conversation towards the latest show-biz news, some drama between our other friends, even the weather, but it's no use. The energy is dead, smothering us like a dark cloud.

When they leave, Alessandra kisses me on both cheeks as if we've had a perfectly pleasant evening. Must be overcompensating, because she didn't do this on the way in. *Three years.* My insecurity and resentment evaporate. The life she thought she was going to lead, the one where she is so much better than me, doesn't exist. She's just a tragic dead girl walking.

Ruth's in the kitchen, scrubbing the plates with a fury not meant for them. There's a half-drunk glass of champagne next to her. When she notices me, she takes a big gulp.

'Aren't you a bit old to take up drinking?' I ask, trying to keep my tone light but knowing I'm not going to be able to dodge these eggshells.

'Zara told me what you said.'

'And did she tell you what she did?'

'I know Alessandra made a bitchy comment. What does that have to do with Zara?'

I can barely contain my frustration. I'm sure the way Zara presented it, my comment was an unprovoked attack. 'She was the one stirring Alessandra up, talking about me behind my back.'

'Are you sure?'

'Yes!'

'Why do you hate her so much? Sometimes I think you don't want me to have other friends.'

In truth, I don't love it. That's mostly why I followed her to Southampton – Ruth went to the 'proper' version, as

Alessandra would say. People have always liked Ruth. The only reason she didn't have many friends as a kid was because she spent so much time in hospital. People don't like me as much. I was worried she'd go to university, make a bunch of new friends and never look back. Whereas I have to hang onto the friends I've got.

'That's ridiculous. I just don't understand why you would be friends with someone who text-dumped you.'

'That's not what happened. I was studying so hard. I just didn't have the headspace for a relationship. She text-dumped me because I said I didn't have time to see her in person.'

'You were busy. It's not like you just couldn't be bothered – you were studying to save lives.'

'I'm not as perfect as you think. And Zara isn't the devil incarnate. You know her dad's under investigation for tax fraud? He fled the country, and there's been no word from him for months. She's devastated. And yet she hardly talks about it because she's always staying strong for everyone else. Then you had to go and make that comment about "Daddy's handouts". Alessandra's been through a lot too. Did you know she's had breast cancer? She's almost finished with the chemo and looks like she'll make a full recovery, but she's been so stoical, working almost the whole way through it because she actually cares about helping people. I was hoping tonight would be a distraction for both of them.'

'Until I ruined it.'

'Not what I said.'

I remember Alessandra's perfect curls and wince at my misplaced envy. Must have been a wig. 'I'm sorry, I didn't know she'd been ill. I'm out of sorts today.'

'What happened? A couple of days ago you were on top of the world, telling me how everything was finally clicking into place.'

'I didn't get the job. I really thought it went well, let myself get excited about it. Then I got a standard rejection just before the others arrived.'

Her icy-blue eyes melt. 'Oh, now I'm the one who's sorry.'

'I wish I hadn't even bothered. At least before, I was under the illusion that I could be a lawyer if I tried. I even told her about my parents. And I mean really told her, about what it feels like to know the person who killed them is out there and I'll never get justice for them.'

She gives me a sympathetic smile. 'Sometimes I wonder what they were like. You don't talk about them much.'

'I wish I knew. I don't really remember much. And the stuff I do remember is stupid. I remember that Dad helped me catch a frog from the garden once, and Mum helped me turn a shoebox into a house for it. There was a tiny dollhouse sofa in there. I kept feeding it leftovers of our dinner. I'm pretty sure it died.' I laugh. 'No wonder Grandad never let me have a pet.'

'Sounds like they were fun, and that they loved you.'

To my surprise she opens the fridge and refills both our glasses. Then she leans against the kitchen counter and slides down onto the floor. I join her, clinking our glasses for luck. We sit in silence for a moment. The vanilla-scented candle on the table extinguishes itself with a small hiss and smoke mingles into the sweetness. I let the quiet linger. If Ruth was just a good friend, I'd want to fill it with noise, but there's no need with someone I've shared every good and bad moment with since we were eight years old.

'You're my best friend, I don't like not being on the same side,' she says.

'You're mine too. I'd do anything for you.' *Quite literally*, I add in my head.

'Truth is, I'm not sure I am okay. I know I said I was just

tired, but it's so much more than that . . .' Her voice cracks and she grasps her throat. She's shaking, then she's sobbing.

'Ruth, what's wrong?' When she doesn't respond I put my arms around her and let her cry into my shoulder. I get that same horrible feeling from the park. I did something dark to save Ruth. In movies, there's always a consequence. I didn't think she'd have to pay it. She catches her breath and I hold her steady. 'I've seen you work seventy-two-hour shifts, but you've never been like this. You can tell me anything.' I pause and look her deep in the eye. 'Even if it sounds crazy, I'll believe you.'

She takes a deep breath. 'Have you ever met someone so good, who deserves to live so much, that you'd give anything to save them?'

She knows.

'There was a bus crash, earlier this week. I've never seen anything like it; we couldn't keep up with the patients being brought in. There was one guy with burns. He wasn't even on the bus. Just an innocent bystander. Apparently he noticed a kid who was stuck, went in to help, then he was caught in it when the engine exploded. I was treating him and . . .' She holds onto her throat and closes her eyes. A couple of tears escape anyway. 'It was my fault. We were understaffed and I was rushing to move onto the next patient. And I made a mistake. I was so focused on the external damage that I missed the internal. He had a bleed on the brain, then he had a stroke. Now he's in a coma and it's all my fault.'

She can't get any more words out and she again descends into tears.

'It's not your fault, Ruth. You're doing your best.'

Selfishly, I'm a little relieved Ruth's been upset about a real-life problem rather than some horrible side effect of what I did to her. Eventually, she stops crying.

'His name's Oliver. He's got two young kids. He runs the largest independent homeless shelter in London. His wife told me he made a fortune in property development and poured every penny back into helping others. Every day a new stack of "get well soon" cards arrives for him with long, heartfelt messages from people whose lives he changed. How can someone like that die?' She pauses and pulls herself up. 'Have you ever heard of Lamed Vavnik?'

I shake my head. 'No.'

'I've been thinking about it a lot. It's an idea in Judaism. Bit of a left-field, mystical idea, but it says that there are thirty-six special people that secretly maintain the world.' Then she pauses and whispers the last part. 'I feel like I've killed one of them.'

'Do you really believe in it, Lame Vavnik?' I ask. Ruth's always been more open to the idea of religion than me, but in the general agnostic 'maybe there's something bigger out there' sense of things rather than taking gospel as truth. Although if Grandad did Christmas like her family does Hanukkah – one present every night for all eight nights – I might not have discounted the whole religion thing.

The corner of her mouth twitches. 'Lamed, not Lame. And, I don't know, not really, but that's what it feels like.'

'How come you didn't tell me any of this earlier?' I ask.

'I wasn't trying to hide it on purpose. I just didn't know what to say. It's not like talking about it can change anything.'

She's right. Whatever I say, she will blame herself if that man dies, and she is too good, too pure, to be tainted by such guilt. To this day Ruth breaks out in visceral hives if I mention the name of a girl who we used to leave out in relay races (she was painfully slow) even though I was the real culprit. She simply can't cope with causing another human being any pain. But I can. If it's a choice between getting my hands dirty and keeping Ruth's conscience clean, then there is no choice. I know exactly what I have to do.

Chapter Eight

*If killing one person will prevent harm to
another, then it's the right thing to do.*

I sneak into the intensive care unit first thing in the morning,
pretending to be Oliver's cousin. Given that I already know his
full name and room number, no one questions me too hard.
I find Oliver in room fifteen, fourth door on the left, and I'm
sure it's him the moment I lay eyes on him.

There's a complicated tangle of tubes taped into place over
his face. There's one long, thick, transparent tube attaching
him to a softly humming ventilator. His white and blue patterned hospital gown is covering everything except his left
shoulder, where I can see the dressings, no doubt covering his
burns. His face is untouched, and underneath the tubes I can
see his soft expression. Even now it's like I can see the trace of
his smile.

'Hi there, Oliver, I'm Thea,' I say dumbly. He's in a med-
ically induced coma and yet I can't help but feel names still
matter.

The bedside table is littered with cards. I pick up one sitting next to a stuffed plush bear, with a bumblebee on it, which says, 'Bee well soon'. It reads:

> *Dear Daddy,*
>   *We hope you feel better soon because we love you more than anything in the whole wide world.*
>   *Love from Milo and Evie xxx*
>   *P.S. We got you this bear in case you're feeling lonely. His name is Bertie.*

I almost find it too trite, but the stuffed bear's earnest eyes provoke a tear. These kids are expecting their dad to come home; they have no idea of the hell that was about to be unleashed upon them. I wonder if they're younger or older than I was when it happened to me. I'd already decided to do this for Ruth alone – this is simply extra motivation. I rest a hand on Oliver's arm, careful to avoid the tubes. *Seven days.*

This time, I can do this right. Oliver Locksley has seven days to live. No need to rush and kill some undeserving bystander, like I did with Greg, or lose control like I did with Frances.

'Don't worry, Oliver, you're going to be home in no time.'

The hunt begins at the magistrates' court. Crown Court is where the important stuff happens, but the trials are long and often nasty, given that it's reserved for only the worst crimes. I have time, but not that much time. Once Oliver is safe, I can figure out a longer-term solution. For now, I only need someone bad enough to justify taking a few months off them; I'm not going to kill anyone.

At the magistrates' court you get to see multiple cases every hour rather than being stuck in a courtroom all day. The downside is that it lacks grandeur. It's like a waiting room at the doctor's, complete with white-grey walls and plastic chairs. I go up to the receptionist and say, 'Hi, I'm a law student. I was wondering what cases I could see today?'

Yes, I know I'm not a student anymore, but it's easier than explaining that I'm a failed lawyer who works in HR but who would quite like to come back to law if only I could find the right opportunity. She nods and highlights three cases with a pen.

'Here and here should be what you're looking for. Keep quiet, follow the judge's rules and turn off your phone.' She passes me the list but snatches it away before I can take it. 'And when I say off, I mean it. Not silent, not mute. Off. Do you understand?'

'Turn it off. Got it,' I say.

She gives me a distrusting glance, then relents and lets me take the list. And with that, I'm waved forward to the metal scanner. I've always found it odd how surprisingly easy it is to go and watch a trial, given how significant a day it is to the defendant. I can see the receptionist has highlighted a murder case, which is not very exciting because it will be all of ten minutes before it'll be forwarded to Crown Court. And I need to actually hear the evidence before I make my decision. But there's also a minor assault, which should be fun.

I take a left and open the door into the courtroom.

I tell Zara I've got the flu and spend the next three days in court. The woman on the front desk no longer scowls at me each morning, trusting me to turn off my own phone. I've acquired a favourite spot in the public gallery and have become accustomed to the courtroom. That's not actually saying much. Almost all courtrooms are the same: magistrates' bench at the front, dominating the room from a height, lawyers and court

legal advisor below, the defendant's dock to one side and witness box to the other. The wood-panelled walls are pine, as are
the tables, the doors and most of the chairs. I have no idea what
the legal profession's obsession with pine is about.

I need to focus. Oliver has just four days left and I'm no
closer to finding a deserving victim.

I've set myself some ground rules.

1. The jury must return a guilty verdict.
2. The crime must be violent.
3. I need to look the defendant in the eye before I take a
   portion of their life.

So far, I've sat through no end of petty thefts that don't warrant
anything but a slap on the wrist, a number of muddy domestic
disputes that I don't feel confident about making a decision on
and an assault I was initially hopeful of, but which returns a
not guilty verdict. Seven days seemed like such a long time at
the beginning of the week, but now time is racing forward.

I head to my next case, a drink-driving charge. It's something
that should be routine, a mild offence, but it sends chills down
my spine because I know exactly what the consequences of
reckless driving can be.

The trial is late starting. Finally, a harassed barrister ushers
her client into the room. He's dressed in a well-fitting grey
suit and has the plump capillary-broken face of someone who
considers alcohol to be a food group. I bet he drinks port. He
just looks like the kind of person who drinks port.

Instead of letting his barrister speak for him, as he should,
he says, 'Terribly sorry, the traffic was a nightmare.'

I press my knuckles into my chair. He *drove* here, to a

drink-driving case. He's so confident in the outcome that he thinks he's walking out of here with his licence. This is unusual. Drink-driving cases are often cut and dried – either you're over the limit or you're not – but I can see from the smug look on his face and his barrister's relaxed posture that something is different here. It's not a Legal Aid lawyer, either. This one has a velvet trouser suit that looks tailor-made, and delicate jewellery that is clearly real gold.

'Let's begin,' the lead magistrate says. 'This is the third time we have seen this case in court. Please tell me I'm right to understand that you have the MGDDA form this time?'

The prosecution blushes and organizes their documents. 'Yes, I have the MGDDA and the breathalyser printout that clearly shows the defendant was over the drink-driving limit.'

The prosecution continues with their case. The magistrates' eyes are glazing over. It's almost lunchtime, they have seen this case before, dismissed it on lack of evidence and given the prosecution one last chance to get their case together. Usually, defendants roll over so quickly, knowing the breathalyser test is damning and they can benefit from a reduced charge, so the prosecution lawyer has been caught unaware by the red-faced defendant's insistence on his innocence. The evidence is damning. It looks like the entire case rested on administrative failure, but finally the CPS has come through.

I hide a smile. My gut is screaming that this will be a guilty verdict. The maximum sentence for excess alcohol is an unlimited fine and six months' imprisonment. To me, six months is not enough. He could have killed someone. I think losing another six is more fitting. Maybe even twelve.

Then the defence lawyer begins. 'I would like to draw your attention to page nineteen in the MGDDA.'

The magistrates follow the instructions. One of them

gestures with her glasses in an exasperated fashion. 'There is no page nineteen.'

'Indeed, the page is missing. That also happens to be the page where the arresting officer signs to confirm that the evidence is correct. In addition, if you could take a glance at the breathalyser statement, you will notice that signature is also missing,' the defence lawyer says, pausing to allow time for verification. 'Therefore, there is no police-verified evidence that any crime took place, and I move that the charges be dismissed.'

The magistrates' eyes narrow on the prosecution. They are now five minutes late to lunch and know exactly who to blame for the inconvenience. The colour drains from the lawyer's face and he exhales. 'The prosecution drops all charges against the defendant.'

I wish I could say I can't believe it – a drink-driver let off scot-free because a police officer didn't sign a piece of paper. The breathalyser report showed he was three times over the limit. Then he drove on the dual carriageway at sixty miles per hour. If he had hit someone, there wouldn't have been enough of them left to clean off the tarmac.

It's not the prosecution's fault. I follow the group outside into the corridor and see him desperately ask the receptionist for courtroom three, then he runs with a hobbled limp to his next case. He was doing his best. God knows how many emails he sent and phone calls he made to get the correct evidence sent over, only to discover the documents were unsigned on the day of the trial.

I cannot help but think of my own parents' deaths. Killed by some idiot who faced no consequences, who's going through life unpunished. Do they ever think of my parents? Do they ever think of the child they left alone on the roadside in the middle of the night? What if someone had possessed the power to stop it? Wouldn't I tell them to do it? Of course I would.

The defendant swings his car keys around his chubby fingers, then claps his lawyer on the back. 'Told you it would be all right. If I'm honest, I drive better drunk than sober anyway.'

The lawyer cringes and looks side to side. 'You can't say things like that to me.'

'Oh, yes, you can't enter a non-guilty plea if I admit guilt, I remember. But the trial's over now – lighten up, old chap.'

The lawyer is neither old nor a chap, but it doesn't seem to matter. She excuses herself. I catch her eye as she walks past and refuse to let go; I'm silently telling her I know what she's done and I do not approve. In law school they tell us that everyone is deserving of a fair trial, and that your only duty is to evaluate the evidence, nothing more. And if a client tells you they are guilty, you can no longer present them as innocent. Lawyers like to use this as a cop-out. As long as their client says they didn't do it, they will defend them as such, but that doesn't stop the deep *knowing* in your bones. Guilt is real and visceral. It leaves a stench impossible to ignore.

Cases like this only reinforce why I wanted to be a prosecution lawyer in the first place. To be the one who doesn't give up, the one who convicts the guilty when no one else can. If there had been someone like me leading my parents' case, perhaps they would have had justice.

My heart lurches as the defendant prances down the corridor, car keys jingling merrily as he goes. It's an arrogant sound impossible to block out, goading me into action. I follow three steps behind him. My blood rushes and I can feel the vein pulsing in my forehead without seeing it. His lawyer failed to find the truth today, but I am here.

Suddenly, six months, twelve months, none of it feels like it would be enough. I already know that he will get behind the wheel of a car again, drunk, barely able to make out the lines on the road. What will happen next time? When someone walks out in front of him as he careers around a corner. It could be a nurse walking home after a long shift, a father coming home with the shopping, or a child who dropped a ball into the road. If I let him walk out of here alive, their deaths are on my conscience.

I move faster. I'm two steps behind him, then one. The cuff of his tweed jacket is riding up and there's plenty of exposed skin. Am I really going to do this? Steal someone's life in a court of justice? I reach out, still unsure how much life I'm planning to take.

'Thea?' a voice calls. I stop automatically, my name cutting through the noise of the court corridor and bringing me to my senses. It's then I realize my heart is in my throat and I'm sweating. What was I thinking? I can't make decisions over whether to take someone's life in the spur of the moment, when I haven't even decided how much I want to take. What if he'd died right here in the hallway?

He walks out the doorway, puts his keys into his pocket and jumps into the back of a taxi. Jesus, were they ... house keys? He wasn't driving himself home, then. That doesn't mean he wasn't guilty, but still, I'd be lying if I said it wasn't what set me off.

'Thea?' they call again.

Then I recognize a flash of red hair, the man it's attached to dressed in robes and waving. It's Sam. My Sam.

Next thing I know, his hand is on my arm, I'm staring into his forest-green eyes and single-dimpled smile, and I forget all about the man I intended to steal from.

Chapter Nine

*Avoid targets who have dependants, or other
people who will miss them when they're gone.
However, this can't always be helped.*

I met Sam during a summer work experience placement, back
when I genuinely believed I was going to be a barrister. Not
only that, but a human rights specialist. I had visions of me
as Amal Clooney, defending the downtrodden on the world
stage, all while wearing designer heels. The far more embarrassing fantasy is how I imagined our names together – Thea
Ellis instead of Thea Greaves. Not actually as catchy, so then
I imagined how he'd insist I'd keep mine out of respect for
my professional reputation. Maybe he'd even take mine. Him
having a girlfriend at the time did nothing to stem my elaborate
fantasies, but it did stop them materializing beyond a drunken
snog in a supply cupboard. Sam, on the other hand, was more
practical. Not once during that work placement did he complain about making the tea or doing the paperwork – and he
did it all with a smile on his face. He applied for all twelve gateway member chambers, and countless non-member chambers,

and received six offers of pupillage. Now he's a barrister, and I work in HR. No update on the girlfriend.

He takes his hand off my arm and says: 'Thea, I haven't seen you around here before. Who are you working for?'

His easy smile steals the words from my brain. I know he's done well for himself. He's wearing a navy suit, simple in design but it fits like it was made for him. And his watch, just a leather strap and a clean face, but it's expensive. One of those things where you have to know the brand to know what it's worth. It's for this reason that I'm struggling to formulate a response.

'No, I'm ... just watching a few cases. I took a break from law a few years back, but now I'm thinking about getting back into it,' I say, fumbling like a useless teenage boy with a bra.

'I'm surprised to hear it. You were always so passionate about what you wanted to do.'

'Well, I did some travelling for a while, wanted to see the world,' I lie. I've never had the money or the impulse to go travelling, but for some reason it's a socially acceptable excuse for not getting on with your life.

A woman opposite us is eyeing Sam awkwardly, clearly not wanting to interrupt but needing his attention. She's cradling a baby, swaying, presumably to keep them quiet.

'Ah, that's my client. I better go,' he says.

She's not who I expected him to be representing. She's wearing ill-fitting trousers and plastic hoop earrings. The baby has drooled on her shiny jumper. And something about the way she won't look anyone in the eye makes me uneasy. Like she's a dog that expects to be hit.

'Good luck with your case,' I say.

He shakes his head. 'Karly's childcare fell through, so we've got to postpone the case.'

'Can't she have the baby with her?' I ask, remembering this exact issue from my training. Single-parent families without support networks or funds for childcare are hardly uncommon.

'Usually, yes, but the baby won't stop crying and Judge Thomas hates kids. I don't want to risk him turning against us. It's a nightmare – it could be months before we get another court date.'

'I can watch the baby for you,' I say, almost without thinking.

'Really? I'm not sure . . .'

'Come on, you know me. And I'm great with kids.'

He stares at me for a few moments, trying to use that analytical brain to figure out if this is safe, then instinct takes over. 'Yeah, that would be great. Let me ask Karly.'

Sam makes the introductions. Karly's sweet. She's got these soulful deep brown eyes and wild curly hair. Her baby is her in miniature. She gently prises him away from her chest so I can see him.

'This is Leo,' she says, and passes into my arms the most beautiful baby boy I have ever seen.

I have always loved things that need taking care of. Plants, animals, babies. Leo nestles straight into me like a slug and doesn't make a sound as we sit at the back of the court. I'm a little smug about this. Sam said nobody could keep him quiet before I came along. He said that shushing and bouncing usually helped, but I haven't needed to. Ideally he wants Karly to be able to see Leo, but I'm under strict instructions to leave if he makes a peep.

I can see why. Judge Thomas rests his eyes on Leo as if I'm holding a rabies-infected badger. Still, court proceeds. I keep

Leo turned into me and make shushing noises in his ear when he wriggles.

Watching Sam in court is the closest I've come to a religious experience. Thankfully, there're no wigs or pomposity in a magistrates' court. Sam's auburn hair is a collection of short fiery waves, effortless, but not so messy as to suggest lack of respect. As he stands to deliver his defence, he meets the judge's eyes and offers a knowing grin, the kind that makes you feel like you're the only people who truly know what's going on. The judge returns the expression and Sam begins, 'Firstly, let me apologize to the court for the time you've had to spend evaluating what is clearly a petty grievance against my client.'

He goes on to outline the case. Seems that Karly's been accused of possessing a Class B substance. Drug offences can go either way – magistrates' or Crown Court can deal with them. It's only a bit of weed. Nothing Sam can't handle. But then it turns out Karly has a prior conviction for assault, which doesn't work in her favour. Leo is a confusing factor too – it helps Karly that she's a primary carer, but it's not a good look that she had drugs in the presence of a child.

Karly also has some dubious character references. She's described as quiet but aggressive, known for unreasonable outbursts. I'm starting to wonder why Sam took her case on.

Leo wakes up. His eyes are wide open, trying to take the world in and look for his mum. I make whisper-quiet shushing noises. His tiny fingers grasp at me, attempting to climb away. He lets out a little squeak. I bounce him gently. He's really pulling at my top now, then the rumbling starts. I dart out of the courtroom before he starts screaming.

If Karly's temperament is anything like her son's, then maybe she is guilty after all, because he howls. I try everything. Rocking, singing, shushing, peek-a-boo, talking, dancing. I've shoved the dummy Karly gave me in Leo's face so many times I'm worried I'll suffocate him. Although I think it's unlikely – this baby has a lengthy eight decades to look forward to. The absolute scathing judgement directed towards me is painful. I want to explain to everyone that this is not my baby, but I don't dare approach them with this demonic screamer, so I keep to a hallway where a receptionist tells me no courts are in session.

My eardrums can't take it much longer. When the courtroom doors open, I throw him to Karly like a hot potato. She accepts him with a wide smile on her face.

Sam's grinning too. 'I got the case thrown out. Inconsistency in the prosecution witnesses.'

Then he asks me to dinner to celebrate.

We go to Middle Temple Inn. All barristers have to join one of the four Inns of Court – they provide training, support and most importantly ... dinner. Seriously, the dinners are not taken lightly. It's a requirement to attend twelve of them before being called to the bar.

I take a breath as we enter the dining hall. It's like walking into Hogwarts. There are chests of armour on top of dark wood cabinets, historic paintings hanging from the walls and stained-glass windows illuminating the end of the hall.

Choosing your inn is an involved affair because membership is for life. I remember the old rhyme about it: Inner for the rich, Middle for the poor, Lincoln's for the scholar, Gray's for the bore. I wonder what it says about Sam that he chose the Middle. His suit doesn't scream poverty to me.

'Are you sure you want to eat here?' Sam asks. He points at the long rows of tables. 'It's not exactly date-friendly.'

I see what he means – we'll be sitting with other people. But hey, it's the same in Wagamama. It's noisy too, young barristers slinging arguments over the table, fighting to earn their place, to be remembered. I don't want to admit to Sam that I used to dream of dining in these halls.

'This is a date?' I ask with a slight smile.

There's always been an inexplicably intense connection between us. We never talked about that snog because we were drunk and he had a girlfriend. And yes, I know that sounds like a giant red flag but we weren't even twenty years old, she was interning abroad and it was the end of a summer spent working together all day, every day. I remember what he said: 'I feel like I've known you for years. If we'd met before, I think things would be different.'

Then the internship ended and he moved to London while I went back to Southampton. It was never going to work back then, but sometimes I'm out on dates with other men and he'll just pop into my head. I know it sounds stupid, but I've always had this feeling that Sam and I met at the wrong time but were meant to be. Weirder shit has happened – recently.

He grins. 'Absolutely.'

We take a seat at the end of a table, leaving a gap between us and our neighbours. Several groups come and go as our date continues – we have plenty to catch up on. Turns out he spent less than a year in criminal law, then moved on to property law, helping to keep London's elite out of trouble and avoid pesky inconveniences like social housing requirements, because what billionaire wants to make blocks of luxury Kensington flats affordable?

The food is surprisingly simple: a beef burger for Sam and halloumi fritters for me. Sam tells me the gourmet service is reserved for the official dining evenings, intended for networking. It's also good value – for London.

'I swear I'm not being cheap,' he says when I mention the prices.

'I believe you.' I wink. 'So, working for the enemy must be treating you well?'

He chuckles, widening the dimple of his left cheek. Possibly his only flaw, the lack of symmetry on an otherwise perfect face caused by a single dimple. It's a stretch to call it an imperfection, though.

'It's certainly a change from Legal Aid. I don't miss working for less than minimum wage, having to choose between heating and food until the next CPS pay cheque comes through. If it ever did, of course.'

'Is that why you ditched criminal law – the money?'

'Wow, we're getting right into it.' Sam gulps his wine as if it's water. 'It's one reason, yeah. You know that the government spends more on giving pensioners free television licences than they do on our legal system?'

'It's not about the money, though, it's about justice.'

'How is justice supposed to be served under such constraints? I've seen murderers go free and the innocent convicted due to nothing but complete and utter state incompetence. Trials get adjourned again and again because of bureaucracy – missing evidence in the case file, the police failing to record testimonies, or the wrong translator appearing in court. Eventually, the judge gets bored of wasting their precious time and throws it out. I got so tired of failing people.'

'So, the answer is to work for a bunch of rich wankers?'

He finishes his wine and winks. 'Someone's going to do it. Why not me? And don't you work in HR, for a bank? What's your excuse for not fighting the good fight?'

'I'm working on it.'

He grins at that. 'Well, maybe I am too. You have to actually have power before you can do any good with it. And there's nothing more powerful than money.'

'If you really believe that, then what was today about? Why are you helping Karly?'

'Sometimes I still take on the odd criminal case. I like the challenge when it's something a bit unusual. You remember Simon, who interned with us? He's a clerk now, so he calls me when it's something interesting.'

'You knew Leo likes being shushed and bounced. I don't believe Karly's just some random case you picked up. Besides, what's unusual about a drugs charge?'

The humour vanishes from his face. He looks at the floor. 'She's . . . penance for a mistake I made. I've been defending her for years. She has a run-in with some authority every couple of months or so and I try to help her the best I can.'

'I don't see how her actions are your fault. What, you lost her trial years ago and now you have to defend her for the rest of your life?'

'If only. No, I won the trial.' He looks up at me. 'I don't want to talk about it.'

The evening has soured. I've made him feel like a bad person and no one wants that. I try hard to repair the damage, asking about his job, his friends, his family, but he has completely clammed shut. He pays for dinner, refusing my offer to split the bill, and walks me back to the Tube station.

If the date had continued in the tone it had started, this walk would have been slow and ambling, pausing under streetlights to catch each other's gaze. We pass a bench underneath a flower garland that would have been a perfect snogging spot, but no, the spark has been well and truly extinguished. Two minutes from the station, he has the nerve to check his phone.

'Shit, I have to go,' he says.

'You don't need to make excuses. I can walk two more streets on my own.'

'I'm not. It's Karly. Her ex has shown up demanding to see Leo, things got violent and she's been taken down to the station again.'

'Wow, that was quick.'

'It's not her fault, it's him. The drugs she was caught with, she was storing them for him. It's like he's got this hold over her. All rationale and logic go out the window when it comes to this guy. He steals, he cheats, he beats her. And she's always convinced he'll suddenly change. But it's not her fault; she doesn't know she's supposed to expect better.'

My heart skips. Not just because Sam gets this intense, deeply stirring look when he's talking like this, but because it's just gone midnight, which means that Oliver has only three days left. 'He's really that bad? And he's violent? How sure are you?'

'Without a shadow of a doubt. Why?'

'Nothing, that's just . . . a shame there's nothing you can do.'

'Trust me, if I had the power to help, I would.'

Chapter Ten

Killing another person is an intensely personal thing. If I've made the decision to take their life, then I owe them the respect of looking them in the eye while I do it. No matter who they are and what they've done.

I need to find Karly's deadbeat boyfriend, and for that I need an address. But I can't ask Sam – what possible reason would I have for that? So instead, I visit the local police station that dealt with the domestic dispute last night, and I pretend to be Sam's assistant. Grandad is always going on about the value of human connection (usually because he's ranting about the dangers of social media) but today I decide it's good advice and go to the police station in person.

The man on the front desk is young with a round, soft face.

'Hi, I'm Thea Greaves.' I use my real name because I expect he'll ID me. I'm not worried about Sam finding out; no police officer is going to call a barrister to inform them about some admin. 'I work for Sam Ellis. One of our clients was brought in last night. We're having issues accessing our system and I wonder if you could print off the report of last night's incident for me.'

He looks side to side. 'I'm not sure I'm supposed to do that.'

'Please, we're preparing for an emergency hearing later today.'

'I don't know,' he starts. He's like a lost lamb, younger than I originally thought. Early twenties, max.

'It's my first week on the job, and it was my fault. I'm the one who got us locked out of the system, and now we can't access any of our records, and the clients are desperate . . .' I let my voice shake. 'Here, I'll call my boss so he can explain, but he's just about to head into court. He's always ready for a fight when he's in courtroom mode. Will you speak to him?'

I take out my phone and start looking for a number I don't intend to call.

'Wait, was it just the record from last night? That's okay, I can give it to you. Wait here.'

Hee-hee. I've just used our generation's worst nightmare against him: talking on the phone.

He returns with an unsealed envelope and a leather satchel. 'Your boss also left this here. Would you mind returning it to him?'

Shit, how will I explain why I've got Sam's bag? And when Sam inevitably comes back for it, they'll tell him his assistant, Thea Greaves, took it. But I can't think of a reason why said assistant would refuse this perfectly sensible request, so I hoist the strap over my shoulder.

'Of course, thanks,' I say, deciding this is a problem for future Thea to solve. I can't be expected to do everything.

I sign for the bag and show my ID, then I'm off. I'm almost out the door when a familiar face scares the life out of me.

'Miss Greaves,' Stewart says in monotone address. 'Now you're showing up on my doorstep. Can I help you?'

'No, I was just leaving.'

I duck and weave under his arm and out the door before he can ask any follow-up questions.

I'm beginning to think I should call this whole thing off. Perhaps the run-in with Stewart was a sign. But then I remember Oliver now has two days and six hours left, and then I find out about the horror show that is Karly's life.

Her case file is in Sam's satchel.

It details years of parental abuse against Karly and her brother, resulting in multiple trips to A&E and concerned calls from neighbours. It never went further. It wasn't until Karly was fifteen that she went to the police and got them to take it seriously. But, when it came to court, her father defended her mother on every count. And the mother's defence lawyer provided a scathing, detailed report on the siblings' behavioural issues in school. In particular, evidence of compulsive lying and elaborate stories. Cases on historic abuse are hard enough to prove anyway, let alone when such doubts are raised on witness credibility.

Sam was the defence lawyer.

He was the one who denied those kids justice, when he clearly knew they were telling the truth.

Karly was taken into social care, separated from her brother, and that's when she met Brendan Steele and the trouble really started. She did a stint in a juvenile detention centre for possession shortly after, and has had run-ins with the law ever since. There are countless domestic incidents, accompanied by photo evidence of the bruises he's left on her. There's one particularly nasty image of Karly's split and swollen eye socket, where you can barely make out it's her.

Sam has handed me exactly what I wanted in a beige file. Brendan Steele should have gone to prison twice over, so by taking a few years away from him, he's not truly losing anything. I don't need to kill him, so it doesn't matter if Stewart is suspicious – there won't be a body this time. This is the right thing to do. Just like Sam said he was, I'm sure beyond a shadow of a doubt.

Brendan works for a garden landscaping business. I decide to use this as a pretence for contacting him.

I tell him I'll come by the office tomorrow after work. I do this because I'm hoping a garden landscaping business will be quiet last thing on a Friday — and I intend to be late, just to be sure. Best as few people see my face as possible. It's on an industrial estate in Crystal Palace and I feel extremely out of place in my favourite blue work dress. I haven't actually been to my job all week but thought I better look the part. It's also raining. I try to dodge the puddles, but by the time I reach the makeshift cabin office my shins are splattered with mud.

The cabin snugly houses two desks and a coffee machine station. I have to move sideways between them to reach the man sitting at the far side.

He's well built, his gym-honed pectoral muscles obvious through a skin-tight blue T-shirt. I think it's supposed to be attractive, but I always think people like this look like LEGO figurines, put together block by block. There's a black and red tribal tattoo snaking its way along his arm, under his sleeve and poking out around his neck again, finishing up by his left ear. I don't mean to stereotype, but he doesn't exactly look like he works for a garden landscaping company.

'Hi, are you Brendan?' I ask.

'We close at six,' he says without looking up.

It's quarter past. The other reason I came when it was quiet was so I could concentrate. I'm certain that if I remain calm, I can control my power. When I accidentally siphoned Zara, I could feel it, and I was able to put it back.

'I'm so sorry, I got stuck on the Tube. My friend recommended you, said you were the best landscaper she'd ever had, and I'm desperate to get a quote from you. Could I just get your opinion?' I ask, being sure to giggle with every spare breath. I need to be quiet and unassuming, clearly not a threat.

He looks up, sees my sodden hair and mud-caked boots, and relents. 'All right, five minutes.'

I pull out the Zoopla photos I got from a random house in the area. 'So, I'm thinking of pulling out the trees at the bottom of the garden and putting in a water feature.' He reaches out for the photos. 'Just here,' I add, taking the opportunity to lean across him and graze his arm. *Fifteen years*. Hmm, shorter than I expected. This matters because it affects the amount of life I feel is reasonable to take. Twenty per cent pops into my head – no, wait, that's gratuity. But just say I did take twenty per cent, that would be three years. I think about what Svetlana said, that the majority of domestic abusers go free. There's no doubt in my mind that Brendan deserves to lose three years to the judicial system, so why not to me? It's for a good cause.

He points to the corner of one photo, where the grass dips down. 'The drainage is gonna be a bugger. It's weird how it dips down and then up again towards the house.' He takes a closer look. 'And the fences don't line up. Are you sure these are recent photos? It's almost like they're different houses . . .'

Oh shit, a bit of a screw-up here. It's not my fault all of suburbia looks the same to me. I feign surprise. 'Hmm, really? Well, that's what the estate agent sent me.'

I need to act fast. I take a deep breath, letting it fill up my

entire body, and allow my mind to go blank. I try to really feel
what it was like with Greg and Frances. First, I have to find the
thread, then I pull. I'm ready.

'I love your tattoo. Can I take a look?' I say, placing my hand
on some angular stripes.

And the energy flows. At first it surges. My instinct is to
resist and push back, but I know that it would be as futile as
holding back a tidal wave. Instead, I relax my muscles completely and picture the wave slowing into a gently ebbing river.
A few seconds later I remove my hand.

It's harder to tune into the exact amount when I'm holding
it. It's like I'm standing too close to see clearly, but I can tell
it's less than fifteen years. I overshot a little. Perhaps four or
five years. What I do know is that it worked. I can control my
power. I gasp with relief and smile.

I only notice the inappropriateness of my facial expres-
sion when I look up and see Brendan's shell-shocked face.
Goosebumps have broken out in angry hives across his skin.
His tanned skin has gone grey. 'I feel sick,' he says.

I get up. 'I'll fetch you a bucket.'

He lunges forward and grabs my wrist. 'What did you do?'

I twist free easily. Maybe it's the extra years of life, or maybe
it's something different altogether, but I can't help the surge
of pride that comes over me. This six-foot monster has been
rendered helpless by me. He's hunched over, holding his side,
and I'm towering above him. Strong. Powerful. Predatory. It's
this boldness that makes me say, 'Nothing you didn't deserve.'

'The photos weren't real. And I haven't done an actual gardening job this year. No one recommended me. Who are you?
Did Lucas send you? I told him I'd pay him for the last batch. I
just need more time to shift it.'

'Lucas didn't send me. You won't see me again, but if you

value your life, leave Karly and Leo alone.' Then I turn away and open the door. I've never felt so powerful in my life. I'm brimming with energy again. It's dark now but the stars illuminate the sky, the traffic from the road sings in chorus and the air is thick with the scent of possibility.

The world is mine because I am invincible.

'Wait,' he says.

I don't finish turning around quickly enough to see him drawing his fist back, and then he's punching me hard in the face.

Nobody has ever hit me before. I'm completely blindsided by the pain. My entire face is on fire and blood pours out of my nose. I'm on the ground. The metallic taste fills me with fury. Does he realize how easy it is to kill someone like this? One knock to the head at the wrong angle and that's it. Dead. Just ask Ruth.

I can't get up. His body casts a shadow over me as he comes closer, then he sits on my torso and closes his hands around my throat. There is absolutely no way I can fight him off. My airway is closing. He's shouting something at me, spit spraying across my face, but I can't hear. All I can think about is the lack of air in my lungs. I flail, I scratch, I shove. Nothing works.

My head feels like it's about to explode when a quiet voice reminds me, I can kill him with one touch. There's no time to debate the right and wrong of it. I need air. I reach one hand up and grab his wrist. I think he assumes I'm trying to fight back, so he smiles and squeezes my neck harder. Then the hand goes still, and his breath goes cold. He knows that something is wrong, because his grip slackens and confusion clouds his eyes, but it's too late for him to do anything about it.

He chokes, and suddenly his hands go to his own neck. Blood bubbles up and leaks out of the corners of his mouth.

Then he wretches, spluttering red liquid over me. I crawl out from under him as he convulses on the floor. I'm frozen on the ground. This wasn't supposed to happen. He made me do this.

Blaming the victim. Sure, that'll hold up in court. Oh shit, three is a pattern. I can't be caught near another dead body.

Something clicks into gear, and I scramble across to him. 'Don't die. Just hold on for one more minute.' The capillaries in his eyes have burst and his face is tomato red. My hands are trembling as I grip his arm. 'I'm sorry, it's all going to be fine. Just hold on.'

I try everything. I relax, I constrict, I soften, I harden, I loosen, I tighten. Nothing works. His eyes are frozen open, staring up at me with a desperate plea. I can feel his twelve years ready and waiting to follow my command, but there's nowhere for it to go. Just an empty host inhospitable to life.

This is the most gruesome scene I've witnessed so far, and I wonder if I should wipe down the surfaces in case I've left DNA. But I don't think I've touched anything except the folder I brought with me, and as there's no visible wound, it's possible people will think it's an outrageously violent blood clot or something. I decide the risk of looking for cleaning supplies puts me at greater risk of leaving evidence behind, so I collect my mismatched garden photos and jam them into my bag.

The door is already open. I'm about to step through it and be on my way when a man climbs the cabin steps. It's Officer Stewart. He looks at the lifeless body on the floor, then back to my bloodstained dress.

Chapter Eleven

Killing in self-defence is not murder.

Jesus fucking Christ, I have killed another person. I was so close to doing things right and now I have screwed it all up beyond belief.

When I'm holding excess life like this, everything is magnified. The lights at the police station are blinding, every scraped chair is deafening and the smell of Stewart's tuna melt, which still lingers on his beard from lunch, is nauseating. It makes me want to run, fight and scream from the pure intensity of it all. This state of being is badly suited to being locked inside a police interrogation cubicle.

'Let me ask you again, Thea, what *were* you doing at Brendan Steele's office this afternoon?' Officer Stewart asks. There's no aggression in his voice. If anything, he's baffled by me, like someone who tried to swat a fly and shocked themselves by catching it instead.

I want to ask what *he* was doing there. Is it possible that a coincidence took him to Brendan Steele's place of work? No, he saw me at the station. He must have found out what I'd asked for, got suspicious and followed me.

'I've requested a lawyer. You're not supposed to continue questioning me until they arrive,' I croak through my flattened windpipe. Despite everything, I still have the sense not to incriminate myself.

I don't expect much from the lawyer. It's 10 p.m. on a Friday, so I'll probably get some inexperienced Legal Aid solicitor who's so desperate for cash that they're hanging by the phone. At least it gives me time to think. There was no weapon at the scene. Brendan Steele choked to death on his own blood. But I need an explanation for why I was in that cabin. I can't claim that I was honestly enquiring about landscaping, because I don't have a garden and it will take them two seconds to work out the photos in my bag aren't mine.

'How's your neck?'

In all honesty, I've barely noticed it. The second I siphoned Brendan Steele's life away, the pain vanished. That's another thing I need to explain away: why he suddenly decided to attack me. But all I say is 'lawyer', because I'm not stupid enough to tell him something I'll regret.

When the door opens several hours later, it's not the exhausted half-drunk Legal Aid lawyer I'm expecting. Instead, it's a man with perfectly coiffed red hair, an easy smile and a single dimple. Sam. I sit up straight.

'Sorry for the delay. I do hope you haven't been questioning my client in my absence, Officer Stewart?' Sam asks, a knowing twinkle in his eye.

The officer shakes his head in disbelief. 'Just keeping an eye on a woman who was found covered in a dead man's blood.'

'Allegedly. May I have a moment to advise my client?'

The officer leaves, and only when the door clicks does Sam's breezy demeanour fall away. 'What the hell is going on, Thea?'

I'm not prepared for this. Sam's not dumb enough to believe this is a coincidence. 'I don't know how to explain.'

'Well, first let's focus on getting you out of here. What have you told the police?'

'Nothing.'

'So, they don't know why you were at Brendan's office?'

'No.'

'Good.' He's scribbling notes in his pad and doesn't look up for a few moments. 'I have an idea of how to help you, you just need to go with it – can you do that?'

I shake my head in disbelief. 'Don't you want to know why I was in that office?'

'Is there any evidence of it?'

'Not really, just a couple of garden photos in my bag.' Sam raises an eyebrow, so I continue: 'Brendan's a landscaper. I asked for a quote. But I also came into the station yesterday pretending to be your assistant so I could get Brendan's address. I've got your bag by the way.'

'Does Stewart know this?'

'Yes,' I say.

'That's fine, I can handle this. Now, let's get into the incident.'

I spend the next few minutes detailing exactly what happened. The train I took, the people I spoke to, my exact movements in the cabin. Sam is in his element. Maybe I'm imagining it, but I can practically hear his brain whirring behind those focused eyes. Thirty minutes later, we're ready and the door opens once again.

For the most part, Sam lets me do the talking. I describe the turn of events, sticking to the truth as closely as possible. That I walked into the cabin, talked to Brendan Steele for a few minutes, then he attacked me and collapsed in a spluttering, choking mess.

'Why didn't you ring for an ambulance?'

'I was in shock. I'd been attacked and then he died in front of me.'

'It's strange, being connected to two deaths so close together.'

'What's your question, officer?' Sam interjects.

Stewart frowns, clearly lacking the confidence to make the accusation. 'Let's go back to how you knew the victim. Why were you in Mr Steele's office?'

'I told you, I'm doing some work experience with Sam. Our client Karly Maxwell was involved in a domestic incident with Brendan a few days ago. I went to serve a restraining order against him.'

The officer turns to Sam. 'I'm sorry, Mr Ellis, you're telling me that you sent your young, female intern to serve legal documents to a man with a history of violence towards women – and you sent her alone at night?'

'Six p.m. is not night. And no, I don't make a habit of putting my colleagues in such vulnerable situations. There was a misunderstanding between us.'

'A misunderstanding?'

Sam shrugs. 'That's what I said. Actually, I'd love to know what you were doing at Brendan's place of business, Officer Stewart. Are you assigned to that case?'

'I don't need to answer that, but I will. No, I'm not connected to that case but I'm familiar with most of our local repeat offenders. Your intern requested a file from us the day before the victim's death. It brought the case to my attention, and I decided to pay Mr Steele a visit, remind him that it would be best to give Miss Maxwell some space. Now if we could get back to that misunderstanding. Please explain.'

Sam smiles. 'No, I don't think I will. You and I both know that you have no evidence with which to charge Miss Greaves. She was witness to an unfortunate death, and rather than support her through this distressing incident, you've decided to interrogate her. You've previously visited her home without prior warning and delayed her from receiving medical attention for her neck injury in the process of a wrongful arrest. Unless you drop this frankly ridiculous charge right now, we will be filing our own lawsuit for police harassment and negligence.'

Stewart goes red in the face. He leans forward and points his finger at me. Before he can speak, the door opens. A woman calls to him, 'Officer Stewart, a word.'

They're gone for a few minutes. Sam stays utterly professional, flicking through his notes, although I don't think he's really reading them. Then the woman reappears. She's wearing a nicely fitted grey suit and has her hair wrapped up in a neat bun. She doesn't look like she's been out throwing criminals to the ground recently. Not that I'm a criminal. Not really.

'You're free to go, Miss Greaves. I apologize for the inconvenience and hope we can put this matter behind us.'

'And Officer Stewart – does he apologize?' Sam asks, head cocked like he's teasing her.

'Absolutely, and you have my word he won't be needlessly bothering you again.'

We get to our feet and walk out the door. I'm exceptionally glad to be out of that cell. We pass Officer Stewart in the hall. And I know I shouldn't do it, but I simply can't help myself; I smirk at him. His eyes widen and his mouth drops open, but he doesn't say anything. Not with his senior officer standing over him like a teacher with a naughty toddler. Which means I did it, I'm out, I'm free.

*

Sam drives me home. I'm relishing the pine scent of his car and the air rushing in through the half-open window. Freedom is invigorating. I spend the entire ride back to my flat recounting Sam's performance, partly to delay the questions I know Sam is going to ask, but also in an expression of genuine admiration. What he was in that interrogation room is everything I imagined a lawyer to be: smart, determined, focused.

'You should get back into criminal law. Really, think how much good you could do for people,' I babble as we turn the corner into my street. There's a space between a van and a car that looks too small for a Mini Cooper, let alone Sam's Audi, but he executes the parallel park effortlessly.

I invite him in, leaving him in the all-in-one kitchen, living and dining area as I slip away to change out of my bloodied clothes. I return to find him leaning over the freezer. He passes me a bag of frozen peas wrapped in a tea towel. 'For your face.' I smile and press them against my jaw.

'Nice flat,' he says.

'Ruth's flat. She gives me mates' rates.'

'Wow, are you sure I'm allowed in?'

'She likes you.'

'Pretty sure she called me a fascist once.'

'I seem to remember you were advocating for society to kill whoever topped the rich list each year.'

'Think how much money they'd donate. I stand by that idea.' He's surveying the place, like he's trying to gather data before making a decision. The silence is growing larger and more awkward by the second.

'Tea?' I ask.

'Sure, I'll have it black.'

Flicking the kettle on and watching it jiggle as the heat boils up gives me something to focus on, a reason to stay turned around and excuse the silence. I pour a dash of milk in mine and hand Sam his. We both take a sip.

'So, how did you do it?' he asks. My breath hitches as I scramble for a response. He continues, his tone excited and quick. 'You obviously did it, but I've heard what the coroner said and I can't figure out how. It's not often I come up against a problem I can't solve.'

'Should the coroner really be speaking to you?' There's admiration in his eyes. I take bizarre pleasure in impressing him. 'What did the coroner say?'

'No, the medical report isn't out yet, but people love to talk about weird cases. Apparently, they think he died of an internal injury consistent with a knife wound. It punctured his lung, which then filled up with blood and killed him. But the kicker is that there was no external stab wound, so how does that happen?'

A stabbing. That's different. Greg died of a heart attack. Frances died of liver failure. It seems plausible that someone would want to stab Brendan Steele and it's giving me a theory: this is how these people were fated to die, and I'm just speeding things along. But I can't tell Sam this. Right now, he thinks I'm some kind of criminal mastermind. If I tell him I have magic murder powers he'll think I'm insane.

So, I ignore his question. Instead, I ask, 'How did you know I'd been arrested?'

'I told you that I still take on the odd criminal case. Simon keeps an eye out for anything . . . challenging. Usually, I would never even meet my client before the court date, but then I realized that you were the murderer.'

'Alleged,' I say, echoing his words in the interrogation room. He hides his smile behind his mug. 'All right, if you're so bloody sure that I killed a person, then why did you help me?' I ask.

'Brendan Steele wasn't a person; he shouldn't even be thought of as human. Whatever you did, it was a good thing. I wish I had your guts.'

We both drink our tea. Sam doesn't say anything else, and I think he might be using some kind of pop psychology trick of goading me into talking with silence. And it's working. I can hardly stand it and I can tell I'm about to confess every little detail of what's happened since that night Ruth collapsed in the smoking area.

Then the door slams and the sound forces the words back down my throat. Ruth comes round the corner and her eyes go wide.

'Oh my God, Thea. What happened?'

I don't think the peas have helped the swelling much. 'It's nothing, just a little accident.'

'Accident?'

'Well, someone hit me,' I say, wondering how much of the truth I can tell without the details. 'Got caught between some brawling idiots on the Tube. It's all fine, though. Sam was there; he brought me home.' She finally looks away from my face and notices him leaning against the counter.

'Ruth, long time no see. How've you been?' Sam asks, his tone genuine.

She blinks a few times, possibly hoping her eyeballs will refresh and Sam will be gone. 'I'm fine thanks. Thanks for bringing her home but I can look after her now.'

Wow, not reciprocating with a question. This is probably the rudest thing I've ever seen Ruth do. For me, totally standard behaviour. For her, she may as well have slapped Sam in the face. I'm not sure how much he realizes, though, so I stay quiet.

He nods and gives a knowing smile. 'Of course, I should leave you both to it.'

I walk Sam all of five metres to the door. His voice drops to a whisper, and he brushes my arm. 'When can I see you again?'

This is honestly baffling. Less than an hour ago he was defending me on a murder charge, now he's asking me out on another date.

'Can I text you?' I ask. 'Today's been a lot and there's something really important I still have to do.'

Chapter Twelve

The transfer of life must occur in such a way
that maximizes social good.

It's a miracle. That's what Ruth keeps saying, along with all the other doctors at the hospital. Oliver Locksley spontaneously recovered in the night. Apart from some light burn scarring, he'll be a picture of health for another twelve years. It's not a lifetime, but at least he's got a second chance to spend more time with his family and continue putting out good into the world. Better than nothing.

I've now killed three people. Technically, that makes me a serial killer. I should feel guilty. Heck, I shouldn't be able to sleep at night. It's for this reason I find an excuse to return to the hospital a few days later. Oliver's out of intensive care now, which makes it easier to visit. But he's not on the ward. I'm about to give up when I spy him through the window. He's outside, sitting in a wheelchair in the courtyard. Nothing fancy, just a couple of trees, some shrubs and a bench. Sitting in nature can speed the recovery process along, according to Ruth. Not that Oliver needs any help.

'Do you mind if I sit?' I ask, pointing at the bench.

'Please do,' he says, his smile warm and inviting. He's wearing tortoiseshell circular-framed glasses that give him the air of a gentle academic. And without the tubes and machines, he's more handsome than I'd realized. I'd say he's around thirty years old. He clearly lost his hair young, but it suits him because it means his relaxed smile is the only thing I focus on. I think you can tell a lot about someone from their smile.

We sit in companionable silence for a while. I enjoy his easy, calming presence.

'I feel like I recognize you,' he says.

'I have that kind of face.'

'Are you visiting someone?'

'Yes, there was an accident. I wanted to come and check up on them.'

'I'm sorry. Were you close?'

'Not exactly. It's hard to explain, but they're important to me.'

'Well, they're in good hands. I was also in an accident. And it was touch and go, so I'm told, but I'm on the mend now. I'm so grateful to the nurses and doctors here – they're an incredible team, so try not to worry too much about your friend.'

'Thanks.'

'Have you got anyone you can talk to? Someone you can turn to for support?'

'Hey, I'm not the patient here. Don't worry about me.'

A petite, dark-haired woman walks over. She's wearing a baby-pink cashmere sweater that looks buttery soft and makes me want to give her a hug. 'Ols,' she calls. 'Are you ready to go?'

'Are you sure you're okay?' he asks me before responding. I nod and he wheels himself towards the door his wife is holding open. Behind her I see two children waiting. I would guess they're around six and eight years old. The girl is holding the stuffed bear I saw in the ICU. Bertie.

The smiles on their tiny little faces as Oliver wheels through the door soften my guilt. I defended myself against a man who only put out harm into the world, and because of it, one who only does good gets to live on.

Later that week Ruth arrives home with a bouquet of white and yellow lilies, freesias and carnations. Apparently, Oliver heard she'd been pulling double shifts to take care of him – although of course only I know this was to alleviate her guilt. He told Ruth that if there was anything he could do for her, she shouldn't hesitate to call. I'm glad for that, because now she can forgive herself and continue leading a life that ripples through the world with goodness.

Ruth arranges the flowers in a vase, smiling to herself. I'm responsible for that. Ruth's other friends may be richer, prettier and more successful than me, but can they do what I can for her? Would they? I think not.

'Maybe you're making it up and you have a secret admirer you're not telling me about,' I tease.

'Talking of admirers, please tell me you're not dating Sam again?'

'Again? We never even dated.'

'You may as well have done. You pined over that mop-haired idiot for a whole summer after the internship ended. I never understood your obsession with him. He likes his own reflection far too much and he needs a haircut.'

I try not to laugh, but bitchy Ruth is such a rare treat I can't help myself.

'Well, you don't need to worry,' I lie. 'We just bumped into each other at court and got caught up talking about work.'

'And about that – I thought you were sick?'

Bloody Zara. 'Surely that's some kind of HR violation for her to tell you that.'

'Don't worry, I'm not going to rat you out. I just don't get why you lied to me about going to court.'

'Well, because of Zara for one. And after the whole interview rejection I just wanted to keep my trying to step back into the legal world to myself.'

'So, it's nothing to do with Sam?'

'What's that supposed to mean?'

'Nothing, it's just that you're not always rational when it comes to him. Remember when you interned together and he forgot to upload those documents to eDiscovery, and you covered for him?'

'Please, it wasn't a big deal. They already hated me at that place whereas Sam actually had a chance of being hired full time. I did a favour for a friend.'

'He let you take the blame for him. That doesn't sit right with me. You deserve someone who's going to put you first.'

I wish I could tell her how much he's already done for me, coming to my defence at the station. But of course, I can't.

'You're being overprotective,' I say, secretly quite enjoying it.

She raises her eyebrows. 'Coming from you?'

She has no idea.

'You're probably right,' she sighs. 'Just be careful. And remember that butterflies in your stomach are sometimes just anxiety.'

'Very romantic.'

Sam has been texting incessantly. I wait a respectable three hours between each text because I have a life and I'm absolutely not obsessed with him. Also because I don't want him to know about the dopamine-spin my head does the second I see his name come up on my phone, and how I instantly read the message without opening it. But mostly the first thing.

We arrange a date for Saturday. He refuses to tell me where we're going, and while I appreciate the mystery, it's quite irritating in practice. I settle on black jeans and my favourite blue top – the type that looks *just thrown on* but happens to make my boobs look amazing – but it's hidden under my usual biker boots and scruffy checked coat. I spend a few minutes snipping at loose coat threads with scissors before I head out, but every time I've cut one straggler away two more appear. It's fine. Don't want him to think I've tried too hard.

I'm glad about this decision when Sam greets me with a bunch of yellow sunflowers, promptly followed up with, 'They're not for you.'

I button up the coat when we first get onto the Tube, then a bus, then walk along a street lined with empty shops and people with nothing better to do than sit and smoke. I'm still holding onto hope this is an elaborate set-up. Any moment now Sam will unveil an underground bar which is secretly the hottest club in the city. That hope is extinguished when Sam stops outside a bleak grey tower block in the middle of nowhere. 'Where the hell are we?' I ask.

Sam shakes his head. 'Trust me. I want to introduce you to someone.'

This keeps getting worse. I don't enjoy meeting new people. I'm bad at small talk and have a habit of saying the wrong thing. But when Sam asks for something, I find it hard to say no.

We ring to be allowed into the building, then Sam approaches the woman working on the reception desk. 'I'm here to see my mum, Linda Ellis. I've brought a guest.'

His mum? Who the hell brings a girl they barely know – a potential killer, no less – to meet their *mother* on a second date?

The woman looks at her notes. 'I'm afraid your mother had an episode in the night, and we had to sedate her for her own safety. She's in no condition for visitors.'

Sam gives a soft, vulnerable smile. His eyes skim over the receptionist's name tag. 'Please, Jane, we'll only be a moment. Mum will be so excited that I've brought a girl by. I think it'll put a smile on her face.'

It seems like everyone else wants to say yes to Sam too, because Jane gets drawn in by his pleading puppy-dog eyes and sighs. She makes a call to see if Sam's mum is awake, then says, 'No more than ten minutes.'

'Thank you, Jane, you're a star.'

She passes us two visitor badges, smiling away at Sam while glaring daggers at me. Her eyes follow us as we disappear into the lift. Sam pushes the button for level six, and I teasingly shake my head at him. 'That was shameless.'

He grins. 'You're just jealous.'

The doors open and Sam leads me to a room at the end of the hall. Before we go in, Sam passes me the sunflowers. The room is small but still able to hold a dressing table, an armchair, a coffee table and a bed. Everything smells of lemon-scented cleaner, which is clearly overcompensating for the background waft of cabbage. A woman I assume to be Sam's mum is asleep.

He goes to her bedside table and takes her hand. 'Hey, Mum, it's Sam.'

She stirs, blinking hard as she tries to focus on him. Then she squeezes his hand and speaks with slow, deliberate effort. 'Hello, darling, I didn't know you were coming. I would have made lunch.'

I don't get the sense that residents are allowed near the

cooking facilities, but Sam says, 'Oh that's okay, Mum, we're only stopping by for a quick visit.' He props up her pillows and helps her lean up a little. 'This is my friend, Thea.'

'Hi, it's lovely to meet you,' I say, feeling like an idiot. I've not spent much time around people who are sick (I don't count Ruth because even with leukaemia she had more energy than me) or old (again, I don't count Grandad because his mind is ten times sharper than mine), and I have no idea how I'm supposed to act or what I'm supposed to say. I wish Sam had warned me, because then I could have googled what to do. His mum stares at me for several long moments, saying nothing. She's not looking directly at me, more around me, as if trying to work out why I'm relevant to this situation. Sam catches my eye and nods his head to what's in my hands. 'We brought you some flowers. I can put them in a vase if you like?'

'No, I'll have my maid do it,' she says.

Sam rolls his eyes. 'Mum, they're nurses, we've been over this.'

There's a vase on the coffee table, so I go ahead and arrange the flowers in them.

The left side of her face breaks into a smile, but the right remains still. 'Sunflowers are my favourite. How did you know?'

'A little bird told her,' Sam says, taking a seat in the armchair. I perch on the coffee table. Sam starts an easy chatter, and I stop worrying about what to say, realizing that I don't really matter in this scenario. He asks her about the food (dreadful, she says, but she's trying to teach the chef), he asks whether she's been for a walk recently (yes, three miles before breakfast) and whether she's watching anything on television (no, the maid keeps hiding the remote).

He doesn't correct any of this. Perhaps it's better to let her believe her constructed reality, to let her have control over something. Sam clearly thinks so.

Her gaze drops to me again. She's doing the same thing, looking around me and not at me, which makes me shuffle uncomfortably.

'There's a darkness around your friend,' she says to Sam. 'Can't you see it, buzzing all around her like smoke?'

'Perhaps we better go,' Sam says.

Both of us get up, but she grabs Sam's wrist. 'I don't like it at all. Stay away from her.'

'Mum, it's okay,' he says.

She's looking at me with panic in her eyes, breathing quickly. Then she gives a faint whisper of a scream, but it's hoarse and catches in her throat. It's more unsettling than any blood-curdling noise someone could make.

'I'll wait outside,' I say, escaping quickly into the hallway.

Sam stays with her for a few minutes. There's no screaming when he opens the door, so I guess he calmed her down. I didn't like the way she looked at me, like she knew something I didn't. Neither Sam nor I say anything until we're outside the building. We stop for lunch at a cafe with metal chairs and plastic tablecloths. When I ask what kind of coffee they have, the answer is 'The caffeinated kind.'

'Why didn't you tell me we were going to see your mum?'

He shrugs. 'I wasn't sure you'd want to come.'

'I'm sorry I upset her.'

'It wasn't your fault; she gets like that. She suffered a stroke a few years ago and never recovered from the brain damage.'

That makes me wonder. I've heard stories about people developing a sixth sense after brain injuries. Obviously, I never believed in anything so stupid, but I also wouldn't have believed what I can do now. Maybe she really did see something in me.

'She said there was darkness around me. Why would she say that?'

'I'm pretty sure you were sitting in a shadow. Don't read too much into it.'

I take a gulp of my ash-flavoured coffee, trying to avoid tasting it any more than necessary. 'So, why did you bring me here?'

'Is this not what you had in mind for our third date?'

'Third? We've only been out for dinner once.'

'And we spent the following evening together.'

'In a police station.' I put down the coffee and lace my fingers together. 'Can you be straight with me for one minute, please?'

'I don't think you trust me yet, or you would have told me the truth about what happened with Brendan Steele. That's fine because, luckily, I'm more patient than you. And although I don't know the details, I understand why you did it. You're like me; you want things to be right, and you want them to be fair. When I told you about Karly and Brendan, you were compelled to help.'

I open my mouth to protest but he continues, 'I wanted you to meet my mother so I can explain why you should trust me.' He takes a deep breath. 'My family didn't have much money when I was growing up, but we were comfortable, and it wasn't important to us. My dad worked for the same delivery company for twenty years, so when they offered him the chance to get in on the ground floor of a new business expansion, he believed they were looking out for him. He mortgaged our house and borrowed against his pension to invest. Then it all went wrong. He couldn't cope with the shame, and he killed himself. Mum found him and she . . . broke. Completely. Tried to drink herself to death. Every time I came home from school I'd wonder if she'd tried to drown herself in the bath or if she'd tripped and hit her head again. But it was a stroke that did it, and she ended up like this.'

'I'm sorry, but I still don't understand. Why are you telling me all of this now?'

'Because my family is one example in thousands. There are so many people who care only about their own selfish greed; they don't care how many lives they ruin in the process. Brendan Steele was a lone thug, a symptom of the rot gripping the system. I don't judge you for what you did, but if you're seeking justice, you're doing it wrong.'

Chapter Thirteen

Money isn't a reason to kill someone, but it helps.

I didn't expect the first step in Sam's plan to show me how I'm *doing it wrong* to be in a block of luxury apartments in Mayfair. A woman walking her chihuahua, talking without regard for volume, pushes me off the pavement. I pull off a ridiculous manoeuvre to avoid falling into a Porsche and then a Jaguar and end up in the middle of the road. Which is thankfully quiet.

Finally, I spot Bartholomew Place, where Sam texted me to meet him. The entrance is framed by well-manicured spiral hedges and two marble water fountains. I'm almost afraid to step inside, certain I'll be recognized for the imposter that I am, but the concierge smiles and waves me over. 'Miss Greaves?'

'Yes.'

'Mr Ellis said you'd be visiting this afternoon. Come right with me,' he says, stepping out from behind the desk and escorting me to the elevator. He swipes a card, the access page on the wall turns green and he calls the elevator. Then he shuttles me inside and presses number sixteen. 'Fifth door on your left. Please do call if you need anything at all.'

Sam answers the door in a plain white T-shirt and jeans. He's holding his phone between his head and shoulder, making a few *hmm*s and *yeah*s to pacify whoever's on the other end, and ushers me into the living room. His laptop is set up on the dining table, alongside a stack of papers and an empty bowl. He covers the phone's audio and whispers to me, 'I'll just be a minute, make yourself at home.'

I keep hold of my bag and perch on the brown leather sofa. The entire wall is glass, leading out onto a balcony big enough for a table, an L-shaped outdoor sofa and several bulbous plants. I can see at least two bedrooms and another room that looks like an at-home cinema. This place is a two-minute walk from Hyde Park. And I thought Ruth's flat was impressive.

I hear Sam clap his phone down on the table, then he joins me on the sofa. 'Sorry about that, I'm all yours now.'

'Is this yours?' I ask, unsure how he could afford it. Sure, lawyers get paid well, but he's not old enough to have accumulated this much and I know there's no family money. It makes me wonder exactly what he's doing for his clients.

'Ha, no, it belongs to my client, but it sits here empty.'

'Why?'

'Most of these places are empty now, the super-rich bought up London years ago. The properties are investments, and most of them can't be bothered to rent them out, not worth the hassle.'

'So, you don't even have to pay rent,' I say, not in question, but in response to my reflection on my salary compared to his.

'And the rich get richer. Irritating, isn't it?'

'I will not kill someone because they've got more money than me.'

'Ahh, so you admit that you could if you wanted to?'

'Anyone *could* kill someone, but they don't.'

He rolls his eyes, as if he's getting bored with the pretence. They land on the Omega on his wrist. 'We had better get ready. I'm taking you to a party.'

Sam takes me to the owner's walk-in closet and tells me to pick something decent. Whoever this woman is, she's thinner than me and has a thing for extremely short, tight dresses. I haven't shaved my legs in a week, so I pick a forest-green silk jumpsuit that's more forgiving.

Sam knocks at the door. 'Did you find something?'

I open the door. A little (big) part of me hopes it'll be like a movie scene, where the love interest is blown away by my transformation from Primark girl to Armani woman. But Sam never does what I want.

'That won't do,' he says. Then he's rifling through a jewellery box. He haphazardly throws me some diamonds, then looks at my boots. 'Take those off, please.'

I swap them for heels that are one size too big but do the job. The diamonds are too much. I once stole a gummy worm from a pick 'n' mix when I was a kid. Grandad told me that thieves are among the worst sinners and made me confess my actions to everyone I met for weeks after. I've never forgotten the sting of it. The diamonds are jewels of guilt glistening on my skin, and I can't help but think people will take one look at me and know exactly what I've done. 'I'm not taking these.'

'You need to look the part.'

'It's wrong. They're not mine.'

'The people who own this flat have another ten just like it.

Every time they acquire a new property, I order exactly the same collection of clothes and products, just in case they ever decide to stay. It's been three years and they've never set foot here. Don't think of this stuff as belonging to anyone. Besides, you're only borrowing them.'

'What if I lose them?'

'Who cares?'

'I do.'

I can see that glint in his eye. It says: *You murdered a person and now you care about taking some jewellery.* To his credit, he does not say this.

'Feeling bad about taking anything from these people is like feeling bad about taking a glass of water from a tap.' He digs deeper into the jewellery box, passing me a thin silver necklace. 'How about this?'

It's simple and I hope it's not particularly expensive. 'Fine.'

For a minute, I think Sam's taking me to a church. The building is sandstone brick, and the front door is an arch with angels carved into the stone. Inside is a quiet circular room with no windows. A woman wearing a gold dress – and maybe it really is gold; who knows anymore? – looks me up and down. There are two six-foot men standing only a few feet away, trying hard to look like casual party guests but it's clear they're her back-up. Not that she needs them. She has the confidence of a woman who doesn't need to wear a bra – not because her breasts are small but because they stay up all by themselves. The way she bites her lip when she spots the simple silver necklace I'm wearing makes me wish I'd worn the diamonds; they would have been the only thing hard enough to reflect her contempt.

Sam gives his name and flashes a smile, which she instantly returns. She presses her fingerprint to a control panel and we're through. Inside is the most jaw-dropping building I have ever seen. The twenty-foot ceiling is Gothic stone stretching across like a ribcage and the windows are stained glass, but that's where the religious overtones end. They've installed lighting so that glass bounces colours across the room and illuminates the dancers who glide through suspended silk. No one gives them more than a second glance, but I'm mesmerized by them. My attention is only broken away by a tiger's roar. It paces the length of a ten-foot cage, trying to evade the idiots who are leaning against the bars for a selfie.

'These,' Sam says, gesturing across the crowd, 'are the very worst people on the planet. Come and meet them.'

And I do.

But they don't seem like the worst people on the planet.

I meet a woman who Sam tells me is a 'middle-woman' running slave-labour textile factories, giving them plausible deniability on how their clothes are made. She compliments my 'shabby chic' hair.

I meet a plump man who looks like he'd be cast as 'friendly grandfather' in a Hallmark movie. Sam tells me there's a constant slew of harassment and assault allegations against him.

Another person tells me she's running an equine therapy programme for asylum seekers. Okay, I would imagine refugees have other priorities, but it's not a malevolent calling. I spend ten minutes with her before Sam pulls me away. 'Careful with her – she likes to collect people, and no one really knows what happens to her little pets.'

'What do you mean?'

'I'm not sure, but she keeps the fixers busy.'

'Fixers?'

'You've got a problem, then you call a fixer. They take care of anything and everything.'

'How do you know all of this?'

Sam nabs a glass of champagne from a waiter and tries to shut me up with it. 'Hard to explain here.'

'If you're so sure of their guilt, then why don't you do something about it? Call the fucking police and turn them in.'

'Don't use the P word around here,' he says. He grasps my hand and leads me onto the dance floor. He lowers his head side by side with mine and we're moving quietly to the music. 'I can't. These people are clever, Thea. Or their lawyers are. If they get caught, they've got ten other people lined up to take the fall. I used to think that I'd work with them, get powerful enough that I could do something real, but it's impossible. If I ever utter a word against them, the prison sentence will be the least of my worries.'

'So, you want me to do your dirty work for you?'

'With me.'

My response is cut off by a piercing scream and a gunshot. The crowd gathers around the tiger's cage. Before panic sets in, a man steps onto one of the silk dancers' podiums.

'No need to concern yourselves. We've had a minor incident with the tiger, which has been contained.'

I stand on my tiptoes. The tiger is dead on the floor, a bullet hole in its head. A clump of black hair extensions lies next to it, and a woman with a messed-up bob is sitting on the floor, being comforted by a small entourage. There's an uneasy atmosphere in the room, like nobody's quite sure what reaction is warranted.

'On the plus side, I've got a new rug!' he adds.

This appears to signal the correct response, and the party-goers chuckle. The tiger cage is wheeled away, the music comes back on and everyone seems collectively to forget what just happened. I can do nothing but stare as the cage rolls by.

This beautiful creature. Dead. For a fucking selfie. And all it warrants is a thirty-second intermission from champagne and caviar.

*

We leave straight away. I told Sam it was either that or I would throw up and cry on the dance floor. He chooses wisely. It's too late and I'm too upset to get myself on the Tube, so I go back to Mayfair. Sam says there's a spare room. Several, actually.

When we get back, I don't complain when Sam helps himself to what's probably very expensive vodka and passes me a glass. I say 'probably' because the bottle is simple frosted glass with a blue label, but rich people seem to do this thing where if something's really expensive, they make it look completely normal. It's like they're saying: if you have to ask, then you can't afford it.

I notice it tastes slightly less like paint stripper than most vodka I've tried. I drink several glasses before I'm able to formulate my thoughts.

'That was awful, but I'm not about to start killing people for being rich twats.'

'I agree, that would be inefficient,' Sam says. He leans closer. 'When I realized what you'd done to Brendan, I knew we were the same. That we both understood there are people who can't be punished in any other way. These people are so much worse than him.'

'I didn't go after Brendan because I wanted to punish him. I did it so I could save someone else.'

'What do you mean?'

I forgot Sam still knows nothing about my power. He's signing up to this on the promise of death, unaware of the ability to give life. I explain how this all started, and why I kept going.

'You're telling me you can save lives by killing people who

fully deserve to die?' He gets to his feet and paces across the room, talking quickly with wide, excited eyes. 'Thea, this is incredible. It's fate. You have this ability, and I can give you the very worst people in existence. Think of what we can do together, think of all the people you could save, and the good they'll do in the world.'

I know this argument well because it's been licking the corner of my brain for some time now. I've been thinking about what Ruth told me, about Lamed Vavnik. Maybe she's right and Oliver is one of these special people that keep the world turning through their good deeds. But is he really one of the thirty-six most special people in the world? Really? I'm not saying I believe in this Lamed Vavnik thing, but if anyone's one of them, it's probably the person with the magic fucking powers.

'Sometimes I think it's selfish not to use my power. Doing the right thing is meant to be hard, and by not using it I'm putting my comfort above someone else's life. But it doesn't change the fact that it's murder – the unlawful premeditated killing of another human being.'

'You're still thinking in black and white, playing a game where you think everyone has agreed to the same rules. But it's all a lie. The people who run the world do not care about right and wrong, only what they want, and they don't care what happens to the people in their way. Your power is an opportunity to tip the balance back in the people's favour.'

It's easy to get swept away by Sam. There would be a joyful relief in allowing it to happen, but I struggle to match his conviction with my own. It all seems so abstract. 'The people, tipping the balance . . . I don't know, Sam.'

'You don't need to worry about the details. Think about what you did for Karly. You punished the man who was ruining her life and, because of you, she's free. Imagine if someone had done that for you.'

I flinch. Sam knows what happened to my parents. He once found me in tears, hiding in the office stationery cupboard on the anniversary of their death, and I blubbered every little detail to him.

He takes my hands in his, then says words I never thought I'd hear. 'I can help you find them. I always thought it was strange how short the investigation into your parents' case was. And after what I've seen, I know things like that usually happen when someone's trying to cover something up. With the contacts I have now, I can find out everything there is to know about what happened. Then you can track them down and give your parents the justice they deserve.'

I've never wanted anything so much in my entire life. The person who killed my parents would no longer be a figment of my nightmares, but a face and a name. Someone real. I could look them in the eye and make them sorry for what they did.

'You would help me do that? Please don't say it if you don't mean it,' I say. The idea is almost too painful to hold, the thought of it being taken away too much to bear.

'I promise. You help me and I'll help you. We can do this – together.'

When Sam looks at me, I matter. It's like there's no one else in the room. I can't speak, so I simply nod because there's no way I can turn back now. I need this more than I need to breathe.

He kisses me, rougher and more certain than before, because it's not some drunken snog, it's an agreement. He pulls the straps of my jumpsuit off my shoulders, and I tear off his shirt. I think he's more beautiful in the dark, because the red of his hair still burns through and his green eyes glisten. He kisses me, teeth grazing my neck and sending goosebumps down my spine. His fingers graze my stomach and I arch my back and moan. This is a partnership now. There's no hesitation as we slide together, our movements taking our breath away long into the night.

Chapter Fourteen

*How can you tell whether someone is a bad
person? The way they treat animals and waiting
staff is a pretty good indication. Personalized
number plates are another.*

How do I sleep at night?

On silk sheets.

I've always wanted to say that, but up to now silk sheets
have been an unachievable dream. Not today. I wake up at
10 o'clock with my face pressed against the pillowcase, trying
to inhale the material. Sam brings me a glass of water and an
espresso in a teeny tiny teacup. He cracks the curtains a little,
so the morning light bathes the room, and he crawls into bed
next to me. Perfect.

The espresso is smooth like caramel, and I don't say a word
until I've finished it. I wish moments like this could be captured
somehow. Whenever I experience something that makes me
so completely happy like this, it always sends a brief spike of
fear through me because I'm already imagining a time when
it's over.

It takes me a while to notice Sam is looking at me with worry lines on his face. 'You okay?' he asks, rubbing my shoulder.

I nod and snuggle into the sheets. Sam does the same, leaving our faces inches apart.

'Fine,' I say. 'Just thinking about that tiger.'

'Wish I could say that's the worst thing I've seen them do,' he says. 'Do you still feel the same ... about what we talked about last night?'

I give the smallest of nods. 'Yeah.'

'So, how does it work?' he asks.

'When I touch people, I know how long they've got to live. It's instant and I can't avoid it.'

I'm surprised how quickly he accepts this. But then I remember his approach to law has always been to gather evidence first and make judgements second. I guess I'm no different.

'Does that mean you know how long I've got?'

Sixty-two years. Lucky Sam. I nod, slowly again. 'Do you want to know?'

He's silent for a moment. His eyes drift away from me, and I can tell his mind has gone elsewhere to find an answer. 'No,' he says. 'I think knowing the end might take the fun out of the journey.'

I understand that. Oddly enough, knowing everyone's death dates but my own has never bothered me. If I knew I was to die at an old age, I don't know if this would be a relief or a burden. Sometimes life is too exhausting to think about in the long term.

'And how do you do it?' he asks.

I don't need to ask what he means by *it*. 'It's hard to explain. All I do is touch them, imagine their life flowing into me, and they die a few moments later.'

His eyes widen. 'One touch and that's it?' I nod. He continues. 'And you can do this to anyone? Even me?'

You would think this would scare him, or at least make him wary about touching me, but instead he intertwines his fingers with mine. He's looking at me with awe, not fear, as he traces my arm. My skin comes alive at his touch. It's like I'm brimming with energy, except I've got nothing except my own right now. The air has stopped moving and I can hardly stand it. I'm afraid of this. This isn't a feeling that can last – it's eating up all the oxygen in the room and choking me. And not in a sexy way.

'I could,' I say. 'But then I'd have to find someone else to bring me those tiny coffees.'

I'm rewarded with Sam's glorious smile. It's warm and safe and silences my racing mind.

'I see, so you're just using me?' he says with a wink. I'm jealous of people who can wink so naturally.

'Definitely,' I reply. I can still feel his smile as he kisses me, drawing me closer like he's trying to steal the air from my lungs.

After I'm reminded that I do indeed need to breathe, we break apart. I'm more than happy to continue rolling about in our silk sheets, but Sam has other ideas. He continues grilling me on the extent of my powers like I'm a case he needs to get all the details on. I can hear that whirring noise again, like the mechanisms in his head have clicked into gear.

He asks a lot of things I haven't thought about and don't have the answers to.

Can you control exactly when someone dies after you touch them?

Are the people you save invulnerable to everything?

Could you make someone immortal?

Can you choose how they die?

It's like I'm in an exam, one I haven't properly prepared for. Eventually, I throw a pillow at his face. 'If I wanted to feel like I'm bad at something, I'd go to work.'

'I don't understand – how can you not want to know everything there is to know?' I glare at him, and he relents. 'Okay, I'm getting carried away. I get it.'

'Indeed. So, what shall we do today?' I ask.

He shrugs. 'There's a bowling alley in the basement.'

Once the coffee kicks in, I check in on tiny phone world and notice a text from Ruth. Hey, you didn't come home last night. Where are you? Just checking you're okay? X

Whoops. We usually let each other know when we're staying out. It's nice. I like having someone care whether I'm alive or dead. I go to text back but can't bring myself to type Sam's name.

> Sorry, all good. Ended up going out
> with Eli, hanging here for the day x

In the grand scheme of things, this tiny white lie shouldn't even register on my conscience. But it does. Everything else has been a lie of omission – Ruth's never specifically asked me if I've been going around killing people on her behalf because she doesn't know about my power. But this is an active lie. It's like the trolley problem, where it's easier to let someone die than it is to actively crush them with a rock. And Ruth and I do not lie to each other. We made a promise.

She hearts my message and I put my phone away. There are only so many things I can think about at one time and today I have other priorities.

Sam thinks the more control I gain over my power, the easier it will be not to get caught. I need to avoid being connected to the scene of the crime. To be fair, I did try this with Brendan before things went pear-shaped, but Sam says this isn't enough. I need to be exact. He's going to help me practise.

Or at least he said he was going to. He went out to get 'supplies' that I assume and sincerely hope means breakfast, but he's been gone for over an hour now. I've been keeping busy. The concierge, Trevor, gives me a tour of the building. There's a shared library where I can work, an executive lounge where I can take meetings and get coffee, a tranquillity room which is pitch black with a ceiling that looks like the night sky, a rooftop terrace, a gym and a pool.

I don't have a costume, but I can't imagine anything more glorious than submerging my hungover body in warm chlorinated water, so I steal an unworn Dolce & Gabbana costume from my host's closet. The tiles are the darkest midnight blue, one shade shy of black, which has the eerie effect of making me feel like I'm swimming in a limitless ocean abyss. I roll in the water, gently sculling on my back so I don't have to stare into the dark.

There are clean towels and a fluffy robe hanging by the pool shower; I doubt either have ever been used because they have that fresh just out of the box smell. I tighten the robe and make my way back to the apartment, marvelling at how everything in this place is so *clean* and so *nice*. It makes me want to grip the gold-painted banisters tighter and sink my feet into the plush living-room carpet.

I eat straight out of the fridge, alternating between sundried tomatoes, Manchego cheese and feta-stuffed olives until the fridge starts beeping because I'm letting out all the cold air. Then I settle into the sofa and find a button on the side to make it recline. It seems like there should be a television in front of me – there's an ornate wooden case on the wall that looks like it could be concealing one. I'm about to get up and investigate, but then I press another sofa button and the casing automatically retracts to show a seventy-inch plasma.

People who say money doesn't buy happiness have a severe lack of imagination. I'm enthusiastically channel flicking when I hear the front door click shut.

Sam's holding a cardboard box. He places it on the coffee table in front of me, grinning as if he's returned from a successful hunt.

'What is it?' I ask, leaning forward, extremely excited we've reached the present stage already.

'Open it.'

The sofa's cushioning is holding onto me like a suction cup, but I manage to shuffle down it by losing all pretence of elegance. The contents of the box are loosely covered by the side panels – Sam's wrapping leaves something to be desired, but I'll forgive him that. I can hardly wait to find out what's inside, so my head's almost in the box when I open it.

It's a rat. A brown rat. And it's huge – a rat that might have eaten all its siblings. It looks up at me with black beady eyes, and I swear it's scowling at me. It's all I can do to stare at it.

'Why have you given me a rat in a box?'

'It's not a rat.'

It's then I notice that its tail is covered in hair, feathering into a small bush at the end. 'Rat-squirrel?'

'Degu. They're Chilean.'

'Why is the Chilean degu here?'

'The pet shop was out of mice, and it was less cute than the rabbit.' I glare at him, and he continues: 'Practice. We need to test the parameters of your abilities. Let's start small by trying to take a small chunk of life off the degu.'

The degu is standing on its hind legs, as if trying to join the conversation, so I close the box. This is not a conversation for its ears.

'I don't think so. You realize killing animals is the mark of a psychopath?' I say. Given how many hours of true crime documentaries I've clocked with Ruth, I consider myself an expert on the subject.

'You've killed multiple people – actual living human beings – but you're drawing the line at degus?'

'Only people who deserved it. This is cruel. Besides, I don't even know if it would work.'

'Isn't it much crueller to practise on people? Come on, just try it.' He swoops down and retrieves the degu from the box. It looks shocked to have been caught so easily but doesn't struggle. Instead, it flares its nose and wrinkles its whiskers as if curious to be suspended mid-air. Sam holds it steady in front of me. I touch the degu's smooth brown fur: *eight years*.

'Jesus, these things live for eight years?' I ask, meeting Sam's gaze.

'So, it works?'

'Oh my God, what if it works? What if I've been taking life from people all this time when I could have been using rats?'

'Degus,' he corrects me.

Eight years. I could have been saving lives without ending others. It simply never occurred to me that my power would work on animals. I've always loved animals, but I hardly spend any time with them – Grandad never let me have a pet when I was young, and Ruth's flat isn't really suitable. My body decides to sit down before I do.

Sam sits beside me. 'It doesn't matter because this isn't only about saving people, it's about those who are escaping justice. About culling the rabid members of the herd before they infect the rest of us.'

But I'm still unconvinced. If I have a choice, I'm not going to keep stealing life from people – even if they deserve it. I reach out and place my hand on the degu. I'm not going to kill it, just take a few days off, as a test. It stops squirming and goes limp in Sam's hand as its life flows into me. I try to concentrate on how much I'm taking, feel for the days so I know when to stop. But I'm fumbling in the dark for the off switch. I take two years, much more than I intended.

'How did it go?' Sam asks.

I ignore him, encircling his wrist. The contrast of cold metal from his watch and warmth from his skin gives me goose-bumps. I need to know if this works. This has become like second nature to me, letting life flow through me as easily as taking a shower or making a coffee. But it doesn't come. I grip Sam's wrist harder, trying to squeeze the Degu's life force out. No response. I drop my hands in my lap and breathe, unsure whether it's relief or disappointment.

I refuse to test my powers on the degu again. Sam tries to convince me that I essentially kill animals every day by eating milk and cheese, and this is basically a rat, but he's arguing with me as if this is a courtroom governed by law and logic. He's not realized that the moment the degu wrinkled its whiskers at me it acquired test-subject immunity. I don't know how many times I can steal life and return it again and I won't risk hurting this oblivious black-eyed rat-squirrel.

'Well, the pet shop had a no-refund policy, so it's yours now,' Sam says. Then he pulls on his coat, zipping it up to the top of the collar. 'Attempt number two, back in a bit.'

As I'm now the proud owner of the degu, I feel entitled to check whether it's a he or a she. Then I give him a name: Diego. And spend the next hour googling how to look after him, ordering a cage and a sand bath – apparently, they go nuts rolling around in it, which is just so cute. Then I fill one porcelain ramekin with water and another with tapenade. He seems to be eating it. He had better not die after my attempts to save him.

Sam returns with a Tupperware full of cockroaches. I have no objection to this, because I cannot stand the sound of their little legs scurrying on the plastic. We learn a lot from the cockroaches.

1. I can transfer life from one cockroach to another, so it appears to only work within species.
2. I can't extend a life beyond its natural limit which, for a cockroach, is a bit less than a year.
3. I can control how much life I take with fairly decent precision. A dozen cockroaches later, I've gotten my accuracy down to a couple of days. Turns out it's less like turning off a tap and more like trying to stop peeing halfway through, but harder. I don't tell Sam this metaphor.

By the end of the day, we have a box of dead cockroaches, all upturned on their backs with the legs pulled into their bodies. I'm starting to notice a nasty smell wafting from them; it's both musty and oily.

'Can you smell that?' I ask.

'I'll get rid of them. You do not want to smell cockroaches once they go bad – it's like rotten piss and takes ages to go,' Sam says.

He dumps them in the outside bin and decides to cook. I suggest a takeaway, but Sam insists he can do a better job. And he can: out of nowhere he produces gnocchi with roasted vegetables and handmade pesto. He covers the gnocchi in boiling water for a few minutes, then drains them and transfers them to the oven so that the little potato pillows are fluffy on the inside and crispy on the outside. Glorious. I'm also rewarded with a present – an actual gift this time, not rats or bugs – a soft rectangle wrapped in blue tissue paper. Inside is a T-shirt. It's grey with a printed pig cartoon and a phrase in white text: *Eat the Rich*.

I laugh. 'I love it. Do they really sell these around here?'

'That was a joke present,' he says, and pulls out a small white box with a silver bow. 'This is to say sorry for making you kill cockroaches all day.'

It's a dainty silver bracelet set with tourmaline stones that match my necklace. I put it on immediately, holding it up to the light to watch the silver sparkle. Two days in and Sam is undoubtedly the best guy I've ever dated. We spend the rest of the weekend holed up in the Mayfair apartment, leaving only for expensive coffees and late-afternoon walks through the park. I'm struck with how wide and clear the streets are around here, and how they are framed by manicured trees. Everything is . . . nicer, cleaner, better.

Late on Sunday evening, I head back to Clapham. I need my work clothes and I don't want to miss my end-of-the-week Thai food and true crime ritual with Ruth. As I open the door, I pull my sleeve over the bracelet Sam gave me. We settle down on the sofa and eat out of the cardboard. I make up a story about Eli butchering 'Angels' by Robbie Williams at karaoke. Ruth pig-snorts when I tell her we were asked to leave due to noise complaints and I try to push down the pit in my stomach that I'm lying to her, again.

The first true crime episode we put on involves a serial killer who started off by putting kittens in vacuum-sealed bags. Now there's a candidate I'd have no qualms about killing.

'Absolutely fucking not,' I say. 'Not watching this.'

Ruth navigates back to the menu. 'That's all right, I already watched that one with . . .' She pauses but it's too late to backtrack '. . . Zara.'

'You TV-cheated on me with Zara. In our flat, our home.' I'm reacting with mock fury of course, but deep down, there's nothing mock about it. This is our ritual and she's shared it with that succubus.

'I'm sorry! There was nothing else on and to be fair you ditched me all weekend. If it helps, I didn't enjoy it. She doesn't like to talk through it like we do.'

'You're just saying that.'

'I swear.'

'Don't let it happen again.'

We put on another episode. This one is about a man obsessed with killing people who remind him of his mother. In the interview, the mother tells us how her son moved to Australia for work and still writes. They're a wealthy family and her non-murderer son makes use of their extensive resources to keep her in the dark. We both agree that this is kind. Lying isn't always a bad thing, if your intentions are good.

I ask Ruth what else she's been up to in my absence. She tells me she's started volunteering at the homeless shelter Oliver runs, helping to establish a medical clinic there. This worries me, given how much the ICU has been getting to her lately.

'Great idea. I often think about how selfish you are, spending all your time saving people in critical conditions. It's about time you helped someone,' I say.

'It's different. I feel energized being there, like I can really get to know people and make an impact. In ICU, I feel like a spare part. When people are that unwell, there's very little I can do. Most of the time, they're either going to die or they're not. It often feels like luck.'

'Is this because of Oliver?' I ask. I guess it must have been a strange experience, going from having thought you've killed a patient to his spontaneous, instantaneous and miraculous recovery. A good outcome, obviously, but disorientating.

'Not in the way you're thinking. He's opened my eyes that there's so much more I could be doing. Structural change that actually helps people.'

Ruth and Sam have more in common than she realizes, and I'm starting to think they might both be right.

We go a little quiet, wrapped up in the episode. There were warning signs before the murderer started killing – stalking, threats, violence. But the family covered it up, used their money to intimidate and bribe. I don't fully understand what Sam's plans are for my power but I do know it's meant for more than saving my bestie.

On Monday morning, reality calls. I'm knee-deep in an employee dispute before I've even had my morning coffee. I nod along at the right moments but all I'm thinking about is Sam, about everything that has transpired between us and everything we're going to do together. In my daydreams, it feels right and good. A few days later Sam texts me: I've got someone. A bolt goes through me, and I don't know if it's anxiety or anticipation. But I do know that I'm going to do this. I'm ready.

Chapter Fifteen

*On the whole, people don't change. And if they
do, they get worse. Once they've done one bad
thing, it just gets easier and easier until they
don't even register it as bad anymore.*

Sam and I don't manage to see each other until the weekend.
It's now 9 a.m. on Friday morning and I'm sitting with Eli in the
conference room, listening to Zara outline quarterly depart-
mental objectives and key results instead of finding out the
details of possibly the most important event of my entire life.
Everything up until now has been messy and accidental, but
what I'm doing with Sam? It's my defining moment. I can feel it.

'And how do you think we can make these goals smarter?'
Zara says in the most unbelievably frustrating voice, as if she's
talking to a child. Zara, who came into my flat and watched
my show with Ruth, and then didn't even appreciate it. 'Thea,
do you have any suggestions?'

'I'm sorry, what? You want to make them smarter?'

'S.M.A.R.T.,' she says, spelling out the word for me.
'It means that the goal should be Specific, Measurable,

Achievable, Relevant and Time-bound.' She turns and points to the slideshow on the wall-mounted screen. 'For example, instead of "improve employee onboarding experience", we can make it more specific by saying, "help employees feel more confident with their roles and responsibilities in their first two weeks".'

I suppose that's quite sensible. Perfectly reasonable really.

'We could introduce a form at the end of the onboarding process to evaluate how they're feeling. To make it measurable,' I say.

Eli narrows his eyes in suspicion, but Zara beams. 'Excellent idea. Thanks, Thea. Let's all take a few minutes to review our personal goals and make them SMART.'

It's a tall order, asking me to care about such trivial things when I could be out there doing something that actually makes a difference. Honestly, I should quit. But keeping some semblance of normality must be healthy – even Superman kept his boring office job. So I try my best. I write my SMART goals out in the neat colour-coded spreadsheet Zara has created. And to my amazement, my focus pays off and it's not long before I've crafted some goals, and I feel a fledging motivation to achieve them.

Then Zara comes over to review my goals. I smell her bergamot and sandalwood perfume before I hear her squeaky voice.

'Hmmm, perhaps what you really mean here is improve employee retention rather than becoming a better employer. And here, why don't we just tweak this . . .'

She pulls my laptop towards her and before I know it, my SMART goals have been rewritten. I barely recognize a word of what I originally wrote and wonder why we had to go through this pretence. Honestly, what is the point of me if she's just going to do it herself?

'That's better. What do you think?' she asks.

'Looks great,' I say.

I bet this never happened to Superman.

I don't go back to the flat. Instead, I take the Tube straight to Mayfair. Sam yanks the door open and welcomes me with a kiss. He asks me about my day, makes me a cup of tea and we sit on the sofa. It's all very sweet but there's a baby elephant dancing in my stomach.

'Sam, are we going to talk about . . . the thing we need to talk about?'

He slaps his hands against his thighs. 'Yes, give me one second.' He jumps up, collects his phone and passes it to me.

The open browser displays a photo of an elegant older blonde woman. She's wearing classy silver spike earrings and has a thin-lipped smile. Her name is Juliette Haimes. I scroll down the Wikipedia article. Never married. No children. Vice president of Omnilert. Why does that company ring a bell?

Then I realize. 'Oh, Sam, this is . . .'

He nods. 'This is the woman responsible for ruining my family.'

'How are you so sure? Surely lots of people were involved?'

'You're right, Omnilert was a huge company. But it was her who pitched the scheme to exploit the bottom rung of struggling companies, her who convinced my dad's company to buy into this insane pyramid scheme. Now Omnilert is bankrupt. No one who invested will ever see a penny of their money again. And she's rebranded herself and moved into pensions. Would you trust a person like that with your life savings?'

I tap on the news tab and skim the articles mentioning her name. There're plenty of articles detailing the Omnilert downfall, but none explicitly blaming her. I find one article where she's given a quote:

> Investing is too rich for most people's blood. I extend my sympathies to the people who lost out to the economic downturn, but everybody involved knew the risks – and the potential rewards. It's only now that things haven't gone their way that some people are claiming otherwise.

My heart twists for Sam. When I look up, I think he senses this because he says: 'This isn't just about my family. They were one in thousands, and she couldn't care less about what she did. Worse than that, she'll keep going. You can stop that happening.'

Sure, but it was Sam's family. He doesn't realize that the moment he promised to find my parents' killer for me, I was going to do anything he asked. The fact that this means something to him just makes it easier. I reach out and squeeze his knee.

'You don't need to convince me. I'm already in.'

The following week is a garbage fire. Zara's bad at the best of times, but something unpleasant has lodged itself in her arse this week, because her eagle-eyed glare spots the smallest of mistakes. The only thing getting me through the week is the thought of Friday night. Sam has given me the address of a club in Belgravia – Hardys. On Thursday afternoon, he sends me a blue velvet dress, stilettos and a bouquet of roses. I know it's cliché, but I don't care – I have always wanted someone to do this for me, and I can almost delude myself into thinking it's simply a glorious date.

Of course, it's not. Hardys is the name of an exclusive club for the super-rich. I've spent the whole week trying to google it, but the internet returns nothing, which only intrigues me more. Not a single Yelp review and no photos of the interior. Even the Google Maps image is blurred out for privacy – I had no idea you could do that. It's where the rich go to snort cocaine and conduct back-room deals. And on Friday night, Juliette Haimes will be there.

Inside the club is a London unlike what I have ever known. Hardys is set over six floors (that I've discovered so far) and includes a spa, a swimming pool, squash courts, a restaurant, a cigar room, a bar and a rooftop terrace with a retractable glass roof and heaters on full blast. It's not child-friendly, but it is dog-friendly and comes with in-house dog walkers and a play area for your pup. I see a goldendoodle curled up on a heated blanket, and I think of the homeless man I pass on my way to work, and what he would do for that blanket.

Sam and I perch near a half-moon table barely large enough to hold both our drinks. Everything here screams indulgence and opulence: the champagne flows in crystal-cut glasses, fresh caviar on the tables comes with generous spoons and, whichever way I turn, there is nothing I can do to escape the haughty laughter that fills every corner of the room. I know what these people pay to be here, just to avoid mingling with the 'common folk'. I'm completely confused as to how I feel about it: one moment I'm sinking into the pure luxury, the next moment I'm sickened by it.

Sam is stiff beside me, eyes fixed firmly on the bar, awaiting our target. His discomfort gives me some relief but also some disappointment. I'm at the most exclusive club I have ever been to, having a drink with the man I like, wearing the most gorgeous dress I've ever owned. Honestly, the way it drapes makes me feel three points higher up the hotness scale than I really am. I don't even need to wear a bra with it because it holds them up all by itself.

I raise my glass and pass him his. 'Come on, we should at least pretend we're enjoying ourselves.'

'Yes, you're right,' he says, taking the smallest of sips. And although he's now looking at me, it's clear his attention is elsewhere. 'My colleague said he was meeting Juliette at eight. Where is she?'

'It's only five past. Relax.'

We're interrupted by a gaggle of whooping noises.

'Sammmyyyyy!' a booming voice calls.

The sea of people part for a group of three men, all around Sam's age, all dressed in a uniform of chinos, open-collared shirts and casual-smart jackets of blue and beige. One of them corners Sam in a friendly headlock.

'It's been too long. Let's get a bottle of the good stuff,' another says, calling a waitress with a single finger.

I stand quietly while Sam greets each one. He seems genuinely happy to see them, the delayed arrival of Juliette Haimes temporarily out of mind. I take a second to rearrange the cowl neck of my dress – I'll admit I'm a little excited to meet Sam's friends and would prefer to do it without a rogue nipple popping out to say hello.

'Thea, these are some of my friends from law school. We all sat the bar together.'

'Ahh, so it's a trauma bond. Nice,' I say, earning me a low chuckle.

'Guys, this is Thea. We met on a placement years ago. She's thinking of getting back into law so I'm helping her out, sending some special projects her way.'

My smile drops onto the floor. It would be bad enough if

he'd introduced me as a friend, but this is so much worse. I'm just a made-up favour. A good deed he's doing.

'Fantastic,' one of his friends says. 'You'll get some great experience working for Sam. He's the best in the biz.'

Suddenly, I feel out of place. My dress is too much – bright blue, velvet and a cowl neck. I'm pretty sure everyone is giving me the side-eye, thinking how tacky I look. Sam's friends barely seem to notice me at all. When the red wine one of them ordered arrives, he loudly complains that the '95 vintage isn't a patch on the '93. There's a delicate gold netting over the bottle, and another friend jokes it's there to keep the riffraff away.

Sam's face gives nothing away. He looks comfortable in their company. I'm betrayed by it. His friends have Rolex watches and Armani shoes. I don't need to ask to know they didn't end up working for the CPS. These are the people he hates the most, the same kind that took everything from his family. How can he stomach it?

My inner monologue is cut short by Sam's hand tight on my arm. I follow his gaze, finding the elegant blonde woman at the bar. She looks just the same as her photos. She greets another guest and settles into friendly conversation.

Sam's breathing has quickened. He's looking from me to her, me to her. Waiting. But something feels off. I'm feeling rushed.

'Remember, leave her with seven days. She'll be abroad by then. They'll be no way to connect her with you,' he whispers in my ear.

She kisses the man she was talking to goodbye, draws her bag up onto her shoulder and turns towards the door. Sam's grasp on my arm tightens. 'She's leaving. You need to do it, do it now.'

His tone is aggressive and demanding. I don't like it and wrench free of his grip. I glare daggers and leave the group, walking towards the opposite exit to the one Juliette is using.

Sam nips at my heels. I walk until we're alone in a hallway and he throws up his hands, exasperated. 'Thea, what was that? She was right there.'

'Oh, I'm sorry, I don't murder on command!'

'Don't say things like that in public.'

'Why, are you embarrassed by me?'

'No, I'm concerned for our privacy. It's my job to keep both of us safe here. What's this about?'

'You basically introduced me to your friends as an intern.'

'What did you want me to say? Girlfriend?'

I wince. Yes, that's exactly what I wanted. So why does it sound so pathetic? My face feels hot and my throat tight. 'Would that have been so hard? I thought we meant something to each other, but maybe we're not on the same page.'

'Maybe we're not, because I thought we both wanted to do some good in the world, not squabble over relationship labels. I thought you agreed to this because you wanted it for yourself, not because of me.' He sighs and massages his temples. 'I need a minute. And, by the way, your nipple's out.'

I hold my dress together while I search for the bathroom. A waitress tells me it's on the floor above, but I must take a wrong turn somewhere because I end up back at the dog crèche. Someone has left the gate open and the goldendoodle puppy I saw earlier pads over to me. I melt immediately. My love of animals comes from Mum. She was a vet. If she'd lived, I'm sure I would have grown up surrounded by animals. Maybe I would have become a vet too, or a groomer or a walker. I forget my dress and crouch down to ruffle its wavy ears. I realize it's a boy when he promptly flops over onto his back for a belly rub.

'He can't just tell me what to do, can he?' I say to the doodle in a baby voice. I can see deep in his hazel eyes that he agrees with me; nice, for once, not to have to justify myself. 'No, no he can't. I'm not the problem here. He is.'

A sharp voice slices around the corner. 'No, Trevor, I won't take no for an answer. The board want results so if you have to get your hands a little dirty, just do it. Stop whining about it and keep my name out of it.'

I recognize that voice from the bar. Her shadow looms around the corner. She drops her sleek black fur coat on the floor and paces down the corridor. I remain tucked away. The goldendoodle squeaks when I stop petting, so I gently shush him and continue tracing little circles on his soft belly.

'Oh I'm sure your share of the profits will go some way to assuaging your conscience. I'm hanging up now. I don't want to hear from you again until it's done.' Then she adds *idiot* under her breath and starts dialling another number.

Sam was right. She hasn't learned from her mistakes. She'll continue to spew out harm into the world for as long as there's money to be had. Unless someone stops her.

In my distraction, the goldendoodle has trotted up the hall, towards Juliette. I try to catch hold of its tail but he slips through my fingers, showing a real interest in the coat. It looks like real fur and the puppy is thrilled about it, wagging his tail and shoving his nose into the pockets to get the smell. Then he cocks a leg. Oh dear.

'Off! Off!' she shrieks. When the goldendoodle doesn't move, she reaches out a heeled foot and kicks him hard. He squeals and scampers back towards the pen. 'Disgusting. They'll never get this out.' She picks up the coat and runs towards what I assume is the bathroom.

I follow her. Automatically I stay low and keep my footsteps quiet. She doesn't notice me enter the bathroom behind her. She's washing the coat in the sink, grumbling to herself about the horror of people keeping animals as pets. And I realize something. Sam is right. I don't need to do this for him; I want to do this for myself and for everyone this woman has hurt and for everyone she'll still hurt if she continues living.

Her hands are occupied with the coat, so she can't move away as I touch her arm, pretending to be moving past her to reach the hand towels. It doesn't matter that Juliette's eyes narrow in suspicion and her thin lips purse, because fifty years flow between us. I squeeze the gateway shut and leave Juliette with seven days to live. It's more than she deserves.

'Beautiful coat. Try some baking soda on it.' Then I release her and slip away.

She seems a bit startled for a moment, eyeing herself in the mirror like she's a stranger, then quickly returns to the coat. I doubt she'll even remember me.

I return downstairs. There are three missed messages on my phone from Sam telling me he's waiting outside, so I quickly exit the building. We take a taxi back to Mayfair and sit in silence until we're inside.

'I'm sorry I snapped at you,' he says.

'No, I'm sorry. And you're right, this isn't just about you. Ever since I got this power, I've felt I'm supposed to do something important with it, and it's only now I have you I know how.'

'Then what happened tonight?'

Talking about my feelings with eye contact genuinely makes me feel quite ill, so I turn away from him. 'Do I have to say it? Seeing you with your friends made me feel insecure. You seemed so different to how you are with me, and it made me worry that everything we talked about was just you using me to get back at Juliette.' I speed up, words tumbling out now. 'You didn't want to go out with me when we worked together, so I can't help but wonder if you only like me now because of what I can do and maybe you don't even care about me at all.'

'How could you think that?' he asks, pushing my hair aside and turning my chin towards him. 'Those people are not my friends. I'm different with them because I have to be, to survive. With you I can be myself. I didn't know how to introduce you because I don't have the right word to describe what we are to each other. Calling you my girlfriend feels so limited when we're so much more than that.'

'Oh.'

He squeezes my hand and I let our foreheads rest together.

'And don't worry about Juliette. She's leaving the country for a few weeks, but she'll be back. We can do it another time.'

'It's already done.'

'What?'

'I told you. I realized you were right, and this wasn't just about you. I ran into her upstairs in the bathroom and left her with seven days.'

He visibly exhales, like it's the first breath he's taken in years. 'You mean it? It's done?'

I nod. 'It's really done.'

He kisses my fingers. 'Thank you. This is a good thing – for me, for everyone.'

When we're alone like this, I have no doubts. Juliette's energy is coursing through me. If I listen closely, I can hear it humming. It's like I can think, see and feel clearly at last. Colours are brighter. Smells are sweeter. I can still feel the wet imprint of Sam's lips on my skin and his tongue on my knuckle. Sparks erupt from my skin. I wonder if he can see it. From his darkened green eyes, he can definitely sense it. Without another word we go upstairs, slip between silk sheets and I find a new use for my excess energy.

Chapter Sixteen

Also deserving: slow walkers.

As Juliette was expected to appear at a conference in Rome in a week's time, we thought it sensible to delay her death until then. Absolutely no one can accuse me of killing a woman across an ocean. While it may have been a sensible decision, it's also torture.

Sam and I are in a strange sort of limbo. We've killed a woman, but she's not dead yet. Neither of us can hold eye contact or a proper conversation. Regardless, I've been staying put in the Mayfair apartment because I'm afraid if I leave, this phase will never pass. Or worse, he'll realize what an awful thing we've done and now that he's got what he wanted he can push the blame onto me and get on with his life unburdened by guilt. And then he'll move into a new block of luxury flats, find some human-rights lawyer model girlfriend with dimples, who knows how to contour properly and actually managed to pass the bar and doesn't kill people, and he'll marry her and forget I ever existed. I bet she's called Eden or Hope or something equally frickin' annoying.

Yeah ... it's fair to say I'm spiralling a bit. I still try to sleep at Ruth's flat every other night because I haven't told her about Sam yet. Thankfully she's been so busy setting up the new medical clinic that she accepts my excuses without much interrogation. And I do my best at work, although frankly I'm sending my body to the office without my mind. Nobody seems to notice. In the evenings, I resolve to keep myself busy by enjoying what's left of my temporary high-end lifestyle. In addition to the concierge service, indoor pool and lounge area, the apartment building has underground tunnels that connect to the hotel across the street – this means unlimited access to a long list of hotel services and a Michelin-starred restaurant. I assume Sam's paying for it. I just told them the apartment number, and lobster mac and cheese materialized at my door.

And the distraction works. The news comes through a few days later when I'm sitting with Sam on the living-room sofa in the Mayfair apartment with my head in his lap. We've been lying here all evening, doing nothing at all. With one hand he's playing with my hair and with the other he's flicking through the internet on his iPad.

His hand freezes in one of my knots and I feel him coil.

'What's up?' I ask.

He passes me the iPad. I'm greeted with Juliette's face, her company's announcement of her death on the open tab.

We regret to inform you that Juliette Haimes, board member and technical advisor for Prosperni Pensions died on 22 March. The family have asked us to share that Juliette died peacefully in her sleep. She was a respected titan of industry known for her formidable business acumen and will be sorely missed by Prosperni Pensions and the wider professional community. We would like to reassure our clients that this unfortunate news will have no impact on investment operations, and we have full confidence in Juliette's successor, Maya Kim, who will be happy to personally discuss any of your concerns.

'Four sentences, one of them not even about Juliette. That's all her life came down to. I'm glad the world cares as little about her as she did about the people in it,' Sam says. His face is expressionless, then a strange noise halfway between a giggle and shriek escapes him. He looks around as if wondering where it came from.

'It's okay, this is a lot to process,' I say, shifting off his lap. I'm desperately trying to keep my voice steady, trying to read his face. 'After I killed Frances, I felt like the world had shifted.'

'No, it's not that. I just still couldn't quite believe this was real. But it is, and there's so much to do.' He jumps to his feet. I fall onto my elbow. 'Who should we take out next? Slumlords, sweatshop owners, arms dealers? The possibilities are endless, Thea.'

'You seem ... excited?' I ask. 'I thought you might feel differently once this was all real. Differently about me.'

He grabs me with both hands and kisses me. 'Not a chance. I'm ecstatic, and this is just the beginning.'

I let out a sigh. 'Thank fuck for that.'

I'm the one sitting on fifty years, but Sam's bouncing off the walls. It's a little disconcerting to be around. I try to remind myself that there's no right or wrong way to respond to this kind of thing. Emotions are weird.

We go for a run together around Hyde Park on Thursday evening and he won't stop talking about a man he knows who works in medical tech. One of the more notable crimes he's committed is selling medical implants that reduce insurance premiums, only for customers to incur extreme maintenance costs not covered by that insurance.

'Marcus Fox. He's perfect, Thea. I met his daughter once and she told me everything after one too many margaritas.'

'He has a family?'

'Hardly. They communicate by hush money only.'

'But he hasn't actually killed anyone, has he?'

'Not with his own two hands, that I know of. But it doesn't matter, Thea. What he's doing is so much worse.'

I break back into a walk. 'We need to slow down. We've only just . . .' I pause as a jogger goes by and whisper the next part '. . . killed someone. Don't you think we need to pause and reflect for a minute?'

'Why? We have so much to do. You know that there are over three thousand billionaires in the world? How many of them do you really think deserve that wealth?'

'Bill Gates is a billionaire.'

'And he's promised his fortune to charity, not his children. Clearly, he's one of the rare few who understand it's wrong to hoard wealth and pass it down to people who've done nothing to deserve it.'

'We haven't even decided who I should give the life to.'

'Whoever you like. No harm is going to come from saving someone.'

'So, you have no thoughts on who deserves Juliette's fifty years?' I ask. I don't know how to explain it to him, but it bothers me that he doesn't care more. That he isn't motivated by the part of my power that's undeniably good.

'None at all. I'll leave that part to you.'

I'm going to give it to Ruth, of course. She's currently safe until she hits forty-seven years old. Another fifty and I'll never have to worry about her again. I should really tell her now's the time to take up parachuting or deep-sea diving.

He puts his arms around me, even though I'm sweaty, and places his nose against mine. 'Hey, I promise I won't make you kill Bill Gates. Does that make you feel better?'

'Moderately. Although we both really stink – can we go home?'

'Only if you can keep up,' he says, taking off at a sprint. I groan and throw my body after him.

On Saturday, I want to wander about town hand-in-hand with Sam like the little lovebirds we are. But he's been annoyingly busy this week. 'Research,' he says. And I text Ruth but she says she'll be at the clinic all day, so I have to entertain myself. Thankfully, I've been hanging around the building so much that I've made a new friend. His name is Othello – apparently his father has a thing for Shakespeare. He seems to spend all his time by the indoor pool. I've never actually seen him swim; he just lounges like a reptile trying to bask under the lounge area's artificial sun and heat lamps – if reptiles wore Givenchy swimming trunks and Armani sunglasses. We don't have much in common, but when he started ordering poolside cocktails at noon, I knew I liked him.

After my morning run, sinking into the Jacuzzi is glorious. Sam's got a work event later and I'd ideally like to be able to walk again for it. I'm not sure what I'm supposed to wear, though, so I ask my newest and richest friend.

'It's an awards dinner, I think, meant to honour people who have been doing philanthropic work in the healthcare sector,' I tell him.

'I'm not obligated to be your fashion advisor just because I'm gay.'

'Rich trumps gay. You know what these people wear. Please,

all my clothes are either cheap or slutty,' I plead. None of the apartment owner's clothes really fit and the dress Sam got me, the nicest thing I own, shows off way too much cleavage. 'If you don't help me, I'm going to end up in a yellow suit with diamante on it. I'm too scared to go into a nice store by myself.'

'That does sound objectively terrible.' He pushes his sunglasses halfway down his nose. 'Okay, I'll help you, but only because I feel sorry for you. And I've always thought it would be fun to have a poor friend.'

Armed with Othello, I head to Harrods. I was expecting to be turned away at the door like Julia Roberts in *Pretty Woman* but instead I'm greeted with people grinning like they're being paid for it. It's Othello they're pleased to see, not me. He knows half of them by name. A woman named Chrissie helps us, and he asks how things are going with her husband's back problem and whether she's still planning that trip to Australia.

Not all rich people are bad. Othello is actually quite sweet underneath the snark. He helps me pick out a classy longsleeved black dress and black pearl earrings that together cost more than my monthly salary. Sam lent me his card and told me to buy something for tonight, but I can't bring myself to spend this much so I head back to the jewellery section to find cheaper earrings. By the time I return to the counter, Othello has already paid for the original extortionate pair.

We stop for a glass of champagne and he makes me try my first oyster. 'Literally like eating snot,' I say. By the time we get back to the building, I'm about to throw up in the lift. He's barely got the door to his apartment open before I burst through and hurl my guts into a high-tech Japanese smart toilet. It informs me that my pH is off.

'How are you feeling?' he asks as I shuffle back into the kitchen.

'Not great. Oysters don't taste any better on the way up.'

He fetches me a glass of water. 'I do enjoy them far more now I can order alcohol to wash them down with.'

I raise an eyebrow. 'How old are you?'

'Eighteen. Why, how old did you think I was?'

'I'm not sure, didn't think about it really. Do your parents live here too, then?'

'No, they're gone. I don't like to talk about it.'

Gone. I know what that means. Not many people under thirty have lost both their parents. Suddenly he looks so much younger. He's got a thin face with these defined cheekbones I thought made him look edgy but now make him seem vulnerable, malnourished in some way. Should I feel bad that I've made him my drinking buddy and accepted such ludicrously expensive pearl earrings from him? Then I remember what Sam said: 'Feeling bad about taking anything from these people is like feeling bad about taking a glass of water from a tap.' That's all money is to Othello. Tap water.

'Don't forget me!' a voice screeches from the living room. Before I can go and look, a flash of grey flies into the room.

I drop my water. 'What the hell. Did that pigeon just talk?'

'Tia, on your perch,' Othello says.

The bird eyes me with suspicion and flies up onto its perch. He strokes its head with his finger and I swear it purrs.

'This is Tia. She's an African grey parrot. They're the world's smartest bird. Lots of parrots can copy very basic speech, but African greys have the intelligence of a five-year-old child. You can have actual conversations with them.'

I picture Othello coming home to his apartment late at night with only the parrot to talk to. It's then I decide to be not just a friend to Othello, but a good one.

*

My dress is perfect. No nip-slips today. Not. For. Me. And
the pearls make me feel like a minor royal, a fib I enjoy telling
three separate guests while Sam schmoozes at the gala dinner.
The awards ceremony is being held in a huge hall with deep
purple lighting. There are probably forty or so tables laid out,
a stage for speeches and a bar no one needs to use because the
champagne is being circulated constantly. For once, I can't
touch the stuff. My stomach won't let me.

It doesn't matter because I'm enjoying tonight enough sober.
Sam keeps introducing me as his girlfriend and it sounds better
every time he says it.

A microphone crackles across the room and the chatter
falls silent. Then a surprisingly familiar face with tortoiseshell
glasses appears. Oliver Locksley takes the stage.

'Good evening, everyone, and a warm welcome to our
annual Desmond Foundation Charity Gala. Last year we raised
an outstanding five million pounds for good causes across
the city. This year, we're hoping to break that record. I'm so
grateful to everyone who's attending tonight, but I also want
to extend a very personal thanks.'

He pauses and takes a breath. 'Five weeks ago I almost died
in an accident. It's only due to the incredible work of the doctors and nurses who cared for me that I'm here at all. With our
help, people like this can do so much more. Save more people,
help more people.'

He pauses, gazing deep into the eyes of what feels like
everyone in the room. Then he claps to break the tension.
'So please reach into your pockets and give generously. And
if you see Dr Levy, who's here tonight and excited to talk
about funding for our new clinic, please give her a big hug
from me. If you could take your seats, dinner will be on its
way shortly.'

People start moving towards their tables and I'm being herded towards the back of the room.

'Table ten,' Sam tells me.

I turn to him. 'What did Oliver just say? I'm sure he said Ruth's name.'

'I thought he said Dr Leroy,' Sam says.

I reach table ten to find Ruth and Zara standing side by side. Zara whispers something into Ruth's ear and Ruth giggles, which makes no sense because Zara was born without a sense of humour. Ruth looks up and spots me. I enjoy two seconds of self-righteous judgement before her eyes find Sam.

We escape dinner, out to the front of the building. It's unreasonably cold and dark for the end of March and we both turn to speak at the same time with the same outraged tone.

'Sam?'

'Zara?'

'How long has it been going on?' I ask, feeling like a mum accusing her teenager of breaking the rules.

Ruth's looking down at the floor, digging her heel into the gravel. 'Not long. I wouldn't even say it's definitely back on. We've been spending more time together and then I invited her tonight thinking things might develop.' She looks up, staring me right in the eye. 'And what about you? How long?'

My turn to play with gravel. 'Argh, a bit longer than that.'

Silence. I don't think either of us knows what to say next. It's hard to be angry at someone when you've separately committed the same offence.

'Well, does this cancel out or something? And neither of us get to be mad about it?' My voice is still raised.

Ruth starts: 'You have been out a lot this week. It's not a huge shock. And I get why you didn't tell me. Is it possible that we're both adults now, and not sharing every detail of our lives is a sign of healthy boundaries and growth rather than a problem in our friendship?'

I think of the promise we made each other at twelve years old, to never lie to each other. Part of me is sad at the thought of losing the purity of that friendship. But it's easier when you're kids. Lying is bad, truth is good. Then you get older and morality becomes a lot greyer.

'How about we try to lie to each other as little as possible, and not about the things that matter?' I say.

'I like it, very enlightened.'

'I know, right? We should start a podcast.'

We wrap each other in a hug and I remember I'm holding fifty years with my best friend's name on them. I grip her tighter and let the energy flow. Ten, twenty, thirty, forty . . . then it stops. I have another ten years in me but no amount of squeezing will push them out. Then I remember the degus and cockroaches and not being able to extend a life beyond its natural limit. I guess I found Ruth's. Still, eighty-seven isn't a terrible end. I release her and we make our way back to dinner.

Dinner is . . . cordial. Sam and Zara have apparently been getting on well in our absence, having discovered a mutual love of coin collecting. For her, this doesn't surprise me. For him, he's lucky he's hot.

Apart from the four of us, there are three other dinner guests and an empty seat. I assume a no-show. It's all going rather well until he arrives.

'I hope I haven't missed the raffle,' he says.

'Marcus, good to see you,' Sam says, standing to greet him.

That name feels familiar. Marcus takes the seat next to me

and offers me his hand. I shake it. Seven years. 'Pleasure to meet you. I'm Marcus Fox, from Titan Medical.'

Of course, this couldn't just be a nice evening out. This is the man Sam told me about on our run, the one he wants me to kill next. 'I'm Thea Greaves, a friend of Sam.'

'Girlfriend,' Sam corrects me. Tee-hee.

'Oh, I was catching up with a few people on my way in. Did I hear you're related to the royals?'

Both Ruth and Sam stare at me.

'No, you must have me confused with someone else,' I say, snapping my breadstick in half and shoving it in my mouth to prevent further questions.

Thankfully he loses interest in me, turning his attention to Sam and Ruth. She's telling him about the work she's doing with Oliver. He seems nice enough, polite and genuinely interested in what she has to say. I guess that's the problem: bad people don't walk around with a badge that says, 'Hey, I'm a piece of shit, you should kill me.'

'A clinic at a homeless shelter could be a great donation opportunity for us,' he says. 'Bit of a bottomless pit but nice optics. And seeing as you're a friend of Sam . . .'

Ruth bites her lip. '*Friend* might be a bit far. Wouldn't that be a conflict of interest, giving money to a personal connection?'

'My dear, we're networking. Making personal connections is the entire point of this event.'

'And what does it matter how you got the money, as long as it's going to people who need it?' Sam adds.

Ruth's glaring a little. 'It matters because there are rules about this kind of thing. Systems to make sure everything's done as fairly – and as ethically – as possibly.'

Both of them look to me and I feel stuck. 'Don't make me

pick sides. Although for the record, I'm generally pro homeless people getting medical attention.'

Zara rolls her eyes. 'Controversial.'

They take our plates and people seem to be circulating again. Ruth excuses herself, and Sam and I find ourselves alone.

'I can't do it,' I say to him. 'Not with Ruth here.'

He squeezes my arm. 'I understand. I just wanted to give you the opportunity. Besides, I think we can do better. This afternoon I met someone involved in the illegal arms trade and, Jesus, what a piece of shit. Maybe I was being a bit rash after Juliette. I just got so caught up in everything we can do together.'

'And we will,' I say. I think back to what Ruth said at dinner. 'But first, we need a better system.'

Chapter Seventeen

I've never been someone who takes pride in my work, but this is different. If I'm going to kill people, I'm going to do it right.

Over the next evenings Sam and I talk endlessly about exactly what our system should be. I steal an A3 flipchart from work and stock up on snacks, and we set up shop in his living room. It's hard to come up with strict rules for imaginary people and future scenarios, so Sam presents me with potential targets and we talk it out, making notes as we go.

A drug dealer linked to a number of deaths after his product was laced with fentanyl. We both agree he doesn't make the list. Sure he's a dirtbag, but he wasn't to know about the fentanyl.

A banker who frequents sex workers. His 'unusual' tastes have put a long list of them in the hospital. Two of them have disappeared in mysterious circumstances. Yet he pays their pimp so disgustingly well that more women keep getting delivered to his door. I vote yes. Someone who's killed, and doesn't appear to be slowing down any time soon, feels like an easy yes. Sam's not against it, but he thinks we can spend our efforts more wisely. I think the sex workers would beg to differ. We put him as a maybe.

A woman responsible for the operation of twenty-eight sweatshops across India and Bangladesh, paying workers pennies an hour to work in hazardous conditions, all so people here can get one more bargain dress for five quid. Six months ago, there was a fire in one of the textile factories in which six people died. The families were intimidated, compensated, and the factory reopened in a matter of weeks. We both agree death couldn't come soon enough for her.

A few days later we have a long list of potential targets and rules, some more nuanced than others. I may have added 'slow walkers' after a glass of wine. We do have a few rules that are particularly important:

1.   The target has caused excessive pain and/or suffering to another human being.
2.   They are aware of the consequences of their actions.
3.   They have taken no action to repent and show no or little remorse for their actions.
4.   They are likely to cause more pain and/or suffering in future.
Bonus points if they have been directly responsible for at least one death.

'I suppose they're more like guidelines. And the more items on the list the target ticks off, the more they deserve to die,' I say.

'Exactly, *An Ethical Guide to Murder*,' Sam says, pouring me another glass of wine.

'Don't call it that.'

'What?'

'Murder. I hate that word.'

'Why? It's what it is.'

'People commit murders because they want to kill people. I don't. I want to put their lives to better use, and they just happen to die as a result.'

'Thea, you're a good person. People who aren't good people don't care about creating ethical guides. All that's left to do is decide when and where to find our first target.'

'Are you sure? It's hardly Magna Carta-level documentation. Maybe we should add a few more guidelines.'

'It's a living document. We'll keep adding as we go. But first, we have to get started.'

It's easier than I ever imagined. Sam does all the work; I show up and do the deed. As long as each item on my list is ticked off, I can walk away guilt-free.

Over the next few weeks, Sam and I serve justice to three deserving victims. The first is Nora Berry, the woman responsible for the sweatshops. It's an especially convenient murder. I find her in a salon in Mayfair, having a fish pedicure, so I take the seat next to her and dip my feet in my own bowl of *Garra rufa*. I yelp at the first nibble, but soon settle into the sensation. Thirty minutes later I leave with softer soles, noticeably shiner cuticles and fifteen years of life.

Our second is Iver Sokolov, a man adjacently connected to the illegal arms trade. He doesn't actually sell weapons; instead he manufactures computer chips. And some of them really are for computers. But some of them are regularly shipped to North Korea and happen to work for long-range missiles. Sam gets me into the man's office and I take his life. No hiccups, nothing out of the ordinary. A few days later his face is plastered over every daily newspaper in the country. Death by Novichok.

Suspected assassination by Russian spies. I feel pretty bad for causing such strife for international relations, and it takes Sam to remind me that I did not poison anyone with Novichok. And if World War Three does break out, well, someone was going to poison the man in three years' time anyway.

The third is a man facilitating modern slavery. Sometimes sexual. Sometimes children. Enough said. I leave the man at his own birthday party with just an hour to live – I don't tell Sam this part because I'm supposed to leave more of a buffer. He dies at the table as the edible gold-leaf-encrusted profiterole cake is wheeled out.

After each one I go to Sam and tell him it's done. He tells me how well I've done and gives me little kisses on my forehead. I don't care to admit how warm and gooey that makes me. Now that Ruth knows about Sam, I don't have to lie about my whereabouts. I switch between Clapham and Mayfair whenever I want. Sam's apartment is closer to work so I've been spending more and more time here. And I really don't care to admit how much I like our morning routine of coffee in bed, the little texts he sends at lunch to check in on my day, the way he always wants to know if I've eaten and immediately feels the need to feed me if I haven't. I didn't know people really did things like this in relationships.

I have a purpose, a nice boyfriend and unlimited lobster mac and cheese. And still, something is wrong.

Why is it so hard for me to be happy? With the steady stream of deserving victims coming my way, I don't even have to suffer the zombie hangovers of gifting life away anymore. I'm like a hamster, stuffing excess stores in my cheeks, only giving away what I can spare. I seem to get a high that lasts a few days, then a downer for few more, then back to normal. Not ideal, but not an excuse to be constantly feeling this irritable. It's a big improvement on the cold sweats and night terrors, anyway.

But this afternoon is day two of a downer. Everything is terrible. I hate being forced to be inside my own body. I want to turn off my brain and come back online tomorrow but trying to close my eyes and go to sleep makes the room spin.

Poolside cocktails with Othello are the only thing that helps. So I waste away my Saturday irritating him with a game I like to play. People want to think there are certain lines they wouldn't cross, but it's all a matter of motivation. Everyone has a price. And I like to find out exactly what they would do for money.

'How much to eat a human toe?' I ask.

He scrunches his face, as if trying to work out if he heard me right, and looks around the poolside searching for confirmation. It's only in the mornings that people actually swim here. In the afternoons, the water is still, save the background bubbling of the Jacuzzi, and the air is deep and relaxing, each breath I take heavy with reed-diffused, aromatherapy-scented calm. So, I suppose it makes sense that it takes Othello a few moments to process my question.

'Ugh, there's no money in the world.'

This game is much harder to play with rich people.

'It's cooked. And it's taken off a corpse, so no one is going to miss it.'

'No.'

I asked Ruth this question once. She also refused.

'You wouldn't eat one toe for a million pounds?'

Othello shakes his head. With Ruth, I guilted her by getting her to think about what that money could do, saying that she could donate it to starving children and that it would be selfish of her not to eat the toe. That's what people don't get sometimes – if the end result is good, then it's selfish not to do a bad thing just because it makes you uncomfortable. She relented and I negotiated her down to one-hundred thousand pounds, which she only agreed to so she could give the money away. I truly believe you get to know a person by establishing how much they would eat a toe for. I try this logic on Othello, but he won't budge. Then I remember the African parrot in his apartment, and how much he dotes on the creature.

'What if I threatened to kill Tia unless you ate the toe?'

'What the hell? In what world would this situation arise?'

'Would you do it?'

'I guess, yeah, I would do it.'

'Finally,' I say, grinning and flopping back onto my cushioned lounger. A fresh-faced bartender from the hotel across the street brings us a mojito and a strawberry daiquiri. She knows us by name now and doesn't need to ask which drink is mine.

'What's your price, then?' he asks.

I don't miss a beat. 'Ten thousand.'

He snorts with laughter and spits out his daiquiri. 'I've spent more on spa days. Have some self-respect, you cheapskate.'

It's plain to see that Othello doesn't know the value of money. The more time I've spent with him, the more I've come to realize this isn't entirely his fault. His whole life is spent in the clouds: luxury apartments, chauffeured cars and private jets. He socializes only in places with a membership fee and talks only to those who can afford it. I expect I am the poorest person he has ever had a conversation with that wasn't about a drink order. It must be easy to become disconnected from the world below when you're so high above.

*

I'm spending too much time in the clouds with him. Sitting around feeling sorry for myself isn't helping, so instead I go for a jog. I'm so much fitter and stronger now and end up running all the way back to my favourite coffee shop in Clapham, Fine Grind. Everyone else in the queue places their order and gives their name, but Terry catches my eye and says, 'Hey, Thea, flat white with oat milk?'

I nod, take my card out of my sports bra and swipe the contactless. Terry makes the best coffee – like genuinely perfect. He sources the beans himself (all about the beans, apparently), uses organic oat milk by default and always makes sure the coffee is actually hot. Some people might think £4.95 is expensive for a small cup, but Terry's coffee is worth every penny. He always asks me how my running is going too.

He passes the coffee directly to me (only his favourite customers get this treatment – the rest have to pick it up from the counter) and, yet again, an accidental brush of fingertips sends shock waves through me: eight months left.

That's when I realize what will make me feel better. Helping people. The second, still unwritten part of the guide.

I don't know anything about Terry. He has a nondescript face, but deep brown eyes that suggest there is something more to him. Does he have a family? Is he happy? Is he a good man? Does any of that affect how much he deserves to live?

Honestly, I'm not saving him just because he makes great coffee. I have a good feeling about him, and I decide that's enough to go on, so I grant him thirty years from my stores. Sam's right – it doesn't matter who I give life to. Nothing but good can come from saving someone.

It might be the caffeine or it might be giving thirty years all in one go, but a headache comes the moment I step outside the coffee shop. Ruth's isn't far, so I waddle back to the flat. She's there when I get back, scouring the oven. The corrosive stench hits me before she says hello.

We briefly catch up and then she says, 'You left your clothes in the dryer, by the way. I put them in the basket.'

'Ugh, I forgot.' I pull myself up off the sofa and find my clothes crumpled together. Oh God, now I have to iron. I have the power over life and death but I still have to do the bloody ironing. 'Oh no, my work shirts. You could have just hung those up.'

Ruth sits back on her legs, blowing her hair out of her face because she's got oven cleaner on her gloves.

'Do I look like your housekeeper?'

She is wearing cleaning gloves but I choose peace. 'Sorry, I'm just in a mood.'

She pulls off the gloves and throws them onto the oven door. 'You've been a bit all over the place lately. Either on top of the world or ready to end it all. I think I know what's wrong.'

'You do?'

'Yeah, the anniversary is coming up. Your parents' death. How could I forget?'

And suddenly I realize why I've been feeling like this. To be honest, I wasn't aware we were so far into April. I've had a lot on my plate lately. But the body doesn't forget these things.

'Yeah, you're right. It always puts me on edge.'

Although it's more than that. I believe in what Sam and I are doing, but it's also a distraction. There's only one person I want dead. I didn't want to think about my parents and face another anniversary without justice.

She gives me a sympathetic smile. 'You can always talk to me about them, if you want.'

I shake my head. 'I'm pretty sure you already know

everything I know about them. My memories of them are so hazy sometimes. Just odd flashes of random stuff like the sandwiches my mum used to make. I don't remember their funeral at all. I know we had it in the church, but I couldn't tell you what colour the flowers were, what hymns we sung or who was there. I feel so bad about it sometimes. Who forgets stuff like that about people they love?'

'Thea, you were there when they died. It wouldn't be surprising if you've repressed a lot of your memories from that time. It's your mind's way of protecting you from trauma.'

'So, it's normal?'

'It's not uncommon. And it doesn't mean you don't love them.'

'You're right, I did love them, and I remember the feeling of being loved by them. That's what I can't understand about Grandad – if you love someone, you should want to keep their memory alive, so why won't he talk about them?'

Chapter Eighteen

*Some people are born evil. Those aren't the
ones that keep me awake at night. It's the ones
who have every reason not to be – wealth, love,
family – and choose it anyway, who are truly
beyond redemption.*

The air is thinner. A slight breeze gives me goosebumps, like
the veil between life and death is more fragile. And maybe this
year, after all that's happened, it feels different. Death isn't a
thing that happened to me anymore, it's a thing that I am.

I take the day off work and visit my parents' graves, just
twenty feet from where I killed Frances Wells. And for the
first time in a long time, I cry. How is this fair? Why are they
dead? When someone dies, you understand that it's simply the
way the world is. Death is inevitable. We're powerless to do
anything but accept it. But that's no longer true. I could have
saved them and instead they're bones in the ground.

And I still don't even know who killed them.

Later, I stop by Grandad's for tea. I did not text because I
knew he would expect me. Every year, I get so worked up and

tell myself it's better for both of us if I stay away. Every year, I go home. We have tea and biscuits. It's a brand-new pack of chocolate digestives. He asks whether I've had any more legal interviews, but not why I'm here.

'Do you miss them?' I ask.

'Of course.'

'Then why don't we talk about them?'

'It does no good to dwell on grief.'

'What about the good times – can't we dwell on those?'

'It's impossible to separate the two. What's important is that they loved you and wanted the best for you.' That's the most he's said about them in decades. 'Would you like some more tea?'

After another cup I excuse myself. Grandad says he'll 'rest his eyes' for a minute in his armchair, which means he'll be asleep in approximately ten seconds. As soon as I hear the inevitable snoring, I creep across the landing and into his room.

It's a small room, taken up by the double bed, single dresser and bedside tables. One side of the bed is lower, the only give-away that someone sleeps there. On the dresser is a collection of jewellery and perfume that belonged to the grandmother I never met. She died when Dad was ten. But I've seen pictures and she was beautiful in a classic old-timey way. Grandad kept pictures of her – he has to have more of my parents. I quietly rummage through his dresser. Yes, I know, invasion of privacy. Pointless anyway because there's nothing but warfarin, beta blockers and omeprazole. Bottom of the cupboard? Nothing. Under the bed? Nada.

I'm about to give up when I notice the corner of a thin box on top of the wardrobe. I reach up and grab it. It's faded beige and covered with dust. Inside are photos of my parents. There's one of them tanned and relaxed on holiday, drinking from coconuts. Another of the three of us, playing in the garden at our house in Croydon. There's more, newspaper cuttings of the crash with details I haven't read before.

'Thea?' a voice calls from downstairs.

I grab a handful of photos and the newspaper cuttings, put the box back on top of the wardrobe and close the door gently behind me.

I proudly smooth out the newspaper cutting on the kitchen bar. 'Look at this,' I say, eagerly awaiting Sam's response. He reads far slower than is acceptable. 'It's about my parents. There's the name of the investigating officer and it mentions a suspect being questioned.'

'Hmm, there's no record of a suspect being questioned,' he says, not nearly as excited as he should be.

'But now we know that there was one. We know what to look for. Let's find the investigating officer and get answers.'

'Sure, I'll make some enquiries.'

'Sam, that's not enough. This is evidence. We need to use it.'

'Evidence of what, Thea? It's great, it's a lead, but let's not get carried away.'

'You wouldn't be saying this if it was Juliette.'

He comes closer and strokes the side of my face. 'I made you a promise. We'll find them, but I don't want you to get your hopes up too early. I remember how awful it felt when clients thought justice was in their grasp, only to have it snatched away.'

I pull away. 'I don't need you to protect me. I need to find out what happened. It's messing with my head and until I know the truth, I'm not going to keep doing what we're doing.'

'Really, that's what we've come to? Ultimatums?'

'No, I—'

'You either trust me or you don't, Thea. And for this to work, you have to trust me.'

Fear shoots through me. He could just leave me. All of this could go away and I'd be back to square one, stuck with a power I don't know what to do with. Alone. I don't know what to say.

'I need some space,' he says, grabbing his coat. 'Let's talk when we're both in a more reasonable state.'

All alone in a flat this size, my thoughts are echoing off the walls. I can't be here. I need to move. Need to do something. Ruth's working. I almost punch a hole through Othello's door before he opens it. He's slow opening it. It's almost midnight, but I know he's usually up until 2 or 3 a.m. Tonight he seems different, though. His eyes are glassy and a little red. I don't realize why until he reaches out and bounces my hair from underneath.

'It's so spiky, like straw,' he says, giggling.

'Are you high?'

'Noooooo,' he says, nodding.

Should I be concerned my eighteen-year-old friend is all alone in his apartment, high as a kite? Probably. Concerned enough for me not to help myself to a brownie? Absolutely not. What am I going to do – call his parents?

Weed takes much longer to kick in when you eat it. I'm still claiming that I'm 'not feeling it' while we're busy making snow angels on the white fur rug in Othello's living room and I'm outlining a detailed argument as to why Blossom is the best Powerpuff girl. I feel like I'm in a cloud.

Either ten minutes or ten hours later I've relaxed into it. It's a completely different kind of high to when I take a life. My muscles are loose, my head is light, and while there are still thoughts in it, they come and go without digging their claws in.

I'm telling Othello about my parents and the newspaper cutting and the fight with Sam when I say without thinking: 'Sometimes I'm so afraid that everyone I love will die. Except now it's different – I know they won't die and I'm scared they'll leave anyway.'

'See, that's where you're going wrong. Friends can't leave you if you don't have any.'

I playfully punch him. 'I'm your friend.'

'No, you're the weird old lady shagging the guy who lives in my building.'

I roll over to face him. 'You have to let people in, trust that they won't leave you. Otherwise you never feel how good it is to love them.'

'That's what stupid people say, the ones who have already made the mistake of getting attached.'

I remind myself how young he is. And I wonder, if it weren't for Ruth, whether I'd be just like him. Strangely, Ruth's leukaemia made her safer to love. I was reassured that the doctors were monitoring her all the time. It meant it wouldn't come out of nowhere and shatter me, like before. Without her, I might have avoided connection altogether too.

'Hey, you've never told me what happened to your parents.'

There's a slight flash of panic in his eyes. 'They're gone. What else is there to say?'

'Sorry, we don't have to talk about it.'

'What did you mean, that you know people won't die?'

'I have a power. I can tell how long someone has to live, just by touching them,' I say, laughing. I touch his arm. 'Don't worry, you're going to have a long happy life.'

'You are so strange sometimes.'

*

Carefully, I make my way back to Sam's apartment, keeping my hands on the walls at all times to stay grounded. He's fallen asleep on the sofa, clearly trying to wait up for me. There's a giant bouquet of flowers on the coffee table. I take them and greedily inhale. None of the guys I've previously dated have ever bought me flowers. Sam has now bought me two bunches.

Sam wakes and pulls himself upright. 'You're back,' he says, gently squeezing my arm. 'I overreacted earlier. I got you the flowers to say that I'm sorry and that if you want to put our plans on hold until we find who killed your parents, of course we can do that.'

I think about how much Sam has done for me already. He came to my defence without a second thought, trusting that whatever I'd done to Brendan Steele, my intentions were good. I owe him the same.

'No, I'm sorry. Of course I trust you.'

'I'm glad to hear it.' Then he sighs. 'But to be honest, what we're doing isn't working anyway.'

For a minute I think he means our relationship and my eyes go wide. I'd just come to terms with him not leaving me.

'It's not enough,' he says. 'We take out one selfish arsehole only for another one to take their place.'

'What do you mean?'

'Remember the woman who ran the sweatshops?'

Ahh yes, the woman I spent twenty-five lovely minutes getting a fish pedicure with.

'Of course.'

'Well, her nephew took over her estate. I thought he was a decent guy, but no, all he did was hire someone to manage the business. As long as the money keeps flowing and he doesn't have to see how it's made, he doesn't care. If anything, we made things worse.'

'Then add him to the list.'

Sam shakes his head. 'No, we're never going to achieve genuine change this way. We have to think bigger.'

I'm struggling to think at all, let alone think bigger. I think the weed is making me blink weird too. How often am I meant to do it? Once a minute? No, it's definitely more than that.

He puts his hand to his brow and smooths out the tension in his face. 'I have to go away for a while for work. Maybe that will give me time to think.'

'Oh, you didn't mention that. How long are you going for?'

'It's last minute. Just a week.'

A week suddenly seems like a long time after spending every spare moment together for the last month. Honestly, I'm starting to feel lonely with the bathroom door closed. Don't want to seem clingy, though.

'Sure, that's not long. I should go back to the flat and see Ruth anyway.'

'Why don't you stay here instead? Everything's taken care of, you can just relax and get high with random rich kids whenever you like.'

I blush. 'You noticed?'

He nods slowly with a wide, knowing grin. 'You're talking like the Cookie Monster. Well, the offer's there if you want it – the flat will just be empty without you.'

The next evening, I pack up my things and then wonder how to transport the degu, Diego. He's been living rent-free in one of the apartment's spare bedrooms – probably the world's most privileged degu. Sam said he'd ask the cleaner to look after him while we're gone, but I decide I'd miss the little guy. The cage is too big to carry. So, I transfer him into a shoebox and make a mental note to order a new cage and supplies to my flat. I can put it on Sam's card – it'll be fine.

I take an Uber back to Clapham, which I know is the height of pure indulgence, but again – Sam's card. Diego is quiet as a mouse during the ride. In fact, I'm worried he can't breathe so I leave the shoebox lid ajar. He's fine, sitting on his hind legs and cleaning his whiskers.

'Maps is saying your road is a one-way street and we're heading in the wrong direction. Okay if I drop you here?' the Uber driver asks.

'Err, I have quite a lot of stuff.'

'It's quite a long way around,' he says.

'Fine,' I say. Although I'd really like to ask why he didn't check this earlier and drive in the right bloody direction?

I pull my backpack on, hoist a tote bag over each shoulder and grab the shoebox. It's a struggle and I have to stand on one leg and gently close the car door with my foot. The driver glares at me; I glare right back. I turn around, barely able to look over the shoebox, and walk straight in front of a moving car. It slams its brakes on. I'm surprised by the complete absence of screeching. The car wasn't going fast, perhaps twenty miles per hour, but still, it responds with ease and the only damage is a clang to my knee. But I've dropped all my stuff. I lean down to collect my things. That's when I notice the shoebox is empty.

Diego is gone.

Shit. I'm desperately searching the grey tarmac for a streak of brown running across, walking further into the road to slow down the cars, holding my hands up. Then I see him. I let out the breath I've been holding. Fuck, it's too late. Diego is a flattened mess of fur and blood on the road. There's no use torturing myself by going to inspect the damage, because he's well and truly dead and several cars are bleating their horns at me. Grandad always said I couldn't be trusted with a pet, and I managed to keep Diego alive for less than a month. Perhaps he's right about me after all.

Chapter Nineteen

*It's worse to steal a loaf of bread from a
starving person than from a rich one.*

One week left to my own devices was bad enough anyway, and
now I'm grieving. I take a day of compassionate leave from
work and spend the day after Diego's death in bed, staring at
his empty shoebox. At 11 a.m. I still haven't moved and Ruth
lets herself in.

'You've got to get up. Let's go somewhere, anywhere you
like.'

'Pub?'

'Not before breakfast.'

We agree on a spa. If I'm going to be sad, I may as well be
sad in hot steam and aromatherapy. It's an underground bath
that Othello once told me about. Inside it's a labyrinth, with
five different baths, each one the size of a small pool, all with
a different nonsense name and a confusing array of buttons to
decode. We're enjoying the 'terrarium' pool, which is encased
in glass and full of tropical plants.

'Feeling better?' Ruth asks.

'I miss his beady little eyes, and the way he used to nibble peanuts with those big orange buck teeth. Even his tiny poos were cute.'

'I can only imagine.'

'Why couldn't I just have held onto the bloody shoebox? Poor little guy, getting squished like that.'

'It was an accident.'

Zara's words are ringing in my ears: *It always is with you, Thea.*

'Distract me. How are things going with you know who?'

'Erm.' She hesitates. 'Please don't say I told you so.'

'What did she do?'

'Nothing really, she just didn't think it was a good idea. Said that if I didn't have time for a relationship back then, she doesn't understand how I would now I'm a fully fledged doctor. And that she doesn't want to risk our friendship.'

'That bitch. Say the word and I'll kill her.'

'And this is why I didn't tell you. I don't blame her really – I'm basically working two full-time jobs and shift work is hard for anyone to deal with. Today's the first day off I've had in weeks.'

'You are a bit compulsive. Why don't you give one up, then? So you can spend more time with me, though, not that she-devil.'

'I'm likely to spend more time at the shelter. But I can't give up ICU this soon after starting. Mum's so proud of it.'

'You're living two lives and you're not getting to enjoy either of them,' I joke, then realize what I've said. Isn't that exactly what I'm doing? Except no one is proud of me for working in HR. 'Christ, everything is shit, isn't it? I'm going to book us both a massage. I'm paying, no arguments.'

'It's not you paying, though, is it? Is Sam really okay with you putting a spa day on his account?'

'It's just another business expense. On Wednesday he spent thousands taking a client out for dinner. Trust me, no one is going to notice a massage.'

'It's not just that, Thea. He pops up out of nowhere and suddenly you're spending his money and every spare moment with him. Don't you think things are moving a bit fast?'

'It's not completely like that. We're working together. It's just a couple of hours after work a few times a week with his firm, but it's good for the CV.' The latter part really is true. After Stewart arrested me, and Sam claimed I was his intern, he thought it was probably a good idea to put me on the books. And I *am* working with Sam, just not in a legal sense.

'Didn't you say he deals in property law? Why don't you volunteer at the shelter to get some experience instead? I'm sure Oliver would welcome your help. Wouldn't that be more relevant for what you want to do?'

'Any experience is good experience. And the work's turned out to be pretty interesting so far.'

'Well, just be careful you don't put all your eggs in one basket.'

'All right, Mum.'

She laughs, but there's a small, concerned smile twitching on her face. 'Come on, you know as well as I do that you tend to rush into things headfirst. You're working together now, practically living together in a matter of weeks. Just try not to get swept away. Balance is healthy.'

'Is that what you tell your patients?'

'Yes, and they don't give me that sarc.'

'You just need to spend some quality one on one time with him, then you'll see what he's really like.'

*

I get Ruth to agree to dinner with Sam and me on Saturday night. I also get the massage because my degu is dead and I am sad. I'm currently lying naked on a massage table, with a hand towel folded over my bum. My face is squished into the hole so I can see the wood flooring and the masseuse's bare feet as she works my shoulders. At first, I'm hyper focused on every curve and knot of the floorboard and the olive green of her toenails, but the Tibetan bowl music soon lulls me into sleep-like relaxation.

'Now, take a deep inhale,' the masseuse says, hovering at the top of my spine. I booked a 'spiritual healing' massage, whatever that means. Figured it couldn't hurt with my current activities. 'Let all the oxygen in the room fill your lungs, bring it deep down into your belly and feel it sink into your blood-stream. Hold it for one, two, three. Now, exhale.'

All I really wanted was someone to rub my back with hot stones for an hour. Nonetheless, I follow her instructions. She 'follows my breath' with deep swooping motions and I feel myself unravel. She occasionally interrupts to tell me things like 'Remember that you are good, you are pure and you are worthy.'

It's nice. The world would be a better place if everyone could afford someone to rub their back in a warm candlelit room and whisper praise in their ear for an hour a week.

My eyes are closed and I'm thirty seconds away from snoring when a jolt of electricity shoots from my collarbone, all the way down my spine. I shoot upright, almost falling off the table. The masseuse holds me steady.

'What was that?'

'Hold still,' she says.

She lifts her hand to my collarbone. She doesn't touch me, just closes her eyes and hovers. Her brow tightens. Her finger-tips twitch. My skin prickles in anticipation.

'What are you doing . . .?' I start.

'Quiet,' she says. 'Let me work.'

The energy in the room has completely shifted. I'm slightly concerned this is going to be like that moment in *The Lion King* where Rafiki imparts wisdom onto Simba by whacking him with a stick.

But then . . . I can only describe it as heat radiating from my collarbone. Clenched cells unravelling and melting into their proper place. I'm still not convinced she's even touched me.

'There, I knew you were carrying your pain in the wrong place. Can be a dangerous thing that, tends to manifest in ugly ways.'

'Is it going to come back?' I ask.

'That's up to you. If you carry on as you are, then yes.'

It's then I realize my eyes are watering from the pure relief of it. They threaten to spill over, and I wipe them away. 'Guess I should get a better office chair.'

'Hmm,' is all she says. She regards me in silence for a moment, then firmly grasps my arms. 'And that's our time for today.'

The masseuse already has thirty-nine years to live but I decide to round it up to an even forty as a thank you.

At the start of the week, I am holding forty-four years in excess life. I've been giving it out in little doses like some kind of benevolent fairy godmother, randomly rewarding people for their acts of kindness. A year to the masseuse who unblocked my negative energy pocket; six months to the goth teenager who gives up his seat to an old lady on the Tube; two years to the retail clerk who manages not to slap the customer demanding to speak to her manager over an out-of-date attempted item return. Plot twist – she was the manager.

It suits me, this new system. Sam's the grand-plan, save-the-world type, whereas I'm more motivated by things I can see and touch. And the after-effects of gifting smaller amounts are better for me. Just a mild headrush and some dizziness. Nothing a glass of water and some paracetamol can't fix.

But it's more than practical. I've started seeing good deeds everywhere I go. The world seems brighter and kinder for it. After Diego's brutal end, I needed this. It's even giving me the patience to cope with whatever sentient stick decided to lodge itself firmly up Zara's arse this week.

On Monday I assist her with a meeting. Everything that the executives like, Zara claims responsibility for; everything they don't, I'm responsible for. Late project? *Thea hasn't finished it yet.* Unresolved employee conflict? *Thea is still handling it.* Employee dissatisfaction, lack of training sessions and the payroll error? *Thea, Thea, Thea.*

None of it matters in the grand scheme of things. Then Thursday comes around. I've been gifting life like candy and am down to ten years. Not a problem. Sam will be back at the weekend and, undoubtedly, I'll have the opportunity to top up my stores. But then a retirement party at work throws a giant spanner in my well-oiled week.

Zara puts me in charge of party planning. Luckily, the beneficiary of my mediocre efforts, Alise from accounting, doesn't like being the centre of attention so it's a quiet affair. Banners and balloons, a Victoria sponge (her favourite, apparently, which I am not impressed with), Buck's Fizz and a thirty-minute gathering in the conference room at 3 p.m. to say goodbye. Our CEO raises a toast to Alise's twenty years of service, gives her a monogrammed leather-bound notebook, and it's all perfectly pleasant.

Afterwards, everyone filters out to finish up their day and I collect the paper plates. Alise stays behind to catch me.

'It's Thea, isn't it? I can't tell you how touched I am by all of this. Thank you for making the effort.'

'It's no trouble,' I say, and I mean it. The Victoria sponge is dry and the Buck's Fizz flat. Sweet that she found out my name, though.

'I've been so nervous about today, but it feels like the right time. I'm ready for the next chapter.'

'Big plans?'

Her heart-shaped face breaks into a big smile. 'Oh yes, I'm about to be a grandmother twice over. I'm sure they'll keep me very busy. My husband is retired too. We're taking a world cruise before the babies arrive. Thirty-one countries in eighty-eight days. I had no idea I'd ever do something so adventurous.'

Alise proceeds to tell me the baby names, the itinerary of the cruise and her fears about norovirus outbreaks on the ship. Either she hasn't realized she doesn't have to stay until 5.30 on her last day or she just wants a friendly ear. Regardless, I listen. A little act of kindness of my own.

'Well, I'd better get going. Reg is taking me out for a cele-bratory dinner. Thank you again, Thea,' she says, brushing my arm. *Ten days.* She is going to die in port at Gibraltar.

I've been avoiding using my power at the office – seems better to compartmentalize. And Alise is sixty-five. Generally, I don't gift life to the over fifties – seems like a poorer return on investment. But I just can't bear the thought of Alise miss-ing her cruise and not meeting her grandkids. She's sweet and earnest and she deserves this. Heck, it's my power and I can use it the way I bloody well want to.

Sam's not back until Saturday but the cruise leaves on Friday. If I don't make the transfer now, I won't be able to at all. So, I gift her almost the whole ten years I'm holding, keeping just a few days to tide me over until the weekend.

It's been a while since I gave away that much life. The headache comes on instantly, pulsing between my temples. The purple, orange and green from the balloons are swirling into a muddy blob across my vision. Every time I blink it grows bigger. I'm nauseous, dizzy and sweaty. I manage to hold on until Alise leaves, then I grab the door, hit the light switch, slump onto the beanbag in the corner and pass out.

I wake up three hours later with Zara looming above me.

It's not that bad, right? People fall asleep at the office all the time. I'll admit the empty bottle of Buck's Fizz next to me was unfortunate, and that I forgot to send out the 'Thursday Tea and Talk' memo at the end of the day, but those things only happened because I did a good thing.

I arrive thirty minutes early on Friday morning, determined to rescue the situation by getting ahead. Coffee wafts from the break room and I realize Zara is already here. She walks by, aggressively clinking her spoon against her mug and says, 'Morning,' in a tone I can't construe.

But then I see an email she sent at 6.30 a.m. It's about the project I've been asking for since I started here, the one I'd finally got my teeth into, the one that would make this whole HR bullshit worth it for the legal experience. She's given it to the newest member on the team, Tim, who can't say boo to a goose. And she's copied me in to do handover.

She's cited *personal circumstances* as the reason for the project transfer. I've been a model employee for weeks and this is how she repays me? I've seen her puking into nightclub toilets. She's not so perfect. Then I remember I have a picture of said nightclub toilet incident. I scroll through my phone and there it is. The club photographer caught it so it's brilliant quality – there's some mushed-up doner kebab stuck on her face and Ruth is holding back Zara's blow-dried hair so you can see her face clearly. Without thinking, I share it in our team WhatsApp group. Obviously the one without Zara in it. But Kate, the idiot, uses WhatsApp on her computer so the image appears on her screen.

And Zara's standing right behind her. She takes one look at it, flushes bright red, then turns to me in deliberate slow motion.

'This is the last straw, Thea,' she says.

'It was only a joke.'

She marches over to Kate's screen, takes a photo of it and shoves her phone into her trouser pocket. 'This is not a joke. You are constantly undermining me in front of other members of staff. You consistently fail to complete basic tasks on time and your attitude in meetings is completely unprofessional. And that's when you're actually here. Nobody in the history of the company has had as many sick days as you. You've never produced a doctor's note, and then there's the constant other absences.'

'Are you kidding? All you do is put me down and treat me like a child. Don't think I don't know what you're doing when you set me such ridiculous tasks – nobody needs to update employee information as often as you make me do it,' I say, my voice rising higher.

'That's your job. Am I supposed to give you a gold star for every project you screw up? Everything I ask you to do, I end up spending twice as long putting it right.'

I cannot stand her voice. It's nasal, grating, but carries the control of the childhood elocution lessons I know she had. Every word is meant to patronize and belittle me.

'I gave you this job because Ruth vouched for you, but I can't keep cutting you slack,' she says. 'I'm going to suspend you for insubordination.'

How dare she mention Ruth. After turning her down – twice. I'm not a violent person. I have never hit another person in my life, but I would very much like to punch Zara straight in her cold veneer of a face, if only to see if she would crack.

'You will receive a formal suspension notice. Please give me your ID card and leave the building immediately.'

We hold each other's gaze for several long seconds. Tim and Kate haven't moved a muscle since this whole situation escalated, and several other employees are rooted to the spot, not even pretending to avert their curiosity. What kind of manager would do this in front of the whole team? This is another classic Zara attempt to humiliate me. But there's nothing I can do. I pull my lanyard over my head and pass Zara the ID card that lets me into the building. Then it occurs to me that there is one thing I can do. Something no one can stop. I press the ID card hard into her hand and let the siphoning begin.

I'm not going to kill her. As I've said many times, I'm not a psychopath. I take a day, a week, then a month. I take my hand back once I reach three months. I take a deep breath. The tension leaves my body and I smile.

'Don't worry, I'll see myself out.'

Technically, I haven't broken the rules Sam and I created to decide whether we can take someone's life, because Zara is still alive. So, I don't tell him what I've done when I see him on Saturday. Just for tonight, I want to enjoy pretending to be a normal couple.

The Mayfair apartment looks glorious for our dinner with Ruth. The countertop is gleaming, wine glasses at the ready, and there's bread, olive oil dip and some fancy cheese bites to nibble on. They weirdly make me think of Diego. I start to well up but pull myself together. It's not often I get to play hostess, and I want tonight to be fun. When Ruth arrives, I beckon her in and gesture to my arrangement. For a while, things are good. Sam and Ruth bond over the lack of funding in the public sector, and the overlap between healthcare and law. Sam's in top form. He's been asking Ruth all about her work with Oliver at the shelter, really listening to what she has to say as if it's truly fascinating. I don't know what I was so worried about – they're both good people and such massive nerds. If anything, I feel a bit left out.

'So, what exactly is it you're doing for Sam?' Ruth asks.

I play for time, reaching for a chunk of ciabatta. 'I'm just helping out where I'm needed at the moment. Jumping between projects, getting involved in a bit of everything.'

'Huh.'

I know it sounds shit. It truly hurts to be carrying out life-changing work but not being able to share it with anyone. Must be how people in MI5 feel.

'And you live here? What is it, four-bedroom? Not to be rude, Sam, but how on earth did you afford it?'

He smirks. 'I can't claim the credit. It belongs to one of my clients.'

'Oh, that's nice of them to let you stay.'

He laughs. 'Oh, these aren't nice people. We manage their estate, make sure everything is kept in prime condition in case they need to liquidate their assets quickly. I don't think they even realize they own this place, let alone that I'm living here.'

Ruth looks like someone's slapped her. 'What? They don't know you're living in their home? That's not right.'

'The real crime is this apartment going to waste. Besides,

they're never going to notice. If they asked us to sell, we'd gut the place anyway.'

I remember Othello making a snide comment about the granite countertops being out of season and feel a strange sting in my pride for my not-apartment.

'Thea, you must realize this is wrong. It's the principle of it.'

I look between them several times. They both look so sure of themselves, both waiting patiently for the obvious outcome that I'll side with them. I know if I pick one, it'll be about more than this conversation.

'I'm not sure. It's a grey area, isn't it?'

They both sigh in the same exasperated tone. Great, I've managed to disappoint both of them.

'No, it really isn't,' Ruth says, getting to her feet. 'It's getting late; I need to head off anyway.'

It's not even 9 o'clock. I follow her to the door, trying to cut her off. 'Ruth, please don't go. We can still have a nice evening.'

She pulls on her coat, spies Sam loading the dishwasher and says in a hushed tone, 'No, we can't. Thea, I didn't even want to come tonight. You know your grandad called me the other day, wondering how you are? It's like you're taking a sabbatical from life, holed up in this fantasy world. But fine, you say you're having fun, so I accept it. But now I find out you're basically squatting in someone else's home, and you've been suspended from work?'

I flinch. 'You spoke to Zara.'

'How could you do that to her, after everything she's done for you?'

My heart quite literally freezes. It doesn't matter how hard I work to convince myself that everything Sam and I are doing is good and right. The thought of Ruth knowing what I've done is unbearable. There's no defence I could offer that would justify it. She is the best person I know. And if she loves me, that means I must be good. If she ever found out the truth, she would not love me anymore.

Ruth shakes her head. 'Zara is so embarrassed.'

'Oh, you mean the photo.'

'Yes. Why? What the hell else did you do?'

'Nothing!'

'Whatever, I'm done. You've always been a taker. I don't know why I keep expecting you to take responsibility.'

'That's not fair, you have no idea what I'm doing at the moment. It's important. I'm helping people.'

'Then tell me!'

'I can't.'

She shakes her head. 'I don't know what the hell you're doing right now, but it all started when he came back into your life. He's not good, Thea, and he's definitely not good for you. If you want to meet people who actually make a difference, come down to the shelter. Until then, enjoy your new life.'

She tries to open the door, fumbling with the lock, getting more irate until I flip the catch and let her leave.

I slump onto the sofa and drink another glass of wine that I don't need.

'Cheer up, it's just a spat,' Sam says.

'You don't know Ruth. I once stole a pencil in primary school, and she wouldn't talk to me again until I fessed up and apologized to the teacher.'

'What a nark.'

'She's principled.'

'Hmm, easy to be principled when you own a flat that's the best part of a million quid without a mortgage. She's not like us.'

'Sometimes it's like you think having money is a crime in itself,' I say. 'I know how hard things were for you growing up, but sometimes you're so angry at other people because they didn't suffer through the same things you did. You know I didn't grow up poor, right? Do you think I'm a bad person too?'

He shuffled closer to me. 'Of course not. That's the trick, you see. They want everyone in the middle to believe they're closer to the top than the bottom because then no one questions the system and the people at the top stay there. People think money is power, but nothing compares to what you have. That's real power. We have the opportunity to create real change, something so much bigger than bumping off a couple of bad apples, only for the next batch to go rotten.'

The wine is sickly sweet, and my head is spinning. There's too much in my brain and I can't process it, like trying to read something too close up and I can't make out the words.

'I know, you're right. It's just getting so complicated, and I want to do the right thing.'

'Then don't think – trust me instead. I know exactly what we need to do next.'

Chapter Twenty

The target has caused excessive pain and/or
suffering to another human being. Amendment:
the cause doesn't need to be direct. If pain and
suffering is a consequence of their actions,
they're eligible to make the list.

The next morning, I roll over to Sam's side of the bed and ask him to clarify what he means when he says, 'I know exactly what we need to do.'

'How well do you know Oliver Locksley?' he replies.

'He's one of the first people I saved, and he's a really decent guy, so what does he have to do with anything?' I ask, fear creeping in. Saving Oliver is one of the best things I've ever done. Because of him, people have found homes; they have access to healthcare, legal advice, a chance to get their lives back. How he has the patience for it I'll never know, but it's like his goodness ripples out across the city.

'Don't panic, that's exactly what I hoped you would say. Oliver's not the target, he's the recipient. See, it's not enough to take out someone at the head of an institution without having the right person in place to take over. The next person we take out, we replace with Oliver, giving him the resources to carry on with the good work he's doing. If we get this right, can you imagine the impact it would have?'

I can imagine: everything Oliver is already doing, without the budgetary constraints and reliance on volunteers and government grants. And all we have to do is help things along.

'Is this why you were asking Ruth so much about the shelter?' I ask.

He nods. 'I was already looking into him, then I remembered why I recognized his name.'

'How can you make sure Oliver gets the money?'

'Oliver already manages the charitable branches of our target's organization. I think, if I lay the proper groundwork, we could get Oliver appointed to head of the board. He'd have full legal control to direct the future of the company.'

'Who's the "target"?'

'Now this you might not like, but hear me out before you say no. Ayesha Bloom. Othello's mum.'

I pull myself up, bringing the duvet with me. 'No, he told me his parents were dead.'

'Well, that says it all. No, they are both very much alive. Bloom's wealth comes from cleaning dirty money from drugs, weapons, prostitution and God knows what else. If it's illegal, she's got a hand in it. She buys multi-million-pound houses for cash and leaves them empty. They all do it; the entire London property market is an elaborate money-laundering scheme.'

'Still, Othello has been a good friend to me. I don't think I can take his mum and his money from him.'

'Thea, think how much good will come from this one solitary act. Just because Othello isn't complicit doesn't mean he deserves to benefit from it. And if it makes you feel any better, we can set up a very generous trust fund for him, more than any one person would ever need.'

'I'll have to think about it,' I say. I can see Sam's about to make his case the way he does with evidence and a tone that makes you feel like an idiot for disagreeing. So I cut him off before he can get going. 'Please, Sam, give me a bit of time to think.'

He bites his tongue and shrugs. 'Okay, but why don't you ask Othello why he told you his parents were dead?'

The next day I knock on Othello's door. No answer. As it turns out, he's jetted off to Milan for a shopping spree. Bit rude that he didn't take his new bestie but, whatever, I won't let that factor into my decision. Sam's busy at work; I'm suspended from work. Lounging around by the pool gets real old, real quick without company and it's only a couple of days before I start to daydream about filing expense reports.

Once at university when I was short of cash, I took part in a study. They left me alone in an ordinary room. Nothing to do. No phone. Just a desk and grey walls. And a red buzzer on the desk wired up to give me an electric shock if I decided to press it. I thought it was a joke at first. Who would voluntarily hurt themselves? I sat there for three minutes before I gave in. Pain is preferable to boredom.

I've spent the last hour spying on Ruth via WhatsApp. I meant to give her the cold shoulder, give her a chance to come to her senses, then I ended up messaging her at 8 a.m., apologizing for last night. But she hasn't responded so I kept our message history open on my laptop. She hasn't seen the message, but she's been online twice. I bet she's pulled down the message at the top of the phone screen to read it, just to leave me on unread without admitting that's what she's doing. Joke's on her because I've got access to her Google calendar, and she can't ignore me if I'm standing right in front of her.

I'm at the hostel by 11 a.m. Sure, I broke quickly but it's better than three minutes, so I count this as personal growth.

The shelter is a hostel. The walls are all painted with the same drab white, with undertones of grey that drag the whole place down with it. Each room is fitted with as many red metal bunk beds as possible, each one with mismatched sheets – in this room I can see one with pink flowers, another with racing cars and two in faded block colours. There's little else of note – just pillowcases, bin liners and the occasional tote bag filled with personal possessions.

I feel deeply, shamefully awful about every time I have joked about being poor.

Ruth has a small room on the first floor, next to the kitchen. I knock gently.

'Oh, it's you,' she says.

'I wanted to come and see what you do here. If the offer is still open.'

She looks at me. Then sighs. 'You can sit in if my patients don't mind. Sit there.' She points to a plastic chair in the corner. The room is mostly empty, except for a small, knitted bird that sits next to Ruth's computer. She boots up the computer and starts organizing the list of patients she has to see today – in a four-hour clinic she needs to get through twenty-two patients. The first is a man with long brown hair peeking out from under his hat and unkempt facial hair, but he has a surprisingly cheeky grin that makes me realize he's younger than me.

'Hello, Dr Levy,' he says, taking a seat on the plastic chair beside her desk.

'Afternoon, Aaron. This is my friend Thea – she's getting to know the place today. Do you mind if she sits in?' Ruth asks. Her voice has a quiet authority to it that I'm not used to. He nods in agreement. 'What can I help you with?' she continues.

He pulls down his sleeve and holds out his arm. In the soft fleshy underside of his elbow sits a red, swollen mass of pus. Ruth pulls on her blue gloves and touches it, making him wince sharply. After a few moments, she sits back in her chair. 'It's an abscess, Aaron. Are you a heroin user?'

'Yes.'

'It's common for them to form at the injection site. I'll need to drain the abscess, then prescribe antibiotics for the infection.'

Ruth continues to run through the procedure until he gives the go-ahead. She first administers a local anaesthetic, then punctures the abscess with a needle. The smell is unreal. A foul odour of rotting flesh and vomit fills the rooms and I'm going to be sick. Really sick. I jump up and skirt out of the room as quickly and quietly as possible. Ruth finds me ten minutes later taking deep steadying breaths in the toilet.

'You okay?' she calls out over the toilet stall door.

I open it. 'Yeah. How the fuck do you do that?'

She shrugs. 'I quite like abscesses; small ones like that are easy enough to fix.'

'So, he's all sorted out?'

'Well, the abscess is. But it wasn't his first and probably won't be his last. I tried to get him to sign up to a methadone programme, but I don't think I made much headway. He did take the leaflets about the free needle exchange, though.'

'Should you be giving them needles?' I ask.

'If it helps him avoid more infections until he's ready to get help, then yes. Sometimes it's all you can do.'

*

Ruth promises to warn me if she does anything else with the potential to make me run for the toilet. I spend the rest of the day watching her work. The list of ailments is endless: mental health breakdowns, deep vein thrombosis, urine infections, chest infections, STIs and a lot more drug-related issues. Before long, people are wrapping up for the day. Time flies when you're horrified at the state of the world.

'Wow, you stuck around for my entire shift,' Ruth says.

We collect our things, lock the medical examination room and begin dawdling back to the Tube station. It takes us ages to leave because everyone wants to say goodbye to Ruth and thank her for her time.

'So, what do you make of it?' she asks.

'Yeah, I think it was good for me to come here. Maybe I've been spending a bit too much time in la la land.'

'I'm glad. Nothing like a bit of pus to give you some perspective on what really matters.'

'Yeah, easier to focus on the simple things.'

'What?'

I catch myself. I really have enjoyed seeing Ruth do what she does today, but part of me resents her for it. No moral quandaries, no ethical dilemmas, just a simple *stick to the Hippocratic oath and do no harm*. But she's only alive because of me. I get to carry the weight of what made that possible while she gets blissful ignorance.

'I mean it must be hard seeing all these people at crisis point, knowing there's not much you can really do about it. There's not enough staff and not enough money. It must feel like you're putting plasters on bullet wounds.'

'Guess you've got it all figured out.'

'No, wait, what you do is amazing. I just meant that you need more help so you can do more of what you're doing.'

'That's okay, you are right, I know that.' We reach the Tube station. 'You know what? I'm going to swing by my cousin's for dinner so I'm going to take the District line. But I'm glad you came. I'll see you at home.'

Ugh, why can't I ever keep my big mouth shut? I wonder how I'll make this latest screw-up good with her. But why is it always me that has to apologize? I'm tired of it. I put my headphones on full volume and put her out of my mind as I make the trip home.

Othello returns a few days later and on Friday night we go to a private club in Mayfair that we like. When the girl on the door side-eyes my trainers, I don't look away in embarrassment. I've learned that if you behave as if you can do whatever you like, then you simply can – as long as people believe you have a limitless credit card in your pocket.

Othello seems to know everyone yet is friends with no one. It takes us fifteen minutes to cross from the threshold to a cosy booth because he stops for everyone he recognizes, enthusiastically kissing them on both cheeks and exclaiming that it's been 'far, far too long' and they 'must catch up'. However, the way he says the exact same thing in an identical tone to everyone makes me realize he doesn't truly know them. They are simply decor that he must acknowledge.

There's a semi-famous singer performing a cappella tracks of her biggest hits near the bar. I say I want to listen for a while, but only so we can stay near the bar and I can ply Othello with alcohol. He didn't fess up last time we were under the influence, despite me bearing my soul, so I need to well and truly obliterate his inhibitions. I want the truth.

'You were so right,' he says, slurring his words. 'I needed to get out.'

'There are only so many poolside daiquiris you can drink before it becomes sad,' I reply, shepherding him to a quieter table in the corner.

He laughs, but he wobbles, because I know there's far too much truth in what I've said.

'That's the upside of not having parents, I guess. Unlimited freedom.'

He raises his glass awkwardly. 'To freedom.'

We drink and I put the glass down hard. 'I know they're not dead, Othello. Why did you say they were?'

'I didn't. At least, not at first. I said they were gone. I meant "weren't around", but then we were having a moment and you started telling me all about your parents and it just felt nice to be the same.'

'Oh, I guess I can see how that happens.'

'To be honest, it felt better to say they were dead than the truth. At least that wouldn't be my fault.' He looks up at me and catches himself. 'I'm sorry. Obviously your parents actually being dead is worse. I shouldn't have said that.'

'It's okay. Why don't you tell me about them now?' I soften my face as much as possible, try to shift into someone a person would trust with their emotional baggage.

'I'm not sure my mum could pick me out of a line-up. She never wanted a kid, and she definitely didn't want one like me. Artistic. Shy. Gay. I think it's her worst nightmare. And it's not like she didn't try to make me into someone else. When I was little, we spent every weekend going to the rugby, trying out sailing, even boxing once – anything she could think of to toughen me up. I tried to fit in for a long time, but there's no pleasing someone like that. I hate her.'

'I'm sorry,' I say, and I am. But another part of me can't help the simmering jealousy – it's hard to hear someone talk about the hard time they had living in luxury, being carted off to endless activities when I would have given anything to do any of those things with my parents.

'And Dad went back to Dubai after the divorce. We talk on the phone occasionally, but he's got a new family now. It's been really tough.'

Tough is watching your family die. Seeing the smoke filling up the car and the only person who could help you drive away. Tough is heroin addiction, homelessness, abuse. Othello wouldn't know hardship if it arrived in cocktail form – the only thing he seems to truly appreciate.

'In truth, I've not had proper parents for a long time. It really does feel like they're already gone.'

If Ayesha's own son can't say anything good about her, why should I spare her? Her death could help so many people. Perhaps Othello would be better off too. He could put her past behind him and make something of himself. I excuse myself to go to the loo and text Sam that I'm on board when – mid-text – I spot none other than Oliver.

I almost don't recognize him. He's wearing a designer shirt and expensive chinos, sitting at a table with his arm around a woman wearing a red dress and a delicate sweep of smoky eyeshadow. I'm pretty sure she's a sex worker – not because of the dress, which is actually quite classy, but because I've seen her in here three times before on the arm of a different, usually much older, man. But there's no misplacing Oliver's signature glasses, with their tortoiseshell frames and circle lenses. Or his booming voice, which travels over the entire room, delighting his guests with details of charity tax breaks they should be taking advantage of. I know two of the others he's sitting with – they're both on Sam's list of people awful enough to be considered for our purposes. What on earth is Oliver doing here with these people?

Chapter Twenty-One

You can never truly know someone. It's only a best guess with the information you have.

I didn't think I would be coming back here, but I need to know what kind of person Oliver is. I walk past an empty kebab shop and ignore two homeless people asking for spare change; no time to think about them today.

I open the door to the red-brick shelter, the one that Ruth introduced me to. She isn't meant to be on shift today. I checked. Still, I walk a little quicker past the room where she conducts her medical examinations, slipping undetected past the older nurse who is on duty today.

'Hi, I'm here to volunteer. Rob's going to get me set up – is he around?' I ask the first person I come across.

'He's in the kitchen; a new delivery just came in.'

I follow the direction the man gestures towards and walk through a swing door. The kitchen is lined with industrial-sized cookers on one side, white plastic counters where volunteers are preparing carrots and tomatoes for a chilli, and a large steel shutter on the other side. To my surprise,

Oliver is here, talking to a delivery driver. He catches my eye and pauses.

'I recognize you,' he says. 'From the hospital.'

I freeze. *Shit*. Didn't think about this. 'Yeah, what a small world. I'm Thea, I heard about this place from a friend and wanted to help out.'

I guess it's okay. I'm allowed to visit people in the hospital. There's no reason for him to suspect anything except a nice coincidence.

'Well, we're glad to have you here. Actually, it's great timing, we could use an extra pair of hands. Rob, can you get started?'

Rob nods and opens the shutter, revealing the delivery truck parked outside. He ropes in a few others, who open the truck door and pull it down into a ramp. They push up out-of-commission supermarket trolleys and start loading them with food. Rob's young but has the lined face of someone who has seen too much for their age. Handsome, with brown eyes and dark hair.

'Grab a trolley,' Rob says.

'Oh, no, I'm here to give legal advice.'

'That's great but we've got a truckload of frozen food that's going to thaw unless we're quick about it.'

I'm causing a blockage in the system, so I step to the side. Rob pushes his trolley into a second room hidden behind plastic flaps. There seems to be a well-oiled conveyor belt of people unloading the food and funnelling it through to the freezers. I suppose I could help, but I feel I'll only slow them down, so I don't. Oliver does, though. It's interesting to watch him work. He's more comfortable here, working to get something done in jeans and a simple blue T-shirt, than he seemed in the club.

Sam insists last night is nothing to worry about. He picked Oliver because of his links to Bloom's business dealing, not in spite of them. Apparently, Oliver spends his time convincing people like Bloom that participating in charitable doings works in their favour. I suppose I saw a glimpse of that at the Charity Gala dinner. He's someone that knows enough about how that world works to take over Bloom's business but remain committed to public good. I can understand that. You have to play the game to reap the benefits. But I have to be sure.

Once the food has been dealt with, Rob makes his way over to me.

'So, you're the lawyer, then?'

'Yes,' I say, hoping he doesn't ask for any more details. I'm trained in law, that should be enough to get me by today.

'Great, so mostly people will need advice on accommodation applications, drug issues and sometimes how to deal with family situations.' Rob leads me to a room that looks much the same as Ruth's medical room. Plain grey walls, two chairs, one desk, a printer and a computer I'm pretty sure has dial-up internet. He gives me a key to the room. 'Most of the people who come here don't have access to a computer, as you can imagine, so they need help submitting the forms. Think you can handle it?'

I nod, ignoring the fluttering in my stomach that says otherwise.

I lose track of time. A couple of my clients just want to tell me how much they hate lawyers, but I file a few housing accommodations that I think have a good chance of coming through. And I meet a young guy who's looking for work. He tells me that he got through to the final interview stage only to be told it's illegal to hire someone who's homeless. I call the potential employer, reassure him that this is not the case and connect him with Jobcentre to take things forward. Once upon a time, this is what I dreamed of doing. It reminds me that I've been getting a little too comfortable spending time in Othello's world. As much as I didn't enjoy being here with Ruth, perhaps it's good for me to spend time here, to stay true to mine and Sam's mission.

I look up to the door when I hear a knock. 'Come in.'

'Just me. You haven't taken a break all day. You hungry?' Rob asks.

My stomach is growling. When I'm at work, I usually start thinking about lunch about an hour after breakfast. And I usually eat it the moment the clock strikes noon – the earliest acceptable time to eat lunch and consume alcohol. But it's two-thirty and I haven't even noticed the hunger pangs.

I follow Rob to the main hall. There are rows and rows of collapsible school dinner tables set up with an assortment of plastic chairs. You can see the kitchen through the open canteen window. It's empty now, only a few people finishing their meals and one person dishing chilli out of a large silver pot. Rob and I head over, grab a bowl and wait our turn.

'Is it veggie?' I ask before I get a ladle dumped into my bowl. The woman narrows her eyes at me as if I've said something very stupid. 'I don't mean to be picky, but I don't eat meat.'

'It's veggie,' Rob says. 'Meat's expensive.'

I shoot back a grateful smile and accept my portion. We take a seat and I learn more about him. He first met Oliver when he was fifteen, on the streets himself. Oliver found him, told Rob he 'deserved so much more', and put him up in the temporary housing he was developing. Rob had no home to go to besides a drugged-up mum and an abusive dad, no qualifications and no professional experience. He's been working with Oliver ever since, trying to give other people the chance Oliver gave him.

'I would do anything for Oliver,' Rob says. 'I owe him my life.'

Maybe I've become cynical. I expect people to disappoint me, so I judge them too quickly, too harshly, before they get the chance. It's not my fault because it has been true for most of my life. But perhaps I'm wrong here. People who dedicate their lives to helping others don't have to have ulterior motives. They can sometimes be genuine.

I let Rob ramble on while I eat my chilli. The onions are underdone and the sauce a bit thin, but otherwise it's not too bad. I'm staring into space when I notice I've been gazing at someone I know for several long minutes. She has olive skin, dark curls that sit on top of her head and a baby cradled into her. Sam's client: Karly Maxwell.

It seems I have properly screwed up Karly's life.

She tells me she met Brendan at sixteen. At first, he seemed to be the answer to all her problems: older, handsome, more money than her and generous with it. He told her not to bother with school – he'd take care of her. Until he didn't, of course. None of that is my fault, of course. What it does mean is that Karly has no qualifications and no work experience. Now she has Leo and can't get a job that covers the cost of childcare. Now she's been evicted because her pathetic excuse for a boyfriend was at least covering the rent, and when I killed him, the money stopped too. The women's shelter is at capacity, and since she's no longer suffering from domestic abuse, they sent her here.

'I can help you apply for emergency housing. You'll be a priority because of Leo,' I say.

'No!' Her arms tighten around him.

'Then where are you going to stay?'

'I don't know, but if I apply for housing, then social services will get involved. Last time I had a run-in with them, I almost lost Leo. They're itching to take him off me. Already tried it once before. Babies and young kids settle better with adoptive families, you see, so if I give them any excuse, he's gone.' She lurches forward and grabs my hand. 'I'll figure this out. Promise me you won't say anything. Promise.'

The panic in her voice convinces me. She truly believes they will take her child from her. Maybe all systems are broken.

'Okay, I'll find another way to help you. I promise.'

Oliver can help, I'm sure of it. I know he has access to plenty of housing, and that he does whatever he can to help people. I do wish I wasn't asking for favours on my first day, but if I explain the situation, I'm sure he'll understand.

I thought killing her boyfriend would set Karly free. But I guess a lifetime of hurt can't be waved away so easily. I'm going to help her – that's decided – but there must be a hundred Karlys who end up here for their own complicated reasons and I don't have time to help each one on an individual level. But I know someone who can – a man who wears tortoiseshell frames and circle lenses. He just needs the resources to do it.

Chapter Twenty-Two

*People are like snakes. All of them can hurt
you but you can't tell which ones are venomous
until it's too late.*

Ayesha Bloom is a paranoid woman. I suppose if I had a billion pounds, I would be too. She lives in a state-of-the-art London townhouse complete with a panic room. She doesn't ever leave the house on foot. Instead, her driver drives down the slope into an underground garage, and presses a button to close the bulletproof shutter doors. Only then will Bloom deactivate the house's security software, use the biometric-operated door and get into the Bentley. She is then chauffeured, by an armed driver, directly to her head office and delivered inside.

Sam has a meeting with her today and is taking me along as his intern. On our way into the office building, we are subjected to a body scan and bag search, and I get an extra pat down for some reason. I've often been told I have a suspicious face. As a kid, Grandad was always sure I was up to something nefarious, even when I wasn't. My presence also had to be authorized in advance, and a copy of my passport given over for background checks. I expect Bloom is one of the most well-defended people in the country. But when all it takes to kill her is a touch, there's really nothing she can do.

However, she's also a germaphobe. When Sam and I arrive for our meeting, Bloom refuses to shake my hand. There's a man with a gun who stands in the corner of the room like a houseplant, and while he appears to be looking off into the distance, he twitches every time I move in a way that suggests he's clocking everything we do. If I tried to touch Bloom, I think this man might shoot me.

This office is unreal. The wall behind Bloom is solid glass. The Thames glistens from below, and I can see straight inside the Gherkin. I can even make out the people working there and the shape of their desks. I force myself to stop window-gazing as Sam gets down to business.

'We're going to have to be more specific about the origin of our capital. There's renewed pressure on solicitors to report money-laundering suspicions,' Sam says. He outlines some of the details. Property law involves a special breed of boredom. No wonder people have to be paid so much to pretend to be interested in it.

'Tell me what you need,' Ayesha says. 'Quickly.'

'We need to be able to demonstrate a legitimate source of income. Some records and contact details for an overseas operation, preferably something that's hard for an outsider to verify the details. These solicitors just need to show they've at least tried to fulfil their legal obligations.'

Bloom stays perfectly still in her chair, her stony face giving nothing away. Thankfully, her and Othello look nothing alike. He's alive and expressive whereas she reminds me of a porcelain doll, not a real person who interacts with the world.

'I'll have Tej set something up. Tech companies are excellent for this kind of thing – no one has any idea what some new algorithm is worth.'

I'm surprised by her brazenness, that she's willing to discuss these things in front of me. It's then I'm reminded of the viciousness hiding behind her calm facade. Sam's told me what happens to people who cross Bloom: a journalist accused of sexual assault before a potential exposé on the Bloom company, a business associate who took early retirement and moved to Australia in a hurry, and one extremely dead lawyer whose details Sam won't share. No, I don't think Ayesha Bloom considers me a threat.

'There's something else. Pressure for the government to reform anti-money-laundering regulators into one cohesive organization. It would be unhelpful for them to become more efficient.'

'Consider that reform dealt with,' she says. 'Anything else?'

A pit in my stomach is growing. Her easy, immediate responses. Sam aiding and abetting criminals with ease. I'm reminded of the club, Hardys, of the nasty feeling that came over me watching Sam in that environment, the way he looks a little too comfortable. But it's all an act, I remind myself. Still, there's something murky about preventing structural reform, the very thing Sam claims we're doing.

'Just a few documents I need you to sign,' he says, and looks at me.

I take out the forms he gave me earlier, stand up and approach the desk. The houseplant in the corner twitches, and I'm reminded of the gun in his holster. Bloom holds out her hand. I notice its youthfulness, like she bathes in milk and honey twice a day.

I pass her the paper, touching the underside of her knuckle ever so slightly, hoping the weight of the papers distracts her from the physical contact. It works. I'm practised now, so skilled that I take her twenty-eight years in a matter of seconds. She reviews the documents, signs them and dismisses us without so much as a thank you. Later this evening, at exactly midnight, she will quietly pass away in her sleep.

I take a special kind of pleasure in this. This woman is one of the most heavily defended on the planet, yet I have taken her life right under their noses.

Sam and I drink a bottle of Moët & Chandon to celebrate. His eyes are electric, like he's been overcharged and now has to keep moving; I'm giddy with Bloom's energy. I haven't decided who to give these years to yet – Othello seems the obvious choice but seeing as he's got fifty years in him already, granting him more seems unnecessary. So, for now, I'll keep hold of them. As a result, Sam and I turn up the speaker system with nineties pop music and dance around the apartment until we're sweating and gasping for breath.

'Think of what this will do, Thea. A billion-pound industry is now going to be headed by someone who cares about this city. Through this one act, we've done more for the world than most people will do in their lifetimes.'

He carries on talking while I pause for a glass of water. The phrases 'social implications', 'trickle-down economics' and 'social mobility' are muttered more times than I care to count.

Sam and I stay awake until midnight. It reminds me of staying up on New Year's Eve, except instead of fireworks, it's the quiet realization of what we have achieved. Sam brings out party poppers anyway. The bang makes me jump and he laughs, his joy taking me along with it. It's not that I'm happy to have killed someone, but it does feel good to be contributing to something that matters.

I wish people like Ruth, Zara and Grandad could understand what I'm doing, that I'm busy changing the world one rich prick at a time. Thinking of them suddenly makes me feel quite alone. I ignore the feeling and take a moment to grab the glass of water, adding ice from the fridge's ice-maker. It's silver, sleek and completely silent, like it's fresh from the box. I think of the fridge in Ruth's flat, with its rounded edges, eggshell blue exterior and the silver handle I once dented; and Grandad's fridge, which is older than me and buzzes like an air-conditioning unit but has never let us down.

The water is tinged with salt. I lick my lips in response, which only makes the taste of stale salt in my mouth worse. The kitchen has two rows of overhead lights and another set built into the cupboards, so I close my eyes and take a breath. This is a significant milestone and I should be revelling in it, not thinking about old kitchen appliances.

'Penny for your thoughts,' Sam says, sliding onto the kitchen barstool. 'Anything interesting in that noodle of yours?'

'Hmm, no,' I say. 'What kind of fridge did you have growing up?'

'I have no idea.' He chuckles. 'Why?'

I can't explain why this matters. It's just that I can't imagine what kind of fridge Sam would have had, I don't know what kind he currently has in the flat I've never been to, or what kind of fridge he would like in the future. If I try to picture Sam standing next to his fridge, there is a blank spot in my mind, one that I would like to fill in.

'What's your favourite colour?' I ask.

'For a fridge?'

'Anything.'

He shrugs. 'Red.'

'Animal?'

'Wolf.'

'Time of day?'

'Thea, why are you asking me these questions?'

'Don't you think it's strange we don't know these things about each other?' I ask. I know all these things about Ruth: purple, meerkat, morning.

Sam leans forward and takes my hand. He pulls me closer, closes his hand around my fist and rests his chin on it.

'I knew it was going to be different between us from the moment we met. We don't feel this way about each other because we like the same food or watch the same movies; we have something deeper: shared values and an understanding of the world. There's no stronger basis for love.'

Love. I stop breathing for what feels like a full minute.

He smirks. 'No, I didn't say that by accident. I love you. But I also have something more important to show you.'

Sam slips off the barstool and darts towards his satchel. He takes out a folder, opens it and passes me a piece of paper. At the top there's a gold letterhead that reads: *Ellis and Greaves*.

'What is this?' I ask.

'You can't run a law firm without your name printed on the stationery.' He reaches back into the folder and passes me a stack of documents. 'There's more. Just boring legalese really. The assistants have already been hired, the office space rented and documents signed.'

My own law firm. I can't take my eyes off the first piece of paper. Every letter of Times New Roman on this soft, magnolia paper is everything I've ever dreamed of. I might have imagined my name first, or on its own, but given my current career progression, I'm in no position to complain.

'I may not know everything about you, but I do know what

you want,' he says, a smile forming. 'We'll use the firm to continue as we have been, vetting potential targets and shifting the money to better-qualified individuals.'

'I don't exactly have the experience for this. What will I do?' I say, thinking about the form rejection I got from my last interview. I want this. I have always wanted this, an opportunity to make real change, but not if Sam is doing it for my own vanity.

'Whatever you like. You like working with the legal clinic at the shelter, right? Now you can get paid for your time too.' He rubs my arm. 'I know you don't like taking handouts, but you can't keep wasting your time working in human resources when you can do so, so much more.'

'When did you have time to do all of this?'

'Always pays to stay two steps ahead. Habit of the job.'

'Where does all the money come from?'

'I've been doing some siphoning of my own.' He winks as if this is something we are both in on. 'Don't worry, it's not stealing if they don't know it's gone. So, what do you say? Are you in?'

I brush the gold lettering with my fingertips. I imagine walking through the doors of my own law firm, instructing younger aspiring lawyers and telling people at the shelter, 'Yes, we can help you with that.'

I'm absolutely not qualified to do this – the sting of failing the bar exam remains strong. But bending the rules seems to be Sam's speciality. Case in point, he's not technically allowed to practise as both a barrister and a solicitor, but he uses split jurisdictions as a loophole. I assume he's found some legal wiggle room for me too. And maybe, just maybe, I deserve this. I'm serving a different, truer kind of justice. I don't need to feel guilty if I happen to benefit as a result.

'Of course I'm in,' I say.

'Good.'

'Oh, and I love you too, just in case you were wondering.'

He grins, his eyes twinkling. 'I know. Two steps ahead, remember?'

Chapter Twenty-Three

The target must be aware of the consequences of their actions.

I don't walk anymore, because I skip, all the way to the pool. My Swarovski crystal-studded sandals clip-clop on the blue mosaic tiles and the gentle hum of the pool heating system welcomes me. I used to wear jeans and a top over my swimming costume, because I was embarrassed to be caught in the elevator in a kaftan, but now I embrace it. The pool has become my natural habitat, although soon I'll be too busy working at Ellis and Greaves to waste away my afternoons drinking cocktails and falling asleep next to softly lapping water.

One thing is missing today: Othello. His lounger looks strangely empty. There's a deep indentation that I recognize as his shape, and his book has been left underneath it.

I wait a few minutes but feel odd sitting here alone. His eerily empty lounger is taunting me, telling me I'm an unwelcome guest. Othello's apartment is on floor fourteen, number fifty-one. I have to knock three times, each one accompanied by the squawking of the African grey parrot, Tia, inside, before heavy footsteps stomp towards the door. I see the peephole darken and hear the haphazard undoing of door chains.

'I'm not in the mood for visitors,' Othello says as he opens the door. He's wearing patterned silk pyjamas, and his wavy brown hair is flat at the back.

I push the door and walk through. 'Are you okay?'

'My mum died.'

'Oh,' I say, trying to sound surprised. 'Sorry.'

There's an awkward silence between us: him wanting to ask me to leave and me struggling to understand the melancholy that's pulsing off him.

'Yeah, I can't believe she's really gone.'

'You weren't close, though, right?'

His eyes snap into focus, and he crosses his arms into his chest. 'What's that supposed to mean? She was my mum.'

It's then I realize what's going on. Othello has never lost anyone before. His grandparents died before he was born, he has almost no extended family and I'm basically his only friend, so he has been completely and utterly sheltered from death.

Without speaking I wrap my arms around him and pull him in close. He resists for a second, then melts into me, sobbing on my kaftan. We stay like this for a while. Quietly. People always think they have to say something in moments like this, to make it better, to alleviate the pain. But that's usually to cover their own discomfort. I know that, in reality, there's nothing you can say to make it better. Nothing you can say to make it worse.

I hate that I did this to him. But I also think about how lucky he is to have got to eighteen with no idea what loss feels like, and that he still doesn't really know the earth-shattering pain of losing someone you truly love. So I need to let him sit with his feelings and experience this. How else will he learn to harden himself and cope with how much worse life will get?

I tell Othello I'll check in on him later and leave him to grieve, because I have a busy day ahead of me. First on the agenda: quit my job. Zara asked me in for a meeting this morning to discuss my suspension, and while I probably could have told her about the good news on the phone, I want to see the look on her face when she realizes she's pushed me too far.

She confiscated my ID card, so I have to wait for a snot-nosed intern that I recruited to escort me into the office. They hardly look at me and don't engage in my good-humoured ribs about the company. It's like I'm being taken to the principal for a telling off and they don't want to be associated with me.

Zara is waiting in one of the frosted-glass-walled meeting rooms, papers laid on the table and a mediation lawyer sitting to her right. I take the empty seat and help myself to the water in the middle of the table.

'Thanks for coming in, Thea. As per our guidelines, an independent assessor has reviewed our case and is here to help resolve our disagreement. This is Martha, our assessor,' Zara says.

Martha looks out of place in this corporate environment in a flowery dress and yellow cardigan. I bet she would be happier working in a gardening centre or a cafe. I also reckon she gives great big warm bear hugs.

'Now,' she says. 'A few guidelines. I would like to encourage you both to use "I feel" statements and to avoid allocation of blame. This is an opportunity to gain insight into the other person's emotional experience.'

We begin.

Zara *feels* disrespected.

I *feel* patronized.

Zara *feels* frustrated.

I *feel* like a caged animal, trapped in this room, playing this game, clawing to get out. Finally, we reach an agreement.

Martha smiles and finishes making her notes. 'Okey dokey, Zara has agreed to undergo training in sensitivity management to prevent future disagreements arising and will apologize for the offences she has acknowledged in this document. In return, Thea, you will receive a warning for the image you shared and also need to apologize and acknowledge that it was wrong to share this with your peers. Future sick leave will also need to be accompanied by a doctor's note. Is this agreeable to you both?'

'Yes,' Zara says.

I nod, curious to see if Zara will really apologize. 'Sure.'

Zara then takes a deep breath, straightens her posture like she's imagining there are puppet strings pulling her up and forcing her movements. 'Thea, I'm sorry that I undermined your confidence and didn't adequately use positive reinforcement to develop your abilities. I acknowledge these shortcomings in my management style and will be working to address them.'

Well, she did it. Albeit the words were clearly pre-prepared and reluctant, but she said them without rolling her eyes or cursing under her breath. Martha nods in approval, then turns to me. Zara lets out some of the tension she was holding and waits for my response.

'I don't want to work here anymore,' I say. 'I'm starting up my own legal firm.'

Zara chokes on her own snicker. 'You? Starting a legal firm? You're nowhere near qualified to do that.'

'This is exactly the kind of undermining stuff that I was talking about,' I say to Martha.

Zara stands up. 'No, don't turn this around on me. You walked in here, got *me* to apologize to *you*, when you had no intention of reciprocating. And now you're saying you don't even want this job? I've given you chance after chance, and all you do is throw it back in my face.'

'You should be happy I'm going. You only gave me this job to suck up to Ruth.'

'That's not true. I interviewed you as a favour to Ruth, but I didn't hire you because of that. I thought you were genuine about your interest in the legal side of things, and that I could use someone like that, but it's all talk with you. You're going to keep screwing up until you finally take some responsibility for your actions.'

I stand up, ready to fight back but struggling to find the right words. It's so easy for people like Zara, who had the best education money can buy and grew up surrounded by people who helped her reach her full potential, to find the right words in the moment and make you feel like you're in the wrong. Thankfully, Martha intervenes.

'This is not productive. Thea, is there anything we can do to change your mind?'

'No, I've already accepted the new job.'

'Okey dokey, then I think the best thing to do is to draw a line under this. Shake hands and be done with it.'

Zara's got her arms crossed. I roll my eyes and hold out my hand, which, after a glare from Martha, she reluctantly takes.

'Thanks for all the opportunities,' I say. I force a smile, although I'm only able to do this because I have the satisfaction of Zara's life flowing into me. Just a few days, then a week.

Zara cuts me off before I can take any more. It's unclear whether she has some sixth sense about me or whether she simply hates being forced to play nice. It doesn't matter. I leave straight after that because I have actual work to do that doesn't take place in an office whose greatest contribution is free annual leave on your birthday.

On Monday I start work at the shelter, doing what I was always meant to do. People aren't queuing up for me yet, like they do Ruth, but that's to be expected. Most of them rank lawyers one rung away from police on their list of trusted allies. But I'm patient. And I know when I see that warm glow of disbelief radiate across just one person's face, amazed that someone is truly taking the time to provide the help they so desperately need, it will make it all worthwhile.

'He's a fucking bastard,' my latest client, Taz, hisses. She hasn't been homeless long enough to remove the crusted mascara on her eyelashes, but she acts like it's been years.

Yeah, I'm still waiting on that warm glow.

'Let's stick to the facts. Your boyfriend has kicked you out of your flat, is that right?'

'Changed the fucking locks, didn't he?'

'Is your name on the tenancy? If so, you are legally entitled to shared occupancy.'

'Yeah, it's my fucking flat.'

'Then I can help you get a court order to return there. Or we can call the police to help you get back into the flat immediately.'

'Don't you dare call those fuckers.'

'Okay, then would you like me to submit the court order? It might take a couple of weeks. Do you have someone you can stay with meanwhile?'

She crosses her arms and sits back in her chair. 'I suppose.'

I force a smile. 'Great, let's get that court order submitted, then.'

*

In better news, Oliver has come through, and I get to tell Karly the good news. She comes by after lunch, cautiously peering around the corner before entering the room. She always does this, as if she's an animal expecting to be cornered at any moment.

'I don't know what to say,' she says. 'I can't afford this.'

'It's okay. Oliver needs you to pay rent so it looks official – it causes a safeguarding issue if he just gives out free accommodation – but he's going to give you a job that'll cover it. It's just answering phones and making appointments for his construction company. It's hardly exciting but it's a job, and there's a crèche so you can take Leo with you.'

She rocks Leo on her knee to keep him from crying and always keeps one eye on the door. 'He's giving me a home and a job? What does he want?'

I'm reminded of the masseuse who pulled that mystical massage on me where a thousand bloody suns exploded from my collarbone and I actually cried. She said I was carrying my pain in the wrong place. I think when bad things happen to you, especially when you're young, you have to store it away somewhere it can't hurt. Except there's usually nowhere deep enough to put it. When you don't deal with the original source of the pain, it comes bubbling up in other places. I can see Karly doing it right now.

'Not everyone is going to disappoint you, Karly. Some people just want to help. This can be a fresh start for you if you let it be.'

One step at a time. I hand her an envelope with the address and the keys. It's not much, a fairly crappy one-bed flat in West Croydon, but at least it's clean and safe.

'A fresh start,' she says, grasping the keys. 'Thank you, Thea. I won't forget this.'

Ah, there's that warm glow I was waiting for.

It makes me want to do more for her. I think about how her parents hurt her. For Karly, that's where the pain started. How does she feel, knowing they are living their lives with no consequences for what they put her through? Brendan's gone. Maybe if they were gone too, she could finally be free.

The last hour of my shift is quiet, so I use it to cyber-stalk Karly's mother. I already know her surname and so track her down easily through her and Karly's mutual Facebook friends. Sue Maxwell lives in a perfectly nice house in East Croydon. She's set up a small bakery business and her Facebook feed is full of blondie brownies, apple pie and chocolate ganache cake. There's even a photo of her in a strawberry-print apron. Shame she didn't discover this maternal side earlier.

I consider calling Sam. We haven't explicitly discussed it but taking a life without his say-so makes me feel a little guilty. Ruth's concerns echo in my head. Maybe I do rely on him for too much. I'm an independent person who can make decisions, or at least I should be. And hey, it's my power, not Sam's.

I place a rush order for ten blondies and leave the clinic early. An hour later I arrive at her shop. I take the blondies and her remaining twenty-two years, minus a day to maintain separation between murder and death.

The blondies are delicious. I eat two of them on the way home, smiling as I imagine how Karly will feel when she hears the good news.

How quickly I've forgotten what a hard day's work feels like. My shoulder muscles are coiled, my back twisted and my brain foggy. Worth it, though, to see the look on Karly's face.

No doubt Sam already has another target queued up, but it feels good to be reminded that it's not just my power that has value, but my knowledge too. No wonder Ruth feels so fulfilled and smug all the time. Philanthropy is addictive.

I get back to Mayfair at 8 p.m. There's a text on my phone from Sam asking what I want for dinner, and I love the idea of him waiting around for me to get home from work. I'm grinning as I press the lift button for floor sixteen. Each button illuminates as I creep higher past each floor. The doors open and I step out, only to realize it's floor fourteen. Othello's floor. Weird, I must have pressed the wrong button.

It's quiet, too quiet. Then I hear Tia squawk loud and clear, making me jump and the hairs on the back of my neck stand up. I can't help but feel something has pulled me onto this floor. I used to think superstition was the mark of an idiot but I'm hardly in a position to be cynical about the supernatural anymore. I'd meant to check in on the kid anyway.

There's a Gucci loafer wedging the front door open. I let myself in, following the low hum of the television to find Othello sitting on the sofa, still in his blue and orange silk pyjamas.

'Hey, have you moved since this morning?' I call out. He doesn't move a muscle. It's then I realize his neck is strained, his head drooping to the side. 'Othello?'

I run around the sofa, cursing the L-shaped seven-seater for slowing me down. He's deathly pale and completely still. There's a bottle of whisky, an empty crystal-cut glass and an empty pill packet on the side table.

'Oh fuck, what have you done?'

I pull up his sleeve and wrap my hand around him. *Three minutes.*

I don't understand. Othello had over fifty years to live. He was safe. How could this have happened?

Two minutes. It doesn't matter how it happened because I

can stop it. I'm holding fifty years and he deserves every last one. I grasp him tight. The energy doesn't flow like normal; it wrenches itself from me. Maybe it's the stress, or maybe I'm out of practice giving out such large amounts. Regardless, every cell in my body has been flayed.

My vision blurs and I can hardly hold myself up. 'Othello?' I mumble, trying to shake him. I can't tell if he's moving or if it's me. My head hits the floor before I manage to find out.

Chapter Twenty-Four

Are some people more responsible for their actions than others?

I have been hit by a thousand trucks. Slowly, I re-enter some lower form of consciousness. The kind you might expect a slug or a jellyfish to have. The room is full of floating objects – I notice an arm, a blanket, a glass – but my brain refuses to put any of this together, leaving me with an incoherent picture of the world.

'Hello, Thea, welcome back to us,' a voice says. 'I know it's probably hard to concentrate right now, but we need to know what you've taken.'

'What?' I mumble.

A brown shadow moves towards me. Ruth's voice speaks. 'Thea, it's really important to tell the doctors what you've taken.'

'I didn't.'

'You won't be in trouble. Just tell the truth.'

This goes on for a while. They seem to be leaving Ruth to coax it out of me. At least an assortment of limbs and hair that make me think my best guess is that it's Ruth. She tells me that Othello is stable too but weak, and it would really help if they knew what had caused this. And she says again and again that no one is angry with me.

'Why would you be angry with me? I saved him. I used my power.'

'Your power?'

'Yes, I saved Othello, Oliver, my barista. Other people. You.'

'Me?'

I notice her eyes. They've always been so round, so empty of judgement. Maybe it's my current state but I swear she's glowing, like a ring of light is haloing her whole self. I'm so tired of lying to her and I feel sure this new, empathetic angel-Ruth will understand.

'Mm-hmm, you died, remember? I had to kill Greg to do it.'

She sits up straight, the movement jarring, and the halo disappears. The other voice comes over and asks her something, to which Ruth replies: 'No, she's talking nonsense. I can't get any information out of her. I'm sorry.'

She leaves the room and I slip down a consciousness level again, back into blissful oblivion.

The next time I wake, I'm strong enough to hold my head up properly. It still takes me a minute to recognize the figure beside my bed. He has square-framed glasses, a grey moustache, long bushy eyebrows and smells faintly of metal polish.

'Grandad?'

'You're awake.' He reaches out to take my hand.

'Where am I?'

'In the hospital. You've been unconscious for three days.'

I groan.

'Follow my finger with your eyes,' he says, moving it from

side to side and up and down. Then he rests two fingers on my wrist. 'Good, your pulse feels steady too.'

'Perhaps I should get the doctor,' another voice says. Sam. Oh God, this is not how I imagined introducing my boyfriend to my family. I hope they've been sitting in complete silence this whole time.

'Well, yes, I suppose we should.' Grandad jumps up with the energy of someone half his age. 'I'll inform them.'

I smile. Always keen to be useful. To be fair, he was a medic during the war, so he's not clueless on these things. He returns moments later with both a doctor and a nurse, although he clearly remains in charge.

They spend the next few hours asking me questions and running every test known to humankind. CT, MRI, blood etc. People don't generally fall unconscious for days at a time without a reason.

The nurse clearly still believes I've taken something because she says nothing showed up in my blood tests but adds, 'Of course, it's hard to keep up with these new party drugs. We can't find something if we don't know what to test for.'

The doctor is less judgemental, and her theory is that the shock of finding Othello put me into a psychosomatic coma. Or, as I like to call it, a sympathy coma. We're just waiting on my MRI results to confirm, and then they'll discharge me – if Grandad will let them, that is.

Ruth called him and he immediately jumped on the first train to London. In the absence of anything medical to fix, he spends his time forcing water down my throat, fluffing my pillows and passing me things well within my reach. Despite my clean bill of health, I'm exhausted, so I don't complain. I've always secretly liked being ill. When I was little, Grandad used to set up the television in my room and bring me anything I said would make me feel better. Ice cream. Always ice cream. Sam reads the room well and stays quiet and out of Grandad's way. But I'm desperate to talk to him alone, so I can tell someone what happened.

I finally manage to get rid of Grandad when he asks, 'Are you sure there's nothing else I can get you?'

'Ice cream?'

He smiles knowingly. I feel closer to him in that little moment than I have in years. He quickly turns and leaves on his mission to find me some frozen goodness.

'Sam, quick, come here,' I say the moment the door closes.

'Are you okay? Do you need the doctor?'

'The doctor won't be any help, Sam. It's my power.'

'Explain.'

I take a deep breath, trying to clear my head. 'Othello was dying. I don't know how or why, but I found him three minutes from death. So, I had to use my power.'

'Othello was dying? I thought he had decades to live?' Sam asks.

'He did. I don't know what happened.'

Sam drums his fingers on the metal railing of my bed. 'So did the degu.'

'What does Diego have to do with any of this?' He doesn't answer me. 'There's more. I gave Othello everything I was holding and it's hard to explain but it felt different. Almost painful.'

'Okay, let's be analytical about this. Clearly your power isn't foolproof. You can tell when someone is meant to die but that doesn't make them invulnerable. And these were both . . . unnatural deaths. Perhaps they weren't supposed to die that way, until they were. And then the second part – you gave Othello fifty years – have you ever given that much before?'

I close my eyes for a moment. 'I don't think so. Not in one go at least.'

'And how long has it been since you've completely depleted your stores?'

'Months.'

He crosses his leg and taps his shin.

'Why, what are you thinking?' I ask.

'Well, it's just a theory. Imagine a heroin addict. If they've been using regularly, they become dependent on the drug, and if they stop, they experience withdrawal effects. If they suddenly stopped using, go cold turkey, you'd rightly expect a severe reaction, which is why doctors put addicts onto methadone to wean them off safely.'

I shudder, reminded of Ruth draining the infected vein abscess of one of her heroin-addicted patients.

'You're comparing me to a heroin addict? I don't steal life because it makes me feel good.'

'It does though, doesn't it? You haven't seen yourself after taking a life. Your eyes are full of wonder, like you're seeing the world for the first time and it's pure magic.' He seems to note my starstruck face and continues. 'You don't have to feel guilty about it. Why shouldn't you get to enjoy the fruits of your labour?'

I'm prevented from answering by Grandad's return. He raises a bowl of vanilla ice cream, complete with rainbow sprinkles and chocolate sauce, in triumph.

After the ice cream, I'm feeling stronger. Grandad has tired himself out and is taking a nap beside my bed. Sam has excused himself to take a work call, so I pull myself out of bed and hobble down the corridor to visit Othello.

'You look beastly. What on earth happened to you?' he says,

propped up in bed with two extra pillows cushioning him. He's even managed to get his silk pyjamas in here, hospital gowns offensive to his fashion sensibilities no doubt.

I drag myself to the chair beside his bed and gasp several short breaths. 'Hey, don't be mean to me. The doctor thinks the shock of seeing you put me into a sympathy coma. God knows why, you look fine.'

'Such a drama queen,' he replies.

We sit in awkward silence for a few moments. I'm not sure what to say. He's awfully chirpy for a boy who just tried to kill himself. Maybe denial is the best policy.

'Right, I can't take this any longer,' he says. 'Let's put this elephant out of its misery. I tried to top myself. It's not as big a deal as you might think. Every London socialite throws out a call for help once in a while, it's basically inevitable. The biggest indignity is that they haven't already transferred me to a private hospital. I'm not supposed to be here.'

'It wasn't inevitable, Othello. This wasn't supposed to happen. Is that what you were doing, asking for help?'

'I left the shoe in the door, didn't I? Besides, I didn't take enough. I wasn't really at risk.'

I wince, wondering if he believes that. 'I should have been kinder this morning, should have said something more helpful. I really am sorry about your mum.'

'It's all right. Not your fault.'

I wince again. If I'd had any idea this would be the consequence, I would have stayed far, far away from Ayesha Bloom. 'I guess losing my parents so young kinda desensitized me to loss. I didn't realize how much you were hurting.'

He gives a pained half-smile. 'When does it stop . . .?'

I know he wants me to tell him that it's all going to be okay. That there's a way through and he'll feel like he did before. But even now, seeing him so vulnerable, I can't bring myself to lie like that. I want to tell him the whole truth and nothing but. I owe him that much, but I can't look him in the eye as I do it.

'It doesn't, but it does get easier to cope with. And after a while you stop wanting it to stop. Sometimes I'm walking around, minding my own business, and I'll think of them out of nowhere. It's always the little things. A loaf of cheap white bread will remind me of the way my mum used to cut smiley faces into my cheese and marmite sandwiches. Or I'll see a stranger on the Tube reading the paper with his glasses halfway down his nose in the exact same way as my dad. And I'll feel it like a stab to the heart. But love and pain aren't so different. Once you realize that, you start to hold onto those pangs even when they hurt, because they are what connects you to the people you've lost long after they've gone.' Othello is quiet. I barely realize how long I've been talking. It's only when I look up that I notice the tears in his eyes. 'I'm sorry. I should have said something more comforting.'

He holds his throat as if trying to release the tension. 'It's not that, it's just . . . those are happy memories you're reminded of. I let things get so bad between me and Mum these past few years. We'd barely spoken since I turned sixteen. She thought I hated her, but the truth was I had so much of my own stuff going on. If I'd just told her, then maybe she would have understood, and she would have died knowing that I loved her.'

I feel hot with shame and guilt. What the fuck have I done?

I can't keep going like this. I let Sam convince me that what is good on paper is good in principle. All I know is that I have caused someone I deeply care for enough pain to want to end his own life. Ruth would never have let me do such a thing.

It's more than that. Ruth is the entire reason I have this

power. I love her so much that the thought of losing her broke the laws of reality. But by lying to her, I'm losing her anyway.

The doctors keep me overnight for observation, then discharge me the next day. Sam says he'll look after me at the Mayfair apartment.

'You can rest up and order unlimited lobster mac and cheese. You've got all your stuff there anyway,' he says.

This is clearly the wrong thing to say in front of Grandad. There was fledging approval when he learned that Sam was a lawyer, but I think the idea of my stuff at Sam's place pushes him over the edge.

'With all due respect,' he says, 'I do not know you. I'd prefer to take Thea home with me. Keep an eye on her.'

'Of course,' Sam says. 'Although I wonder if getting the train back to the countryside is good for her?'

I don't want to be around Sam right now. I killed Ayesha, but I did it because of him. And I know I need to take responsibility for my actions, but he's just so convincing. I don't trust myself with his voice in my ear. Not until I've got another one to balance him out. I need Ruth.

'Hey, I can look after myself,' I interject. 'I'm going back to Clapham. Neither of you can object to me having a literal doctor around to look after me.'

Both struggle to argue with that. I send them both home. Sam seems a little put out that I've chosen Ruth over him, but I promise I'll send regular text updates on how I'm doing.

Later that afternoon, I find her in our kitchen, chopping a carrot into batons. She puts ten batons in little plastic bags, so she has on-the-go snacks for the week ahead. How I love that freak.

'Ruth, I need to talk to you about what I said when I woke up.'

'Yeah, you were saying some crazy things, but you were pretty out of it. It's okay, you should hear the things people say when they come round from anaesthetics. A woman once told me she was the universe itself, that she was every person that had ever been and ever was and she loved them all.'

I can't produce even the slightest giggle. 'And I bet sometimes people tell the truth.'

'Sure, being that out of it can cause disinhibition. Kinda like when you drink alcohol.'

'Ruth, I was telling you the truth.'

'I'm sorry?'

'You were supposed to die. That night at Supernova when you fell, you cracked your head on the concrete step and you would have died, but I saved you.'

She rolls her eyes. 'That's insane.'

'I know, but it's the truth.'

She steps forward, looking me straight in the eye. 'You really sound as if you believe this. Are you feeling okay? You must be suffering from some neurological side effect of whatever you took. I really wish you would just tell me what it was.'

She reaches up to feel my forehead with the back of her hand. I snatch it mid-air.

'I didn't take anything. Othello tried to kill himself. He was dying and I saved him too.'

'Wow, with those skills we should keep you on the ICU full time,' she says in her soothing doctor voice. She really does think I'm crazy. Of course she does – any sane, rational person would.

'Take me there right now. I can tell you which patient will die next and exactly when it's going to happen.'

'Easy, tiger. You can't just waltz into ICU. It's for really sick patients.'

'I've been in before. I pretended to be Oliver's cousin so I could save him. I remember the cards by his bed and the stuffed teddy, Bertie, from his kids.'

'How do you know that?'

'Because I'm telling you the truth.'

Rule-abiding citizen that she is, Ruth refuses to take me to the ICU and frog-marches me back to hospital. The doctor takes my temperature, shines a light in my eyes and promises to run more tests. Ruth relays our conversation to the doctor. I deny everything.

'Hmm, there could be some amnesia. Let's run a CT scan as soon as possible to rule out any bleeding.'

I submit to yet another scan. Not a peep as I follow instructions and lie under the machine that makes me feel like I'm inside a massive doughnut. While we wait for my results, Ruth chatters incessantly. She does this when she's nervous, and despite her outward conviction of my insanity, I can see there's a flicker of doubt in the corner of her eye. It's like she won't quite look at me properly, because then she'll know I can see it.

The scan comes back clear. The doctor says they've already run every test they normally would in this situation, while I was coming around from my inexplicable coma. They want to schedule a number of follow-up appointments to keep track of my progress and refer me to a psychiatrist but, by all accounts, I'm perfectly healthy and there's no reason to keep me here.

'Unless you've had any other delusional episodes?'

'No, totally sane now. Sorry for the trouble.'

Before we go, I excuse myself from Ruth's company, telling her that I forgot something and I'll meet her downstairs. I need proof. This is a hospital. Someone has to be dying soon and I need a test subject. I check on each patient until finally I find who I'm looking for. Doris Brown is ninety-two years

old, recovering from a routine kidney-stone removal procedure. She's going to die in exactly twenty-six hours' time, at
8.28 p.m.

I tell Ruth this thirty minutes before Doris's time of death,
when we are curled up on the sofa in our flat, eating Thai food
and watching the latest *Love Island* copycat TV show. I ask
her to go to the hospital right this minute and see for herself.
As expected, she thinks I'm having another episode and curses
herself for not making more fuss with the doctor who assessed
me. I tell her that if she does this, I will put my medical decisions solely in her hands now and forever.

To her credit, she does it. And then she doesn't come back.

Chapter Twenty-Five

If they knew they could get away with it, most people would commit murder. All it takes is motive and opportunity.

'How much?' Grandad asks.

'Sixteen ninety-nine, sir,' the waiter replies.

'For a sandwich?'

'It's not just a sandwich, it's Smørrebrø, Grandad,' I interject, earning me a blank look. 'It's a set of open sandwiches – more like a meal.'

'It's daylight robbery, that's what it is.'

The waiter looks to me for help.

'We'll have two of the Sorgenfri specials,' I say, adding to Grandad, 'It's my treat.'

'No wonder you can't afford to buy anywhere if you're spending the best part of twenty pounds on lunch.'

I remind myself not to retaliate by saying houses don't cost a shilling anymore. 'I wanted to take you somewhere nice to thank you for coming to take care of me in hospital, and for coming up to check on me again. I know how much you hate London.'

'There's no need for that,' is all he says.

We sit in awkward silence. Our usual distance has returned. Without a purpose for being here, a medical reason to show care, he simply doesn't know how to be. It doesn't help when the trio of open sandwiches arrives and each is small enough to pick up with two fingers.

'How's the museum?' I ask. Getting him onto the war is usually a safe bet.

He nods. 'Good. We're hoping to acquire a new set of Second World War diaries.'

'That's exciting.'

'Quite.'

'Are you going to set up a stall for the village fete this year?'

'Yes.'

'Is it going to be a busy one?'

'Fairly.'

We continue like this for a while. Each answer shorter and coarser than the last. Until finally I break.

'Grandad, I'm trying here and you're not helping me out much.'

'That's because I know you're hiding something, and I don't appreciate being taken for a fool.'

I choke on some watercress. The pepperiness of it stings the back of my throat and makes my eyes water.

'The doctors seemed to think you'd taken something. Look me in the eye and tell me the truth.'

'I didn't take anything. Honest,' I say, grateful that this is in fact the truth. I've never been able to lie to Grandad.

He squares me up, trying to uncover deception behind my pupils. 'Well, that worries me even more. At least drugs would have explained things.'

'You seem angry with me.'

'I'm not. I'm disappointed.'

Christ, that is so much worse.

'Disappointed? Grandad, I'm doing well. I told you about my new job. I'm giving out legal advice at a homeless shelter. I'm helping people.'

'I know it wasn't easy for you, coming to live with me after your parents died, but I did my best. I tried to teach you right from wrong and how to get on in the world.'

'I know you did. I don't understand why you're being like this.'

My protests do no good. Once I've paid for our extortionate sandwiches, he leaves. We don't make plans to see each other again but our next visit has a hard deadline. He's only got just over seven months left – 20 January. I realized it at the hospital, but there was too much going on to properly process it and I'm not holding any life to give him. It's okay, though. Seven months is practically a lifetime.

I head back to my flat. Every time I open the door, I get my hopes up that Ruth will be back. It's been five days since I've heard from her. There's an unwashed bowl of half-eaten quinoa-and-kale salad that's still sitting by the sink. It's really starting to stink but I'm leaving it there as a crude Ruth-alarm because there's no way she would come back inside the flat and leave it there. But yet again, it's untouched; the only change is the fly that's crawled up and died there.

I put the TV on to mask the emptiness of the flat. I hate living alone but Ruth has to come back at some point, if only to restock on knickers. I'm determined to wait her out. Lunch with Grandad was my longest outing all week.

Sam's been texting me every morning and every evening to check I'm okay. I'm not. I haven't taken a life since I gave my stores to Othello, and I'm suffering for it. Without the excess energy I'm used to running on, I'm like a ninety-year-old with chronic fatigue. Everything is exhausting. And yet I can't sleep either. For the first time in a long time my nightmares are back. Always the same one. My parents, the crash, their deaths.

I stay up on the sofa drinking the half-open bottle of wine from last night, trying to resist the pull of sleep because I know what I'll see if I succumb. But, eventually, I do.

It's midnight when the crash of a ceramic dish wakes me up. I jolt awake. There's a figure in the kitchen, crouched down in the dark. I turn on the lights.

'Ruth?'

'Ugh, you caught me.'

She's squatting down, picking up the smashed pieces of bowl strangely slowly. When she tries to get up, she falls back onto her arse and laughs. Her elbow is dangerously close to a shard of ceramic as she tries but fails to pull herself up.

'Ruth, stop. Stay still,' I say, and rush over to help her.

'I'll just wait until the room stops spinning,' she says. It's then I realize she's completely trashed. She doesn't even try to get up, just lies down on the wooden floor and closes her eyes.

I leave her for a moment, fetch a dustpan and brush and sweep away the broken bowl. Then I grab hold of both her wrists and pull her up. She makes no effort to help. Instead, she lies like a dead weight in my arms, finding the whole thing quite entertaining. She brings us both down to the floor.

'Ruth, what the hell?'

'What? I'm just having some fun. You always told me I should have more fun.'

She is distracted by the zip on her hoodie, zipping it up and back down like a child. I leave her propped against the kitchen counter while I get her a glass of water and some toast. This has never happened before; she's always the one looking after me and the role reversal is alien to me. I remember the first party we went to as teenagers, which involved drinking alcopops in a random field with two older girls we thought were extremely cool at the time. Anyway, I graduated to vodka in an attempt to impress our new friends and ended up puking my guts up. Ruth stayed with me, holding my hair back and not making me feel guilty for a second, even when I vomited on her brand-new Doc Martens.

She drinks the water and manages half the toast. Her eyes are focusing a little, to the point that I feel confident she can see me clearly.

'Ruth, are you okay?' I ask, hoping she can hear the sincerity in my voice. Most of the time, when people ask this question, they don't really want an answer, just reassurance. But I mean exactly what I'm asking.

'Why wouldn't I be? I'm alive, and lucky to be, aren't I?' She shrugs and forces down the second half of the toast. The air tenses in my lungs. I don't speak. I wait for her to swallow the toast. 'You know, I've always felt this sense of guilt, since I was a kid. Like I didn't really deserve anything, but if I was good enough, if my grades were high enough, if I worked hard enough, then I could earn it and I wouldn't have to feel so guilty all the time. But now, what's the point?'

'What do you mean?'

'Someone else died so I could live. You killed Greg for me. And then you said you carried on saving people, which must mean you carried on killing them too. I'm responsible for that and there's no amount of doctoring and good Samaritaning that can make up for it. I don't deserve the air I'm breathing right now.'

Part of me wants to put my arms around her and tell her that there's nothing she could do that would make her more or less worthy of life, but another part of me wants to slap her for being so naive. I'm sick of hearing people spout nonsense about how everyone is equal. It's a lovely sentiment, sure. But I've seen Ruth at work. People need her. I can't bear the pain I've caused her right now but, if it came down to it, I would kill every single one of her patients if it bought her some extra time. She is simply worth more than them.

'I'm not going to apologize for saving you. It was the right thing to do.'

'There's nothing right about what you've done. You lied to me.'

'We updated our agreement, remember? Lie as little as possible . . .' I stop when I remember the second half.

'And not about the things that matter,' she finishes. 'This isn't about who you're dating, Thea. It's about who you're killing. You can't possibly think that doesn't matter.'

'I did it to protect you.'

'I want you to leave.'

'Sure, it's your flat. I'll go and stay with Sam for a while.'

'No, I don't want you in my life anymore. I can't do anything to change what's happened, and no one would believe me if I told them the truth. So, I need you to go. I don't ever want to see you again.'

At this time of night, it takes me two hours to make the short hop from Clapham to Mayfair. Station closure, incident on a carriage and a group of creepy drunk men I'd rather avoid all slow me down. It's late by the time I get back, but I want to check on Othello – I can't afford to lose another friend today. True to form, he's awake like the pathological night owl he is and greets me with a bony hug. I don't think his hospital stay did him any favours.

'How are you doing?' I ask.

He answers but I struggle to take in the words. All I can hear is Ruth's voice over and over. Every time she tells me to leave it's like her words grip me by the throat and punch me in the chest. She can't have meant it. It's the shock. She'll come to her senses. Why don't I believe it?

'I've decided I will eat a human toe. Fifty pounds, final offer.'

I've been nodding along, wondering if Ruth is asleep already or if she's lying awake replaying our argument like me. Then I realize what Othello has said.

'Sorry, what?'

'I knew you weren't listening. Jesus, I've only been out of the hospital for a few days and you're already bored. People have killed themselves over less, you know.'

'I'm so sorry. I had a fight with a friend and it's all just chaos up here,' I say, gesturing to my head. I put my hand on his arm. 'I promise I'm listening now.'

After some side-eye, he relents. 'I was telling you that I've been speaking to my dad. He heard what happened. I was posting a story for some of my followers who were dead curious what the inside of a NHS hospital looked like, and one of my half-sisters saw it and told him.'

'That's great that you're talking. It's the least he can do.'

'Well, that's the other thing I wanted to tell you. He wants me to go stay with him for a while, in Dubai.'

It's then I notice the suitcases by the sofa. Three huge ones with extra duffel bags all emblazoned with the Chanel logo.

'How long are you going for?'

'TBD. A while though, I think. It's not like I have anything keeping me here.'

Fear jolts through me. Two friends gone in the space of a few hours.

'Are you sure about this? Your dad left you. You should be with people you trust right now, people who will look after you.'

'And who's going to do that here? You? And it's not like that, anyway. Apparently, Mum had warned him off, told him I didn't want anything to do with him. Can't understand why. It's not like she wanted to spend the time with me. Feels like I was some kind of asset she won in the divorce.'

'Are you coming back?'

'Of course. I'll visit,' he says, but his tone does not agree.

'I doubt it,' I say, shrugging as if I don't care. It makes sense that he would leave. It's not like our relationship ever made sense anyway. If a friendship of seventeen years can't last, what hope would ours have? I can already picture Othello in Dubai. Towering skyscrapers, luxury fashion, exotic animals and extravagant parties. I know when he gets there, he won't look back. 'You'll have plenty of drinking buddies in Dubai.'

'I will. And you can come out and see me. Apparently, there are vending machines that spit out bars of gold. We'll have fun. Please say you'll come? You're basically my only friend.'

Shit. He sounds so sad. I'm older; I should know better than to get abandonment issues triggered by an eighteen-year-old whose mum has just died. I can't pretend it doesn't hurt but of course he should go and be with the family he has left – and get as far away from the person who killed his mum as he can.

'Thought I was just the weird old lady shagging the guy upstairs? Won't I cramp your style?'

'No more than usual.'

*

Ruth's cut me out. Othello will be four thousand miles away by morning. By the time I'm heading back to Sam's apartment, I'm on the edge of tears. Then I stub my toe in the door, so of course I kick the door back to teach it a lesson, and now my entire foot hurts and I'm completely dissolving.

Sam waddles out of the bedroom, half asleep and dressed in his checked pyjama bottoms and a soft white T-shirt. He finds me on the floor cradling my injured extremity.

'What are you doing? It's late.'

'Oh, I'm sorry to be such an inconvenience to you.'

He sits cross-legged on the floor with me. 'Tell me what's wrong.'

I tell him about my lunch with Grandad, the incident with Ruth, and Othello leaving. 'I just feel like I'm messing everything up and losing everyone I care about.'

'Why do you let them have such a hold over you? Especially Ruth. She's just a person, you know, just as flawed as everyone else. Not some paragon of virtue that can dish out objective moral judgement.'

'When I was a kid, Grandad had this way of making me feel like I'd already done something wrong before I'd even done it. Every time I did slip up, I could see I'd just confirmed his low expectations. More disappointment. It's so tiring having someone you love think so little of you. Then I met Ruth, and she believed in me. Even when I really was being an arsehole, it didn't change how she thought of me as a person. She'd just tell me to stop being an arsehole. So for her to think I'm a bad person, it must be true.'

'Why do you care about being good or bad? It's all relative anyway.'

'That's not true. Some things are objectively bad.'

'Like what?'

'Torture.'

'What if torturing someone helped you get information that saved lives?'

'Murdering children.'

'What if they'd killed your child first?'

'War.'

'The Civil War ended slavery.'

'Can you stop?' I ask, almost shouting.

'I'm just trying to make the point that all morality is subjective. What's evil to one person is justified to another. All we can do is what we think is best in the systems we create for ourselves.'

'I can't think straight. You were right, what you said about me liking the way it feels when I take a life. Everything looks brighter, tastes sweeter, feels more intense. It's overwhelming sometimes. After what could have happened to Othello, I think I need a break, to give myself some time to separate my own thoughts from everyone else's.'

'Of course, whatever you think is best,' Sam says, nodding and stroking my arm. Then he stops and bites his lip.

'What is it?'

'Ahh, I had something I wanted to tell you, but now I'm not so sure. Maybe it's best we put all of this to bed for a while.'

'Tell me,' I say, knowing I will quite literally be unable to think of anything else until he does.

'I found one of the lawyers involved in your parents' case.'

My heart stops.

'I still don't have the name of who killed your parents. But it turns out that you were right – there was a suspect they investigated more seriously. I finally tracked down an officer who was willing to talk. Well, they were when I offered them enough money. They ran forensics on the car, they took statements, they checked alibis. But suddenly the investigation just stopped. No charge was made and the records that are supposed to be kept on the system are gone.'

I overlook that he bribed a police officer. Morality is subjective, after all.

'I don't understand.'

'Someone went to considerable effort to remove any possible connection between your parents and this suspect. Someone who could throw money at a problem and expect it to go away.'

'But if there was no evidence, maybe they were innocent?'

'Then I would be able to find a name, and the evidence would be accessible. Innocent people don't cover up crimes they didn't commit.'

I don't respond. All I can think about is finally seeing the face of the person who killed my family.

'You've no idea what you did for me when you killed Juliette. It was like I'd been carrying around this shard of metal all my life, and then you pulled it out. Ever since then I've felt clear, like I can move on unburdened by what happened. You set me free and I want to do the same for you. I just need more time.'

I imagine what it would be like to confront the person who killed my parents, to tell them I know what they did all those years ago. I want to see the look of panic on their face as they realize they haven't escaped justice. I've been lurking in the shadows all this time, waiting for them. I want it so fiercely it burns.

I reach forward and pull Sam into me. I have never needed anyone like this before. And, most importantly, he needs me too. There is a certainty in the way his fingers clasp the side of my neck that tells me he couldn't let go if he wanted to. And he's never afraid to look me deep in the eye, as if the act itself is not so important, but what matters is that we are together.

After the way Ruth severed our lifelong friendship with mere words, I gain comfort from Sam showing me how he feels. Actions are what matter. Bodies do not lie.

Chapter Twenty-Six

Nothing but good can come from saving someone.

My nightmares always start the same way: that sunny evening in the forest with a McDonald's picnic. Mum's soft voice and sweet perfume; Dad's booming laughter and the promise of excitement in the air.

I am eight years old, and all I want to do is stay in this moment. If I could make them wait ten minutes or take a different route home, then maybe we wouldn't crash. Maybe we would get home, maybe we would have pudding before bed, maybe they would read to me and maybe they would tuck me in. Maybe.

But the words have been said and our actions have been decided. There is nothing I can do but watch this scene unfold.

The headlights of another car approach us, blinding us. I remember how it burned my eyes and I looked down to avoid the intensity. Then the impact hits. My seat belt tightening like a punch to my chest. Glass shattering, wheels screaming.

Mum's head hits the dashboard. Dad's entire body lurches forward.

When I can breathe again, I call out their names. No response. Panic rises because I know the outcome and yet the eight-year-old doesn't and I want to save her from the images that will haunt the rest of her life. But I cannot stop her small hands unbuckling the seat belt on the third attempt, her feet crunching on the glass as she gets out of the car and calls out for help.

The other car has been scraped all down the side, red paint etched into blue. There is a figure standing a few feet away from it, tall and imposing. I don't remember if this was accurate or just in the way all adults are to eight-year-olds. The headlights blind me, and I can't see their face.

But lately, I get glimpses of it. It's almost like looking directly at the sun. For just a second, I can grasp it before having to look away.

A large nose. Blood streaked through golden hair. The glint of a silver watch as they hold up their arm to shield their eyes from the light.

'Stop!' I scream.

They get inside the car, slam the door and drive away.

I wake up. My heart is pounding and sweat soaks my forehead, hands and the backs of my legs.

I go to the bathroom, wash my face and wait for my body to stop shaking. Sam's right. All of this will make sense once we find the person who left me alone on that road. Everything else has been a distraction, practice for when the time comes. I just need to keep going until then.

I busy myself with the legal clinic. It's not hard to do. There's a weird effect I've noticed where doing work creates more of it. When I was an inefficient HR assistant, no one asked me to do anything because they knew it wasn't worth the hassle. But now people actually want my help.

Sam hired a bunch of recent law graduates to help me keep up with demand. One of them, Syed, has interrupted me three times this morning with queries. The most recent being how to establish which council to submit a homelessness application to if the client isn't sure which he belongs to.

'Section five point eight of the guide, Syed. There's a list of what qualifies for local connection; if there's more than one, ask the client where they'd prefer to live.'

'Oh, yes, the guide, sorry.'

'That's okay,' I say through gritted teeth. Everything's in the guide, every time.

He scampers away as Oliver turns the corner with a bemused smile. 'It's all a bit new to him, isn't it?'

I nod, exhausted after my long shift.

'But it's all worth it. That's what I wanted to talk to you about, actually. Our new proposal has been accepted. We'll be turning the empty tower block, Vale House, into forty-eight long-term homes. The building needs some work, but we should be ready for new residents in about eight weeks. And while all applications need to go through the council, I think it's fair to say we'll have priority.'

'That's amazing!'

'I'm so grateful to you and Sam. I know he had a big hand in securing us that additional funding.'

And maybe I misread it, but I think he's going in for a hug, which I fully embrace. He looks a little startled, but I don't care. All I can think about is the number of people who are going to have homes. I can't believe I ever doubted Oliver. It's good though. Now he's my touchstone. When I'm feeling unsure about whether I'm doing the right thing, I can remind myself I once doubted him too. But I know deep in my core he was worth saving. I just wish Ruth could see that.

'I just wish we could do more,' he adds.

'More? This was a big win!'

'I know, but there are so many people who fall through the cracks.'

'Rob told me how you found a way to help him. And you found a way to help my friend Karly. She must have moved in by now. I should go check in on her.'

'Yes, well, the rules aren't always right. And usually not for everyone.' Then he adds, 'I didn't realize you were friends.'

'Well, no. An acquaintance. I'd met her once before, but sometimes you just get a gut feeling about people.'

'Be a bit careful about visiting her. It's important to keep professional boundaries in place.'

Maybe I shouldn't have hugged him. 'Yeah, you're right. I have a lot to do anyway.'

The awkward pause is disrupted by a knock at the door. To my surprise, it's Ruth.

'Ruth, my star doctor. I was just thanking Thea for what an incredible job she's been doing here, but it's you I really have to thank. First you save my life, then you lend me your medical expertise and bring me a lawyer. What will you do for me next?'

She blushes. 'Just doing my job.'

Oliver prances out of the room as quickly as he came in. If I'd left his life in her hands, he'd be dead right now. But I refrain from making this comment. I don't want to hurt Ruth more than I already have.

'I didn't think you were on shift today?' I ask.

She's carrying a wad of files, clutching them close to her chest and barely making eye contact. 'I wasn't, but then I thought I'd try and catch you.'

I cannot keep the hurt out of my voice. 'I thought you wanted to cut me out completely.'

'I know, but I was drunk. Maybe I was being hasty. I think it might help me to know the full story, every detail, so I have all the information. I want to know who you killed and when, where and how you killed them.'

It's then I realize something is not right. Her lips are tight, her eyes are darting around the room and she's shuffling her feet. I'm having serious déjà vu.

'Do you remember that game we used to play when we were kids, the one where we ran a triage clinic with your stuffed toys? And one day we found that bear in the cupboard, manky old thing. And I decided to cut it open for emergency surgery. Only it wasn't a manky old bear but a limited edition Steiff teddy bear.'

She smiles. 'It was worth thousands. I don't think Mum ever forgave you.'

'And we made a pact, promised to say the dog got it. You got about three words into the lie before spilling your guts.'

'I don't get why this is relevant.'

'Well, you have the exact same expression on your face right now. You've always been a terrible liar.'

I step forward and pull down the files. Sure enough, her phone is concealed behind them, recording our conversation. I tap the red button to end it.

She resolves her face into stone. 'You don't get to kill people and get away with it. I don't know what else you expected of me.'

I shrug. 'Me neither. I guess things are pretty clear now, though.'

I spend the next few days stewing. I would do anything for Ruth. Shit, I have done anything for her. People think the measure of love is whether you'd die for someone. It's not. It's only when you're willing to kill for them – again and again and again – that's when you know it's real. And she still can't see past her primary school code of ethics. Right is right and wrong is wrong. I'm tired of Ruth walking around with her moral superiority intact, all because I've done the dirty work for her.

It doesn't matter what I say to her. All logic and argument about how this is for the greater good will fall on deaf ears. You simply can't convince someone of something they don't want to hear. I have to show her instead.

So, I head to the hospital on a sunny Thursday afternoon. I make a fake ID card that looks like the one I've seen Ruth wear on a lanyard and order a set of scrubs identical to hers – you can get anything online these days. I change into them in the toilet. As I come out, a woman nearly opens a door into my face. She doesn't even apologize. *Twenty-nine years*. I notice this as she brushes my arm in her hurry to get past me. I'm desperately craving to feel good again. It's been weeks since I've taken a life and I'm still feeling the effects. Maybe this is just what life is now. Grey. Monotone. Empty. Sometimes I feel like there's a realer, rawer version of me trapped inside and I'd like it to crawl up and burst out of my flesh just to feel alive for a second.

But I let her pass without taking so much as a day. I made a promise to myself not to use my power until I have the clarity I need. I'm not going to break because I need a sugar rush.

I do let the elevator door close on her though. I even smile a little as she runs for it, shouting at me to hold it open.

I wait until someone's holding the ICU door open and slip inside without challenge. The power of a lanyard and a uniform is truly transformative. I quickly scope out the patients. The next person to die is a man in the bed by the window. I'd guess he's in his late fifties, with a greying beard and full belly.

And he's perfect for what I'm about to do. I spot Ruth standing over someone's bedside.

'You're not supposed to be in here,' she says.

'Well, I'm not supposed to do a lot of things. What's wrong with her?' I ask, pointing to the girl in the bed. She has a soft face that makes her look about twelve years old. Although if it's who I think it is, she's actually sixteen. And I already know what's wrong.

'Leukaemia. She had it when she was a child. Now it's back. It's been touch and go but she's finally responding to treatment so we're hopeful.'

'You shouldn't be. She's supposed to die today.'

'What? How?'

'I don't know how, only when. Don't worry, though, I've sorted it.'

'I don't want your help.'

I point to the man in the bed by the window, who is quietly wheezing. 'He was supposed to leave the ICU and live another thirty-nine years. Sienna here was supposed to die at three twenty-eight this afternoon. I remember you telling me about Sienna, how bright and brave she was through all of her treatment, and how sad you were when her symptoms came back. I think she deserves those years more than he does.'

'No one is more deserving of life, Thea.'

'If that's true, then tell me to switch them back. Let fate take its natural course and let Sienna die right here and now. You decide who gets to live and die today.'

Ruth clutches the edge of the bed as she watches Sienna, quietly breathing through a tube. She goes to say something but stops and looks to the man by the window, then once again back to Sienna.

'Why are you doing this?'

'Because I want you to know it's not so fucking easy as keeping your hands clean, Ruth. I didn't ask for this power, but I have it, and I can't just ignore it. Every time I choose not to kill one person, I'm choosing to let another die. Now it's your turn.'

'I can't.'

'That's okay, I know how hard this is. Just remember that no decision is still a decision. I'm going to grab a blueberry muffin from the cafe – give me a call if you want me to come back up.'

She doesn't call. Sienna leaves with thirty-nine years to live, and the nameless man dies at 3.28 p.m. As they were always supposed to, because I never switched them. I just wanted Ruth to think I did.

Talking of good things, Karly moved into her new accommodation today. It's in West Croydon, which is only a short train ride away so when I finish supervising the clinic, I decide to pay her a visit.

The building is nothing to rave about. A grey tower block that looks like it was put up in a hurry, but the area's not too bad. There's a set of monkey bars and a swing, some overcrowded parking and a few trees. It feels safe here in the daytime. It probably wouldn't at night but, hey, what do you expect with London property prices? Above all, Karly's got it for a token rent. She and Leo can get back on their feet in relative comfort while not worrying about social services.

The door buzzer is broken so I let myself in. Karly lives on the eighth floor, but the lift looks a bit ... rusty. I'm sure it's fine, but I could use the exercise anyway, so I take the stairs.

There's no answer when I knock on the door. I double check the address – number fifteen, eighth floor – and knock again. Maybe I should have called first, but I didn't know what time I'd be finished at the clinic, and I just assumed she'd be at home seeing as it's move-in-day. I call out her name, knock again, then once more. I'm about to turn around when I hear a crash.

'Karly, are you okay?' I say, trying to yell through the door.

'Yeah, just a second.'

She opens the door, then scuttles back to the broken mug on the floor, scooping it into a dustpan. The flat looks good. It's a bit stuffy, but what do you expect from a high-rise in summer? The kitchen and living area are all one room, with a bedroom to the side and a small balcony with some plants. There are not many personal items, but a stack of empty boxes next to the door suggests she's finished unpacking. Karly seems agitated. She's fretting that she might have missed a shard of china and telling me not to step anywhere. For a moment I have a horrible feeling that I've misjudged the situation again, like I did with Othello, and learning about her mum's death has had some psychological fallout I didn't anticipate. No, Othello and Karly are not the same. She's probably stressed from the move, and because she's got a kid to think about.

Leo's lying on a blanket in a playpen. I leap over the area Karly is still fussing over and into the living room where Leo is, pick him up and start rattling his favourite giraffe to keep him busy. Then I sneak a sniff of his soft baby head. There's nothing like it to brighten my day.

'How are you settling in?' I ask.

'It's fine. More than fine. It's great.'

'Leo seems to be happy here,' I say. He's currently staring out the balcony window, seemingly calmed by the view.

'Yeah, we need this,' she says, but even though I'm hardly looking in her direction, she's nodding furiously and clutching the kitchen counter. I get the sense she's trying to convince herself more than me.

I put Leo back into his playpen. He tries to keep hold of me, gripping as tightly as he can, and I have to be careful, gently prising his tiny fingers off my arm.

'Are you okay?' I ask.

'Of course. Fancy a cuppa?' she says, smiling widely. It's the type of smile where all your muscles are straining to keep it in place, and when she turns around to flick on the kettle, I can tell the smile has dropped by the way her shoulders relax.

I notice there's a lone mug of half-finished tea on the kitchen table. There's also tea on the floor from the one she dropped. My own post-baby-sniff smile drops. Karly doesn't have any friends she would invite over for tea. I step closer to her and place a hand on her arm. It's meant to be a reassuring gesture, to tell her I am here for her, but she flinches.

'Sorry, you made me jump,' she says.

She pushes back the hair that has fallen from her ponytail, and I notice two small purpling bruises on her arm. She turns away and pulls down her sleeve.

'Karly, who did that to you?'

'It's nothing,' she says.

I look her straight in the eye. 'Tell me now.'

'I was playing with Leo.'

'No baby leaves marks like that. Stop messing me around. Did you start seeing someone?' I ask, because I know how terrible her taste in men is.

'No,' she says with a conviction that makes me believe her.

Her eyes dart towards a pair of glasses on the counter. I don't clock them at first, but when she finishes making the tea and tries to lead me into the living room, I realize the significance of them. Karly doesn't wear glasses. I take a closer look at them – tortoiseshell frames and circle lenses. I would recognize those glasses anywhere.

Chapter Twenty-Seven

*Not everyone who makes the list presents an
ethical dilemma. Sometimes simple is best.*

I'm going to kill Oliver.

It's a scorching hot day and I'm boiling inside and out. It's
rare that I feel this level of violence towards someone. But I
wish he was a cockroach so I could pull off his legs one by
one and watch him flail from side to side as he realizes what's
being done to him. Then I would explain my reasoning to him,
slowly, so he knew that he only had himself to blame for his
predicament. Then I'd leave him there. Wait for some passer-by
to crush him like the bug he is.

He paid Karly a surprise visit, told her he wanted to check
how she was settling in. So, she opened the door, told him
to make himself comfortable and made him a cup of tea.
She turned round to look for biscuits and found him right
behind her. He told her about how many people were on the
waiting list for temporary housing, and how lucky she was
to get it. There were literally hundreds of young women like
her, and wouldn't it be awful if she lost it, just as she'd got

social services off her back? A mother should do anything for her child. Other women certainly did, and they were grateful for it.

Karly said she tried to step away, tried to explain that she was very grateful but actually she had to run some errands so perhaps they should wrap this up. He grabbed her wrist and told her this was simply the way it worked. She tried to free her wrist, pushed him back with her other hand, but he only tightened his grip. Other than punching him or screaming, she didn't know how to escape the situation. Not in a way that wouldn't get her kicked out. Not in a way that wouldn't jeopardize custody of her son. So, she did what was asked, the only route available to her at the time.

Karly is confused. She's more focused on returning his glasses than anything else — apparently, he got a call from his wife and forgot them in his hurry to leave. When I try to talk to her about what happened, she keeps saying it wasn't that bad and makes me promise not to say anything. She won't even hear the R-word, even though she told him to stop, asked him to leave and pushed him away. Oliver knows exactly what he did.

I cannot sit on the train; I hold onto the railing, clenching it tight and tapping my foot to keep me sane. I can't believe how stupid I was to trust him. Throughout all of this, he's been my one reliable sign that everything I've done has been worth it. Because Oliver is supposed to be good. He's supposed to help people and be a force for social good. But no, behind the innocent smile and wise eyes he's just another rapey bastard. Not for long, though.

I go home first because I want to share this betrayal with Sam. He's still at the office so I pace across our Mayfair apartment's marble-floored kitchen with my arms crossed. Then I get bored, so I turn on the TV, stress-eat pistachios and throw the shells onto the floor. Then I imagine Grandad's face if he saw them scattered like that and pick them all up.

I accost Sam the moment he comes through the door. He doesn't have a chance to put down his bag or take off his shoes before I've finished recounting what Karly told me.

'This is a lot to take in,' he says, then grabs my shoulders and gently but firmly moves me aside. 'Give me a minute.'

I follow him into the kitchen, exercising great patience by staying silent while he drinks from the tap and undoes his collar. He drinks the water like a sloth. Long gulp after gulp after gulp until finally I can't handle it. 'He'll be at the shelter in thirty minutes. I'm going to deal with him.'

Sam raises an eyebrow. 'And by deal with him you mean . . .'

'You know exactly what I mean. I'm going to put an end to this,' I say.

'Whoa, wait a minute. Don't you think that's rash?'

I'm struggling to understand Sam's problem. Together, we have ended plenty of lives, so if he's having a crisis of conscience, it's a bit bloody late.

'I gave him his life, which means it's mine to take.'

'Thea, we've put so much work into setting this up. Oliver is doing good in the world, and everything is finally falling into place. Let's take a minute before we kill London's leading philanthropist – a man who, let's not forget, has a wife and two kids.'

'Why are you defending the person who raped Karly?'

'Thea, I'm not defending him. I just want to make sure we have the whole story before we jump straight to murder. You're forgetting that I know Karly much better than you do. Trust me, she's not just some victim. She's made false accusations before. I've always fought for her because I owed her, and it's not her fault what happened to her as a child. But that doesn't mean we throw away everything we've worked for on her say-so.'

Suddenly, I don't recognize Sam. Whatever my doubts about our relationship, I have always been certain that he was the one person that was unequivocally on my side. There is supposed to be something that runs deeper between us. Something real and binding between our souls. People like Ruth don't understand my actions because she doesn't see the world for what it truly is, but Sam does – did – see the world through my eyes. Until now. A feeling akin to grief washes over me, because I loved the person I thought Sam was, and there's no way I can restore that version of him.

I storm into our bedroom, collect my toothbrush and the scattering of other belongings.

'Thea, what are you doing? Calm down.'

'Don't tell me to calm down. I have to get out of here.'

'Let's talk about this.'

'She didn't twist her own wrist until it was black and blue, Sam. But you've made it clear you don't believe her, and you don't believe me, either.'

'I didn't say I didn't believe her. I'm just suggesting that there's another possibility here and we need to gather all the relevant information. Stop being so impulsive. You can't go off dealing with matters of life and death without thinking things through. It's stupid.'

'There we go, I'm stupid. You really would prefer it if I blindly did everything you said, wouldn't you?'

It slips out, but the more I think about it, the more I realize it's true. Sam always leaves it to the last minute to show me the proof of our target's guilt, and he doesn't listen when I question certain aspects of it. Usually, I enjoy our fights (and sometimes

I provoke them because they often end in spectacular sex) but I have no interest in this one. All I want is not to be here, occupying the same physical space as him.

'I know you killed Karly's mum,' he says.

'What's that got to do with anything?'

'Because I know your heart is in the right place, but sometimes you don't think things through. Did you know there was CCTV on that street, which clearly shows you at her shop the day before she died under suspicious circumstances?'

Karly's mum was found dead in her bakery kitchen, blunt force trauma to the head. Her husband is the prime suspect. 'So? I wasn't there on the day of the murder. It's not a crime to collect baked goods.'

'No, but you were arrested for murdering the ex-boyfriend of her daughter. It's suspicious. All you need is for Officer Stewart to pick up the trail again. A few sloppy mistakes like that and I won't be able to protect you.' He steps forward and tries to take my hand, which I snatch away. 'But I took care of it. I had the CCTV footage erased because I'm on *your* side. Take a minute to think of all the people who rely on the shelter, who will be helped by that money. If you go down there and take out Oliver right now, the money will be under the board's control and I've no idea how it will be used. We have a plan, Thea, and we need to stick to it.'

Logically, I know he's right. I can't mess up our entire plan over one person. But I really want to. 'So, she's just collateral damage?'

'We'll get Karly the help she needs. I promise. I'm not even saying don't kill him. I'm just asking you not to kill him today, so that I can put things in place and we can get this right. Can you do that?'

The genuine question in his voice goads me into agreeing. As if I'm not capable of controlling myself. 'Fine, I'll wait a couple of days, but no more.'

I'm going to show Sam just how wrong he was to doubt Karly, even for a moment. And I'll do it in his language – with hard evidence. It occurs to me that in the long list of people who voiced their support for Oliver, none of them were women. This is the fuel behind my growing fear that this isn't Oliver's first offence – nice people don't just wake up one day and do things like this. So, I decide to look back through the shelter's records for people who were placed in homes through the system. There's a lot to go through, so I restrict my search to young women who weren't eligible for accommodation for whatever reason, assuming that Oliver likes potential victims who are easier to exploit.

I come up with a list of ten names. The first two don't answer. The third and fourth have nothing but good things to say about Oliver. They tell me that he changed their lives, gave them the chance they needed to lift themselves out of poverty. I'm not deterred. Just because Oliver hasn't raped every woman in his care doesn't mean I'm wrong about him. The fifth woman won't let me speak long enough to explain my purpose. She repeatedly says she's not buying whatever I'm selling and hangs up.

I'm praying to a God I don't believe in for some luck with number six. She didn't admit to anything on the phone, but when I mentioned Oliver's name, she caught her breath. I've decided she might be more willing to talk in person.

Her home is modest but comfortable. Semi-detached with parking for two cars (if one blocks the other in) and a patch of grass for a side garden. I open the porch, clocking the two pairs of children's boots before I ring the doorbell. Iveska opens the door. Her hair is tied up in a messy bun that sits on her neck and flour is dusted across her black T-shirt. There's something about the wide-eyed innocence on her face that reminds me of Karly, and I'm both hoping and dreading that this will be the one.

'Can I help you?' she asks, her voice gentle and enquiring.

'Hi, yes, I hope so. I'm Thea Greaves. I work for the crisis support shelter that I believe you used a few years ago.'

She steps forward and looks side to side at her neighbour's houses. Her shoulders drop when she realizes nobody is outside. 'I don't want to talk about that. I have a new life now.'

'I provide the shelter with legal advice. Please, I just have a couple of questions,' I say, passing her my business card. There's nothing like a business card to instil a fake sense of authority in people.

The turn of the neighbour's key in the door makes her dip her head out the door again. 'Come inside, then.'

She ushers me into the kitchen. There are twelve cupcake holders filled with batter, the rest waiting in a tub. On the counter there is butter, flour and eggshells. She does not apologize for the mess.

'I haven't done anything wrong,' she says, struggling to look me in the eye. 'I've been minding my own business and getting on with things, like we agreed.'

'Iveska, I think you've misunderstood. I offer legal advice for the people who come to the shelter, not for the shelter. I don't work for Oliver.'

'Oh, then what do you want?' She crosses her arms and manages to look in the general direction of my face, if not my eyes.

I try to keep my voice as soft as possible. 'This is awkward, but I noticed you weren't eligible for temporary accommodation when Oliver offered it to you. I wanted to ask whether he ever asked for anything in return?'

'No idea what you are talking about.' She snorts incredulously, three times as if she's playing for time, trying to block out my questions with the noise.

'I'll never mention your name. I just need to know if it happened.'

She scoffs, a bitter noise in her throat she's been holding onto for years. 'Of course it happened. Everyone knows it happened.'

'I'm sorry that it did. What if I told you that it's still happening – would you help me then?'

She eyes me like a nervous animal, caught between fight and flight. Then she gives in. Her shoulders slump and she uncrosses her arms. 'Tell me what you need.'

Ruth is calling me. Odd. We haven't spoken since the hospital; perhaps she wants me to pick up the rest of my stuff from her apartment. I'm both not ready for that and genuinely too busy to worry about packing boxes. I swipe the red to reject her call.

I'm in my new office, conducting research. Iveska gave me the names of two other women who were assaulted by Oliver, which is a great starting point. I've just finished assembling my new ergonomic desk chair, organizing my collection of succulents (fake, because after Diego I don't want the responsibility of a living thing) and smoothing open a gorgeous brand-new purple leather notebook with gold-edged pages. My three hungry young interns are hard at work on their assignments; I've asked them to investigate any charges raised against Oliver, even the ones that might have been scrubbed from the record, so I can compile a list of people involved. They are incredibly proactive, all of them scouring the internet and making phone calls non-stop since I asked them to. I don't even think they've peed yet this morning.

Sam comes to visit me at lunch. I only allow him to stay because he brings me hot lobster mac and cheese and I'm starving. I reject Ruth's second call, and her third, but it's more difficult to ignore her face staring through the glass walls of my office. She's dressed in creased scrubs and most of her hair has fallen down from her ponytail. She pulls open the door and marches up to my desk.

'Why aren't you answering my calls?'

'And make it easier for you to incriminate her?' Sam answers for me.

'She's not your client. Can you get out, please?'

'No, I don't think I will.'

Ruth bites her lip like she wants to chomp straight through it. 'Oh my God, how did I not realize? You've known all along, haven't you? It all makes sense. If your "connection" was really so strong, then you would have reached out years ago. You didn't. Thea, he only wants you because he can use you.'

'She's capable of making her own decisions.'

'But not of speaking for herself, apparently?'

'Ruth, why are you here?' I ask, quietly and calmly.

'Phone,' Sam says.

She throws her phone onto the desk and pats herself down. 'Happy? Why are you looking into Oliver's past clients?'

'How do you know that?'

'Oliver told me. He asked me if I knew what was going on.'

'How does he know that?' I ask, my heart beating faster. My investigation is less than a month old and already my target knows I'm on to him.

'How should I know? All he said was you've been turning up uninvited at the houses of some extremely vulnerable past clients of his, interrogating them. So, you tell me what you're up to.'

Well, that explains it. I bet it was the third woman I interviewed – Evangeline. That well-dressed, snot-nosed snitch.

'You need to stay away from him, Ruth. Oliver is not who
he says he is. He attacked a client of mine, Karly, said he'd
chuck her out of the flat if she resisted. He's been doing the
same thing for years. That's why I've been contacting those
women – they're all his victims.'

Ruth's rosy cheeks go white, like all the colour has been
sucked out with a sponge. 'That's bullshit. It doesn't make any
sense. Oliver knows exactly what it's like to be exploited, to
be in impossible situations, so he wouldn't do that to someone
else.'

Sam's unusually quiet, like he's figuring out how to best
play this. He wants the same as Ruth, for me not to kill Oliver.
But I think he's enjoying us fighting too much to try using her
argument to his advantage. I think he's trying to hide a smile.

God, first him, now Ruth. I cannot believe Oliver has got
to her. Smart of him though. When you get accused of being a
rapey-bastard, helpful to have a smart, credible woman ready
to vouch for you. I wonder who else he's got in his corner.

I throw my hands up in the air. 'Why is everyone so quick to
defend that psychopath? Karly told me this herself. You need
to believe her.'

Ruth stands up. 'It's you I don't believe, Thea. You rush into
things, make these judgements before you get the complete
story.'

'I've literally spent weeks investigating this so I get the whole
story. I'm not going to keep making the same mistakes. I'm
going to make damn sure people are who they say before I act.'

'Act?' Ruth's eyes go wide. I hate it when she does that,
makes me feel like she's seeing me in my entirety. 'You're going
to use your power on Oliver, aren't you?'

'He has to be punished.'

'If Oliver dies, I will know it was you who did it. And I will never forgive you.'

I don't say anything in response, and she leaves. A threat from Ruth would have once rendered me useless, but now there's no force on earth that can stop me dealing with Oliver as I see fit.

Sam leaves shortly afterwards, kissing me goodbye with far too much enthusiasm. A few minutes later, intern number one knocks on the door (I've decided not to learn their names until they've earned it).

'Excuse me, I've found a few things you might find interesting,' she says.

I beckon her in, and she places a folder on my desk. She's compiled the list for me. Inside are the details of six women who went to the police to report Oliver, but all of their accusations were quashed before any charges were made. There are other names that keep cropping up too: the same police officer handling the cases, and several of Oliver's protégés come up as alibis and character references. There's one case that actually went to court, which ruled in Oliver's favour, of course. A drug addict with a history of mental-health issues was never going to stand a chance against Oliver. Individually, none of these women do. But if my intern can find this much dirt in a matter of hours, then I can only imagine what we'll eventually uncover. Buckets of it. Wheelbarrows full.

'Have you contacted any of the women?' I ask.

'Not yet. I wasn't sure if you wanted to make the calls, as it's your case?'

My case.

'No, that's okay. You get started, set up some meetings as soon as possible,' I say. She obediently gets to her feet and walks to the door. Before she goes, I add, 'Oh, and good work, Cecelia.'

Ruth can rest easy. I'm not going to kill Oliver – not when I have a genuine legal case against him. This is the career-making case of a lifetime, and it's fallen right into my lap. I can picture Oliver's face splashed across the newspapers. Me, standing behind Karly as she tells the truth to the world. Yes, Oliver stays alive. Let him feel the heat of an angry public. By the end of it, he'll wish I'd killed him.

I'm outside Karly's flat, ready to tell her the good news. I can hardly keep my smile to myself, but I do try when she opens the door because she looks terrible. Bags under her eyes and a whitehead on her chin that I'm desperate to burst. She lets me in.

'Sorry about the mess,' she says.

'No worries. I've got important things to tell you. I've looked into it, and Oliver's done the same thing to countless other women. I've started building a case and I think we have a good shot of winning.' I pull out Cecelia's folder and push it towards Karly.

'I didn't ask you to do any of this,' Karly says, leafing through the documents.

'Don't worry about any of the details. I'll take care of everything, but historic assault cases are much harder to prove. Given that something happened to you so recently, you're the most important victim.'

I don't understand the look on her face. Her eyes have narrowed and her face is darkening with red. 'I don't want anything to do with this.'

'But this is important. It's about a systemic abuse of power, about male violence against women.'

She closes the folder and shoves it across the counter. 'I'm not going through this again. I know exactly how the courts will treat me, and how they will use my history against me. They'll pit me against Oliver, then ask twelve strangers who they believe. They didn't believe me before and they won't this time. I want no part in it.'

'Karly, six other women were assaulted!'

'Please stop sounding so excited about it.'

I remember how afraid Iveska was to speak to me. And the bribe that Cecelia uncovered.

'Tell me the truth. Has he threatened you, or offered you something?'

'Why is it so hard for you to understand? This is my best shot at a better life. I'm not about to throw that away to be part of your pet legal project.'

We continue arguing like this for the next thirty minutes. I try to make her see the bigger picture, but she doesn't care. She's too afraid of Oliver, of courtrooms and the judgement of strangers. And too afraid of losing what little she has because of Leo. I try to offer her money, support, but she refuses again and again. I don't understand her. Why do people make it so difficult for me to help them?

I'm beginning to feel like we're stuck in a *Groundhog Day* loop, and that we will keep repeating the same points until one of us dies. Then Karly snaps.

'Will you just fuck off and leave me alone? I never asked for your help. Why are you so obsessed with meddling in my life?'

'Because what happened to you isn't fair,' I say softly.

Her expression hardens, her mouth pursed tightly. 'Get out.'

There's no further discussion to be had. I leave, defeated. Sure, we can still try to build a legal case against Oliver, but it will fall apart without Karly. He'll intimidate the witnesses, bribe the authorities and win over the public with that arrogant smile. People like him think the rules do not apply to them. They are wrong, but I'm still not going to simply kill him. I have a much better idea.

Chapter Twenty-Eight

Bad things happen when good people do nothing. Enablers are just as guilty, just as deserving of punishment.

I need to talk to Rob away from the clinic so I catch him on his walk home. I ask him for a quick chat, say it's important and offer to buy him a coffee, and that's all it takes for him to come along. Silly Rob.

I order an avocado latte for me and an Americano with milk for him. He asked for 'just normal coffee' so I had to improvise. I hate it when people say that – we've had fancy coffee shops for years now, so if you're under eighty there's no excuse for not knowing the basic menu rundown.

'So, Rob, as you know, I'm part of Oliver's legal team,' I say, waiting for his response. He nods as if this is common knowledge. 'I need to confirm some old statements, where you were Oliver's alibi – is that okay?'

'Fine,' he says. He doesn't sound vaguely interested in why I might want to know this.

'March twenty-fourth, 2017. Oliver says that you were both

working at the shelter. Mark and Tess were also present that evening. Is that correct?'

Most people would need a minute to recall their where-abouts on a random day years ago. Not Rob. He drinks a big gulp of his coffee and replies, 'Yes, that's right.'

That's his first mistake. Mark wasn't present that evening. Rob doesn't remember who was there because the event didn't take place. More importantly, in a single question he's already shown me his willingness to blindly lie for Oliver. I want to be sure before I take action. No more mistakes.

I carry on questioning him on different dates. He agrees to everything without a second thought. Then, the most impor-tant part of my faux interview. 'There's been a new accusation against Oliver. It's from Karly Maxwell. Oliver says that he was with you all evening, that you stayed in, watched a film and ate pizza. Is that correct?'

'Absolutely,' he says without hesitation.

'This is a rape allegation, so it's very important that you're sure about this,' I say, trying to give him one last chance.

Rob presents as a nice guy. He's got a friendly face, smiles whenever a person with a dog walks past the coffee shop window and refuses to put down his coffee stirrer because he doesn't want to mark the table. Yet he's willing to protect his friend no matter what the crime. Nice guys like Rob let bad things happen to people like Karly, and they too deserve to die.

'Well, you know what women like that are like. They make this shit up. Looking for some payout or something.'

I don't know whether he's trying to convince me or himself, but I'm not deterred because nobody provides multiple fake alibis without knowing something bad is happening. Rob's signed his own confession.

This coffee shop has no cameras, so it doesn't matter that

I'm the last person who will see Rob alive. There will be no evidence of it. Rob has a watch on, so I pretend to look at it for the time and turn it towards me. I simultaneously take his remaining twenty-eight years. Sam's insistence on repeatedly testing my abilities has improved my control, and I leave Rob with exactly fifteen minutes to live. Enough time for me to get far away from him, but hopefully not enough time for him to call Oliver. Just to make sure, I slide his phone under a napkin and leave it behind the bin. It's not difficult to do. People always seem to be a bit dazed after I've siphoned their life away.

There's something else I want from him. A pin on his bag. Oliver gave it to him to mark his first year off the street, and Rob has had it on his bag ever since. I get up and say I must head off and make no motion to clear up our disposable coffee cups, but Rob does. Such a gentleman. He clears the lot and tips it into the bin, leaving his bag unattended on the floor for me to swipe the pin.

Outside, I clean the pin down for prints, enclose it in an envelope with Oliver's address and drop it into the postbox. Rob's still in the coffee shop looking for his phone. I walk down the road and hop onto the 29b bus – I pre-planned my route. As the bus drives past the coffee shop, I notice Rob walking outside. I see him clutching his throat, struggling to breathe, but there's no one around to help him. I later find out that he choked on a hazelnut.

Oliver's losing it. He's hired a bodyguard. Well, he says the six-foot tank of a man who's now following his every move is a personal assistant, but the timing's odd. The PA wears chinos and a shirt and wool jumper combo. I've never seen someone look so uncomfortable in their own skin.

Oliver used to spend his time helping out in the kitchen and chatting to people to find out how things are going. I used to think that was admirable, that he really cared. Now I realize he just likes the feeling of being in charge. I think that's why he's been doing these awful things. It's not about sex – he's got a smoking-hot wife and is good-looking enough himself to have extra-marital things on the go – it's about power. Always is with these fuckers. They love the fact that people can't say no to them.

I wonder what he felt when he opened the envelope with Rob's pin inside. Before then, he'd presumably thought Rob's death was an unfortunate accident. Sad, but no one to blame but Rob's own lazy chewing. But there's no explanation for why Rob would have sent him the pin – something so important to him he never takes it off – moments before his death.

I bump off Oliver's lawyer next, Kamryn Bond. Nothing worse than someone who wields the law against those who need its protection the most. A blood clot, followed up with a single business card posted to Oliver's address. If he'd had any doubt about foul play in Rob's death, I'm sure this erased it. That's when the bodyguard showed up, anyway.

I'm currently holding Rob and the lawyer's remaining life – fifty-four years between them. With that much excess energy, I'm processing cases this morning faster than the queue is forming, an unheard-of occurrence at the clinic. Undoubtedly, the most common legal advice we provide is help with emergency accommodation. Without a fixed postcode, homeless people can't apply for jobs. Without a job, they have very little chance of getting off the streets. We try to do this through official channels, but Oliver has access to his own accommodation, for the ones who get their applications for government support rejected or for those who cannot access it for whatever reason – like Karly. The recent increase in Oliver's resources means I'm able to deliver plenty of good news this morning.

The only thing that gets me to pause is Oliver's head poking around the door to my tiny, dank meeting room. Until now, I've been managing to avoid him. Now he's blocking the doorway and I can hear my own pulse beating in my ears. It's as clear as a ticking clock. Beat, beat, beat. Each one seems to slow down time, letting me properly see Oliver for what feels like the first time. One of his front teeth is chipped. I hadn't noticed it before, but from a certain angle it makes the welcoming smile I was so fond of quite menacing.

'You've been busy, apparently,' he says, a pleasantness on his face but a nastiness lurking in his voice.

Is that an accusation? No, he's messing with me, trying to put me on edge. But I've dealt with worse than him.

'Yes, lots of people need my help.'

He looks me straight in the eye. I can sense his mind trying to work me out. *Why is she asking questions? How much does she know? What is she capable of?* 'Well, I just wanted to say how much I appreciate it. Must be difficult to fit in alongside your other work – where is it that you're working?'

Now I'm the one wondering what he knows. I don't think Sam's properly filed the paperwork yet for Ellis and Greaves, so there's no public link between us. I'd prefer to keep it that way – in Oliver's eyes, at least.

'It's easy to find the time when the work is so meaningful. You must be so proud of what you've created here,' I say with a chirpy smile.

'I am. The people who run this place mean everything to me.'

There's a crash from the corridor and Oliver jumps like he's been hit. I can see his chest rising in short, heavy breaths. The 'personal assistant' is standing guard outside my office.

'Just some boxes,' the personal assistant calls out.

'Bit of a nervous nellie,' I say teasingly.

Oliver laughs and visibly relaxes. 'I better get going. Good work today.'

'Thanks,' I say. 'Oh, and sorry to hear about Rob. I know you were good friends.'

It was cruel to add, but I can't help the twisted joy I feel at seeing the visible lump in Oliver's throat. He deserves it. What does it matter if I revel in my punishment's success a little?

I keep hold of the fifty-four years for several days. I've decided there's no need to rush any of this – I can enjoy it a little. No word from Ruth, so I assume she's not suspicious of Rob's and the lawyer's deaths. I would be surprised if she's even heard about the latter, and there's still no reason to connect it to me. Sam's being extremely attentive, trying to keep me placated with over-the-top dinners, gifts and a steady supply of champagne. I'm not complaining. And my running is the best it's ever been. I'm now managing ten kilometres in forty minutes, easily. All thanks to the excess life I'm carrying and my new trainers. They are glorious. Sweat-wicking and blister-proof, with memory foam soles that are like running on clouds. It's been a good few days.

I'm still wearing the trainers when I walk into the office that morning. Cecelia comments on my latest run – we're friends on Strava – and I reward her by getting her name right. She's my favourite intern; the others hate her.

Once I'm settled in my office, Cecelia knocks on the door, only entering after I wave her in.

'I heard back from my contact. That police officer, Mark Thompson, is definitely involved with getting the charges against Oliver dropped. He convinced junior officers to pass the case over to him, and there are multiple counts of missing interview evidence that is clearly down to him,' Cecelia says, dropping more documents on my desk.

There's a lot to go through, but I'm glad for it because at least it means we're being as thorough as possible. Thompson is clearly next on my list.

'Great. Anything else?' I ask.

I'm still getting the law students to work the case, even though it will never see a courtroom. It's good experience for them and useful for me.

'Iveska called. She said she wanted to meet, and that it was important. You had a gap in your diary at two p.m., so I've provisionally said then.'

'Okay, fine.'

'Oh, and she wanted to meet in the coffee shop down the road. She got all nervous about coming here.'

That raises plenty of questions, but I know Cecelia doesn't have the answers, so I let her go and start reviewing the documents she's given me. Two p.m. comes around in no time. It's amazing how being genuinely interested in your work makes the day fly by.

It takes me several moments to spot Iveska because she's wearing a headscarf and sunglasses like she's the femme fatale in a spy movie. She briefly waves at me, then slinks back down into her chair. She's got a green tea and doesn't ask if I want anything.

'Oliver called me,' she says.

'Why? I didn't mention your name to anyone.'

'I don't know, but he wanted to know if I'd been talking to anyone, and he threatened me.'

'That fucker. What did you say?'

'You have to understand: before the shelter I was in a very bad way. I had no money, I needed drugs and I had to find a way to pay for them. I was a sex worker. Oliver knows this and he's always used it against me. Now he's threatening to tell my husband, so I had to tell him about you and the questions you asked me.'

Shit. Clearly Oliver's paranoia is more organized than I had realized. He knows the deaths are connected to the women he abused, so he's been doing some investigating of his own. I wonder how many have talked.

'It's okay, Iveska. When did this happen?'

'Yesterday evening. I'm sorry. I had no choice, but I thought you should know.'

'It's fine.'

'So, you will keep my name out of your court case, yes?' she asks, her eyes wide and pleading.

She's clutching her tea with both hands, and I can see it's the only thing keeping her together. Oliver did a number on her. I suddenly realize who I should give those years to. Making sure Oliver's victims live long healthy lives is the best revenge I can think of.

I take her hand, having to prise it away from the mug, and enclose it in mine. I let the energy flow, her hands warm under my touch and they stop shaking.

'Don't worry, Iveska. You won't need to worry about Oliver for much longer.'

I need to escalate. If Oliver knows I'm the one who's been snooping around, then he'll figure out who's on my list and warn them about me. Tonight will be the third of Oliver's friends that I've killed. Three is a solid number. It will do. Then Oliver.

The police officer lives alone in a roomy two-bedroom flat in Richmond. Wonder where that money came from? Not his government salary, that's for sure. I don't have time for sneaky coffee-shop meetings, so I wait for someone to open the front door to his building, slip in behind them and take the lift to the fifth floor. Cecelia has assured me of his guilt, so there's no need to conduct my little interview. Four long steps and I'm at his door. I knock hurriedly, then keep knocking until I hear footsteps.

I can tell exactly what kind of person Thompson is by his front door. It has a 'No Entry' hazard sticker at the top and the knocker is two bulbous breasts in a red bikini. I bet he wears a Female Body Inspector T-shirt too. Ending his life is truly a public service.

The door swings open. I'm ready with my excuse to come inside – that I got locked out of my friend's flat and need a wee – but it's not Thompson who opens the door. It's Sam. He's got an accusing glare in his eye like I've eaten his leftovers without asking.

'What are you doing here?' I ask.

'Stopping you from making a mistake.'

My blood's heating up again. 'Don't be so patronizing. You've no idea the work I've put into this case. And your advocacy for a bunch of rape cover-uppers is not a good look, Sam. How did you even get in here?'

He holds up a key. 'I'm pretty adept at talking my way into luxury flats by now. And the management company who owns the building is a client.'

'Where is he?'

'On his way to falsify evidence for a well-paying client. He really is a scumbag. Barely thought twice before taking the money. He'll figure out it's fake eventually, but until then he'll be out of the city for a while. Out of reach.'

'If he's such a scumbag, why do you even care if I kill him?'

'Because I know Oliver will be next on your list, and I need more time. So I want to make a deal instead. Leave Oliver alone until I've done what I need to do, and I'll tell you who killed your parents.'

'Wow, now who's making ultimatums?' I realize that I can just agree to this and kill Oliver anyway. Getting Thompson out of the way isn't going to stop me. It's not a good plan.

'I'm always practical.' Then he says, as if reading my mind: 'I've texted you a location. Go there now. When you get there, I'll send you a file that tells you exactly what happened to your parents. If you don't, I'll delete it.'

'You wouldn't do that to me. Not after Juliette.'

'I'm doing this *for* you. Once you do this, you'll be able to think clearly again. You'll see.'

Chapter Twenty-Nine

It doesn't matter if I feel good or bad about doing something. It's not like I'm going to stop doing it.

In less than an hour, I arrive in a village straight out of a children's picture book or a yummy mummy's wet dream.

There is a church, small with stained-glass windows and lovingly restored stone angel carvings at the front door. Three pubs: the Cock & Bull, the White Lion and the Royal Oak. Each has a roaring fire and a grey-bearded man in a tweed cap nursing an ale at the window who is undoubtedly there from midday to midnight. There's even a duck pond, which has a sweet little bridge to walk over and, when you do, the plump little creatures gather, quacking in expectation of the bread that people throw from above.

Sam thinks this place is the answer to my problems, that if I confront the point in my life where everything went wrong, I can move on. I hate that phrase – *move on* – because all it really means is that people are getting tired of your pain. I wonder if Sam is tired of me too. He said I should do this by myself and only come back when I'm feeling ready. I guess a superpowered girlfriend is more of a liability when she won't follow instructions.

And I think he knew that the second I set foot in this village, I wouldn't be able to turn back. Sometimes, when I fantasize about the life I could have had if my parents had been alive, this is the kind of place I imagine us living. But that's all it is: a fantasy. My parents are dead. Now I know the reason why.

Once I sent proof of my location, Sam sent me – in his words – 'a gift'. A detailed, full-length transcript of the police interview with my parents' killer. A seventeen-year-old boy was on the road that night, driving a red Nissan Micra, the same colour as the paint left scraped into the side of my parents' car. Except by the time the police questioned him, the car had been sold and shipped to Bulgaria for scrap. A coincidence, I'm sure. There's more: an officer breathalysed him at his home. He was four times over the drink-drive limit. But it was several hours after the crash, he claimed he'd been drinking at home and, although it was mentioned in the interview, there's no evidence of the test results. The boy's father was Johann Grey, a world-famous political correspondent who came from old money. His son, Elias, winner of the Global Young Journalist Award and recently accepted to Oxford University, was poised to follow in his footsteps. Wouldn't want to mess up such a bright future over a little accident, would we, now?

The first time I see him, he's at the grocery store. It's the only one in the village. Everything is locally sourced and costs three times what it should. Elias buys bread, milk, porcini mushrooms and some craft ales. I think about the interview transcript that Sam gave me, how the breathalyser test was missing from the police report, and wonder exactly how much Elias had to drink before he got behind the wheel that night.

He pays for his food, turns and looks straight at me. For a moment, I think there must be a flicker of recognition, an immediate connection to someone he has so terribly wronged, because his eyes lock with mine and don't let go.

'Excuse me,' he says.

Then I realize I'm blocking the aisle, and he's only looking at me because I'm in his way. A completely innocuous interaction between two strangers. I step aside and he smiles.

'Thanks,' he says in a chirpy tone, one cultivated by friendly neighbours and a happy life.

This is not right. He is not supposed to be happy, but I think he really is. He looks young for his age, with clear skin and a lightly muscled body that suggests he has time to work out. The picture of health. I brush his arm as he moves past me to confirm what I already suspect: *forty-two years left*. Elias will grow old in the village, eating his £6 sundried tomatoes and drinking his craft ales until the day he dies.

I could end his life on the spot, but I don't. That would be too quick, too easy, too final. He doesn't deserve such mercy. No, I need to know exactly how to hurt Elias Grey, so that he knows what it means to lose what you love.

All the village pubs have rooms upstairs. I check into the Cock & Bull for no other reason than I'm an overgrown child who finds the name entertaining. The room is tiny, with pink floral bedding, pine furniture, faded beige carpet and no television. I dump the heavy stuff from my bag – portable charger, book, make-up and notepad – in my room and head straight out. The investigation of Elias Grey begins.

Over the next few days I learn that he works for the local

newspaper, and volunteers for charity in his spare time. At the church, he organizes a youth outreach programme. They plant trees in the local community, discuss mental health and do fundraising activities. They call him El and don't even cringe when he goes in for a high five. It's all very touching.

On Saturday, I go to their bake sale and buy a fairy cake from an extremely smiley girl who tells me to 'have a heavenly day'. And when I ask about Elias, she has nothing but praise for him.

The next three kids I question say the same thing.

This is irritating because I'm still committed to the system Sam and I have devised: that transfer of life must occur in a way that maximizes social good. I only take the lives of people who are truly deserving and represent a continued threat to society. But, as Elias carries mountains of Tupperware, following the orders of teenagers with a smile on his face, I'm struggling to summon my rage. Perhaps Sam didn't get the full story about Elias. Or perhaps he's changed. If Elias had gone to prison for what he did to my parents, I imagine he would have served his time by now. Sam and I didn't really factor historically unpunished crimes into the system.

Even worse, he has a child. A six-year-old boy who wears a Spiderman T-shirt that chokes me up. All superheroes have tragic backstories. Case in point: me. Do I want to be part of that kid's origin story?

The kid runs out to meet his dad when he gets home. I see what must be Elias's wife leaning against the door frame, watching them with a contented look on her face. She looks a few years older than Elias. Sweet, but plain. Her waterfall cardigan skims her rounded stomach. I imagine she's self-conscious about the post-child weight gain, but from the way he looks at her, I also imagine Elias tells her she gets more beautiful every day.

I need more time, so I go back to the Cock & Bull. I kick off my boots and get into the bed fully dressed, wishing I'd brought some other clothes with me so I could go for a run. The tick-tock of the bedside alarm clock is driving me nuts. Not even shoving it into the wardrobe helps, so the possibility of a nap is out. I watch cat videos on my phone instead until I run out of battery. Then I realize the portable charger is dead and I've forgotten the cable.

I'm alone, staring at the off-white ceiling with nothing but my own thoughts. Sam has manipulated me by sending me here. That doesn't particularly bother me because he wasn't trying to hide it. However, I'm struggling to reconcile the Sam refusing to let me end Oliver's life with the Sam encouraging me to hop on a train and kill Elias. My personal vendetta doesn't aid the greater good, and yet Sam keeps saying that's all he cares about, which makes him, at best, a massive hypo-crite. And what does that say about me, that I've been using said hypocrite as my moral compass, putting life and death decisions in his hands so I can wash mine of the guilt?

Nope. Definitely not. Can't be dealing with this.

I pull my boots back on and head downstairs to ask if they've got a spare charger. The bar is busy. There's a queue and the bartenders are struggling to hear drink orders over the raucous laughter from a large corner table.

Elias's table. He's here with six friends, some of whom I recognize from the bake sale and are still wearing their church T-shirts. He's holding court, delighting them with a story. Of course, appearances can be deceptive. Enough people have taught me that: Oliver, using his position to exploit others in the name of social good; Frances, masquerading as a pillar of the community. Elias is no different. Just because someone has the church on their side doesn't mean they're a good person.

In fact, I think people are often drawn to it to legitimize their own bile.

I finally get to the bar to ask about the charger. The bartender is weirdly reluctant about it. He only relents when I explain that I'm a guest here, and says he'll lend me his for a bit, but he makes it seem like such a big favour that I order a glass of wine as well.

'What kind?' he asks.

'Cheapest,' I say in reflex, forgetting that I no longer have credit card debt to worry about. I have always had to worry about money, and had it instilled in me early on that to spend it is vulgar. It's hard to correct a misbelief that you've spent your whole life thinking is true.

He pours me a yellowish Spanish wine with cartoon grapes on the label. I take it and sit at a small circular table slightly hidden behind a wall, but still with a clear view of Elias. I plug my phone into the wall socket and pretend to search through Instagram.

I don't take my eyes off him. Someone asks if they can take the second stool at my table, and I grunt in agreement. Someone else tries to buy me a drink, to which I refuse without explanation and am called a bitch for my troubles. I let it slide. Elias keeps drinking and laughing. He's had three beers and a glass of red wine. It's clearly gone to his head, because his face has reddened and he's taken his jumper off, complaining about the nearby fire, but it's not that close. Not really.

Still, I can't kill him for any of this. I wonder what could justify it? Maybe he spends a bit too much time with those underage church girls or maybe he's skimming the profits off the bake sale? I seem to have developed a rather dismal outlook on the world, but when the shoe fits . . .

Then Elias does the hard work for me. He stands up,

exclaims that he's already late for dinner and moves to leave. He's holding his car keys in his hand. I try not to get ahead of myself – after all, this happened once before, and the suspect got into a taxi. I give Elias the benefit of the doubt as he walks towards the front door, almost tripping over a woman's handbag.

'Elias, you parked round the back, you plonker,' one of his friends shouts.

Elias jingles his keys. 'Too right. Thanks, Jim.'

Yeah, thanks, Jim.

I follow Elias into the car park and watch him get into a Range Rover. Four drinks. That's not even defensible as on the limit; it's blatant disregard for the havoc he could wreak with that grill-bumpered four by four. How could anyone do such a thing when they already know full well what could happen?

It's settled, then. Elias is a dead man. But I'm still not ready to end his life. I can't let him go out as a local hero, another good man who died too young. It's not enough. I need to obliterate who he is so that *Elias Grey* and *a good man* never appear in the same sentence again.

Obviously, I can't kill Elias in front of his family. I also need some one-on-one time with him. So I continue following him for a few more days, looking for an opportunity. I order some new T-shirts, yoga pants, running trainers and a charger on Amazon Prime, which thankfully delivers here. The bartender is getting pissy with me about all the parcels.

Elias's wife commutes to the city. The local newspaper he works for shares offices with the town council, so he spends his days in the heart of the community. And their family-friendly policies mean that it's Elias who does the school runs. Every time I see him behind the wheel of that car, I'm nothing but a living, fuming ball of seething rage. It almost makes me forget about the kid and I'm close to ending Elias's life right there on the spot. I only just get a hold of myself. I can't believe I entertained the thought that Elias might have changed.

Between his family, his work and volunteering with whatever do-gooder project of the month is top of the list at church, Elias is tricky to get hold of. It takes three days before I get my chance. The wife comes home early on Tuesday, picks up the kid and takes him to swimming club, followed by pizza with the other kids. Elias gets the night off parent duty. He's at home, watching television on the sofa, feet kicked up and a beer in hand.

I can see him through the living-room window. Elias doesn't lock his garage door. It's very easy to prise open with a stick, so I'm inside the house in no time. I have to act now. Who knows when I'll get such a clear window of opportunity again?

Elias is a big guy, so I need to take him by surprise. I ordered a taser off the dark web. Sure, they're technically illegal, but so is a lot of stuff I've done over the past few months, and I really don't want to get punched in the face again. So, with my taser at the ready, I plan to get Elias's attention by half pushing the wine rack over. Three wine bottles crash to the floor. Shattered glass lies across the pool of Sauvignon Blanc; I hop over it, crouch behind the door and wait. Elias's footsteps approach, his socks padding against the wooden floor. I hope he isn't the type to approach all suspicious situations with a baseball bat.

The door opens and I lunge. I yank down the back of his collar as I press the taser against his neck. His entire body convulses from the shock, scrunching up like an insect, reacting instinctively against an unknown threat. He drops to the floor. I waste no time. Tasers don't render people unconscious for long, so I get behind him, hold his arms together and fasten them with a cable tie. I push him against the car and fasten him to the alloy wheel with a second cable tie. I'm so glad I didn't try to tie him to a chair. He's like a sack of heavy flour and it takes all my strength to shove him one foot across the floor.

It's done. I rest my weight, leaning on my knees, and take a few deep breaths. Minutes later, Elias is fidgeting in his restraints. His eyes are fractionally bouncing around the room, unable to understand what's going on.

I crouch down, but not much, so that I still impose from above. 'Do you know who I am, Elias?'

'I saw you in the shop. And at the church.'

'Very observant of you. Do you know why I'm here?'

'To kill me,' he says calmly, as if he has been expecting it.

I don't know what to say. He's put a bit of a spanner in the speech I have been rehearsing since I was a little girl. 'What?' I ask.

'You're the girl from the crash. Thea Greaves. Your parents, Lucy and—'

'Don't say their names. So, what? You looked me up?'

It doesn't matter. This doesn't change what he did to my family. Perhaps he googled me out of morbid curiosity. He still left an eight-year-old child alone at the scene of her parents' murder. Some things cannot be forgiven.

He nods. 'I wanted to know that you were okay. What I did has haunted me, in my dreams and out of them. I always wondered if you would track me down some day.'

I don't like this. He's not supposed to be like this, and I'm not meant to feel guilty about what I have to do. That's not fair. After what I've been through, I should be able to enjoy this. It's my defining moment. I've won.

'If you didn't want to feel guilty, perhaps you shouldn't have driven off.'

He nods. 'I know. I'll never forgive myself – and I don't expect you to – but I was a stupid kid. I'd been out to the pub with friends, and I was over the limit. My life would have been over. So, I've been trying to make amends ever since.'

'So, you were drunk?' I ask to confirm. He nods. I lean forward. 'Then this is what's going to happen. You are going to write a letter confessing to exactly what you did that night, every detail, and you are going to send it to everyone in this town – the church, your friends, your colleagues. Everyone.'

I can see the realization on his face. Right now, his mind is imagining everyone he's ever known reading about the worst thing he's ever done. His reputation as the town do-gooder obliterated.

'Will that make you happy?' he asks. Why does he keep taking the punch out of this? He's supposed to fight this, then I'll have a reason to threaten him. Now my back-up plan seems cruel.

'Extremely. And in case you think of not following through, you should know I've put insurance in place.' I move forward onto my knees and place my hand on his wrist. 'Pay attention,' I say, and very deliberately, as slowly as I can manage, I siphon his life into me. It's like the drip of a tap. I turn the faucet on his last few hours.

'What was that?' he asks.

'You tell me. What did it feel like?'

'Cold. Bleak. Nothingness. Like you drained the life out of me.'

The look on his face is one of terror. Sharing this secret with him is strangely and intensely personal because I think Elias is the reason why I have my power. I couldn't save my parents, but the grief I carried for them sparked this in me – a natural response to a desperate need – and when I needed it to save Ruth, it answered.

'That's exactly what I did. If you don't follow my instructions, you'll be dead before your family gets home.'

'I'm not afraid of death.'

'What about your wife, your kid?'

'Ella and Charles.' His head snaps up. 'Please, they're completely innocent. You wouldn't?'

Of course I wouldn't, but he doesn't know that.

'Not if you give me what I want. Right now, I'm holding your life and your family's lives in my hands. Write the email to the town confessing what you did, that you have decided you can't live with the guilt anymore, and I'll make sure it's only you who dies. Make a different choice, and you can lose your family too, just like I did.'

'My laptop is in the kitchen,' he says, his words urgent.

I fetch it, place it on his lap and cut the cable ties with my penknife. I'm not worried that he'll attack me because, if he does, his entire family will die. At least, that's what he thinks. I'm really not into murdering children but there's simply no other threat so effective. I think almost all movies could be finished in thirty minutes if the villain had threatened the kids at the start. Elias types like a man who's used to working to a deadline, fingers flying over the keyboard in the rush to destroy his legacy.

'Done,' he says, and passes me the laptop.

I skim-read it, wanting to avoid reliving my parents' deaths but needing to check he's been completely honest. It's all there: the crash, the girl he left alone, the alcohol, the bribed judges and perversion of justice. He says he's sorry. And that this is goodbye. When Elias dies, there will be no big sappy funeral,

no obituary in the town newspaper, no legacy. Just shame. I
pass it back to him.

'Send it.'

He presses without hesitation. The whoosh of the email
being sent is overly jolly for the situation, but at least it con-
firms what he's done.

'My family?' he asks.

I stand up, brushing the dust of the garage floor off my jeans.
'I never took their lives from them – only yours.'

He breathes a sigh of relief. No anger, just gratitude. 'How
long do I have?'

Acceptance. 'Not long. Maybe enough for one last drink.'

I look at the smashed wine bottle on the floor – the reason
Elias destroyed both our lives. Then I notice something else.
In small faded grey lettering: 0.05 per cent alcohol content.
I look at the wine rack, pulling out the bottles that didn't
fall and throwing them down. Every single one is the same.
Alcohol free.

'I saw you drinking at the pub. Three beers and a glass of
red wine. Then you got into the car and drove.'

He stays silent but I can see the truth in his face. Elias doesn't
drink.

The doorbell rings, followed by a knock and a man shouting
Elias's name. He doesn't move; he's completely accepted my
control. Then, red marks blister around Elias's neck. Rope
marks. Thin and burning into the skin. He tries to take a
breath but can't. It's like watching someone drown. His eyes
bulge. He claws at his throat, trying to remove the invisible
rope, but he can't.

There's more shouting at the door. Whacking again and
again, like someone is throwing their entire body against it. It's
not supposed to be like this. There's a crash. The door is down

and a man is still calling out for Elias. I reach down and touch his neck, let his energy return to him, and when I retract the marks have all but disappeared. I leave Elias breathless on the floor and escape out the side door.

Chapter Thirty

Is redemption possible? If so, how can you know when it's done? Is it something you can give to yourself, or is it only something other people can give to you?

My first instinct is to get straight on the first train to London Victoria, put this all behind me and forget about it because – once again – I've royally screwed up. I'm so tired of it. But if I don't use my powers, justice goes unserved. It's selfish to keep them to myself. All I want to do is help people, but I can't seem to get it right.

I buy a ticket, and I'm about to step onto the train when I stop. My feet will not move. I'm frozen to the spot as the train quietly pulls out of the station, leaving me alone at the platform. It's so quiet. It's like the air itself has gone to sleep, expecting nothing to disturb it until morning.

A portly train conductor strolls over and says, 'Last train's gone, miss. You best be heading home now.'

He has a kindly face, genuinely worried about leaving a young woman alone at night.

'I'm leaving,' I say. 'Thanks.'

I go back to the Cock & Bull, but I don't sleep that night. Instead, I look for patterns in the ceiling, swirls that if I squint hard enough look like rabbits, cats and dogs. After a while all I can see is the rabbits – I think I'm looking for them now and can't see anything else.

The night slowly gives way to morning. I watch as the sunlight tears straight through the paper-thin curtains, heating up for the day. I'm too tired to be either asleep or awake. Returning Elias's life to him has drained me in more ways than one.

Still wearing my clothes from yesterday, I float down the stairs in my semi-fugue state and ask the barman for a coffee. It's bitter instant granules in a thin paper cup. I grimace as I drink it. No less than I deserve.

Elias is at home today, and his wife's car is in the drive. I sit on a neighbour's wall opposite the house and watch countless friends drop off casseroles and get-well-soon cards. They must all think Elias attempted suicide. There's no way I could get to him, and even if I could, I'm not sure what I would do.

Instead, I decide to spend a day in Elias's life. I walk into town, buy some bread, feed the ducks, walk around the church grounds and then I head to the town council. I claim to be a reporter doing a piece on 'best villages for families in the southeast', because I want to know what these people really think of Elias, to help me decide what to do about him.

The town hall is a small but grand building. From the outside, it could be anything, constructed from large, sandy-coloured stones and with griffins carved above the double wooden doors. Inside, there's a simple reception desk and plastic chairs for people waiting. Time moves slowly here. I imagine they hold staff meetings to fully consider the potential merits and drawbacks of a new signpost in the village.

So, I'm surprised when I'm ushered through to the mayor after just ten minutes in the plastic chair. The mayor is not what I expected for this town – young, female, beautiful. She has a stylish pixie haircut and is wearing leopard-print court shoes.

'What would you like to know about our village?' she asks. I get the sense they're keen to get me out of here, so I assume they all received Elias's email. Doesn't look good – pillar of the community admitting to a criminal offence, then offing himself. Or trying to, anyway.

I ask about daily life, about the local community and the church. The mayor paints a rosy picture, her genuine enthusiasm for her home putting her at ease and loosening her tongue. I smile and laugh and take dutiful notes.

'Now, there's one name that keeps being mentioned by everyone I talk to. Elias Grey. I'd love to do a feature on someone who's contributed so much to the community,' I say, not dropping my smile for a moment.

She freezes and swallows her discomfort. 'Actually, he's not very well at the moment. I don't think he'd welcome the media attention.'

'It's only a puff piece. I don't even need to speak to him. Your endorsement and a few anecdotes would do the trick.'

'Look, this isn't common knowledge, but Elias just made an attempt on his own life.' She pauses. 'This is all off the record, yes?'

'Of course.' I close my notebook.

'All you need to know is that whatever else you hear, Elias is a good man. He's put everything into this village. We depend on him. Last year, he raised ten thousand pounds for new speed bumps. And he leads the yearly driving safety talk at school. He's the only one they really listen to.'

'What's that? Driving safety?'

'Yes, it's always been a passion of his. He says careless driving is the biggest risk to our safety since the cigarette. I never really knew why but . . .' She looks down into her lap. I guess she knows why now. 'Look, they're going through a tough time at the moment. A nice comment in the paper would be great for Elias but anything else and the village would never forgive you.'

Her tone has changed; the threat is obvious. Knowing what Elias has done doesn't diminish their affection for him.

'Of course not. You've given me plenty of material to work with here. Thanks for your help.'

I'm done with stealth mode. All this sneaking around, asking questions and gathering evidence. No wonder no law firm ever hired me. I'm starting to realize that I'm completely unsuited to the job. I'm someone who acts, who gets things done, even if I have to crack a few eggs in the process.

I walk straight up to Elias's front door and bring the silver knocker down three times, hard. His wife answers. Her eyes are red, puffy and underlined by dark circles. She probably got less sleep than I did.

'I need to speak to Elias. Now.'

She shakes her head. 'I'm afraid he's not in a condition for visitors.'

I don't have time for this. I barge past her. People must not behave like this in this sleepy village – she's so stunned that I'm at the top of the stairs before she reacts.

'Stop!' she yells. I ignore her and start opening doors until I find Elias. She comes in after me. 'You can't be in here. He's . . .'

Elias is propped up in bed on a small mountain of pillows.

He has a lap table across him, on which sits a sandwich, a cup of tea and a magazine about fishing.

'Ella, it's okay,' he says. 'Thea and I need to talk.'

'But ...'

'It's important,' he adds.

Ella turns to look at me, clearly boiling over with questions, but then nods. I wait for her slipper-covered footsteps to pad down the stairs before I pull up a chair beside Elias.

'You don't drink,' I say. It's not a question, more of an accusation.

'Not a drop since that night.'

'And you give talks about driving safety and raise money for speed bumps.'

'Yes.'

'Why?'

He takes a deep breath, then winces and holds his throat. Faint red marks peek out at me from between his fingers.

'Because I have thought about what happened every day since. Before I go to sleep, in the middle of the night and when I wake up. Sometimes, I'll be with Ella and Charles, feeling happier than any man has a right to be, and I'll remember that I don't deserve to feel that way. It's a gloom that washes over me and reminds me that I did a terrible thing, that I am a bad person who is worthy of nothing but torment. So, I do everything I can to make things right, even though I know I never can.'

'And you didn't think to tell me any of this?'

'I knew you were watching me in the pub – drinking. I wanted to make you angry because part of me was glad when you showed up. Finally I was going to pay for my sins. Besides, what does it matter if I feel guilty? It doesn't change what happened.'

'It does to me.'

'Why?' he asks.

I think about the legal system, about how Elias would have been punished for his crime with incarceration. That's what I used to believe would give me peace. But what good would that have done? If I just wanted him punished, then I couldn't have asked for more than for him to torture himself with the guilt, trying to find some arbitrary redemption that doesn't exist. And really, my hatred for him was born of each time that the system passed over my parents' death, the way it fell to the bottom of the pile, faded from public memory, when their friends stopped remembering their birthdays and when Grandad stopped saying their names. So it does matter that Elias feels guilty about them. It matters that someone else cared enough to think about them.

I suppose I could explain all of this to him. It's probably also the moment I should give a big speech and forgive him. Let him move on with his life unhindered.

'It just does,' I say, and get to my feet. 'You're not about to drop dead anymore. If you stay away from me and don't run over anyone else, then I've got no reason to come back here. Okay?'

He nods, too shocked to answer. My last chance to forgive him. There's a look in his eye that tells me this will continue to haunt him, and I can't help being comforted by it. I leave him to his quaint village life, content to know that my parents will be remembered every time he gets behind the wheel and whenever he sees a little girl that reminds him of me. They will live in his nightmares and haunt his days. That's a fair enough trade for the gift of life I've left with him.

Chapter Thirty-One

*It's important not to make big decisions when
you're not in your right mind – if someone who
kills can ever be considered in their right mind.*

I'm going home. Not to Mayfair, not Clapham, but to Grandad.
Because it doesn't matter how old I get, or what I've done,
there's nothing like home to make me feel like myself again.

The next few days are exactly what I wanted. Grandad
keeps a tight schedule and insists I follow it too. Every morning
he walks into town, buys the *Telegraph* from the local post
office, reads it during breakfast, then spends the rest of the
morning gardening or pottering around the house. Our village
is home to one of the country's only Spitfire museums. Grandad
volunteers there in the afternoon and, thankfully, I'm not
expected to go with him. But he's found a list of chores to leave
me with. Today I'm cleaning the oven. A task that I've never
seen the point of – it's not like the dirt touches the food, so who
cares? But I don't complain because today I'm glad to be busy,
to have my mind occupied by something uncomplicated and
without consequence. I go for a run while the cleaner soaks.

After I get back, I finish scrubbing the oven, then treat myself to a bath to remove my own grime. I've been back for three days and haven't checked my phone since I got here. Actually, it's gone dead and I haven't bothered to charge it. No Sam, no Ruth, no Oliver, no Karly. Not my problem. Not my responsibility. I've not put my head in the sand; I've submerged my entire body in thick, noise-cancelling cement. And I've got no plans to dig it out.

On Sunday we have visitors. Grandad insists on cooking a full roast. He's currently defrosting a whole chicken in the sink. He flicks the kettle on, not asking if I want tea, because he knows the answer is always yes, and passes me a knife and chopping board.

'Carrots need doing,' he says.

I peel them, take off the ends and cut them into thin half-moon slices. There's something extremely comforting about following simple instructions. I don't utter a word of complaint as Grandad orders me to prepare broccoli, roast potatoes and cauliflower cheese. He refuses to let me stuff the chicken because I don't know the 'secret ingredient'. I'm pretty sure it's just sage. Then I pick strawberries from the garden. It's August now so it's a little late for them but they're still plump and perfect. There is nothing more delicious in this world than strawberries from Grandad's garden, served with nothing else but cream.

Grandad's friends Elizabeth and Kenny arrive at 3 p.m. They remark on how much older I look, which I try not to take to heart, but I suppose it's true because I haven't seen them in years. The questions are fired across the table like bullets.

What are you working on? Where are you living? Have you met someone yet? When are you having children?

I excuse myself as often as possible to check on the roast, to nip to the loo, to stand in the hall and take a deep breath. Their questions no longer seem relevant; they are for Thea Greaves, and I don't know who she is anymore.

Worse is Grandad's response. He takes my silence and fills it.

'Thea is a lawyer now, works for some fancy firm in the city on – what did you call it? – social justice issues. She always said it was what she wanted to do. Even when I told her to stop living with her head in the clouds and be grateful for the job she had, she never stopped working towards her goal. You don't see much of that persistence, that moral core, in this generation anymore. I've never been so proud to be proved wrong.'

He has never smiled at me like this before. Genuine pride lights up his face with a youthful glow I haven't seen in years. Red wine encourages him to continue. He tells them about the cases I've been working on, about Karly and Oliver. He refers to the latter only as a 'sorry excuse for a man'. He knows every detail, every name. I had no idea how much he'd truly listened to our fortnightly phone calls.

It makes it all so much worse. How can I tell him it's all a lie? I'm not a lawyer. The job is simply a cover Sam created for me, one that appealed to my vanity and enabled my worst impulses. Grandad believes that the good are rewarded and sinners are damned for eternity. How could he ever reconcile his faith with my actions?

I cannot bear to look at him, with his wispy caterpillar eyebrows and kind, soulful eyes. All he ever wanted for me was to lead a good life, a quiet life, and I've failed him completely.

Our neighbours leave once the wine is gone. Without hesitation, I begin clearing the table. We don't have a dishwasher, so I stack the plates high beside the sink, scrape off the leftovers and start washing up. I leave the clean items on the rack, then

Grandad dries them with a dish cloth and puts them back into the cupboard. I would have left them to air dry, but he doesn't like to leave a job unfinished.

'You were quiet tonight,' he says, not looking up from the spoons he's wiping dry.

'Was I? Must be tired, end of the week and all.'

'Yes, a busy week of cleaning the oven and jogging,' he says, raising an eyebrow. When I don't reply, he continues: 'I'm not complaining because I'm glad to spend more time with you, but why are you here? During the week no less – surely the firm is missing you?'

'It's a quiet week.'

He drops the cutlery into the drawer with a crash. 'Thea, lies are for children and cowards. Now, tell me what is wrong.'

I stare into the sink. The soap bubbles gently pop, the foam dissipating on my hands. And I don't know if it's the red wine, or the lack of sleep, or something else that I can't explain, but I start talking.

'I've made a mess, Grandad. All I wanted to do was fix things, change people's lives for the better, but whatever I do, it seems to make things worse. There's this ... thing ... inside me. It's corrupting everything I touch, and I don't know how to stop.'

I look up, expecting him to look at me like I've well and truly lost my mind. But that's not what I see. He's not confused at what I've said. Instead, he's deathly pale. He looks as though I've walked up to him and plunged a knife into his heart and is still processing the shock of it.

'Grandad?'

'It's happened, hasn't it?'

'What do you mean?' I ask, because I need to hear him say it. I need to know exactly what he knows in his own words.

'Your power. Something triggered it. Just like it did for your father.'

Grandad takes a step towards me. I take one step back.

'Thea, you must understand. I thought it was best that you didn't know, that if I raised you with a strong enough sense of right and wrong, then you would never be tempted.' He pauses and gives me a look of crushing disappointment. 'I suppose I was wrong.'

'You've known about this power my entire life – and you said nothing?'

'You had so much of your childhood taken from you. I couldn't bear to burden you with something so dark, not after what it did to your father.'

'What do you mean – what did it do to him?'

Grandad shakes his head. There is more emotion across his face right now than I have ever seen in twenty-six years. It is one of pain. Of strange contortions and muscles never used.

'I can't talk about it,' he says.

'*Try*,' I say, forceful and insistent. Grandad walks away from me. I follow and ask again, softer this time. 'Please, Grandad, I need to know.'

He nods, once. 'I don't have the words, but he can tell you in his.'

We walk up the stairs. The creak of the old timber frame is the only thing to distract from our silence. He opens the hatch to the roof, pulls down the ladder and hauls himself up. I hold the torch. To this day, I've never been up here. It's dark, we have mice, and one wrong step and you'll put your foot through the ceiling. Grandad retrieves a box. Hidden under carefully preserved antique magazines from the wartime, there's a set of black leather notebooks. They are coated in a film of dust, the pages yellowed, with frayed pieces of red ribbon poking out of the top. Even if I had ever ventured up here, I would have assumed they were more of the same – wartime stories I have absolutely no interest in.

But I open one to the first page and the handwriting is unmistakably my dad's. Grandad quietly leaves me and all I can hear is my dad's voice, speaking to me from the page.

My father's power first came to him when he was a child. Just ten years old. His own mother was dying in the hospital and, like me, he felt it clear as day: three hours to live. She'd gone in for a routine operation to remove some kidney stones and was sitting up in bed, happily chatting away and drinking her tea. He'd thought himself mad at first, so he didn't say a word.

I understand the instinct to disbelieve. The brain doesn't like contradictions – its entire purpose is to ride shotgun to your adventures, providing you with a real-time script of what's happening. When something doesn't make sense, it doesn't know what to do, so it finds an explanation. Not enough sleep. Paranoia. A weird hangover from a bad dream. Much easier to accept than the fact that you've developed the spontaneous power over life and death.

He didn't believe it until Grandad passed him one of the sandwiches he'd brought from home. Cheese and pickle. Always consistent, that's Grandad. That's when Dad felt it again: fifty-two years. Real and visceral as if seeing a timer in his mind's eye. That's when he told Grandad what he'd felt.

Of course, Grandad didn't put much stock into the delusion of a ten-year-old child.

Dad pleaded, insisted, asked to speak to a doctor, but children in those days were meant to be seen and not heard. And his mother was getting tired. Dragged out of the hospital without debate, then left in the car with the child-lock on, Dad was stuck in the car when his mother died of hypovolemia, a rare side effect of anaesthetic.

It's strange to think of him as a child, discovering this inexplicable power just like I did. And in the same way. It's fear of loss that triggers it, I'm sure of it. When the idea of losing someone you love is so unbearable that you simply can't let it happen. Until now, I assumed I was the only one. Maybe it's just our family, some supernatural kink in our DNA. There's one question I can't find an answer for – why couldn't I save my parents? I loved them, needed them, so why didn't I know they were about to die?

Dad doesn't describe the events of his childhood in any great detail, or in any semblance of order at all. I only get the full story in snippets written in the margins, crossed-out sentences and bracketed thoughts. What he really writes about is far more disturbing. Most of the journal reads like this . . .

Faces. So many faces. When I sleep, when I wake. All I see are the dead. Rotting flesh and shards of bone pulled back to earth to torment me.

Charlie Robinson, the first life I took, at the foot of my bed, growling. Eyes glowing like cats in the road, never blinking, never looking away. He'll take me with him one day. He'll grow claws and tear at my flesh until he takes me away from here, from Lucy, from Thea.

He's only a boy. His uniform tattered and grey. Nine years old, three months and a day. I never forget. How could I? Charlie won't. He exists in endless turmoil knowing he will never grow old, never see his family, never find peace. And for what? A playground dispute over who won at bulldog that went too far, a flash of rage I could not control. Dead. Over. Gone. But not for me. Never for me.

Mrs Kirke, my decomposing teacher, finds me at breakfast. They say she died of a broken heart, but I am the one who stopped it beating. Another moment of my weakness, another victim of my curse. She watches as I eat. Presses her icy hand against my chest to test my pulse, tries to trick it into stopping. Her wails fill the room every time she fails, every time I smile or laugh. And when I spend a moment too long with Dad, her gaze wanders, and I fear even my power isn't enough to save him.

On the way to school, a deadbeat with a skull tattooed on his neck. If he could reach through the void and rip out my spine, he would. He stands in my path, daring me to come closer. Spiders scuttle across his arms and onto the path. Great monsters with twelve legs and four red eyes.

School. Marcus Stafford. He sits at the desk to my right, waves at me with skeletal fingers and missing teeth. His eye pops up, rolls across the floor and a snake slithers from the socket. When will it end? I want it to stop. Anything would be better than this hell I'm living.

I read until my eye begins to twitch, which reminds me of the snake. I don't recognize the man in these pages. Where is the soft tone of my father? His poems? His love of nature?

Pages and pages of horrifying visions; hallucinations I suppose. But hadn't I had the same? Greg once appeared on the television, for Christ's sake. But that was simply guilt. Perhaps it's not possible to kill a person and not feel some form of guilt.

There were times the hallucinations lessened, where his grip on the world improved. At these times, my mother was there with him.

> Lucy. Calm, bright Lucy with her sea-green eyes and ocean frizz ringlets. When she speaks, it's the only sound I hear. She's the sun blocking out the darkness with her rays, her presence a warm summer's day dancing across my skin. I bask in her.
>
> She works with animals, so she knows how to communicate without speaking. And make me feel safe with a single touch. I think this is it. If I stay by her side, the void will stay closed. No screams in the night, no spectres of death in the living room. Even the noise in my head is not so bad when she's with me.

I remember that feeling, the way Mum would embrace me with a warmth that enveloped. As long as I was with her, nothing else seemed to matter. But it hadn't worked for Dad, not really. There are long gaps in the journal. From the entries I can read, I piece together that the gaps are long stints when he was admitted to psychiatric hospitals, bedridden by whichever tranquillizer could keep him down, lacking the energy to write. I do remember that Dad would go away sometimes when I was little. Mum told me it was for work. I never even questioned it but even if I had, I would have never imagined . . . this.

Then each time he was released, he wrote about how sure this would be the time everything was okay. In every entry after a long gap, he mentioned the smile on Mum's face when she took him home from the facility. Reading the same pattern over and over feels like a form of madness. Years go by and the words blend together. Six months. That's the longest stretch he went without visions.

I don't know how she coped with it. I guess love often fails to make sense.

I come across my own name during the final journal.

Thea looks so much like her mother. This is a good thing. That child should be cursed with as little of me as possible. I wonder if they would be better off without me. Probably. Lucy would surely be glad not to have to care for two people, and Thea would have a better chance of normality without a father who brings the dead into our kitchen.

There is one thing stopping me. What if Thea is like me? Sometimes, I think she sees what I do, or at least senses it. Yesterday, Charlie Robinson sat on the floor as she played with building blocks. He started combing her hair with his fingers, her golden strands getting caught on his loose pieces of flesh. I can only watch. Reacting just encourages him and makes the smug grin of satisfaction spread across his face. Then, she looked right at him. He knew it. I knew it.

She burst into tears, and he dissipated into smoke.

Dad used to tell me that if you make a mess, you'd better clean it up. I remember one time, I was playing with some friends from school, shooting stones out of slingshots. We aimed at the small branches, trying to snap them, and listened to the clunk as the stones came back down. Until one didn't come down. Instead, a small bird fell from the tree, landing with a thud on the ground. Half its skull caved in. Still alive. Until Dad told me to put it out of its misery. Sometimes death is kinder than life.

So, I can't leave them. I pick Thea up, sing a soft lullaby until she quiets in my arms. Her tiny heart fluttering against my chest like a baby bird, and her infant fingers clutching the zip of my jumper. It's easy to forget what darkness could be lurking inside my little girl. If she develops my power, will she act as I have? Will she suffer like I have? Can I truly let that happen?

As much as I try to think of her as Lucy's child, I can't ignore my flecks of green in her eyes and the ridge in her nose that mirrors mine.

There's no doubt that she's mine. My responsibility. My problem to solve.

It's the last entry I can find. Part of me is glad for that because I don't think I could stomach one more word. My childhood is a lie. On the day of the crash, I wasn't robbed of the perfect family; it was a sad end to troubled lives. I have always felt more connected to my dad, for reasons that are only just beginning to make sense, but right now my mum is the only one I want to speak to. She's the only one who saw everything, stuck by him, and could possibly tell me the truth. Right now, emptiness dominates. But bubbling beneath it is fear. Elias doesn't remember the crash. He was drunk so assumed it was his fault, but what if it wasn't? There was only one person there that night who had a history of ending lives.

The problem with dead people is that they can't explain themselves. I can't be sure of what happened that day. All I know is that the person who was supposed to love me most in the world, the person I trusted to protect and nurture me, wrapped his arms around me and thought my life belonged to him.

This fear saps my energy. I stare at the dresser, paint peeling from its corners. Grandad never cared for appearances. It occurs to me that my anger has been misdirected all these years. He was there for me, kept me fed and in clean clothes when he didn't ask for any of it. He lost his wife, then his son, and I never thanked him for being a constant in my life.

My entire life has been built on rage. Anger at a wrong that went unpunished. Without it, I feel hollow. I close my eyes, breathe, and try to feel what else is there. Every life force has a distinct imprint. It's like a tuning fork, and only by blocking out all the noise can you find its unique thread. This is the first time I've felt mine. *Forty-eight years.*

It's thin, fraying and yellow. Not like sunshine or gold, but the pale kind you might paint on the walls. It's tired and bruised, like someone's used twine to tie boulders together.

I keep my eyes squeezed shut, fascinated by the energy I've discovered despite its unflattering image. I prod at it in my mind, picking at the threads in an attempt to understand it. What happens next is an accident; I'm too far outside my own body to consider the consequences. I manage to wrap my mind around a piece of it and pull. Like a loose strand on a woolly jumper I can't resist. I keep pulling until I feel it unspooling in my hand. My eyes still closed, I can picture it glowing. With this comes an indescribable relief. This ugly yellow thing that is my life is not mine. It's toxic waste expelled from my body. No longer part of me. Not my responsibility.

When I open my eyes, the dresser appears so hazy that it looks new. No broken handles and chipped paintwork marring its wood. My mind is quiet as I slip from my position slouched against the bed and into the carpeted oblivion of the floor.

Once again, I wake up with Grandad by my bedside. This time I'm in my bedroom. The retro record-covered orange and green wallpaper orients me immediately.

'We must stop meeting like this,' I groan. I'm tucked into bed so tight I can't move my arms. Grandad has to help me escape and I hoist myself up into a seated position.

'Here, drink this,' he says, passing me a glass of water. 'How are you feeling?'

'Rubbish. How long was I out?'

'Three days.'

'What? And you didn't take me to hospital?'

'No, I knew they wouldn't be able to do anything for you. Just like they couldn't for your father.'

'I still can't believe you've known about me this whole time, and you said nothing,' I say, barely managing to meet his eyes.

'I didn't know, not with any certainty. I always believed if I instilled you with a moral compass, then you'd be able to make the right decision regardless of the situation. And I thought I'd done my job well enough. It wasn't until the hospital that I suspected you'd been ... corrupted. Still, I was a coward. I couldn't admit the truth to either of us.'

'It didn't start like that. I wanted to do the right thing. I just wanted to save Ruth, and I wanted to help people, but it all went wrong ...'

'There is no world where killing a person is the right thing to do.'

'But you've killed people, in the war?'

'And a piece of my soul has been missing ever since. Why do you think you're trying so hard to justify your own actions? We need to be the heroes of our own stories. It's much harder to admit that we're not.'

'Sometimes it's too hard; I just wish it would stop.'

'Is that what happened? Did you try to make it stop?' he says, levelling me with owl-like wisdom.

I don't know how to answer that question. I remember pulling at the threads of my life force, how watching it unravel felt like relief.

'Not on purpose,' is all I can say.

'Well, that's something.'

'Why aren't you angrier with me?' I ask.

'Because this is not your fault. You and your father were given a power too great for one person, and I failed to save you both from it.'

'You know, I remember that last evening with them. Dad took us up to the forest for a McDonald's picnic. He kept saying it was a special occasion and I never understood what he meant. And the more I think about it, he was so strange that evening. I used to think he was just being fun, but it was ... manic. Then it got so late and I fell asleep in the car and I don't remember anything before the crash. All this time I thought we were the victims of a terrible accident, but do you ... do you think he did it on purpose?'

Grandad considers me carefully for a moment. 'Does it truly make a difference? I know how much he loved you. He wasn't in his right mind but if he did do it on purpose, then he meant to end his own life too. It wasn't something he could bear to live with.'

What happened to my parents has haunted me my entire life. I thought I needed justice, then truth, but now ... perhaps there's something freeing in letting go altogether. In accepting there's no answer that could make it all okay.

'You need your rest,' Grandad says. 'But first, ice cream.'

He wheels the television into my room and brings me a bowl of vanilla ice cream with rainbow sprinkles and chocolate sauce. I'm licking the bowl when Oliver's voice invades my peace.

'I'm pleased to announce the construction of our new homeless shelter on York Street has been approved. The shelter will be part of a number of new homes, of which many will be designated affordable living.'

I stifle a bitter laugh. There's a legal requirement for a certain percentage of new builds to meet 'affordable living' requirements, as if slightly discounted luxury apartments in central London are going to help the housing crisis. Oliver is simply the charitable face of an industry that doesn't give two shits where people sleep at night.

'None of this could have been possible without the hard work of our volunteers and the generous contributions of our donors,' he says. 'So, I'd like to say thank you. And remember, everyone deserves a second chance.'

I reach for the remote and try to turn off the television. The standby button is sticky, and I have to dig my nail into the squidgy silicone to shut Oliver up. I slam the remote down on the side table and cross my arms.

There's a line in my dad's journal that has stuck with me – that I was his responsibility, his problem to solve. And I can't help but think he might have been right.

Chapter Thirty-Two

Ending a life means the end of possibility. For growth, for healing, for change.

This is my mess. Time to clean it up.

Oliver's family lives in a countryside mansion – a fleet of cars, several pools, a gym, games room, the works. But Oliver only spends his weekends there because he's too busy *helping people* to cope with the two-and-a-half-hour train ride home. Instead, Oliver spends weekday nights alone in his Fitzrovia penthouse.

Except tonight, he has a visitor. I've become comfortable in these environments now. No longer put off by marble-floored lobbies with gold-rimmed banisters and artwork I don't understand. Even the air smells sweeter in places like this, as if the rich cannot risk an unperfumed breath. The doorman smiles as if he's genuinely happy to see me, calls Oliver to confirm my visit, then walks me to the lift and presses the button for floor eighteen for me.

'Do let me know if you and Oliver should need anything. No request too big or too small,' he says, then lets the door go.

I'm reminded of all the time Sam and I have spent in our luxury apartment, where gourmet food and luxury are fetched before you can blink. I wonder whether Oliver was born malicious, or whether being surrounded by people who make you feel there's something truly special about you makes you that way. I know the seductive allure of power better than anyone. Oliver may be a rapist, but I'm a murderer. Perhaps power will always trump good intentions. Then again, Sam's always remained true to his ideals, and Ruth was born into money, so maybe Oliver's just a massive prick.

Oliver welcomes me into his flat with a smile and a glass of red wine in hand. He floats back to the kitchen counter-top, gets another bottle of wine from the rack and pulls out the cork with exaggerated flair.

'You have to try this. It's a Bordeaux 1974 vintage. Divine.'

'As I said, we have something important to discuss.'

'There is no conversation that cannot be improved by a glass of wine.'

He pours me a glass, but I don't touch it. I don't think I could enjoy anything Oliver tried to give to me. Plus, I've always thought anyone who spends more than a fiver on wine is an idiot or a snob.

He pours himself another glass, puts on a calm background beat and reclines on his leather sofa. I do not like this. The music, the wine, the sofa. It makes me think of how many other women have been here, Oliver's entitled hands all over them. I wonder if his wife really buys that he *needs* to stay in the city all week, or whether she's accepted the hand she's been dealt.

'I want to know why you did it,' I say, without taking a seat. He gives me a blank look, quizzical, as if I'm starting to make a joke and he's curious to hear the punchline. 'Karly, Iveska and the others. I would like to know why you feel entitled to assault the women you promised to help.'

'Your generation has forgotten what hard work is. I'm one of the last people to have genuinely pulled himself up by his bootstraps. Now you're all looking for handouts and expecting things. So, if you're looking to vilify me because a couple of bitches decided to whine about having to earn something for once in their lives, go ahead.'

At least he's honest. No bullshit about sex addiction or not understanding the meaning of consent.

'Why are you really here?' he adds.

'To give you one last chance to do the right thing. If you don't, then I promise you I will never stop hounding you. I know what you've done, and I'll make bloody sure that every person in the country knows it too.'

He laughs. 'With your *legal acumen* and lack of willing witness testimonies, I doubt I have much to worry about.'

'You're right, I'm a terrible lawyer. I did manage to uncover some pretty important details, though, which Svetlana Tate found very promising.'

'Svetlana Tate?'

'She specializes in domestic violence cases. Highest success rate of any prosecution barrister in the country. You might have heard of the Travis Broverstock trial last year? She built the entire thing single-handed.'

Oliver tightens his grip on his glass. Travis Broverstock was a famous film director and minor royal. He should have been untouchable but Svetlana had him sentenced to sixteen years in prison for charges of rape and sexual assault. I was an idiot for thinking I could even pretend to emulate her, so I had my interns send her everything we found on Oliver, all gift-wrapped with a neat bow on top.

'I'm sure you'll fight it but it doesn't matter because tomorrow the biggest newspaper in the country will have your name in the headline. Every sordid detail of what you've been doing will be exposed, and there's nothing you can do about it.'

'There's no way you pulled that off. No journalist is going to print unsubstantiated claims like that.'

One who is trying to make amends for potentially killing my parents will. Elias may work for the local newspaper, but with family connections like his, he can make it happen. I keep this information to myself. I gesture to Oliver's surroundings.

'You do know that all this, all the power you've had since Ayesha conveniently died, is all because of me?'

He scoffs. 'I think Sam might have something to say about that.'

'Rob. Your lawyer. All me. You have no idea how much power I really have. So, when I say that story is ready to go, you should know I'm telling the truth.'

He stiffens at Rob's name and speaks through gritted teeth. 'Sam seems to think there's something special about you. I'm not so sure. My gut tells me you're a narcissist who believes her own fantasy.'

'Are you willing to stake everything you have on it?'

'All right, let's say for argument's sake I believe you. What's your price to let this all go?'

I smile, thinking of the game Othello and I once played. People have always joked that I'm cheap, but I think I understand the value of money and seeing Oliver punished is worth all the money in the world.

'It's no use. You're going down for this. I'm simply offering you the opportunity to handle it with dignity. Think of your kids.'

He doesn't like my comment, and quickly moves to the edge

of the sofa. Much quicker than I anticipated. 'I think you're going to want to hear what I have to say before you go making threats like that.'

'Why is that?'

'Because if I'm going down for this, I'm bringing you all down with me.'

I really don't want to kill Oliver, but he's backed me into a corner.

Sam's been stealing and Ruth's been caught with class A drugs. The former doesn't come as a surprise, given that stealing from the rich was the entire basis of Sam's and my plan for system-wide reform, but he's taken so much more than he told me about. He's moved millions to an offshore account, not for *Ellis and Greaves* or any other apparent purpose. Just for him.

If I don't back off, Oliver will press charges against them both. Of course, that's only if he's alive to do so.

As I leave Oliver's apartment, I take the shiny black credit card Sam gave me out of my purse. I'm not sure what's more corrosive, my power or this tiny piece of plastic. I close my eyes, count down from three and make myself snap it on two, surprising even myself. Possibly the adult part of my brain knew I wouldn't be able to go through with it once I opened my eyes.

I've enabled Sam, and my guilt stops me from directing too much of my anger at him. It's Ruth I can't get over. She'd be dead if it weren't for me. How dare she take drugs? Especially after she's seen the consequences. I only have to think about the pus-filled heroin-induced abscess I saw and it's enough to taste vomit.

I turn up on her doorstep at 11 p.m. The flat we used to share. The Poundland gnomes I bought are still sitting on every other step.

She opens the door in her fluffy dressing gown, patterned with blue butterflies. 'Thea? What are you doing here?'

'I need to talk to you.' I barge in without waiting for an invitation. Once you've lived somewhere, you don't really need permission to go inside.

She follows me into the kitchen/living room. It makes my heart twinge a little to be back here. The personal touches and lived-in feeling are in stark contrast to the lifeless penthouse apartment I've become so comfortable in. The television is on standby, a bowl of half-eaten popcorn's been left on the coffee table and the sofa cushions are squashed into the corners. Our porcelain cat – the one I thought was funny and Ruth thought was creepy – is tucked away on the television stand, but not gone. Seeing it melts my anger away. Ruth was convinced it would bring bad luck, but she's kept it anyway.

'What is it?' she asks.

I hesitate. I still have to say what I came here to say, but I deliver it in a softer voice than I'd originally planned. 'It's Oliver. He told me that he caught you with drugs. Now he's using it to threaten me.'

Her face pales. She pulls her dressing gown tighter across herself. 'Oh.'

'Ruth, what happened? After everything you've seen, how could you have done something so stupid?'

'No, they weren't mine,' she says. 'A patient came in, said he was in crisis and I had to take the drugs away from him. So, I did, but I didn't know the format for logging them. I thought I could throw them away. I know it was stupid, but I thought it was for the best. Then I dropped my bag in front of Rob, he told Oliver and ... well, I thought they believed me.'

Tension evaporates from my shoulders. For a moment I

really thought I'd pushed Ruth into a darker place than I could have imagined.

'Oh, I think he does. He just doesn't care what the truth is.'

At that moment, Zara walks in, wearing a fluffy pink dressing gown – Ruth's spare. She awkwardly waves at me and flicks the kettle on. I don't even have it in me to find her presence irritating. I've always held such a special place of hatred in my heart for Zara, and I'm not sure she ever really deserved it. It simply felt safer to keep Ruth to myself than to let her grow with someone else.

'I don't understand. What is Oliver threatening you about?' Ruth asks.

I give a sideways glance to Zara, wondering how much I should say in front of her.

'Zara knows all about the drug incident,' Ruth says.

'Well, you know I told you about what happened to Karly? Turns out there were others, and I've been working to put a legal case together against Oliver. He found out and ... well, he clearly thought this threat would make me stop.'

'A legal case? So, you're not going to ...' Ruth trails off. Clearly there are some things Zara doesn't know.

'Well, I was trying to do things differently. Then this happened.'

'Then I want you to keep going. Don't let him escape justice – real justice – because of me.'

Of course Ruth would say that. She's never put herself ahead of anyone else. I would – I always have – but maybe it's time to stop.

Zara brings over three chamomile teas and sits beside Ruth on the sofa. She brushes Ruth's hand. 'Are you sure? It could end up on your permanent record. You could go to prison.'

Ruth nods. 'I'm sure.'

They exchange another look like the one before. One of unspoken words and safe places.

'So you two are together again?' I ask.

'Yeah, after ... what happened ... recently, I realized how lucky I am to be alive. And I don't want to waste my life on things that don't make me happy. So I gave in my notice at the ICU, and I'm going to specialize in family medicine. It means I'll really get to know my patients, and I'll have more time for the people I care about,' she says, softly smiling at Zara.

'I'm happy for you.' And I realize I am. I may have been angry at Ruth for turning her back on me, but I never want her to be in pain. I'm glad Zara's there for her. 'Sorry for being such a shit employee,' I add.

She laughs. Not a sound I've heard much of from her, but it suits her. 'You weren't all bad. It's certainly less fun without you around.'

Kind of her to say. She leans forward to pick up her tea. As she does, her cropped black hair falls into her face and I catch a whiff of her bergamot and sandalwood perfume, the one that reminds me of Frances, of bursts of rage and childhood shame. Then I remember something else. *Fuck*. I've taken three and a bit months off Zara's life because she pissed me off at work. Zara, who is now Ruth's girlfriend. Ruth would smash that creepy porcelain cat into a million pieces if she ever found out what I'd done. I make a promise to fix this too, somehow, but one problem at a time.

Ruth follows me to the door. Zara excuses herself, diplomatically, I think.

'It was nice to see you,' I say.

Ruth shakes her head. 'This doesn't make us okay, Thea.'

I want to tell her about Elias, about Dad, about everything.

But there's too much distance between us. I have to find a way to make it up to her.

'I'm sorry for what I did to you. Christ, I'm sorry about a lot of things.'

'You killed people. Sorry isn't enough. Not even close.'

'How do I put things right?'

'I have no idea. Just ... don't kill Oliver, okay? That's a start.'

If I let Oliver live, Ruth and Sam could go to prison.

If I kill him, I'm afraid I might never stop. It's not like a diet; I can't restart it in the morning.

Regardless, I've made my choice and set things in motion. At 8 a.m. tomorrow morning, Oliver will get the justice he deserves. It's taking every ounce of my strength not to turn around, barge back into his apartment and reverse my decision.

I can't stay with Ruth, and I can't go to Mayfair because the idea of a confrontation with Sam is about as appealing as staring directly into the sun. The only places that are open in Clapham this late are loud and have horrible lighting. Nevertheless, I go to a place with sparkly walls and order three shots of vodka. I miss the days when this was my typical evening. How sensible I've become.

There's a luminous pink digital clock looming above the bar. It's 2 a.m. I notice a cup full of cocktail sticks and wonder if sticking one into my hand would be preferable to the waiting. Killing Oliver would be murder. That word has always bothered me. *Murder*. It's so fraught with associations to acts of evil, and I wanted to believe that I was different, better than everyone else who kills a person, because I had noble intentions.

I'm under no such illusions now. Lots of people will kill

under the right circumstances. To save their own life, the lives of others. Heck, soldiers and police get rewarded for handing out death. Dress it up however you like, taking a human life is murder. Each one will chip away at my soul. I have now accepted this as fact.

But is that an excuse not to do it?

I order three more shots, downing them so I don't have to taste it. There's a group of university students by the bar, drinking in much better spirits. Ha, a pun. Oh dear – I think the shots are kicking in. I keep up a steady routine in time with the music. Thump, thump. Shot, Shot. Until I'm good and hammered.

I start dancing to an R & B song I can't name. The university girls have adopted me into their group and within minutes we are old friends, bouncing when another even greater song comes on and singing the chorus in mangled cat wails. Until the vodka turns into potato churn in my stomach and I have to run to the bathroom.

My new best friend, who is either called Tatiana or Tabitha, comes after me and holds back my hair while I hurl into the toilet. There's nothing purer than friendships formed in night-club toilets.

'Are you okay?' she asks.

'Yes,' I say, once I'm finished retching fumes. 'No,' I add in a second, smaller voice.

She passes me water and some toilet paper.

'I've done something that will hurt my friends, but it's the right thing to do,' I whisper. Although, truthfully, there was no choice available that could have prevented that entirely.

'You had better not be telling the bouncer about the molly in my purse,' she hisses. There's something fierce about her, a fighter. I shake my head. 'Good,' she says. 'Well, I don't know who your friends are, but bitches got to make their own deci-sions. It's not up to you to go round fixing their problems.'

I'm not sure if she's right, or if the alcohol is imbuing her words with more meaning than they're worth, but I finally commit to my decision. I stay with her while she fixes her make-up, takes a pee and tells me all about her university debt and shitty minimum wage jobs. She says she works at a pet shop cleaning cages, earning dog shit while cleaning up after them. She's out celebrating because she just quit. I don't think it sounds so bad. At least she gets to be around animals and doesn't have to worry about whose life she's currently ruining on a daily basis, but I'm happy to mutter, 'That's crap,' and, 'You should have definitely quit,' in the right places.

I admire how thoroughly she denies absolutely anything being her fault. By the time 8 a.m. comes around, I'm sitting on a park bench with Tatiana or Tabitha, stroking her hair as she comes back down to reality.

I don't notice the time until my phone buzzes. Oliver's face flashes up in the news alert alongside a headline: 'NOBODY SAYS NO TO DADDY': AN EXPOSÉ OF ABUSE. It's a multi-page spread detailing how Oliver used his position to exploit those in his care, case details provided by Svetlana Tate, pub-lished by Elias Grey in one of the country's most widely read newspapers.

Chapter Thirty-Three

*When is someone beyond redemption? The
moment they first take a human life? When
they do it with intent? Or when they do it with
malice?*

I can't help it; I'm feeling a little smug. Oliver is now the most
hated man in the city, perhaps the country, and it's all thanks
to me. And I didn't even have to kill anyone to do it. It's nice to
know my power isn't the only thing I have to offer, especially
since I don't plan on using it again.

I'm working at the pet shop that Tatiana/Tabitha told me
about. I still don't know her name, but it's not important
because I deleted her number the next day. Some friendships
should stay in the toilet where they were made.

After that night, I walked past the pet shop on my morning
hunt for coffee, assumed they would be looking for staff as
their last employee had just quit, and they were. The manager
didn't ask much, just wanted to know when I could come in for
a trial. Nothing burned down on my watch, so I got the job.

I've also got a house share. It's a bit of a step down from

Ruth's flat, but I never could have afforded that if she'd charged me a proper rent. It's mould-free and I have a decent-sized cupboard, so I can't complain. The house comes with four other renters of varying ages. They don't seem to know each other either, our social lives so far limited to grunts as we eat breakfast and a discussion about washing machine priority when we get home. It's fine. Normal. Where I'm supposed to be.

Talking of Ruth, I guess we're friends again. Or at least a tentative friendship consisting of weekly coffee dates that feel slightly more like probation appointments, but hey, it's progress.

The charges against her were immediately dropped. I don't know the details, but I guess no one really wants to see a good doctor dragged through the courts on the say-so of the country's current public enemy number one. Sam, on the other hand ... let's just say his assets have been frozen and the law firm is under investigation. Turns out my name wasn't really on anything official except the letterheads, so the police have been leaving me alone for now.

Almost every week, Ruth asks me the same question. 'How could you bring yourself to do it, Thea? To kill people?'

And I tell her the same thing – I love her, I had to save her, I was trying to protect her.

But this week she cuts me off. 'Not the normal crap. You might have started doing this for me, but that's not why you kept going.'

I take a deep breath. If she really wants the truth, she can have it.

'You know how many people make it through life without killing anyone? Literally almost everyone. It shouldn't be hard. And yet, somehow, I found myself having killed multiple people. Ever since I was a kid I've been on this downhill trajectory – everyone in my life thought I was a fuck-up, and then I proved them all right and failed the bar, but I never thought I'd be capable of this. I never set out to do this. The only way to make it all right was to believe I had this power for a good reason and to ignore anything to the contrary.'

She is watching me intently, assessing me for signs of deceit. 'You killed people because you were afraid of being a bad person?'

'Yes.'

'Is that why you created it – the *Ethical Guide to Murder*?' she says, sipping her cappuccino.

'You know about that?'

'Found it in the flat. I threw it out.'

'Oh,' is all I can say. I don't even remember taking it to the flat. It must have been in the bags I brought back when Sam went away, that weekend when Diego died.

'How can I trust you not to do it again?'

'Isn't that why you're here right now – to keep an eye on me? It's okay, I'm grateful for it. I promise you, Ruth, I've learned my lesson. I'm done running away and shifting the blame. I'll find a way to prove it to you, however long it takes.'

Today is my fifth shift. I arrive five minutes before I'm expected and get straight to work. First, I need to check and feed the animals in the back room, which are just small reptiles and rodents. I love this job. People bring their dogs in all day long, so what's not to like? The khaki uniform is a bit military, but it's comfortable. My boss, Carl, checks in to make sure I've taken my breaks (because of a union threat a previous employee made). And cleaning cages isn't that bad – it's only mice droppings, which if I'm perfectly honest are so tiny that I find them cute.

The pet shop has a wall of dog collars and leads, two vertical aisles of food and treats, and three horizontal aisles of beds, treatments and other supplies. This morning, a whole family came in with a schnauzer puppy. There's nothing cuter than baby barks combined with an old man's beard. I helped them pick out the works. I also recommended a feed known to help schnauzers with their problem skin – Carl told me about it, but I've also been reading our books on pet care during the quiet periods. I'm learning. Maybe I'll even get another pet that won't get run over, in the distant future when I can afford to live somewhere that allows animals.

All is well until a customer I recognize from last week walks through the door. I remember her because she insisted on pronouncing my name as 'Tay-ah' rather than 'Thee-ah', even after I corrected her. She came in to get probiotics for her yappy Yorkshire terrier with uncontrollable diarrhoea.

'I want a refund,' she says, banging down the sunshine yellow tub of 'Happy Tums' probiotics I sold her. The plastic seal has been ripped open.

The customer is always right. Always right. Always. I take a breath and smile.

'I'm sorry, we don't usually refund opened supplements. Is there a problem with the product?'

'You could certainly say that. Poor Tiddles has been vomiting for days, and he's completely ...' she looks side to side and her voice drops to a whisper '... backed up, if you know what I mean?'

'Constipated.'

She raises her eyebrows, as if to scold me. 'Well, yes.'

'You know, it's quite normal for dogs to take a few days to adjust to probiotics. The vet recommended them, right? Sometimes you have to introduce supplements gradually.' I pause to open the tub, intending to show her what she could cut the portion down to. At least a quarter of the finely ground chicken-flavoured powder has been used. 'Erm, how much have you been giving him? This is a three-month supply.'

She smiles in a fake, pursed-lip effort, as if I've said something incredibly stupid and she doesn't want to embarrass me by calling it out.

'I would like to speak to a manager,' she says, turning around before my response, searching for someone else in a khaki uniform to accost.

Her hand rests on the counter. Three rings: two diamonds and one sapphire. Why she would care about a refund for an £8.99 tub is beyond me. Especially as there's nothing wrong with it – she's just using it incorrectly. It takes me back to every time someone has tried to make me feel small just because they can – they're important and I'm not. I think about how easy it would be to reach over and shorten her life. Every retail worker should have my abilities. Even if they didn't use them, customers would certainly change their tune if they knew that one rude interaction could be their doom.

But no. I'm reformed. Anger cannot be allowed to rule my decisions anymore.

Carl takes over my irritating customer. He's about forty and one of those men who get better with age. She clearly prefers talking to him because her laugh echoes over the aisles where I've slunk off to. He repeats the same advice I gave her but offers her a refund if there's no improvement in a week. She leaves the store with a wave and the same tub tucked under her arm.

At the end of my shift, I walk home with a pep in my step. I made a good decision today. Very adult, mature even.

Grandad and I speak most days now. He's finally relented and allowed me to pick him out a smartphone, and is fairly blown away that he can send me pictures over WhatsApp. Today he's sent me a photo of the sky with a message that reads: Look what I just saw. Incredible. I'm not sure what he means so I ring him as I walk.

'You got it already?' he asks.

'Yes, Grandad. I can just see the sky though. What is it?'

'It's a Spitfire. They were flying them over the golf course. Haven't seen one in the wild like that for years. Can you see it?'

I see a small dot that looks like a bird. 'Oh yeah, amazing.'

He tells me about his day and I tell him about mine, even the woman with the Yorkshire terrier.

'You didn't get angry?' he asks.

'A bit, but I'm in control.'

'I didn't mean you weren't.'

'It's okay, Grandad. It actually feels good that I have someone to talk to about it, someone who understands and can hold me accountable.'

'I'm so sorry, Thea. I genuinely believed if you didn't know about your power, then you wouldn't be tempted to use it. I thought I was protecting you by keeping it a secret. Now I wonder if you'd been able to talk about it, maybe you wouldn't have been so influenced by that lawyer, and none of this would have happened.'

'Grandad, no one is responsible for my actions but me. Definitely not you. But not even Sam. And I get why you didn't tell me about the power. There's no guide for how you're supposed to deal with that situation – trust me, I've tried to find it. But there is one thing I don't understand – why wouldn't you talk to me about my parents? There's so much I wish I knew about them.'

'You were always so close to your father. Two peas in a pod, your mother used to say. I was afraid that if you felt connected to him, you'd start to think like him, be like him.'

'And Mum?'

'Every time I picture her face ...' He pauses, swallowing hard enough that I hear it through the phone. 'I simply cannot bear it. I think about everything she should have had in life. She wanted more children – another girl and a boy at least. She wanted to live abroad for a while, somewhere in Europe. And she wanted to open a little shop – she loved restoring old furniture and antiques. I told myself that you were so young when they died, it would be better if you could forget and move on.'

I stop walking in the middle of the pavement. My eyes are stinging. I've just learned three new things about my mum, and they are precious. I keep a hold of myself though, because I don't want to set Grandad off and have him end this call.

'Do you have any idea how good it feels to hear you talk about them? About her?'

'I could tell you more?'

I settle down on a bench. It's covered in fresh pigeon shit and I still don't care.

'I'd like that.'

I'm about to get onto the Tube when my phone dings again. I wonder if it's another Spitfire from Grandad, but it's a message from my housemate: The washing machine has flooded the kitchen. Are you coming back soon?

I thank some higher power that I dragged the message down instead of clicking on it. Instead of replying, I leave it unread and put the phone back into my pocket. Not very nice, I know, but I've done worse. One step at a time.

Instead of heading home to the washing machine drama, I

text Sam and head to Mayfair. I've been dodging him for several weeks, letting my anger towards him simmer. But he hasn't called or texted me for three days now. I can't help wondering if I'm thinking about him again simply because he's stopped chasing me; I'm always wanting what I can't have. I don't think that's all it is – sometimes you have to let time smooth away the sting of betrayal before a productive conversation can be had. Now it's time to talk. Finish things with an air of amicability. Also, I left my favourite trainers in the flat. I cannot keep running in these cheap things, with no heel support, that I ordered off Amazon when I was desperate for an outlet in Elias's village.

I still have the key, and the doorman only glances my way as I head past him and push the button for the elevator. Sam hasn't replied to my message. What if he doesn't want to see me? I've turned up uninvited, wearing my khaki uniform, dry shampoo no longer hiding my unwashed hair, and I think there's some lizard shit on my sleeve. Why do I still care? It's not like I want to maintain our relationship. We're bad for each other. Together, our worst qualities shine bright and combine into something monstrous. But, despite all of that, I do love him. Sometimes the heart is slower than the head.

The elevator door opens and I get the shock of my life. Oliver. My heart misses a full beat, and I have to reorient myself, checking I'm still in the lobby, looking at my hands to make sure I have ten fingers to confirm this isn't a dream.

'Thea,' he says. Bizarrely he is grinning. 'I'm so pleased to see you.'

'Fuck off. What are you doing here?'

'I'm allowed to visit my lawyer. Gossip rags don't mean much to me.'

'Hardly a gossip rag.'

'Well, he didn't answer anyway. Maybe you'll have better luck.'

I propel myself into the elevator and press for floor seventeen. If it wasn't for the lift buttons illuminating past each floor, I'd hardly know I was moving. The quiet ease of it puts me on edge.

The doors glide apart. I force my brain to take charge and stride forward. I knock three times. No answer. Oliver said he wasn't in but now that I think about it, that doesn't make sense. The concierge wouldn't have let Oliver up if Sam wasn't home, and I can hear the faint sound of evening news television coming from under the door. Sam won't mind if I let myself in. If he's really not there, then I'll grab my trainers and try him another day.

I unpick the chewing gum that's stuck to my key and open the door. I head down the corridor, first door to the left into the kitchen. 'Sam?'

Then I see him, motionless on the floor. His hand on his throat, but without the strength to grasp. There's blood. Too much blood. Red leaking out onto the marbled kitchen floor, staining his white shirt and seeping out through his fingers.

I'm not sure when my heart last pumped. There is no air in the room. I sink down to the floor, feeling the blood seep through my jeans. It's colder than it should be. Sam's eyes are open, staring at the ceiling, non-responsive as I gently call his name.

I put my fingers to his neck to check for a pulse, but I find something stranger. He is empty. No time of death because he is already gone. Sam is dead.

But ... people get resuscitated all the time, right? Maybe if I can jump-start his heart with a bolt of energy, it'll work just the same as the defibrillator paddles.

But I'm not holding any life. I've got nothing. I desperately try to think up solutions. Oliver's long gone by now. Who else could I find quickly enough? The concierge is too far away. I think of Mrs Maple, the widower who lives in the flat next door. She's always in, watching daytime television and calling management to complain about the cleaners stealing from her. Spoiler alert: they never steal.

I can feel Ruth's judgement condemning the thoughts entering my mind. Or maybe my own moral compass has finally kicked in. But what am I supposed to do, just let death take Sam?

Oh, I know.

There is someone with life I could take, and she's right here in this room. Can I really do it? Give up years of my life for a man who manipulated me? But how can I blame him? I pulled him into this because the decisions were too much to cope with on my own. Neither of us is well suited to power.

Sam's green eyes are like dry summer grass. Since that day at Grandad's, when I read Dad's journals and pulled my life force out from me, I've been able to see it clearly. All forty-eight years of it. I decide to give him half. Our crimes are shared, so our punishment should be too.

I take his hand and close my eyes. The outside world falls away. I see nothing, taste nothing, hear nothing. Instead, focusing only on my breath, reaching inwards until I can pull the thread. There it is, that ugly, frayed and yellow thing. I wrap my mind around it and pull. It's different to all the times I've done this before. It's like my body knows what I'm trying to do and is resisting the threat. Taking life from someone else is easy because they don't expect it, so they don't even try to hold on. And last time I tried this on myself, it wasn't intentional. Not really. This time, my body is wiser and stronger. I keep pulling, trying to visualize my life force coming loose, unravelling through me and curling into my fingertips.

I let it flow, straight into Sam.

I've almost managed it when the door bursts open behind me. Words. Footsteps. Shouting. I ignore it, trying to stay focused on the task at hand. Then two hands grab me, shoving me back hard into the kitchen cabinet.

There are men and women flooding the room, circling Sam.

'Wait!' I shout. 'Let me see him.'

As I scramble forward, someone pulls me back. 'Oh no you don't.'

I recognize that rat-toned voice. It's Stewart.

Once again, he says, 'Thea Greaves, you are under arrest.'

Chapter Thirty-Four

Is it ever possible for the punishment to fit the crime?

There is no Sam to come to my rescue this time. I know the transfer didn't work. As Stewart pulled me away, I felt my life force snap back into me like a rubber band. All forty-eight years of it. Instead, I get the shitty Legal Aid lawyer I was dreading for my previous arrest. I've been waiting in the police holding cell for three hours before she arrives. Anya Broadman is in her twenties; she has dark circles like caverns under her eyes and a stain on her suit jacket I don't think she's noticed.

'Is he dead then?' I ask the moment she enters the room.

'Who?'

'Sam.' When she doesn't respond, I gesture at my blood-soaked T-shirt. 'The man whose blood is on me.'

'Oh, there's been no update. He's been taken to the hospital.'

That's weird. They don't take corpses to the hospital.

'Let's go through your case, Emma,' she says.

'It's Thea.'

She stares at her notes. 'Oh, I see.' Then she slips the file into her bag and leafs through a stack of ten more. 'Here we go.'

She quickly scans my file. Her eyes widen as she reads it for what is clearly the first time. I'm fucked.

'Okay, you've been charged with the attempted murder of Sam Ellis. However, you weren't in possession of a weapon. I've seen cases like this before where the charges have been dropped to assault. It really all depends on whether he survives.'

Anya stops reading and looks at me cautiously. People keep giving me this particular look, one where they are trying to appraise my level of humanity. I've seen it from Ruth, and I've seen it from Grandad.

'I don't understand. Why haven't they arrested Oliver? He was leaving Sam's building as I got there. He must be on CCTV,' I say.

'Unfortunately, the CCTV inside the building was down due to a wiring fault. The concierge has testified that he only saw you today, not Mr Locksley – who also has an alibi.'

I should have realized Oliver wouldn't have tried to kill Sam unless he was sure he'd get away with it. He's not exactly a fan of a fair fight. Then I showed up and gift-wrapped myself as a prime suspect. No wonder he was pleased to see me.

'It's bullshit.'

Anya continues: 'This is clearly going to Crown Court. The prosecution will use your relationship with the victim as a motivation. But without a weapon, we can argue your presence at the scene of the crime as circumstantial evidence. Even without the CCTV, we can still make the case that Mr Locksley should be considered as a suspect. And it seems Sam had other enemies we can cast aspersions on, which could be enough to give the jury reasonable doubt. My advice is to plead not guilty.'

It's then I realize there's a quiet intelligence in Anya's eyes.

She's tired and overworked, of course, but I think she cares. She's not phoning it in on my case, even though it's a tricky one and she'll undoubtedly end up putting hundreds of hours into it for a pittance of a paycheque. Anya's no Sam, but she's not what I'd expected, either.

'Okay,' I say. 'Not guilty.'

I'm held in the police cell overnight and processed in the magistrates' court the next day. This has to be the first morning in years that I've woken up without a coffee. My back is in knots from the bed, which is a thin blue plastic mattress thrown on top of a cement block. And the light from the barred window has been coming through bright and strong since around 7 a.m. I miss luxury apartments, silk sheets and caramel espresso. I miss Ruth's colourful flat with its cosy cushions and fluffy rugs. I even miss my substandard house share.

I didn't actually expect to be taken to court today because I'd assumed the charge would be upped from attempted murder to murder. Then we'd have to go through the formalities all over again. So Sam's somehow still alive. I've no idea how. No way to find out. So it's extra bizarre to be standing in the defendant's dock. Everybody's eyes are on me. I can almost hear them wondering whether I'm guilty and speculating on why I did it. I stay focused on the public gallery, hoping that I'll see a familiar face. A few more spectators trickle in, most likely aspiring law students. There's a girl who looks like me: short blonde hair and an asymmetrical face. And then, finally, Grandad shuffles onto the aisle seat. He gives me a small nod of encouragement. I take a deep breath.

The prosecution stands first – a man in his fifties with piercing blue eyes. I recognize him from when I used to listen in on trials, back when I wanted to be a lawyer. He's got a decent reputation. One of the rare individuals that stays with the CPS for their entire career, even though he's good enough not to.

I dip my head in shame while he outlines my crimes. When he says my name, I look to the door and notice as the blonde girl with the asymmetric face stops chewing her pen and lets her eyes go wide.

'Given the serious and violent nature of these allegations, I recommend that the trial is immediately sent forward to Crown Court and that bail is denied,' he says.

Solicitors can't represent their clients in court, so there's no sign of Anya. Instead, a barrister I've never met gives my defence. He's young, and the first thing I notice about him is his pit stains, even though it's barely twelve degrees.

'My client has no history of violent offences and no prior convictions,' he says. 'There is no reason to think that if she was released on bail she would commit another offence.'

He doesn't fight my corner too hard though – Anya's recommendation – because there is no point. Bail is something given to petty thieves and teenagers with weed, not suspected murderers. Magistrates' court is not our battleground, and there's no sense in pissing off the system.

'The defendant will be held at HMP Bronzefield until such a time when the case can be tried at Crown Court,' the magistrate says.

And that's it. No crack of the gavel, no drama. I'm processed in less than fifteen minutes, and I overhear the magistrates discussing whether they can squeeze in another case before lunch.

My chariot awaits. Or, rather, a police Transit van to deliver me to Bronzefield, the largest women's prison in the country. My barrister walks with me.

'Remember, you're not a criminal and they can't treat you as such. You'll get your own clothes, greater visitation rights and access to activities. They can only hold you on remand for a maximum of a hundred and eighty-two days, and that time will come off your sentence.'

'What if they find me not guilty?' I ask.

'Oh, well . . .' His professional veneer cracks. Clearly, he hasn't considered this option. 'Anya will outline all of your options in due course.'

'Sign this,' the prison officer says, passing me a form. She's a short, squat woman who reminds me of a pit bull.

'What is it?' I ask.

'A non-disclosure agreement.'

The other women I came in with signed it without reading it and have been taken through to discover their new home. However, to the pit bull's great displeasure, I read the document. It says that I cannot contact any media about anything that happens inside the prison, which has the effect of making goosebumps rise on my forearms. I have already watched them rifle through my possessions as if they did not belong to me. My phone, my credit card, my driving licence, all taken from me and wrapped in plastic. Maybe that's why, despite the pit bull's glare, I cannot make myself sign this document. It's the last part of my freedom.

I put the pen down. 'Sorry, I can't give up the few rights I have left.'

She huffs. 'We can't process you until you sign it.'

I say nothing. Maybe I've discovered an incredible loophole in the prison system and they will have to let me go.

'You'll have to stay in isolation until we can find a solution.'

I'm given three pairs of granny pants, grey trackies and a nightie. Every garment is itchy and smells of cheap detergent, but I do not complain. The officer that takes me to isolation has been muttering about the inconvenience of it, and I don't want to piss them off further.

The isolation room has four walls, a bed, a toilet and nothing else. There's no air, no light, no noise. My heartbeat quickens. I cannot be in here. The officer smiles as he locks the door behind me.

The night is gripped by ghosts.

I'm in the nightclub, Supernova, smoke filling the air and Ruth dying on the floor. Greg is there. The first person I killed, the reason all of this started.

'Murderer,' he says, gripping my arm when I try to escape.

Then I'm back at church. Sitting at my parents' graves when Frances Wells spits venom in my ear. 'Selfish little liar. It should be you who's dead.'

I am a child again. It's a moment of reprieve, and my parents are alive. Dad sits beside me, stroking my hair. 'It's not your fault,' he says. 'You were my mistake.'

And then there's Sam. He cannot speak. Every time I see him floating through my mind, his throat opens up and blood pours out. He tries to force the words, but all that comes out is a strangled gurgle. I wake up and blink away the image of him, but he's there every time I close my eyes and sometimes even when they're open. I stare at the wall, but all I see is his flame-haired silhouette imprinted on the grey.

I sign the non-disclosure agreement the next day.

My cell is a welcome upgrade. There is a television, a kettle and a welcome pack on my bed, like I'm in the world's worst spa facility.

I find institution life suits me. The prison follows a strict schedule from 8.15 a.m. to 6.15 p.m. Not being able to choose what I wear, eat or do is a relief. The outside world is full of decisions, each one an opportunity to set your day down a wrong path. But here, nothing is expected of me. The assumption is that I'm already a bad person simply for being here. Sometimes I even get little green slips under my door for good behaviour (the standard of which is simply not starting fights or telling guards to go fuck themselves) and each one gives me a little dopamine kick.

Newcomers often get themselves into trouble here – sit at the wrong table, look at the wrong person – but I'm generally left alone. It's like I've been giving off an energy that warns people away. Until today.

I've been on remand for twenty-seven days. Today, I'm in the cafeteria queue, waiting for soggy mashed potatoes and burnt cauliflower (veggie food in prison means I get an extra portion of whatever non-meat option is there), when something pushes me forward and I smack my head against the canteen. When I go to touch the spot, I find blood.

'What the hell?' I say, without thinking, without noticing who I am speaking to.

There's a woman on the floor – undoubtedly the weight that crashed into me. But I accidentally lock eyes with another. She's tall and lean, built like an athlete with a long red scar across her broad shoulders.

'What did you say to me?' she asks, although it is not a question.

'Sorry, I didn't mean anything by it.' I hold up my hands to placate her and try to look for an officer to help. This is not the correct course of action.

'Who are you looking for?' She steps closer. 'Are you going to tell on me? Report me to the teacher? Do you really think that's how things work around here?'

Then she grabs the back of my head and smashes me into the canteen again. I'm blinded by the shock of it, as well as the droplets of blood rolling into my eyes. I try to jerk myself out of her grip, but her hands are entwined with my hair, and she does it again. Her eyes are shining with hatred and something in me gives way. I stop trying to escape. She can do whatever she wants to me. I deserve it.

She cocks her head to the side. 'What's wrong with you?'

That's when the guard finally shows up.

'What's going on here?' he asks with the interest of a man forcefully dragged on his wife's shopping spree.

My attacker roughly pushes me away. 'Nothing.'

He looks to me.

'I slipped. Sorry for the fuss.'

Sam is still in a coma. I asked Anya to find out for me and to my surprise she called. He's apparently stable but not showing any signs of recovery. I don't understand it. I failed to make the transfer. He should be dead. This in-between state has never happened before, but there's nothing I can do about it. No one is about to let me anywhere near him.

It's another week before Anya comes to discuss my case. I'm delivered into a bland meeting room and the officer waits by the door, pretending not to listen to our conversation.

'I'm sorry to tell you that the prosecution would like to move forward with your case.'

'But what if Sam wakes up? He can tell them I didn't do it.'

'According to the doctors, when a patient is stable but unresponsive like this, there's no way of knowing when and if they'll wake up. It could be years. And, after being in a coma for an extended period of time like this, memory problems are extremely likely. And they think they can get the charges to stick.'

'Did they find the weapon?' I ask, wondering if Oliver some-how got it back into the apartment.

'No. It's because of what else they found. All the evidence has now been entered into discovery. I have to warn you that what they've collected is going to cause ... obstacles,' Anya says, passing me a binder. 'Go to page ten.'

The contents of my notebook have been photocopied and logged into evidence. The notebook Sam jokingly titled *An Ethical Guide to Murder*, pages upon pages of us brainstorm-ing who we'd kill and why. Ruth threw it out so how did they get it? There are also various texts Sam sent to me, articles detailing the crimes of some of our targets. Cryptic messages about what they deserve to happen to them. And CCTV plac-ing me near some of those targets shortly before they died. But, crucially, never on the day they actually died. Whatever Stewart is trying to pin on me here, even he can't make out I killed these people just because there's evidence of Sam and me talking about them.

'The dates of some of the diary entries correspond with several of the victims' deaths, and the descriptions could be argued to represent some of them. Is there anything you can tell me to explain this?'

'I don't understand. Are they charging me with more mur-ders? Most of these people died from natural causes.'

'There's been pressure from the police to reopen the Brendan Steele case, but they aren't charging you with anything else. Yet.'

'Pressure from the police – you mean Stewart?'

She nods. 'The courts are usually reluctant to reopen a closed case. I believe what they're actually doing is preparing an argument about your state of mind. My guess is that they'll say all of this is some kind of delusion concocted by you and the victim, and then you took it further and killed him. But you'll know better than I.'

I shake my head. 'It's nothing, just a creative exercise. Some ramblings in my personal diary.'

'Well, it's not personal anymore.'

I continue flicking through the evidence. Then I reach the list of prosecution witnesses, and I read a name that cuts me cold. Ruth Levy.

'Ruth is testifying against me?'

Anya nods. 'As a character witness. Do you have any idea what she might say?'

It's then I realize why the police never came for Ruth about the drug charges. Why she's listed as a prosecution and not a defence witness. She's been working for the police. That's how they got the notebook, that's how they knew where to go looking for evidence.

I must have been quiet for a while because Anya says, 'I know this can be difficult. Were you and Ruth close?'

I can't even be angry with Ruth. She wanted me to face justice, and she told me this clearly and repeatedly to my face. It would be like being angry at the sky for being blue.

'I'm fine. She's going to say that I killed all these people because of her.' Then I add, 'Or she'll say that I think I did.'

I wonder if they're going to try and find me not guilty by way of insanity. Perhaps Ruth thought a mental hospital would be a kinder place to hold me. Or perhaps by making me out to be a violent maniac, she hopes they can keep me for longer.

Anya doesn't ask if it's true – if I admit this, she can no longer present my not-guilty plea.

Instead, she leans forward. 'I should tell you that CPS have offered another plea bargain. They're willing to reduce the charge to second degree attempted murder if you plead guilty.

It carries a prison sentence of five to fifteen years. And, of course, a third off your sentence for saving the court time. I think it's unlikely they'd reopen the Brendan Steele case if you accepted the plea.'

It's strange that the true outcome of so many legal cases is settled this way. Not in a courtroom, but behind closed doors with quiet agreements. A 'we know you're guilty but we're not sure we can prove it, so take the deal'. It's a good offer. I could manage five years, I think. The alternative could be life imprisonment. Worse than that, if the trial goes ahead, I will have to face Ruth standing up in court, tearing apart my character and condemning my soul.

I remember what she said to me the last time I saw her: 'You killed people. Sorry isn't enough. Not even close.'

I think I understand now. I need to accept my punishment; no more running away. Ruth thinks I deserve to be here, so perhaps I do.

Anya continues, 'So, Thea, how do you want to plead?'

I'm waiting in the visitors' hall, wearing a hi-viz jacket over my grey trackies. I got us a decent table – number thirteen – which is in the corner. It has a view of the running track and is close but not too close to the vending machine.

The door opens and the visitors pour in. The woman next to me chokes on a sob as her partner walks over with two small children, but she cannot move from her chair, not unless she wants this visit to be cut short. Her kids move as quickly as walking allows.

Grandad is more hesitant, uncomfortable in his unfamiliar surroundings. He's been calling me every few days or so, but this is his first visit.

'How are you, Thea?'

'I'm pretty good. I've been gardening this morning.'

'I'm sorry. Perhaps that was a tactless question.'

'No, Grandad, I wasn't being sarcastic. The prison has a vegetable garden. They think it's good for us to have something to nurture. Plus it keeps costs down.'

'I see. Well, I've always said gardening is good for the soul. It's almost November. I hope you've planted hardier veg for the winter season: broccoli, brussels sprouts, cabbages, kale, leeks and parsnips . . .' Then, before I can respond, he adds: 'Not that you'll be here in winter, of course. You'll be home by then.'

'Actually, Grandad, I'm not so sure about that. The case doesn't look so good and, well, I've decided to plead guilty.'

His eyebrows crease. Then he clasps the armrests of the plastic chair and tries to shimmy it closer.

'It's bolted to the floor,' I say.

'Oh,' he says, looking at the silver bolts. He settles for leaning forward. 'Thea, I know you've made mistakes, but you're young. You could get up to fifteen years. I don't want to see you waste your life away in here.'

'I know it sounds strange, but this feels . . . right. And fifteen years is unlikely – Anya will get them to agree to less. Whatever I get won't make up for what I've done but it's a start. For now, this is where I'm supposed to be.'

'Well, you sound as though your mind is made up.'

'It is. I want this.'

'Can I get you anything?' he asks, pointing at the vending machine.

'I'll take a Curly Wurly.'

For the first time in a long time, I sleep soundly through the night. And the next. And the one after that. The key to prison is routine. First up, a hundred sit-ups – I like to start the day right – then cereal and sugarless tea (they deliver the food to our cells the night before). Next, my morning gardening shift. Grandad's right, we need hardier vegetables. After that, yoga. Yes, I know, prison has yoga. At least my cell block does because there's a hippy who runs the sessions, and the guards allow it because it helps keep the peace.

And it really does help keep us calm. I focus on my breath. Inhale. Exhale. Inhale. Exhale. It reminds me of the strange mystical massage I had all those months ago. I can still feel the pain she found in my collarbone – grief, regret and anger all wrapped up into a tight ball of muscle – but I'm managing it. I try to remind myself that this moment is all there is. All I can do is accept it and make the best of the little things.

And I have accepted it. Anya has argued the prosecutor down to seven years. Now it's up to the judge to approve it and pass my sentence. My court date is looming, but it doesn't matter. I'm already where I'm supposed to be.

Then, three weeks before I'm due to appear at Crown Court, I get a phone call. Odd. Grandad's the only one who calls me – every Sunday afternoon at exactly 3 p.m. – and it's only Friday.

'Hey, Thea,' comes the familiar voice, the one that used to send goosebumps down my spine in all the right ways.

Sam is awake.

Chapter Thirty-Five

*I want to lie as little as possible, especially
to the people I love. If I have to lie, it should
be kind.*

I'm free.

After the story about Oliver came out, Sam realized there was only one way things were going to go. So, true to form, he tried to move as much cash as possible away from Oliver. Once Oliver realized this, he reacted badly, to say the least. And that's how Sam ended up bleeding out on his kitchen floor. But he finally woke up and told the police everything. Oliver was arrested. All charges against me were dropped.

Stewart has been suspended pending investigation. Apparently, his supervisor had explicitly told him to stay away from me after Brendan Steele. She'd had no idea he'd continued to investigate me. Then he'd tried to go over her head to reopen Brendan's case, only for the whole thing to come crashing down and the police left facing the public embarrassment of holding an innocent woman on remand for over a month. I even received a formal apology from the police commissioner saying that, while it was no excuse, Stewart had been under a huge amount of stress in his personal life. Of course, Stewart's not the only one to blame – it's the prosecution who decided to pursue the case – but he makes a better scapegoat.

So, I'm free. Free to wake up whenever I like, go wherever I like, do whatever I like. I'm not exactly sure what to do with that freedom, so after my first private shower in almost two months, I head to the hospital to see Sam.

He's sitting up by himself, fresh-faced and chirpy. There's still a dressing on his neck. It's a strain but he can speak, although the nurses are flabbergasted at his speedy recovery. It's odd, though. Ruth recovered almost instantly, Othello in a few days. But Sam's been in a coma for weeks.

'What's your theory, then?' I ask. 'Come on, you always have one.'

'Don't make me laugh,' he says, hand going to his throat.

'You do have one though, don't you?'

'Well, of course,' he says. 'I think it has to do with how close we all got to death. Ruth had a few minutes, Othello even less, and from what you told me, I was already dead. Couple of weeks recovery time isn't so bad, considering.'

'Hmm, maybe.'

'So, how long do I have left?'

This is the other thing that's confusing. Sam has exactly the same number of years left as before: sixty-two years. I didn't give them to him. It's like Oliver knocked Sam off his pre-planned course, and I stopped things long enough to get him back on track.

'You asked me that once before. Do you really want to know?'

He shakes his head. 'No, you're right. I like life better with some surprises. Although if it's on the shorter side and you're feeling charitable, do feel free to top me up.'

'I'm not going to use my power again, Sam. You compared me to an addict once and you were right. Once I start, I can't be trusted to control myself.'

'I don't understand you sometimes. I'd give anything to be able to do what you can do. Anything.'

He looks at me with such intensity I feel myself getting swept up in those green eyes again. But I can't shake the feeling it's not me he's looking at.

'Tell me honestly, did you ever really love me, or just my power?'

He hesitates for much longer than he should. 'I don't know how to answer that. I can't separate you from your power – you're one and the same to me.'

'My power is death, Sam. All I've done is make things worse.'

'You can't just ignore it.'

'Of course I can. I made it twenty-six years without killing anyone, there's nothing hard about it.'

Sam's making a weird cutting motion near his throat which feels in extremely poor taste. Then I realize a nurse is standing behind me, her eyes wide.

'Oh, sorry, we're writing a screenplay together. Just practising,' I say.

'That's so wonderful. My son's writing a screenplay too, so I know what a hard business it is. What's yours called?'

Jesus, who cares what's in some Gen Z twat's screenplay? 'Erm, *Murder . . .*' I scramble, '*Murder Book.*'

'How intriguing. I'll watch out for that,' she says, giving me an encouraging pat on my bare shoulder. *Ten years.* Not long enough. She briefly checks on Sam and tells him not to push himself too hard, then leaves the room.

'Thea, you don't think I know when you're doing it! You're in the middle of giving me a righteous speech about how you're going to stop using your ability, then you use it right in front of me.'

'That's not my fault. I can't help it when people touch me. It would be like walking around with my eyes closed.'

'Exactly, and one day you're going to meet someone you have to save. It's not your fault. Nobody could have a power like yours and not use it. Sooner or later, you will.'

Why did this have to happen? Guilty people are supposed to go to prison. They pay penance and atone for their sins. I'd accepted my fate. Heck, I was grateful for it because for the first time since Ruth cracked her head on that concrete, everything made sense. There is a relief in certainty and surrender. Now all I have is overpriced rent and student debt.

I can't turn myself in. Sam's alive and nobody would believe me about the rest. And my old life holds no appeal. There isn't a single part of me that wants to work in law anymore, or even an office, because I know it'll only be a matter of time before I murder someone over an expenses form. So what the hell do I do with the burden that is the rest of my life?

Somehow, I get my job back at the pet shop. Carl barely questions my sudden absence. I'm not sure if he's kind or negligent, but I'm grateful and not in a position to ask. My old housemates threw out my stuff after a month and replaced me with a friendly student, so I find another bland grey box room, except this one does have mould. It's great really because it reminds me of prison and I'm trying to keep my routine as similar to being behind bars as possible. I start the day with a hundred sit-ups, followed by the same breakfast of cereal and tea. Usually cornflakes, but Coco Pops if I'm feeling fancy. I meditate on the way to work. It's a one-hour bus ride and I try to pick a seat not facing anyone, so they don't think the trance-like stare on my face is about them. I go for a run as often as my blister-prone feet allow. Then I spend most of my evenings alone in my room, watching reality TV until I fall asleep. No alcohol, no caffeine and only a little sugar. Anything to calm my dopamine-driven arsehole of a brain. Rinse and repeat. I'm fully committed to maintaining this beige lifestyle until the day I die. Shame I have to wait so bloody long.

I've accepted the dull ache in my chest as fact when I notice a new poster on the bus. *Are you lonely? Change is easier together. Come to your first meeting today.* There's a photo of a very depressed-looking man hunched over, holding his head in his hands. It's for Alcoholics Anonymous.

Alcohol might not be my problem but I'm starting to think Sam's right about my addiction. That's still not enough to make me sign up. But I can't stop thinking about how nice it would be to have help, to not have to find all the answers myself, to talk to people who understand what it's like to be out of control. The fifth time I see the poster I decide it must be a sign and I cave. I never have been very good at resisting my impulses.

My nearest meeting is held in the local church. A strangely modern building with yellow panels on the outside, tinted blue windows and a glass revolving door. Nothing like the one I grew up attending; I'm not sure if Grandad would approve.

Inside the room, there are around thirty people seated in a semicircle. I procrastinate as long as possible by pouring myself a cup of instant coffee, then take the seat nearest the door.

A woman sits in the middle of the circle. She begins by

reading the preamble, 'Alcoholics Anonymous is a fellowship of men and women who share their experience, strength and hope with each other that they may solve their common problem and help others to recover from alcoholism . . .'

Then the serenity prayer:

> *God, grant me the serenity*
> *To accept the things I cannot change;*
> *The courage to change the things I can;*
> *and the wisdom to know the difference.*

The religious undertones take me by surprise. I'd thought the location was just a coincidence.

'Now I'll hand over to Harry, who is going to read for us today.'

I later learn that it's typical for different members to read sections of writing from the *Alcoholics Anonymous Big Book* and the *Twelve Steps and Twelve Traditions*.

Today, Harry is focusing on forgiveness. 'Step nine begins with,' he says, 'make direct amends to such people wherever possible, except when to do so would injure them or others.'

We discuss what this means. Sometimes making amends can include an apology, but that's not all it is. An amend is a clear, purposeful act to repair the damage inflicted on a person. It's a way to put the past behind and stop old problems resurfacing later down the line.

After this, some people share their stories. Some people don't. I sit and listen. For once, it's a relief to focus on other people's problems.

If I'd attended the previous session then I would have learned about step eight, which includes making a list of all the people you've hurt and want to make amends to. The next evening, I stay up late reading about it, then I open a brand-new leather notebook and start a new list.

I start with the people I've killed:

Greg Ferguson
Frances Wells
Brendan Steele
Juliette Haimes
Marcus Fox

Nora Berry
Iver Sokolov
Howard Peaty
Ayesha Bloom
Susan Maxwell
Rob Saunders
Kamryn Bond

This is the first time I've tallied them up. Eleven people. Christ, I've killed more people than I've had sex with. That's not a statistic anyone should aspire to. Regardless, I've made my list. Now for the amends.

AA says you should try and make your amends directly to the person you harmed. Problem is, how do you make amends to the dead?

I ask this question in the next session. Harry's chairing today so he takes this one.

'We can't make amends to someone who has died so, in this instance, we may have to make indirect amends. Perhaps contributing to a charity they cared about, visiting their grave and apologizing to their memory, or making amends to their loved ones if it feels appropriate.'

For most of the people on my list, I don't know what they cared about, who their loved ones were or what could possibly constitute amends to those people. I start with the easiest. I go home and visit Frances Wells's grave. It's overly ornate, practically a miniature tombstone in the church grounds, just three rows away from my parents. I try hard not to resent her for that. She didn't pick her burial spot. I even try and put my bus-route meditation practice to good use. There's something called a 'loving-kindness meditation' where you try to extend compassion to both yourself and others, even the people you hate.

You start with yourself. Saying things like:

> *May I be well*
> *May I be happy*
> *May I be peaceful*
> *May I live with ease*
> *May I find deep joy*
> *May I be free of pain*
> *May I be free from harm*
> *May I be free of suffering*
> *May I feel safe*

Then you redirect this to others. I decide to give it a go but *May you be well* sticks in my throat. Wow, I couldn't even say number one on the list. I don't think loving-kindness applies to people you've killed. I'm not sure any of this stuff does, because people who commit murders aren't supposed to move on with their lives. Healing is for other people.

'I'm sorry I killed you. I shouldn't have done that,' is all I manage to say to Frances. *Even thought you were a massive bitch*, I add in my head. I put the bouquet of freesias and lilies down on the ground and leave her be.

I relay this experience to Harry, illegal details redacted.

'There's no use in making empty amends. The path to healing begins with a genuine desire to change, and amends are about breaking old patterns, making a promise to do things differently.'

'What amends did you make?'

'Well, I'm still making them,' he says. 'Actually, I have to admit something to you. I'm not an alcoholic, but I am an addict. After our son died, my wife turned to alcohol, but I decided to wallow in my own pain. I became obsessed with the idea that he'd been murdered, even though it was a freak accident, because it gave me something to focus on, a way of keeping his memory alive. I left my wife alone with her grief, and it nearly killed her. She refuses to see me, so I can't truly make amends to her, but I can turn my pain into service to the people who want my help.'

'I'm sorry about your son. What was his name?'

'Greg.'

I see the resemblance in his face and the blood drains from mine.

My need to make amends goes so much further beyond the people I've killed. Before me, Harry and his wife, Margaret, were happy parents to a happy son. Then I murdered him and drove them both off the edge.

Margaret lives alone in a small house much like Grandad's. The front garden is a forest of overgrown weeds. I pop by one weekend on a sunny winter morning, armed with garden shears and a trowel. I knock and she greets me with the stench of pure ethanol.

'Do I know you?' she says, each word slow and deliberate.

'Sort of. This might sound a bit weird, but I wonder if I could do your gardening? I don't want any money. It's just that I find it really therapeutic, and I don't have a garden where I live.'

'I guess,' she says and closes the door.

For the first three visits, I do the gardening and nothing else. Until one evening she's watching me wrestling with a patch of crabgrass and invites me in for a cup of tea.

The house is mostly bare, stacks of cardboard boxes left unpacked. I'm fairly sure the milk has gone off, but I drink it anyway. No milk for her. Instead, she tops up with whisky while she thinks I'm not looking.

'Do you live here alone?' I ask.

'Yes. I was married, but not anymore.'

'I'm sorry.'

'I'm not.'

I don't know whether it's too soon, but I risk it. 'Any kids?'

She clenches her mug tightly. 'Yes, but he's . . . away. He went abroad. Hong Kong.'

'How exciting.'

She smiles. 'Yes, he worries about me being here on my own, of course. But it was an incredible work opportunity, so I told him he had to go. He works in finance, you know.'

'Tell me more about him.'

I visit once a week, then twice because the tea breaks mean not much gardening is getting done. She delights in telling me stories about Greg. I learn that he used to volunteer at an animal shelter every school summer holiday and that he got a first in economics from Warwick University. He was the first member of their family to go to university and she made sure everyone knew it. It was always his dream to work abroad. His girlfriend is a veterinarian and once they move back to England, they plan to get married and start a family.

Providing Greg's mum with some company twice a week seems like the very least I can do. I'm not sure if it counts as amends, but I do think our chats provide a momentary escape. For a short time, she can pretend her son is not dead but living out his fantasy. When she speaks of him, she is alive, so I indulge her as often as I can.

I have started bringing my own milk, though. I deserve to be punished, but drinking white vomit benefits no one.

Doing good is a lot less complicated than I thought. Turns out, when you're up all night wracked with guilt over what you've done, it's a pretty good sign you should stop. Doing good feels good. I wish I'd known this sooner.

Greg's mum is just one of the people I want to help. I'm going to spend the rest of my life thinking of ways to make amends to everyone I've hurt. I'll probably never tip the scales back in my favour, but that's no reason not to keep trying.

But today I get a break from earning my redemption because it's Puppy Sunday. We turn half the store into a playpen and customers bring in their puppies to socialize. It's my favourite day of the week by far.

I volunteer to get more toys from the back, but as I return with an armful of stuffed rabbits and pheasants, I freeze. Officer Stewart is standing with his arms crossed, gazing at a tiny goldendoodle.

I need to run. Hide.

'Thea, can you get over here, please?' Carl calls out.

Stewart turns. His eyes lock firmly on me. I feel like he sees straight through me, into the same wretched core that

I found that day when I pulled my yellow fraying life into my hand.

I drop the toys and make for the exit. Stewart catches up with me in the car park.

'Wait,' he says. 'I owe you an apology.'

What the fuck? He wants to apologize?

'I've not been thinking straight the past few months. It's not an excuse, but I've had . . . trouble at home, and I think having something to focus on gave me an escape. I became obsessed, making you out to be some larger-than-life monster, wanting to see patterns where there was only coincidence. I'm truly sorry.'

Is it weird that I'm extremely compelled to confess right now? I admire his tenacity. He knew there was something wrong about me and he followed his instincts. Only to be publicly humiliated and have his career ruined because he hadn't factored in the supernatural.

'That's okay, it was just a misunderstanding.'

'That's very decent of you,' he says, and I can see those detective eyes analysing me, wondering why I would forgive him so easily.

'Well, you did get suspended, right? I guess you've already been punished.'

'Right, yeah, I did. Turns out it was the best thing to ever happen to me. Spending time with my family showed me what's really important. You'll be glad to know I'm not a police officer anymore, and I don't intend to go anywhere near law enforcement ever again.'

'Oh, congrats, I think?'

'Thanks.'

There's an awkward silence. What do I say to a man who tried to send me to prison for life? I settle on 'The salmon and quinoa is better on their tummies.'

'Excuse me?'

I point at the chicken liver pâté food pellets tucked under his arm. 'If you have a new puppy, I mean.'

'Oh right, yeah, we just got a goldendoodle for my daughter. She's eight, been begging for a dog since the moment she was born.' There's a hint of a sad smile I don't quite understand. He coughs. 'Salmon and quinoa sounds good.'

'Come with me and I'll get it for you.'

When we get back to the store, his daughter runs to join us at the counter, goldendoodle in her arms, even though it looks like it weighs more than her. It's not a giant dog; she's just extremely slight. A strong gust of wind could blow her over. But still she's cradling it proudly, desperate for everyone to know it's hers.

'Can we get these too? She loves them. Please, Dad?' she asks, passing up a bucket of gravy bones, a rubber duck toy and an antler chew.

'She loves them, does she? Okay, then.'

I ring it all up. Stewart slaps his credit card on the machine and hauls the bag of puppy pellets under his arm. I pass him the tub of gravy bones and the antler, but he doesn't have another hand for the rubber duck.

'I'll take that,' the girl says, putting the puppy down and taking the duck from me. Our hands touch. *Three months.*

My heart doesn't just sink, it drops into the abyss. His daughter is dying, and there's nothing I can do about it. I know that I did a lot of bad things with my power. And I regret most of it – but not saving kids.

Stewart's 'troubles at home' all make sense now. I stare into his eyes, and there's a moment of recognition between us. I've always felt he can see through my exterior, right into my core, but right now I'm doing the same – and I'm sure he can feel it.

He steps between us, shielding the girl from me. 'Let's go, sweetheart.'

What the hell am I supposed to do?

Chapter Thirty-Six

*Why am I like this? Is it because I've
experienced bad things or because I am a bad
thing? Does it make a difference?*

Sam can't be right about me – I won't let him be. This morning,
I meditate for an extra fifteen minutes. All I need to do is stick
to my routine, and everything will be fine.

'*Focus on your breath,*' the guided audio from my phone
calls out. Her voice is serene; I let her calm wash over me. '*Pay
attention to the way it feels in your body as you inhale . . . and
exhale.*'

It's working. Screw Sam – what does he know?

'*If your mind wanders, acknowledge it, and gently bring it
back to your breath.*'

Shit, focus, forget about Sam. Focus on my breath, the way
it feels. I've never noticed before, but air feels slightly cold
when it's inhaled, turning warm as soon as it's inside. It's a
miracle really, that we can breathe, that we remember to do it
every minute of the day, that we're alive at all. Wow, I sound
really enlightened; this is really helping. Let's go through every

metaphor I can – that'll keep me focused on my breath. Hmm, how about balloons? I try to picture the air inflating my lungs like long pink balloons, then slowly leaving again, like I'm holding the end, controlling the flow.

Balloons.

Kids' birthday parties.

Kids.

Stewart's daughter.

Death.

'And if your mind wanders, acknowledge the thought, and bring your mind back to your breath.'

I try, over and over, until I give myself a headache, but all I can see is that little girl's face. Just from those few minutes, I could see what she meant to Stewart, how loved she was. I imagine the hopes and dreams he had for her: maybe she'd become a police officer like her dad or follow her love of animals and become a vet. It doesn't matter now. All their hopes and dreams will be buried in a child-sized coffin.

How is that fair?

Nope. That's the thinking that got me into this mess. I don't kill people anymore. No exceptions. This impulse to swoop in and save the day will pass, like everything does in the end.

I tell Grandad about the girl, hoping the anticipation of his disappointment will be enough to stop me. He listens. He's empathetic. And he reminds me that if I save her there will be another one, and another one, and another. So the killing would have to go on.

Time passes. Christmas is a nice distraction. Grandad and I have lunch with his neighbours. He gives me a woolly Fair Isle jumper, which is the warmest thing I've ever owned. I get him a subscription to an app that lets him track live air traffic and set it up on his phone.

Then it's January, which is depressing at the best of times, and now I can't even drink through it because I'm committed to staying in control of myself at all times. The world does not need Thea Greaves with her inhibitions lowered. I double my AA meetings; I now go on both Tuesdays and Thursdays. Harry is my sponsor. It feels a bit perverted that he's helping me, but he offered, and I can only assume the constant reminder of what I did to his son is a good thing for me. And yes, I owe Harry his own amends but, in this case, the truth would harm him, so I feel only a little guilt about the lie.

'Would anyone like to share?' he asks the group.

For the first time, I do. I stand. 'Hi, I'm Rachel. I'm an alcoholic.'

'Hi, Rachel,' the circle chorus my fake name – it is Alcoholics Anonymous, after all.

'So, I've been doing pretty good lately. I made my list of people I've harmed, and I've been making amends where I can. But then, something happened recently, and I felt myself tempted to slip back into old habits. It was like this primal need inside me.' I stop, embarrassed at my intensity, suddenly aware of the group staring at me. 'It's hard to explain.'

'We all understand that feeling, Rachel. Shame and guilt are dangerous emotions, serving only to disconnect us from each other. Bringing them out into the open like this lessens their hold,' Harry says. 'You've not been with us long, and you've already reached step nine. Perhaps you're expecting too much of yourself too soon?'

'Well, step nine seemed the most important. I've got a lot of amends to make so I needed to get a jump on them,' I say, laughing. No one joins me.

'So, you haven't done step one?' a woman next to me chimes in. 'You have to start with step one.'

'It's okay. The twelve steps are more like guidelines. But most people do find it helpful to follow them in order. Step one is about honesty, about admitting that you are powerless to your addiction so you can begin your recovery. Why don't you give it a go now?'

'I wouldn't say I'm powerless.'

'Yes, you are. This first step is one of the most difficult ones, but it's important to break the cycle of denial and lies.'

Fuck's sake, don't take my progress from me, Harry. This is weird, and not what I expected. Isn't AA supposed to boost you up, not tear you down?

'Yeah, but I'm here, I'm fighting my cravings, so I must have some control over them.'

'No, you don't. It's okay if you're not ready to admit this just yet. We'll be here for you when you are.'

I'm not powerless; I just need to try harder to make amends. Elias dedicated his life to making up for what he did to my parents – or what he thought he'd done, at least. And that was just for one wrong. I have so much more to put right.

So, I'm taking a leaf out of Sam's book. I'm going to make amends in such a way that maximizes their impact. I begin at the bar of a hotel lobby. Svetlana Tate is waiting, elegantly perched on a high stool in a taupe pencil dress. She watches without comment as I scrabble to haul myself onto the stool next to her.

The bartender brings her a gin and tonic in a classy short crystal-cut glass. 'Drink?' he asks me.

As part of my commitment to my zero-impulsivity beige lifestyle, I've been off the booze. But, quite honestly, having a drink with Svetlana in a swanky hotel bar is a remnant fantasy from my past life. 'I'll have the same, please.'

'So, how are you adjusting to unincarcerated life?' she asks.

'It's harder than I imagined. How's the case going?'

She laughs softly. 'Rape tends to get downgraded when the accused is facing an attempted murder charge, but we'll get there. After public backlash, more witnesses stepped forward, and there's no way he'll risk intimidation and bribery after all this. It's just going to take a bit more time. I can't thank you enough for handing me this case. Perhaps I should have hired you after all.'

My gin and tonic arrives, although he's poured mine into a less sophisticated balloon glass with a pink straw.

'I'm just glad justice is being served. And thanks, but I would have made a terrible lawyer. Too impulsive, no attention to detail, jumping to conclusions – I'm well aware of my flaws now.'

'That's not why I decided against you.'

'No?'

'No. When I asked what justice meant to you, you said, "Justice means doing the right thing, even when it's hard." It's not. Justice is about seeking the truth, and accepting what you find. I knew you weren't someone who could put their own feelings aside to uphold the law. God knows how many ethical lines you crossed to gather some of that evidence against Oliver.'

'You used it.'

'It's up to the judge to decide if it's admissible, not me. The point is that I did not unfairly attempt to obtain evidence.'

I reach down to pick up my backpack, almost falling off my stool in the process. The bloody gin and tonic has gone to my head already. Once I've steadied myself, I pass Svetlana a black leather-bound notebook.

'Well, I'll leave it up to you whether you use this.'

She opens it and flicks through the pages. 'This is—'

'Yep, dirt on some of the worst sexual predators in the city. There's some non-sex stuff in there too, in case you're interested, or know anyone who might be.'

'Where did it come from? What do you want me to do with this?'

I copied the contents of Sam's computer when I first started seeing red flags. Given he's currently fighting embezzlement charges, I don't want to draw any more heat his way. 'You don't need to know where it came from. And in terms of what to do with it – whatever you feel is right. I trust your judgement more than mine.'

Svetlana is still poring through the pages, eyes going wider and wider as she skims. Then she says, 'I need to make a call,' and excuses herself.

I'm taking a big gulp of my drink when I lock eyes with the last person I want to see right now. Harry. From AA. He makes a beeline for me.

'What the hell do you think you're doing?'

'It's not what it looks like.'

He takes the glass out of my hand and sniffs. 'Gin. I think this is exactly what it looks like.'

'I was just having one.'

'No, it's a disease. You can't "just have one" because it doesn't work that way. Total and utter abstinence, anything less and you'll fail. Is that what you want? To fail?'

'No.'

'I'm sorry to do this, Rachel, but give me your chip.' My thirty-day sobriety chip. I wince as I pull it out of my pocket and hand it over. 'So, tell me what happened,' he says.

'I can't, not right now.' I nod my head towards Svetlana.

'Please, she's a work colleague. This would be really embarrassing for me.'

'Okay, I'll let you wrap things up if you promise to call me later. I want to hear from you, sober. Then see you at AA on Tuesday, without fail.' He gives me a reassuring squeeze. 'It's okay, this happens. The important thing is to stop before you're too far gone.'

'I'll see you Tuesday, I promise.'

As I arrive for Tuesday's meeting, Harry hands me a twenty-four-hour sobriety chip. 'Remember, it's okay to slip up. Now you start again.'

Today we focus on the fifth step: acceptance. Apparently, this means accepting your flaws as they are and letting them go. The light from the window is shining in my eyes. I keep having to move my head to avoid it and it's very distracting. I've barely heard a word of the readings when we reach the sharing portion of the day.

There's a guy who always brings doughnuts, Aaron. Usually he's quiet, but today he decides to share. I only catch the tail end.

'My little girl was alone in the flat for two weeks. Her mum left us, cheated on me. I didn't handle it well and I took off. She was just five years old. No food, no one to take care of her.'

'You could have killed her,' I say before I can help myself.

I've shocked the room into silence.

'We don't judge here, Rachel. Honesty is required for progress.'

'I'm sorry, but that's bullshit. Downing a few bottles of Chardonnay is not the same as what he did.'

He stands up, pointing his tattooed finger at me.

'At least I'm trying. You've been sitting her for weeks and

all you've shared is some vague shit about making amends. It's weak and pathetic. Actually share something real. Are you proud of everything you've done?'

'No, but at least I can say I've never hurt a child.'

He's shouting now. I can feel tiny droplets of spit on my face. 'So fucking high and mighty, but you're just some bitch, just like the rest of them.'

He's shaking with rage. He wants to hit me; I can feel the energy pulsing across from him. His knuckles are white. I imagine how many times he's thrown a punch at someone, and don't doubt for a second he would have already done so if we weren't in this room, surrounded by witnesses. I want him to do it. I want him to show everyone exactly what he really is.

'Is this how you talked to your girlfriend? No wonder she left you.'

Harry steps in. 'Rachel, stop it.'

'You fucking bitch,' Aaron snarls. 'Don't you dare talk to me that way.'

I smile. I've always loved it when they talk like that, when someone thinks they are so much more powerful than me. He's taking me in, probably thinking he could snap me like a twig. Little does he know I could sap his life before he even blinked. The little hairs on my arm are standing up on end. I forgot what this was like, the rush, the power.

I step around Harry, quick as a cat, until my face is just inches from Aaron's. 'Your little girl would be better off with you dead.'

Yeah, that does it. He lunges at me, throwing me down on the floor and drawing back his fist. One punch from a guy like that could kill me, so I really have no choice but to defend myself. I grab his fist and pull his life into me. I'm out of practice and it comes out fast, all at once. He's so shocked, he freezes. So does everyone else for a moment. They were ready to dive in and help, but they don't know what they're looking at.

Finally, Harry breaks, pulling Aaron off me, just as I've finished taking his life. He clutches his chest. Heart attack, most likely. I don't move, don't react as he writhes on the ground. Should I really return twenty-five years that could save Stewart's little girl? Really?

'Call an ambulance,' Harry shouts, pulling at my sleeve. As he does, my twenty-four-hour chip falls to the floor.

Oh shit, I can't do this. I don't get to pick and choose life. If I do, I know it won't be the last. I drop to the ground, put my hand on Aaron's shoulder and let his life flow back where it belongs. I wait long enough for proof of life. He takes several steady breaths before I slip out the side door, knowing I can't go back.

Harry keeps calling and texting to check on me. Or rather, to check on Rachel. He doesn't have my address but he doesn't let up. He's a good man, a good sponsor. I wish I could explain to him that this has nothing to do with him, that I'm simply beyond his help. Eventually, I cave and say that the group's not working for me – too much macho energy – and that I've found a women's only support group. It's the only thing that finally makes him leave me alone, so I can focus on what I have to do.

There's no ethical guide to murder, but there's also no ethical way to let a child die. Whatever I do will be the wrong choice. Except, there is a third option. Once I realize what it is, I can see the solution has been staring me in the face the whole time, like that stupid painting of the man and the apple I once mocked to Ruth. I'm simply doing what feels right to me. Decision made. No backsies.

Stewart placed a standing order for monthly pet food deliveries to his home address. He didn't do it through me. Probably online. We're a national chain and I doubt he imagined I'd bother – or even be able – to look him up.

But I did and here I am standing outside his house. It's nice. A two-bed maisonette with a Juliet balcony. Stewart takes his daughter to school every morning in the van he parks outside the house. I think he's a handyman now. Makes sense – he was always good at getting to the bottom of a problem. I hear him call her Hayley as he drops her at the school gate and kisses her goodbye. It's too difficult to get to her at school. Bloody paedophiles, ruining it for the rest of us.

I don't get my chance until later that afternoon. Stewart and Hayley are back just before 4 p.m. They close the door behind them and I'm about to give up. How the hell is one supposed to save a child's life when the parents keep them so well surrounded? Then the door opens again. It's Hayley and the goldendoodle puppy.

'Don't go far. The end of the road and back,' Stewart calls out.

'Okay, Dad!'

This is it. I wait for her to walk fifteen metres or so, then I follow her. As instructed, she goes to the end of the road and no further. I break out into a grin and drop to the floor to pet the goldendoodle. It jumps up to lick my face, nails scratching against my jeans. 'She's so cute. What's her name?'

'Nala.'

'Like the Lion King?'

She nods, tucking her chin proudly into her chest as she grins.

Nala is extremely interested in the treats in my pocket. 'Sit,' I say, which she does. 'Can I give her a treat?' I ask Hayley.

'Sure.'

I take one out and throw it. Nala catches it in the air.

'How did you do that?' Hayley asks, eyes full of wonder.

I pass her a handful of treats. 'Here, let me show you.'

She's distracted. It's time. I focus on my breath and turn inwards. The street fades into blurred colours and shapes. I keep digging down and down until I find that frayed edge. My life force. And I tug. This time, it doesn't fight so hard. It's sitting coiled and waiting for instruction.

On the third attempt, Nala catches the treat and Hayley squeals in delight. I congratulate her, clasp her hand in a high-five and let my energy flow to her.

'I better go now. Thanks for teaching me that trick,' she says.

'Bye, Hayley. Look after that puppy of yours.'

She trots away with my whole life ahead of her.

Chapter Thirty-Seven

I am no closer to answers at the end than at the beginning. All I know is that nothing is absolutely right or wrong, nothing good or bad. Not even death.

Not long left now.

I didn't give it all away. I saved six months for Zara, which I have now given to her, so I have repaid my debt to her with interest. And I saved myself three weeks to put my affairs in order.

I take the contents of my room to the charity shop down the road and say goodbye to my flatmates. I could just have easily told them I was going to the shops and got the same reaction. Actually, probably a better response because they would have been pleased to have someone get snacks. With a single bag of clothes I can easily carry on one shoulder, I hop on the train home to Grandad.

He doesn't question my sudden reappearance, nor ask how long I'm staying for. Every morning at exactly 8 a.m., he takes his tea in the front room and reads the paper. Then he walks into town. It's a fifteen-minute trip that takes the best part of an hour because everyone knows Grandad, and everyone wants to stop and chat. Monday, Wednesday and Friday he does a four-hour shift at the museum. He's home by 5 p.m., we have dinner at 6.30 p.m. and watch television until bedtime. I spend every moment I can with him.

On the fifth morning, he looks up from his newspaper and says, 'I'm dying, aren't I?'

'Yes.'

'Soon?'

'Yes. Do you want to know when?'

'Indeed, best to be prepared for this sort of thing.'

'January twentieth. In the afternoon.'

'Next Tuesday. Very good, I suppose it had to happen at some point,' he says.

Then he goes back to reading his paper. I take my cue from him, and we don't speak of it again. I keep asking if there's anything he wants to do or any people he wants to see, but he refuses. I suppose I had to get my love of routine from somewhere. The rest of the week goes by quietly and without deviation.

Thursday morning rolls in.

I'm willing time to slow down but the sun starts to creep in underneath my curtains anyway. He's already downstairs. I can hear the kettle boiling. I sigh, pull on jeans and my Fair Isle jumper and join him in the front room. He seems quieter today, his breathing laboured and his eyes glassy. I catch him staring out the window for a long time as if not connected to the world around him. We follow our usual routine until after lunch when he asks, 'Thea, will you take me somewhere, please?'

He's not up to driving so I volunteer despite not having

operated a car for seven years and not having any insurance. It's difficult to say no to the requests of the dying. He leans heavily against me as we make the laboured trip to the Rover, and takes a deep sigh of relief as I ungracefully deposit him into the passenger seat. Miraculously, the engine bursts into life on the first try, as if it's grateful for the opportunity to shine.

'Where are we going?' I ask.

'Home.'

'Right, that's clarifying,' I say, gritting my teeth as I reverse out of our driveway and the cottage disappears from the rear-view mirror.

I manage the driving well enough. Grandad gives me directions, seemingly seconds before he expects me to follow them, and I only forget which way to go around roundabouts twice. There are no casualties, and the engine is still humming with joy, delighted for the outing. The only real problem is when we get out of town and into the forest.

I'm conscious of the time. We've been driving for about thirty minutes when we come up behind a line of four stationary cars. We bump over a cattle grid, then I roll to a stop behind a green Volkswagen.

I try to peer around them, leaning forward over the steering wheel. 'What the frick are they doing?'

'There's no need for language like that.'

'Really, Grandad, after everything I've done, you're still scolding me over word choice? I said frick, anyway, not fuck.'

'It's the sentiment that matters.' He pauses and gives me a wry smile. 'And now you've said both.'

I can't help but laugh, then Grandad does too. A lovely sound that warms the frost from the windshield.

'But seriously, what are they doing?' The cars ahead still

haven't moved. The one in front is sitting on the bend, but I still have fairly good vision. The green Volkswagen beeps its horn, then I do the same.

'Just wait, Thea, we're in no rush.' He closes his eyes, settling in for a long wait, and it strikes fear through me. He looks so fragile. The person who raised me, just a bundle of skin, sinew and bone. It seems so odd to me that we would waste our time accumulating experience, putting so much effort into becoming fully functioning adults, only to encase it all in such careless packaging. Any moment could be the one where his body can't hold him any longer.

'No, you wanted to show me something, so we're not going to sit here, wasting our lives in traffic.'

I turn the wheel, ready to cross onto the other side of the road and overtake this random traffic jam without a cause, when he grabs my arm with surprising strength.

'Do you remember that trip we took to Cornwall, for your mother's birthday?'

Great, now he's really losing it. I need to get us out of here.

'Sort of, I was a kid.'

'You were seven. It was three days before your mother's birthday, and we were spending the bank holiday weekend by the beach. Your mother wanted to leave at the crack of dawn. But your father just laughed, and we left after breakfast.'

'Well, he didn't always have the best ideas, did he? I remember we sat on the motorway for hours. What a nightmare.' But despite myself, I smile. The soft sad smile I always get when I think about my parents.

'What would they give to be sitting in a traffic jam with us right now?'

'Oh,' I say, and let the wheel slip back into place.

Then the first car starts moving. And finally, I see it: two huge black cows and a calf, meandering across the road with all the time in the world.

'Here it is,' Grandad says, pointing at a clump of trees.

I park beside them and help him out of the car, then we walk down the path. The trail is uneven and he stumbles a few times before we reach a bench. We sit and he catches his breath.

'Wow, it's beautiful here,' I say.

The bench is at the top of a hill, overlooking miles of forest and, in the distance, rolling farmlands. I've never seen anything so quintessentially English before. Like something out of a kid's storybook.

'Your grandmother is down there,' he says.

She died before I was born, but still I look. Not a soul but us.

'Can you see her?' I say.

'No, the tree.' He nods with his eyes. There's an oak tree, much taller and set apart from the others. 'This is where I asked your grandmother to marry me. It's our special place.'

'Oh, that makes more sense. Why haven't you brought me here before?'

'You had enough graves to visit. But I came every afternoon before I picked you up from school. I want to be close to her when I go. No use keeping her waiting any longer than I already have.'

'It won't be long now.'

'Good.'

'Are you not afraid?'

'No, I feel lucky. How many people get to appreciate their last moments like this, with the person they love most by their side? People would be a lot less afraid of death if they knew it could end like this.'

My heart aches. 'Aren't you at least a little . . . sad?'

'There's nothing sad about a full life coming to its natural conclusion.'

His gaze rests on the oak tree and he's quiet, closing his eyes every now and then. I take his hand and lean against him. We stay like this until 3.01 p.m., when I know he's already gone.

I still have the ache in my chest, but I wouldn't describe it as pain. It's a bittersweet longing to stay in this moment and capture the unexpected gratitude I feel for it.

Now it's my turn. I didn't want to hurt Grandad with the knowledge of what I've done to myself. He deserved the peaceful death he got.

I called an ambulance to the place where he died. By the time they found us the sun had set and the cold air had set in. I didn't bring a coat so after all that time sitting there, I'm frozen to the bone by the time I get home. Even with a blanket and a hot drink I can't warm up. It's like the house has given up now that it doesn't have Grandad here to nurture.

There's a letter in the kitchen. A final, unceremonious good-bye from Grandad that's mainly practical instructions for his cremation, funeral and how to deal with his will. The house and his savings are mine. I expected this, and I've already arranged for everything to be left to Karly once I'm gone. It's not much but hopefully it will go some way towards an apology for what I put her through.

I regret not making more progress on my list of people to make amends to, but I can't risk any delays. Making these amends could take a lifetime. And I know that after what happened with Stewart's daughter, it's not a case of if but when. I can't control knowing the fate of every single person I cross paths with. If not Hayley, then there will be someone else who tugs my heartstrings in such a way I can't let go. All I need is a bad day and the right trigger. That's where the addiction analogy ends. If an alcoholic makes a mistake, they can go to rehab. If I slip up, someone dies.

That's why this was the only course of action left that made sense to me. I did consider alternatives – taking little chunks off several thousand people, for example. But taking myself out of the equation is the greatest amend I have to offer, the only way I can stay true to my promise not to hurt anyone else.

I spend the time I have left writing letters to everyone I've harmed in some way. I admit, this is more for me than for them. I can't shake the need to unburden myself now the end has come.

In some, I tell the truth. For Stewart, I tell him he was right about me, but that I hope this doesn't tempt him back to the police. He seems happy. I tell him this and more. How his daughter will live to become a grown woman and exactly how I know this.

I send Elias my dad's journals. I tell him that I don't know the truth about what happened that night, but that regardless, I hope he continues to live a life he's proud of.

In others, I lie. I write to Harry and tell him what a great sponsor he was, that I've moved abroad and am doing so much better now. I write to Greg's mother. I tell her I'm going travel-ling, just like Greg, and that I'd love it if she'd write to me. I've paid a woman in the Philippines to write back on my behalf. I've briefed her thoroughly. She'll listen to Margaret's stories, ask about the garden and encourage her to reconnect with the outside world wherever she can.

My final letter is also the hardest. Ruth. By the time I'm done I have a blister on my index finger, but my soul feels lighter than it has in years.

Other than that, I cook, I clean, I tend the garden. The days blend together. It's warm for this time of year and the sun is shining. The house looks like something out of a fairytale. Ivy has crawled up the walls and encircled the windows. Winter honeysuckle has bloomed in the front garden. A family of robins has taken residence in the bird house and their chatter creates a pleasant background tune. The cranberry bush is still bearing fruit. I squat on the grass and eat one. It explodes in my mouth. It's by far the juiciest, sweetest thing I have ever tasted.

I've never cared much for my home, but today it is beautiful.

I'm going to die today.

I resolve to face it with the same quiet dignity Grandad did. I follow his routine. Tea in the front room. Walk into town, nodding and giving a cordial 'Good morning!' to everyone I see. Then lunchtime comes around and I'm alone in the house. Nothing left to do and no one to talk to.

The clock on the mantelpiece is deafening. I'm an idiot. I've wasted my last precious days on this earth with busywork. I even cleaned the shower, for fuck's sake. My mind is racing with things I've never done:

- Bungee jumping.
- Scuba diving.
- Running a marathon.
- Spending a night in a haunted house.
- Shark cage diving.
- Volcano surfing.
- Seeing a polar bear.
- Going to Paris. And taking one of those stupid tourist photos where I'm holding the Eiffel Tower like it's a teeny tiny toy.

My heart is racing. I can't breathe. All I can think about is that I'm going to die alone in the house I grew up in, voluntarily giving up all the joy life has to offer. I'm crying now. I try to bite back the tears, but they won't be denied. Why am I like this?

The doorbell rings. It's Ruth. She goes to speak but her voice sticks in her throat. I don't wait for it to clear. I wrap my arms around her and squeeze her tighter than I ever have before.

She got my letter. I explained everything from beginning to end so I could leave with no more lies between us. She isn't here to change my mind because she respects my choice.

'I just didn't want you to be alone,' she says.

I'm grateful. Her being here means everything.

'When will it happen?'

'Eleven twenty-four p.m. Same time I was born.'

'Okay, so what do you want to do until then?' Her voice is more controlled than I expected. I think she's forced herself into caretaker mode. I tell her about my bucket list, and she chuckles. 'Do you actually want to go cage diving with sharks?'

'No. Just seemed like something I should do.'

'Take a moment and picture the perfect day. Forget about everything else that's going on, don't think about anything you should be doing and focus on what you would really enjoy.'

I take her instructions to heart and don't speak for several minutes.

'I just want us to spend the day together, having pointless fun, like we used to when we were young. I want to go to an art gallery and make fun of the paintings while you try to convince me of their deeper meaning. I want to pick up a book in a bookshop and yell, "Here's that erotic fiction you were after" across the store so you turn red. I want to go to a restaurant and pretend it's my birthday so I get free cake. I want to draw funny faces on all the eggs in a supermarket. I want to leave one of our garden gnomes outside someone's door, ring the bell and run away. Then I want to go back to our flat and eat Thai food and ice cream until I throw up.

'Well, that's sounds doable. Let's go.'

We do everything on my list.

Ruth scowls at me when I tell her I've met children more artistically gifted than Picasso.

She turns crimson when I say I'm not sure the book has enough BDSM for her.

The waitress brings me warm chocolate cake with a lone candle stuck on top.

The eggs are not enough so we start on the bananas.

Our neighbour keeps our garden gnome. She puts it on her windowsill.

We go home, sit on the sofa and eat Thai food and ice cream until my stomach churns. I'm glad to be surrounded by mismatched cushions and photo frames with real photos and clutter on the tables again.

Ruth turns on the lamp closest to us as it gets dark. We sit on the sofa talking until late, drinking the last of the ice cream. She talks about the future, about how she'd like to move back to the countryside and someday start a family.

'It makes me sad not to think of you here, in our flat,' I say.

'I'll miss it, but it feels like the right time. I need to put all of this behind me.'

'Of course.'

'Not like that. I just mean I need to move forward.'

'I know. I'm glad.'

Time is marching on. We can both feel it. Without a word I grab a blanket and cuddle up next to my friend.

'Thank you for today. I know you don't forgive me, but I

think that might even mean more to me, that you're still willing to be here in spite of how angry you are with me.'

'I can't offer you forgiveness, but you're wrong about how I feel. I still don't agree with what you did but . . . I've never lost anyone before and it's unbearable. If what you felt that night was anything like what I'm feeling now, then I understand how it happened and why you did it. And I'm not sure it's possible to be angry at someone you understand.'

It's more than I deserve, but I'm getting tired now, too tired to argue. My eyes stay closed for a few seconds each time I rest them.

'What do you think it will be like?' I ask, fear creeping into my voice. 'Do you think I'll be judged – that they'll decide whether to send me up or down?'

She squeezes me tight and cradles my head into her. 'I don't think it will be like that. I've watched a lot of people die, and so often there's this look on their face before they go, like everything finally makes sense and it's all okay.'

I feel myself slipping, my life unravelling inside me. Not yet. I pull it tight, just a little longer.

'But what do you really think is there?'

'I think it will be different to anything we can imagine. We'll have no concept of time or space, no physical form to embody. It will just be peace. No shame, no guilt, no pain. Just endless peace.'

'Well, that doesn't sound so bad.'

She strokes my hair. 'No, it doesn't, does it?'

'I love you, Ruth.'

'I love you too, Thea.'

Our flat is blurring around me. I focus long enough to notice the porcelain cat is back on the mantelpiece, then it disappears in a swirl of pastel colours and mismatched patterns. It's dizzying, and I have to close my eyes to stop the whole room from spinning. Ruth holds me steady. I open my eyes again, using her as my focal point. I can see her future. She will move to the countryside, a quaint village somewhere close enough to her parents but not too close. She'll love being the local doctor, someone who is part of the community and knows the residents by name. And she'll have a family. She'll love them so much it will frighten her, and they'll love her back just as much.

This is the end of my story but the beginning of hers. Finally, I loosen my grip on the thread holding me here. I do not need to know what comes next because, when I look at her, I am already at peace. It's more than I deserve, I know. But despite every bad thing I did, nobody can argue that I didn't do at least one good one.

Acknowledgements

So obviously the most important place to start is with you – thank you so much for picking up my book and reading to the very end. You've given me elevenish hours of your life, and I don't take that for granted. I hope Thea's story has made you laugh, cry and think about things you never expected to. One of which being 'Would I kill a bad person to save a good one?' and another being 'How much would I eat a human toe for?'

I always loved books growing up (shocking), but it simply never occurred to me that I would write one. Then, when I was twenty-two, one of my closest friends – and simply one of the best people I have ever known – unexpectedly and suddenly died. Writing this book helped me (somewhat) to process the unfairness of losing her. I hope you've found this book a bit of fun but – if you've needed it – I hope it's been of some comfort too.

Thank you to Katherine Armstrong, my editor at Simon & Schuster. I know how much you've championed *Ethical Guide* from the beginning and I'm beyond grateful for your support. I remember receiving your editorial comments and thinking, *Oh my god, why have I not asked myself these questions?* and genuinely loving the chance to add more depth and complexity to the novel. And thank you to the whole team at Simon &

Schuster who have helped make *Ethical Guide* a reality – so much work goes into creating a book and I'm so lucky to have had such amazing people working on mine.

Thank you to Francesca Riccardi, who picked my book out of a slush pile and said, "Well it's just fucking great, isn't it?" I'm sorry I didn't email you back for a whole day. I swear it wasn't a mind game I just have a really weird junk filter. I can't imagine having a more supportive agent who also makes the whole process seem easy and fun.

My beta readers who've read and helped refine earlier drafts: Sarrah Qureshi, Miranda Osmelak, Ian Muir, Karen Gill, Bijal Trivadi. Miriam Steiner for helping me with random philosophy questions – I love how you always just answer the question instead of asking, "What, why the hell are you asking me that?" And the whole crew from Faber Academy who really helped me learn how to write in the first place and read the very first chapters of Ethical Guide.

And finally, my family aka the wetskins (sorry, inside joke, they'll get it). If there's one thing writing a book will help you understand, it's how much you love the people that are always there for you. The patience of coping with having a writer in the family is immeasurable.

Mum, you read my first (terrible) short story and believed in it. You're the reason I had the confidence to pursue writing, to do the Faber course and never gave up on *Ethical Guide* – even when I wanted to! I quite genuinely have the most special mum in the world.

Al Pal, you're the best brother and my best friend wrapped up in one. Whether you're making me laugh, talking through tricky plot points, or providing essential details about Spitfires, you're always there for me. Your book allergy might be severe, but that hasn't stopped you from supporting my writing.

And Dad, sometimes I feel unlucky that you're not here to see this. But not really, because I'm so much luckier to know exactly how proud you would have been.

Family, I know you'll all understand why the dedication in this book isn't for you but trust me – you'll be getting the next one and probably everything else I write for the rest of my life. I love you.